I0692072

CAUGHT STEALING

SEATTLE CASCADES
BOOK 2

C.M. KANE

COPYRIGHT

Published 2022
Text Copyright © 2022 Magic Cat Press

ISBN: 978-1-958386-01-9

No part of this book may be reproduced in any form or by an electronic or mechanical means, including information storage and retrieval systems, without written permission from the author, except for the use of brief quotations in a book review.

    This is a work of fiction. The names, characters, businesses, places, events, and incidents are either the products of the author's imagination or used in a fictitious manner and are not to be construed as real except where noted and authorized. Any resemblance to actual persons, living or dead, or actual events are purely coincidental. Any trademarks, service marks, product names, or names featured are assumed to be the property of their respective owners, and are used only for reference. There is no implied endorsement if any of these terms are used.

    The author acknowledges the trademarked status and trademark owners of various products referenced in this work, which have been used without permission. The publication/use of these trademarks is not authorized, associated with or sponsored by the trademark owners.

∼

Editing & book design by Maggie Kern @ Ms.K Edits
Cover art by Golden Czermak @ FuriousFotog

BOOK TWO

DEDICATION

For those who love the game, and those who do everything they can to keep it pure.

PROLOGUE

*B*eckett…

"Oh, yeah, baby," I groaned. "Just like that."

I watched my dick disappear into her mouth, in and out, over and over. I held her ponytail tight, controlling the tempo, not allowing her any freedom in sucking me off. Moving her head faster as I felt the buildup begin, she tried to tap out, but I wasn't having any of that. No, this was what I wanted, this was what I was gonna get.

"Fuck yeah," I said as I exploded into her mouth, spilling down her throat without giving her any time to catch her breath.

"Son of a bitch," she said as I let go of her head. "I told you not to do that. You fucking suck."

"So do you." I smirked down at her. "Just like I told you to."

"Screw you," she said, getting up from her knees and putting her tits back into her top. "Lose my number, asshole," she continued as she tugged her skirt down, then stormed out of the hotel room.

"Never kept it to begin with," I mumbled as I dropped to the edge of the bed.

All these bullpen bunnies were the same. They wanted to find themselves a rich ball player they could hitch themselves to. I wasn't about to get stuck with one of these fucking bitches. Give me head, let me fuck you, walk away. That's the way I wanted my women to be, and it was the way things had been since I came up to the big leagues this year.

There were some issues at the beginning of the year, but I'd learned to keep things as clear as possible when hooking up. This was for fun only—no strings, no expectations, no demands. We get to business and they walk away. Eventually, maybe, I might want to settle down, but that wasn't going to be anytime soon.

Toeing my shoes off, I dropped my jeans and pulled them off with my socks, then pulled my shirt over my head and walked to the bathroom naked. A shower to get the bitch off me, then I'd be ready to head to the hotel bar and see if anyone else might be up for a round of fucking before curfew. Houston was hot and hopping and I was down for getting some love in the Lone Star state.

CHAPTER ONE

F i...

"Hey," I said as my big brother stepped out of his truck. "You look great."

"You too, sis," he replied with a hug. "You need help with your bags?"

"Nah," I replied. "Just the carryon. Want me to put it in the back seat?"

"Yeah," he said as he opened the back door. "You ready for a good time?"

"I am so ready for the sunshine you have here," I said as I climbed into the truck.

"It gets hot, though," he said. "Think your wet-weather loving ass can handle the heat?"

"It's not that hot," I said, which was actually a lie.

When I landed in Houston, the pilot said the temp was still eighty-seven, and it was almost nine at night. I loved the sunshine, but I wasn't used to it being this intense.

"Good thing I got AC," he said as he pulled away from the curb at the airport to head onto the freeway.

"Quentin," I said. "Where are you taking me?"

I'd visited him a few times, and I'd always stayed at his apartment, but he'd passed the exit and we were continuing into the downtown area.

"I got a hotel room for you," he said.

"But why?" I asked.

"I didn't want to subject you to my apartment," he said. "It kinda needs some work."

"You sure it isn't because you got some babe you're shacking up with?"

I laughed because this was the furthest thing from what my big brother would do. I mean, he dated, don't get me wrong. It's just that he was more of a guy-next-door, good-old boy kind of dude. He was the clean-cut kind of guy my best friend McKenzie went for. Me, on the other hand, I tended toward the bad boy, as long as he wasn't too bad.

"I put you up where the Cascades are staying," he said, as if that explained everything.

"Who cares about them?" I asked. "You're a Dragon, the best team in the league. What do you need to rub elbows with them for?"

"Research," he said. "Let's get you checked in and drop your bag off. Then we can hit the bar."

"I mean…" I hedged, but didn't go further.

We drove up to the valet, and he climbed out, handing his keys to the man that was standing there. I pulled my suitcase from the back seat and followed him into the hotel after shutting my door.

"Room for Quentin Belinsky," he said at the desk.

"Yes, sir," the woman behind the counter replied, clicking on her computer to pull up the reservation. "And how many keys do you need?"

"Just one," he said. "I'm paying, but my sister is the one staying. Do you need anything from her?"

"I just need your card and ID," she said. "I will also need your ID," she continued, looking at me. "Just to add you to the reservation."

"Sure thing," I replied, pulling my wallet out from the purse strapped across my chest.

After a bit, she got everything into the computer, had my brother sign for the room, and me sign that I wasn't going to be smoking in there. Once that was done, she handed over the key card and gave us instructions on how to get to the room.

"Thanks," Quentin said, then led me to the elevators across the lobby.

We rode up in silence and, when the door opened, headed down the hall to my room. This hotel was a pretty nice place, from the looks of the lobby, and when we opened the door to the room, I was in heaven. The space was big and open, with a bank of windows along the back wall overlooking the city and the stadium.

"This is amazing," I said, wheeling my little suitcase into the room. "You sure you're good to pay for this? I don't want to put you out or anything."

"Sweet little sister," he said. "I could buy you this room for the month and still have plenty of money left over. You forget that I'm in the big leagues now."

"But still," I said.

"It's fine," he said. "It isn't that expensive. A bit more than one of those no-tell motels, but it ain't the Ritz Carlton."

"Not sure I'd want to stay there," I said.

"Okay," he said, clapping his hands together. "Let's hit the bar and have some drinks. Maybe dinner?"

"Am I dressed okay?"

"You're fine," he said. "This is a baseball hotel for a baseball team. You're wearing the right colors, so you'll do just fine."

"All right," I said, then turned back to look at the amazing view of the city lit up one more time before following him out of the room.

He handed me my key after the door closed, then we walked back down the hall and waited for the elevator. Again, we rode in silence, then stepped out into the lobby. The bar was easy to find, just next to the check-in desk. When we stepped in, I realized he had been right about it being a baseball hotel. The televisions that lined the walls were all showing baseball games from the entire league.

My brother had been with Houston's baseball team for four years, and they'd been in the playoffs every year, winning the championship the last two. He'd worked his ass off to get here, and me staying somewhere players from another team were staying just didn't seem right. I mean, I loved that he was putting me somewhere I could see the city from my room, but I could have stayed at his apartment, too.

It was loud in the bar, but not overly crowded. We walked in and sat at one of those high tables with the taller stools. I picked up the drink menu that was standing in the middle of the table, perusing my options. Quentin would end up with a beer on tap, but I liked my girly drinks, so wanted to find something fruity and fun. Since he was paying, I didn't even bother to look at the prices, and opted for a tequila sunrise.

The waitress came over, took our drink order, and left food menus for us to review. I'd already decided that I was going to get some mozzarella sticks with ranch, and then a big burger. My brother always laughed at me when I'd out eat him, but I worked hard and eating was my reward for that.

"Right there," he said, thrusting his chin out toward the door. "That's their shortstop. He's a punk rookie and thinks he's hot shit. Not saying he can't play, just that his attitude needs some improvement."

"Are you here to fight with a player from the other team?" I asked, laughing.

"Nah," he said. "I just want to try to figure out what makes him tick. His fielding is at ninety-eight percent and he's hitting .350 for the season."

"You got a crush?" I asked.

"Shut up," he said. "Can you go try to talk him up? See if he'll open up to you about his play?"

"Seriously?"

"What?" He looked back at me. "I need to know what he's doing that makes him so damn good."

"I'm your spy?"

I was incredulous. My brother and I had a great relationship, one built on mutual respect for each other. This, however, was never something we did. We'd watch film together, help each other out with our respective opinion on what we saw that was an issue, and even work out together, but being wingman for each other, even in this context, was not what we were about.

"Come on, Ophelia," he begged. "I need to know what makes him work."

"Go watch the film," I suggested. "I'm not going to go over there and ask him for all his trade secrets."

"You can get him to talk," he insisted. "He's always trying to impress the women, and he is a known playboy."

"You trying to pimp me out?"

"God." He sighed. "You make it sound so awful."

"Because it is," I insisted. "I am not your spy, not your whore to pimp out, and I came here to have fun with my brother, visit my best friend, and watch some baseball."

"Fine," he said, and I could tell he was upset.

The guy wasn't bad to look at, but he was on a different team, and my heart belonged to the Dragons. I mean, growing up, sure, we had all been fans of the Cascades, but since Quentin had been drafted, we switched our allegiance to the Dragons and never looked back.

"Well, well, well," the player said as he sidled up to the table. "If it isn't Belinsky, the soon-to-be unseated MVP of the American league."

"What's up, Hennings?" my brother said. "Looks like you're all alone tonight."

"Nah," he said. "I've had my first date already. Just looking for a second. This your girlfriend?"

"My sister," Quentin said. "And she's off-limits."

"Don't you think she should be the one to determine that?"

He reached out his hand, offering it to me in a most gentlemanly manner, and I took it. Never taking his eyes off mine, he raised it to his lips and laid a gentle kiss on the back, his beard rough against my skin.

"My lady," he said, still holding my hand.

"Dude," my brother said, smacking his shoulder. "Knock it off. You are not allowed to screw my sister. Especially since you've screwed everything in a skirt from here to Seattle and back."

"I've obviously missed the most beautiful one," he said, and I hated myself for the way my pulse quickened.

"I'll pass," I said, pulling my hand away.

"You don't even know me," the other player said. "I might be exactly what you're looking for tonight."

"Highly doubt it," I said.

Just then, the waitress came back with our drinks.

"Hey," the Cascades player said to the waitress, and the way he looked at her, as if he were sizing up a steak, was awful.

"Can I get you something?" she asked him.

"Just you in my bed," he replied, and I choked on the sip of my drink I'd just taken.

"I meant to drink," she corrected, and I was impressed.

"Jack and Coke," he said. "And this dude is paying," he added, indicating Quentin.

"The fuck I am," my brother replied. "You got a fucking contract. Pay for your own damn booze."

"I usually just pay for the ladies," he said, winking at me.

"I'm good," I said, and he quickly replied, "I'm sure you are."

"Jesus, dude," my brother said. "Do you ever quit?"

"Not if I can help it," he said and sat on the stool next to me. "I'm like the damn Energizer bunny. I keep going and going and going."

The waitress came back with his Jack and Coke and we ordered appetizers and our meal.

"I like a girl that likes her meat," he said, and I couldn't help but laugh. "Hey," he said, looking at my brother. "I think she likes me."

"Don't bet on it," Quentin said. "She's just laughing because you're an idiot."

"Can we not talk about me while I'm sitting right here?" I asked.

"I could talk about you all night long," the player from the other team said. "Especially if you come back to my room. I'm sure we can find all sorts of good things to talk about."

"Ballsy, ain't ya," I said.

"They're big," he replied. "Wanna feel?"

"Enough," Quentin barked. "My sister is off-limits. You try to screw her, you're gonna have to deal with my whole team coming after you."

I sat there and shook my head. My brother was the protector, for sure, but I was a big girl and could take care of myself. Honestly, I didn't even think this guy was that bad. Maybe it was my perception, but he just seemed to keep going because it was pissing Quentin off, which made it even funnier.

"At least give me your number," he begged. "I promise, I'll only send you good angled dick pics."

"I swear to God, dude," my brother said just as the waitress brought the appetizers.

CHAPTER TWO

*B*eckett...

Belinsky's sister was hot, and not just in the way she looked, although that was true, too. No, she had sass and was not at all afraid to talk back. I could totally get into her if she weren't attached to the enemy.

"So," she said once the appetizers were set on the table. "You're the short stop for the Cascades. Anyone ever make comments on your height?"

"What I lack in height," I replied, pouring on the charm, "I make up for in length and girth. You know, where it counts the most."

She laughed, which just meant that she understood my reference. Maybe there was something there I could work with and keep the whole baseball enemy thing out of it.

"That's my baby sister," Quentin said. "Can you just not?"

"Have you seen her?" I asked. "She's fucking rockin' in that beautiful bod of hers. I'd love to see it without the Dragons' jersey, though."

"Forget it," he said, as if he could rule who his sister screwed around with.

I kept watching her, though, and she seemed like she was starting to warm up to me and my antics, so I just filed that shit away for use later. Maybe I'd be able to find out where she lived or at least get a number for her so we could maybe hook up. Honestly, I was getting hard watching her down the mozzarella sticks. If she started eating a banana that way, I might just blow my load in my pants, cause she had a mouth I'd love to fuck.

"I don't know, man," I said. "She's drinking, which I'm pretty sure makes her an adult. Which means she can screw anyone she wants."

"Don't talk about her like she's some trash ho you picked up," her brother said.

"I'm right here," she said. "I do have vocal cords and can speak for myself."

"Chime in, baby doll," I said. "I wanna hear everything going on in that gorgeous head of yours."

I stared at her, and she blinked, like she wasn't expecting that. It was true, though. Her voice had a quality I could totally get into, and hearing more just gave me that much more ammunition to use to beat off to later. Either that, or I could pretend she was the bitch I was fucking if she didn't let me do her.

"I just find it a little ridiculous that my brother thinks he can dictate what I do," she began. "Not that I would be doing you, mind you."

"My heart," I groaned, putting a hand to my chest. "You're killing me."

"I'm sure you'll find someone to fill the void," she said. "I mean, you're a charmer, obviously."

The backhanded compliment didn't bruise my ego, not nearly as much as her rejection did. Somehow, though, she still looked like she might be interested. Maybe she wasn't willing to say anything in front of her brother, but there was something there, just under the surface. When the waitress came back with their burgers, I decided I'd let myself be tortured enough for one evening.

"Tell you what," I said. "I'll just give you this little coaster with my number on it, and you can call if you find yourself lonely."

I'd scribbled my cell number down on one of the extra ones on the table and slid it over to her. She smirked, but stuffed it in her back pocket. I'd take that as progress any day.

"Enjoy your meat," I added with a wink, downed what was left of my drink, then walked away.

I could hear her laughing and her brother said something about me being an asshole, but I didn't care. She hadn't tossed it, shoved it back at me, or completely ignored it. No, she'd picked it up and would likely be taking it with her. Whether she called me or not was another story.

Stepping out of the bar and into the lobby of the hotel, I thought about walking outside to find another bar to hit up and find some desperate whore to bring back to my room, but it just didn't sit right for some reason. I headed up to see if I could find something that would keep me busy until I passed out. We started our series here in Houston the next day, and I did actually have some film I should be watching, figuring out how they were gonna hit our pitchers, what they'd done so far this season, and looking at the pitching we were likely to face throughout the next four days.

Decision made, I made a beeline for the elevators, punched my floor number, then rode it up. The walk down the hall to my room wasn't long, and the more I thought about her, the more I wanted to get her under me and me inside her. It was more than just a quick fuck, though. Maybe she could be my girl in this port, as the sailors used to say. I'd be down for banging her the handful of times a year we were here, and Houston wasn't that far from Dallas, either, so I could maybe hit it more often.

The more I thought about it, the more I liked the idea of banging little Miss Belinsky. If I was lucky, I could even get her to dress up in some naughty schoolgirl outfit or be the naughty librarian, or honestly, anything with naughty in front of it. That long brown hair pulled up in pigtails would be mighty fine to hold on to while I fucked her from behind. Damn, just the thought of it was making me hard.

Guess another shower would come sooner than planned, but that was fine. I'd just imagine her on her knees, me fucking her mouth. Yeah, not a bad way to go.

CHAPTER THREE

Fi...

"You're not gonna call him, are you?" Quentin asked.

"Thought you wanted me to get on his good side and get you some insights," I replied.

"Ophelia," he said.

"What?" I asked, feigning innocence.

"Fi," he began. "That dude is a dick. On and off the field. Every guy on his team has complained about his womanizing ways. I don't want to see you get hurt."

"Like he said," I countered. "I am an adult. Besides, I can take care of myself."

"If I forbid it?"

"The temptation of the forbidden fruit ring any bells?"

"Fine," he said. "But don't say I didn't warn you."

"Wouldn't dream of it, big brother," I said, then dug into my burger.

Quentin had always been a bit overbearing when it came to me dating. I once dated one of the players on his high school team. Apparently, the dude was bragging about taking my virginity and going on and on about everything he did to me at a practice. My brother punched him in the face and was suspended for a couple of days for it, but I just turned the whole thing around on the dude. By the time my brother came back to school, the dude was off the team and was the laughingstock of the entire school. Let's just say that my love of trashy romance novels and my ability to be petty as fuck led the entire school to thinking he had a tiny pecker and couldn't even get a rise out of it, no matter how hard I tried.

After that incident, he realized that I was more than capable of taking care of myself, and didn't need him to be my bodyguard. The fact that we were so close together in age had always bothered him, but now that we were adults, it was great. We hung out any time we could, and I was always a great supporter of his endeavors, especially base-ball, which I absolutely loved.

"What time do you have to be at the stadium tomorrow?" I asked.

"Why?" he asked.

"I just want to know how much time I have to get into trouble before you go," I replied. "I mean, I do like to cause trouble."

"I thought you were hanging out with McKenzie," he said.

"Oh, we are," I replied. "But we gotta get into trouble. I mean, it's been ages since we hung out."

"Really?" he asked.

"Dude," I said around a mouthful of burger. "She lives here now. I live in Seattle. We don't see each other all the time. I mean, we chat, talk on the phone, even video chat often, but it's been almost a year since I've seen her in person, and I miss her. We're doing the whole weekend hang out thing, and doing all the girly things you hate."

"I guess I didn't realize it had been that long," he said.

"She was in school when I came down last time," I replied. "She hasn't been back home since Christmas, and I didn't see her then because I was super busy with work. She said she had the weekend available for me to come see her, so we're gonna hang out. You did get us both tickets to the game, right?"

"You told me to get two," he said. "I just assumed you were bringing a friend."

"You're a dork," I said.

We'd finished our burgers, and it was late enough that I was getting tired.

"I think I need to turn in," I said with a yawn. "You should clean up your apartment."

"Why?" he asked.

"I mean," I began. "Never mind. You don't need to let me in. I'll see it another time. I'm gonna text McKenzie when I get to my room so we can make a plan for tomorrow. You wanna meet up with us?"

"Not if you guys are just doing girly things," he said. "I'll let you have fun. I should go home, anyway. I have some film to watch before the game tomorrow. You know how to get to the stadium?"

"There is this magic thing called Uber," I said. "I've used it before. Besides, I think McKenzie is gonna drive tomorrow, so don't worry about me."

"Well," he said, dropping cash on the table. "I'll see you at the game tomorrow."

He stood up, and so did I.

"See you then," I said and hugged him.

Walking from the bar, he turned to go out the front doors of the hotel and I headed for the elevators. Yeah, I could feel the travel day hitting me. I never slept well before flying somewhere, and with it being a late flight, I was beat. Guess I'd just head to bed after texting my friend. I had to tell her where I was, since we usually met up at my brother's place. When I stepped out of the elevator on my floor, I wasn't paying attention and I ran right into the player who had been in the bar earlier.

"Hey, sweetheart," he said, steadying me on my feet.

"I'm sorry," I apologized. "I wasn't watching where I was going."

"No worries," he said. "You coming to find me?"

"Actually," I replied. "I am heading to bed."

"I make great company," he said with a smirk. "I'm all kinds of warm and fuzzy."

"My brother told me you had a reputation," I said.

"I am good with the ladies," he replied.

I had moved away from the elevator and had been walking down the hall. He'd fallen in step beside me and had accompanied me along the way. We were now standing in front of my room, and I was a little uncomfortable.

"I'm sure you're great and all…" I began.

"But big brother Quentin wants you to stay away from the big bad wolf, right?"

"Something like that," I agreed. "I mean, I'll see you at the stadium tomorrow, since I'm going to the game."

"That mean you're looking forward to seeing me?"

He sounded hopeful, and standing this close to him, even though I was a few inches taller, he was actually really good looking. No, I couldn't do this. It would be too weird.

"I guess," I said, trying not to give any of my discomfort away. "But I gotta crash."

"Sleep well, angel," he said, then turned and headed back down the hall.

He stopped in front of a room just a few down from mine and I realized that we were on the same floor.

"If you need anything," he called down the hall, "don't be afraid to come knocking. I'm right here, you know, for whatever you might need."

I used my key to get into my room and locked the door behind me. This could either end up being a really good thing or a terrible one. Only time would tell.

CHAPTER FOUR

*B*eckett...

"If you need anything," I called down the hall, "don't be afraid to come knocking. I'm right here, you know, for whatever you might need."

The way she slunk into her room was a little bit of a blow off, but there had been a moment where she looked like she might be open to something. I opened my door and went inside. Originally, I'd planned to see if I could find someone to hook up with, but running into Miss Belinsky was divine intervention if ever there was such a thing. Now, knowing she was just a few doors down from me, I was determined to plot at least one more meetup before I left town.

My biggest question was why she was staying in a hotel. I mean, her brother lived here, so she should be staying with him. Then again, I figured they were from here, and that's why she was with her brother in the bar. There were many things I needed to get to the bottom of, and it all started with a search of the baseball website.

I grabbed my laptop from the desk and flopped down onto the bed, opening it up and signing in. The hotel had free Wi-Fi for all the players because it was part of our contract to stay here. Logging in, I went to the website and did a search of the players. Fortunately, I could start typing his last name and he was easy to find from the drop-down list of active players. Once I clicked on his profile, I looked at his bio.

"Shit," I muttered.

They were actually from Washington state. I had no idea where the hell Auburn was, but that's the town he grew up in. Maybe that was on the eastern side of the state and it wouldn't be an issue of me running into her at a game up there. Or, he moved his family to Houston to be closer to him. Honestly, though, she probably didn't go to many, and likely only to the ones her brother was in, so I didn't have too much to worry about. At least I hoped I didn't.

I also went to Google to see if there was a mention of her first name. We didn't get introduced, but I assumed it would be somewhere. Just my luck, she was actually an athlete, too, although not at the level of her brother. She played softball for the University of Washington, at short stop no less, and they'd won the Women's College World Series her senior year, which was just now over.

"That's interesting," I said to nobody.

The question then became, did I call her on it? Tell her I knew she played, and that she played the same position as me? Or did I pretend I didn't know a thing?

"Not a question I need to answer now," I muttered, then went to the team's website to review film for tomorrow's game.

Four game sets were both a blessing and a curse. It was good that you got to do it on the same field several days in a row, but you also had to deal with the fact that if you were off, even a little bit, it could be absolute hell. Their starting pitcher for the first game was their number five guy, so his ERA was higher than the rest. With any luck, it would end up being a bullpen game and we'd see several pitchers who wouldn't have enough time to get into a rhythm, and that always favored the hitters. Either way, I needed to prepare, so off I went to find all the answers to baseball's questions, at least as it pertained to the Houston Dragons.

~

MY PHONE WENT OFF, AND I TURNED THE ALARM OFF, ROLLING OVER to look at the curtained windows. They did a decent job of keeping out the light, but it still leaked in around them, and I could see that it was already bright out. I threw back the covers and climbed out of bed, heading to the bathroom to start the day. Once I'd cleaned up, I threw on my slacks and a button-down and headed out to the coffee shop in the lobby. Some guys said it was horrible for their system and wouldn't touch it, but I needed it in order to people as much as I had to.

I was a bit disappointed that I didn't run into Miss Belinsky on the way down, or even in the lobby. Ophelia turned out to be her first name, but it didn't seem to fit, so I'd stick with the Miss part and forgo the first name business. Maybe there was a nickname, but it didn't really matter. I'd make sure she knew my name, though. I wanted to hear her call it out in ecstasy at some point, hopefully in the near future.

After coffee, I checked the schedule on my phone and was a little disappointed I didn't have a text or missed call from an unknown number. She'd call or text. I knew it. My schedule said we were to meet the bus at two, so I had a few hours to kill before we had to head out. I went to the restaurant and ordered some breakfast to be sent to my room, then headed back up to figure out whether a workout before heading to the park would be worth it.

"Hey," Bridge said as he stepped out of the elevator as I was stepping in. "Breakfast?"

"Ordered it to be sent up," I replied as the doors closed.

The dude was nice and all, but he had that dad vibe going on, and I was plenty old enough to not need a parental figure in my life. I mean, my sperm donor was an asshole and left me and Mom high and dry once he found out I was on the way. Said he never signed up for parenthood and wasn't gonna do it. Mom filed for child support, but it was sporadic at best. By the time I was in middle school, she was holding down two jobs to keep us in a shitty apartment.

Then I found baseball. I tried out for the team and actually turned out to be natural at it. The school had a scholarship program that helped with equipment for underprivileged kids, and I was definitely in that category. They paid for a glove and cleats, and I just wore the team uniform for the first three years. By the time I hit high school, I was the talk of the town, and some rich son of a bitch decided that he'd take me under his wing and help me out.

He paid for everything. New glove, new equipment for the school, all the pieces that I needed to play. It was amazing to begin with, and the fact that I just flat out excelled at the game was really great. After the first year, though, the rich asshole wanted to call in his repayment plan by way of sexual favors. The booze was great, the weed was great, but him fucking with me downstairs was awful.

I tried to tell my mom about it, but she was barely home, and when she was, she was exhausted. She kept telling me it couldn't be an issue because he was paying so much. No one would do that and then expect something in return.

Turns out, he wasn't just fucking with me. One of the other players who was in the "underprivileged" category like me, went to the cops. Before anyone knew it, the dude was on the news, being arrested and they were looking for any other victims to come forward to corroborate his story. I told my mom I was gonna come forward, and she freaked out. Said I was going to take a good man down with some lies.

After the trial, when there were more than a dozen kids all saying the same thing, my mom finally realized that I had been telling the truth. At least that's what she told me after it was all over. By then, though, our relationship had suffered beyond repair. First chance I got, I bailed and hadn't talked to her in years.

When Coach gave me a letter they received near the start of the year, I didn't think anything of it. Opening it opened all the shit I'd tried to bury. Mom had cancer, something awful that was killing her from the inside. There was nothing they could do, and she only had a few months at most. She'd begged me to come see her, or at least to call her, but I couldn't. Too much time had passed, and I wasn't the scared little boy who left her.

Fuck, I thought. Why the hell had all this come up now? Must have been the whole taking care of me thing J did at the beginning of the last season that made me see him in a way that brought it out of me.

This was why I didn't do relationships of any kind—no friends, no family, certainly no girlfriend or wife. Nah, the rest of the guys could do that, but not me. I was all about being wild and free and able to fuck 'em and leave 'em.

Letting myself into my room, I grabbed my laptop and opened it up to get on the team website and make sure nothing had changed since the lobby. There was still a tab open with little Miss Belinsky's information on it, and I clicked over to it. Even when she was all sweaty with black eye running down her cheeks, she was hot as fuck, maybe even hotter. Yeah, I was definitely gonna have to hit that before I left town.

CHAPTER FIVE

*F*i...

"Fi," McKenzie screamed when she got to the hotel and saw me. "I missed you so much."

She gave me the biggest hug, and I returned it likewise.

"Girl," I said when we pulled apart. "You are looking fine as wine. How have you been?"

"Life is insane right now," she said. "I have a couple of interviews next week for some really great jobs, but this weekend is about you and me and being total girls."

"You're gonna stay in Houston?" I asked.

When she headed off to college, she wanted to experience some-place different from where we grew up, and Texas was about as different as it could get.

"I kinda love it here," she said. "Besides, I get to see your brother play all the time, so that's a bonus."

"You still crushing on him?" I laughed.

"Never stopped," she replied. "First thing first, let's get breakfast."

"Lead the way," I said as we stepped out of the door.

She walked to the other side of a pretty nice car and I kind of looked at her, but she didn't notice and climbed into the driver's seat. I got into the passenger seat and we headed out.

"There's this really cool brunch place I love to go to," she said as we drove down the street.

"Nice car," I said as we went along.

"Oh, yeah," she said, blushing. "A friend helped me get it."

"This friend a guy?" I asked.

"Just a friend," she said, but the blush running up her cheeks told me she was lying.

"Okay," I replied.

No need to call her out on it when it didn't really matter. She pulled up to this little out-of-the-way place that was one of those hole-in-the-wall ones that likely had great food. She parked, and we climbed out, heading up to the door. When she pulled it open, the scents that were coming out made my mouth water.

"It smells so good," I said.

"Best brunch in town," she replied.

We walked up to the front counter, and the hostess took us to a little table away from the door. It was pretty small inside, maybe a dozen tables at most.

"They do takeout as their main business," she said when we were seated. "I love picking something up and taking it home. It travels really well, and they have a huge variety of options. Everyone can get what they want and no one will go hungry. Their portions are huge."

"Should we share something?" I asked.

"We can drop the leftovers at your hotel," she said. "You do have a fridge, right?"

"Yeah," I replied. "So, what's good?"

"Everything," she said. "I'm gonna go with biscuits and gravy. Their gravy is bomb."

"You have officially become a southern girl," I said.

The waitress came back and took our order and then headed off to put it in. Once she was gone, I started the inquisition.

"Who's the guy?" I asked. "And don't try to tell me there isn't one."

"Just a guy," she said. "He's nice, but we're not serious."

"But he got you a car," I added. "That sounds serious."

"He helped me out," she countered.

"You living together?"

"God, Fi," she said. "Do you need to know everything?"

"We're supposed to be best friends," I said. "That means we share everything."

"So," she said. "Who's your guy?"

"I don't have a guy," I said.

"Then why are you all dressed up and shit?"

"Cause we're out on the town," I said. "I like dressing up, and this was just the excuse I needed. Besides, I bought this sundress just for this trip, and I gotta get as much use out of it as possible."

I wasn't about to tell her that I hoped to run into a certain baseball player while I was at the hotel, or that I planned to be as dressed up as possible in case he happened to see me in the stands, or at the hotel, or anywhere in town. No, not gonna tell her that, 'cause it just isn't a good look.

"Fine," she said. "There's a guy. He's really nice, and he treats me well. I'm not going to tell you anything else about him because I don't want to jinx anything."

"See," I said. "That wasn't so hard, was it?"

The waitress brought our food and McKenzie wasn't kidding when she said they gave big portions. I didn't even know whether I could eat a quarter of what was on the plate. This would feed me for the rest of my trip to be honest. Once we'd stuffed ourselves as much as possible, we got boxes to take the rest back to the hotel before heading out for our day of girl time.

"I'll wait here," she said when we pulled up to the hotel. "Just run in, put it in the fridge, then come back out."

"Okay," I said. "I'll be quick."

The automatic doors opened as I walked up and then hushed shut behind me. I walked across the lobby to the elevator, paper bag in my hand, and pressed the button to go up. A couple of guys stepped out of the elevator who were likely players for the Cascades. They had the build and were dressed pretty nice. I stepped in after they got out and pressed the button to my floor and rode up all alone in the music-infused space.

When the door opened, I went to step out, but stopped.

"Welcome back," the player said. "You miss me?"

I stood there staring, and the doors started to close, but he stuck his arm in to keep them open.

"You coming out?"

"Oh, yeah," I stuttered and stepped out.

When he didn't step in, I stopped and looked at him.

"Just gonna watch the show," he said, smirking. "Go on now."

"Jackass," I said, but turned and made sure that my hips swung just a little more than normal. I mean, if he wants a show, I'd give him one.

"Hate to see you go," he called down the hall. "But love watching you leave. Damn, if you ain't the finest thing I've seen since I got to town."

I rolled my eyes so damn hard I checked out my own ass, but I didn't turn around. No, if I did that, he'd know I had a thing going for him, and I didn't want him to know. When I got to my door, I pulled out my key card and stuck it in the lock. When I opened my door, I took a peek down the hall and he was just standing there, leaning against the wall, like he was waiting for me.

"Shit," I said and ducked into my room.

I opened the fridge and had to pull the little cartons out of the bag in order to fit them into the small space. Once that was done, I popped into the bathroom and checked my makeup. No reason to go back out there right away. If I was lucky, he'd be gone when I went back down the hall. Without anything left to delay me, and knowing McKenzie was waiting, I took a deep breath and let it out, then went to the door and opened it. Stepping out of my room, I looked down the hall, and he hadn't moved.

"Son of a bitch," I mumbled as I let the door close behind me.

Whatever, I could handle this. I did fine with him in the bar, so this should be easy.

"You look just as good coming as you do going," he said.

"Although, I'd prefer to see you coming in a different manner. You know, for research purposes."

"Do these lines actually work for you?" I asked as he pressed the button to recall the elevator.

"Usually women just look at me and fall to their knees in worship," he replied. "You know, like you wanna do right now."

"Pretty sure you're imagining things," I said. "No worshipping coming from me. Hate to burst your bubble."

"I'm not worried," he said. "Eventually you'll come around. See, there we go, talking about you coming. This could get interesting."

"Wow," I said. "I'm surprised you've actually slept with anyone if these are the lines you've used."

"Oh, baby," he said and I kind of gave a little shiver. "I'm better than you've ever had. I guarantee it. Try me out, you'll see."

I just rolled my eyes as we rode down to the lobby. Once the doors opened, I walked as fast as possible away from the man.

"See you soon," he called across the space.

"Not if I see you first," I muttered and walked out into the heat of Houston.

CHAPTER SIX

*B*eckett...

"You look to be in a good mood," Decker said as I sat next to him on the bus.

"Always a reason to smile," I replied.

He was one of the few players that hadn't been pissed at me the whole season so far. Maybe because he was new to the team, too. Of course, he was a little older than me, though not much. I think he had two, maybe three years on me, but he had been in the bigs for both of those, so that made him a bit more aware of what was what when it came to this level.

"Yours is usually a girl," he said, laughing.

"Girls are often good things," I replied.

Plugging my AirPods into my ears, I switched on my music and zoned out, working through the plan for the night. I wasn't too worried about the starter the Dragons had for the night, but there were a couple of guys in their pen who were not easy to read. No matter how much film I watched, I couldn't figure out what they were throwing. That was never a good thing. Oh sure, we could figure out what we thought they *may* throw, but if you guessed wrong, you ended up taking that long walk back to the dugout. No one wanted to do that.

Afternoon traffic in the city wasn't horrible, so we were able to get to the stadium easily, then we all got off the bus and made the walk to the clubhouse. Our team was fairly young, with the handful of veterans who were good to chat up and find out how to work our bats against the opposing team's pitchers. I figured I'd see if my babysitter from the beginning of the year had any insight.

"Hey, J," I said as I walked past him.

"What's up, kid?" he asked.

"You been here a while," I said. "What's your approach to this guy that's starting tonight?"

"Honestly," he said. "I think he's gonna struggle to get the ball in the zone. Wait him out. Sit dead red, but otherwise wait and see. At least for your first at bat."

"Kinda what I was thinking," I replied. "He seems to have been hit a bit, so figured he'd struggle."

"Yeah," Huffman added, coming into the conversation. "He can't locate his curve, and the slider tanks too soon. Sit dead red, you'll be fine."

"Thanks," I said.

I'd taken a bit more of a team approach to the season after the first month or so. Figured out that being pissed, and pissing everyone off, wasn't going to win me anything, so settled down and shut up, so to speak. Don't get me wrong, I was still smack talking the opposing team's players when they got close to me. I just worked to hold my tongue when I had to deal with my own team.

Turned out, the team actually appreciated my work ethic once I'd let my plays do the talking. I think the whole thing with my mom sending me that letter just fucked me up, and I needed to get it out of my system. The team hadn't received any other letters from her, so I don't know if she died or what, but it really didn't matter.

What mattered the most was the game, the time spent between the chalk lines. If I kept my work ethic aboveboard there, most everything else could be excused. Bridge still reminded me every time we went to a new town to not screw the fans, but I had just learned to smile and nod, then do whatever the fuck I wanted. Made things a whole lot easier. And I was careful, always ensuring that they were legal age, they weren't drunk or high, and that they left without any way to trap me.

"Hey, Hennings," Cote, our second baseman, called. "You coming?"

I laughed, remembering the conversation with Miss Belinsky from the hotel, and then called out, "Yeah."

I grabbed my mitt and headed out to the field to begin warm-ups. Our infield coach, Rodriguez, wanted to work on some drills with me and Cote. We'd been turning double plays pretty well, but they'd always started with him throwing to me. Coach wanted us to work on the other way around, with him doing the catch-and-release throw to first.

～

"GOOD THING WE DID THOSE DRILLS," COTE SAID AS WE TROTTED OFF the field.

"Seems like Coach knows exactly when to work on things," I replied.

"Nice job, guys," Coach said as we dropped into the dugout. "You're really playing to your potential tonight."

"Thanks," I said, with Cote copying my gratitude a moment later, saying, "Thanks, Coach."

I was up first, so I stuffed my glove and hat into my cubby after pulling out the helmet and batting gloves that were in there. I grabbed my bat and headed to the on-deck circle, adding weight to the bat to get stretched out. Watching the pitcher, I swung the bat back and forth behind my head, pulling my shoulders to their full extension, then brought it back around my head to in front of me.

Pounding the handle of the bat on the ground, I dislodged the weight, then stood in my stance to try to time out the pitcher. It was a bit difficult, being on the third base side and hitting left-handed, but I made it work, moving further behind home plate than where the circle actually was. Feeling confident with my timing by the time the catcher made the toss to second and the ball went around the horn, I moved toward home plate to step into the batter's box.

"Let's go," the catcher said, then squatted behind the plate.

The pitcher stared in, looking at the sign the catcher was putting down. I watched the middle infielders to see where they were gonna line up. That would give me a little bit of a hint as to what I might see when he finally threw the ball. He stood up, went to his set, then wound up and let the ball go.

"Ball," the umpire said.

It was a curveball that went into the dirt. Huffman was right, this guy couldn't put it where he wanted. I stepped out of the box with my right foot, took a couple of swings, then stepped back in, getting my back foot toed into the dirt. The second baseman had moved closer to first, and the short stop had stepped a couple paces toward second, so I figured the pitcher was going to try to throw inside.

The set, the wind up, and the throw, and it was inside so far I almost fell on my ass trying to get away from it.

"Really?" I shouted toward the pitcher.

He just shrugged after taking a new ball from the catcher. I took a couple of practice swings outside the box, then toed my back foot in before pulling my right into the box.

"Two and oh," the umpire said, indicating there were two balls and no strikes.

This time, the middle infielders moved the other direction, which likely meant that the pitcher was going to throw it outside. The set, the wind up, and the release, but the ball didn't move outside. It stayed straight, right down the middle. I pulled my lead foot up and swung right into the ball, feeling the jar run up my arms as the bat connected. My follow-through was perfect, and I watched the ball as it left my bat and soared high and far, going the other way down the left field line, clearing the out-of-town scoreboard, and landing behind the fans seated there and onto the concourse behind.

I dropped my bat as I left the batter's box to take my trot around the bases, giving a high five to the first base coach.

"Only way you're gonna score tonight," Belinsky said as I passed him on the infield.

"Not the way your sister was looking at me earlier," I barked back, laughing.

"Asshole," he called after me as I rounded third and gave the third base coach a high five as well.

I stepped on home, then turned and gave Huffman a high five before dropping into the dugout for hat slaps and high fives.

"Nice hit, kid," Bridge said as he patted my head.

"Thanks," I replied.

There were more congratulations down the line as I went, then I pulled my helmet off and stuffed my batting gloves inside before swapping it out for my hat and mitt. After a hit, strike out, and a double play, we were heading back out for defense and my counterpart was set to be first up to bat. We did our pre-inning warm-ups, catching grounders from our first baseman, Matsui, then throwing them back until our pitcher was warmed up. I took the throw from Decker, our catcher, did the sweep across the base, then threw it to Cote who threw it over to Matsui, who then tossed it to Sammy.

Watching Belinsky step up to the plate, hearing his walk-up music, I was confused. He stood just outside the batter's box and watched the third base coach, who was looking into the dugout. Now, this is a normal thing, in that the third base or first base coach gets the sign on whether to swing or take a ball, as well as what other things are set up for the pitch like hit and run or a steal. What was odd was their manager was looking behind him and down the ramp to the clubhouse. He turned around just after Belinsky stepped into the box and sent out the sign after Decker threw down his fingers.

Sammy was set to throw a curve that should break into the batter in the right-hand batter's box. I took my hand and rubbed it across my chest, then patted my knee twice. Decker caught it and called time, standing up behind the base.

I walked to the mound on the guise of grabbing some rosin from the bag at the back and said to Sammy, "They're stealing signs."

I picked up the rosin bag, let it bounce on the back of my wrist, then dropped it back down behind the pitcher.

"Throw it in his ear," I said before walking back to my position. "Let's go," I shouted to the rest of the team.

Sammy took the sign from Decker again, but didn't throw the pitch that was called, and instead threw right up and in on Belinsky, who had to fall on his ass to avoid being hit. The crowd booed us, and the players in their dugout came up to the top step. Decker called time and walked the new ball out to Sammy after the previous one had gone all the way to the backstop and the umpire had thrown it out of play, pulling me into the conversation.

"What the fuck?" he asked when I got there.

"I don't know how," I explained, my glove covering my mouth, "but they're stealing signs. Their manager is watching something down the hall, then relaying it to their base coaches."

"What do we do?" Sammy asked.

"You guys know what you want to pitch," I said, looking between my teammates. "Don't throw down signs."

"How will you field?" Decker asked.

"We all know what's gonna happen," I explained. "We'll play it by ear. Think middle school rules here. No signs, play it straight, strike them all out."

"You sure?" Decker asked.

"Absolutely," I replied. "I'll make sure the rest of the infield knows what's up."

I walked away from the mound toward second and told Cote, letting him know we were going without signs for the rest of the inning. I told him to give the word to Matsui and I would tell Cameron, our third baseman.

After we were all on the same page, we lined up, fairly straight away, shifting every so often to one side or the other, and waited for Sammy to pitch. It started with a fastball, low and outside, but still within the strike zone. Then he threw a cutter that had the bottom drop out of it and had Belinsky swinging over the top. After that, it was the same curve he was going to start the inning off with that the batter was way too fast to try to hit it.

When he walked away from the plate after the strike three call, he glared at me for some reason. Did he know I figured out what they were doing? Or was he just pissed that he didn't get a hit when I'd gone yard on his guy? Neither question needed to be answered.

With the next two batters, Decker threw down random signs, but we all knew what was going to be thrown. Each pitch was missed, either late on a fastball they thought was going to be an off-speed pitch, or way ahead on one that was slower. It honestly was a beautiful thing to watch, and I was happy we all knew what actually was going on. We walked off the field with three strike outs and our manager scratching his head.

"What the hell was that?" he asked when Sammy came into the dugout.

"Ask Hennings," he replied.

"Well?" the coach asked, looking at me.

"Don't ask me how," I said. "But they're stealing signs without players on the bases."

"The fuck they are," he barked.

"Watch them next inning," I said. "Their manager is looking down the hall, then giving a signal as soon as the signs are thrown down."

"How did he strike them all out?"

"Didn't use signs," I said. "Or threw down shit that wasn't what he was actually throwing. Beat them at their own game."

"Can you prove it?" he asked.

"Not yet," I replied. "But give me a bit and we'll figure it out."

"That's a hell of a lot of trust you're asking me to put in you, kid," he said.

"Give me two innings," I said. "I should be able to figure it out."

He just shook his head, but let me go. I walked down the dugout toward the outfielders. They would be able to help me figure out what was going on, or at least I hoped they would.

"What up, short stack?" Huffman asked.

"Got a project," I said. "You up for screwing with these guys?"

"Let me have it," he replied, a smile crossing his face that held a bit of malice in it. Exactly what I wanted to see.

CHAPTER SEVEN

*F*i...

   "Quentin said there are tickets for both of us," I said when we got back from our girly time.

My nails were done up in a great deep purple that matched the color of my Dragons' jersey. We'd also gotten facials, waxing, and hair that my brother had graciously set up for us.

"That's nice of him," McKenzie said. "Did he know we were hanging out?"

"Oh yeah," I said. "Told him it was my girly day, then we were gonna come to the game, and made sure he had tickets for both of us."

"He's really nice," she said.

"Oh yeah," I replied. "Stupid that he won't let me stay at his place, though. He said it was kind of a wreck, which if that's the only thing, I could have dealt with it. I honestly think he's hiding something from me. Like, he's got a girl living with him or something."

"Oh," she replied, but it was a bit distracted.

She had been texting on her phone since I mentioned that we were going to the game, like she had some secret plans she had to cancel or something. Whatever it was, she definitely was hiding something, too.

"Breaking a date?" I asked when she shoved her phone into her purse.

"Yeah," she said, but it wasn't quite believable.

"What's up with you?" I asked.

"What?" she countered.

"You just seem really distracted," I said. "You're on your phone, looking like you're afraid to tell me something, and just kind of all over the place. You okay?"

"Just had to get some things squared away," she said. "You know, since we're going to the game and all."

"If you'd rather—" I began, but she cut me off.

"No, no," she said. "I just..."

She stopped, mid-sentence, like she was going to tell me something, but then decided against it.

"If you're in trouble..." I said.

"Nothing like that," she replied. "Can we talk about something else?"

"Sure," I said. "Like what?"

"What's going on with you?" she asked.

"I don't even want to talk about it," I said. "It just sucks that there aren't too many pro women's sports and I have to find a real job now that college is over."

"I feel that," she said. "I'm just glad I landed something so quickly. It was almost like it was meant to be or something."

"Yeah," I said. "How did this come about?"

"I applied," she said. "Sent my resume and a cover letter and they apparently loved me without even meeting me. Once I had the official interview, they asked about my plans moving forward, whether I was going to be staying in the area or moving back home. When I told them I was planning on staying, they offered me an amazing opportunity."

"That's awesome," I said. "I can't even tell you how many resumes I've sent out. It's like the Pacific Northwest isn't hiring anyone for anything right now."

"You could always come here," she suggested.

"I can't handle this heat," I replied.

"You get used to it," she said. "It actually didn't take that long, either."

"I guess," I said. "I did line something up, though, and it starts on Monday, so I'm not totally on my own without a job or anything."

"That's good," she said.

We'd pulled up to the parking garage for the stadium and followed the long line of cars in. McKenzie held out a pass of some sort and they told us to head to the third floor.

"What's that?" I asked when we pulled away from the attendant.

"Oh," she said, a little bit awkwardly. "Your brother gave me a pass thing for if I ever came to a game. I didn't even think about it."

"He's cool like that," I said, but filed that information away for later dissection.

She parked in an area of some pretty nice cars, so it must have been the place where families parked or something. Once she shut the car off, we got out and headed to the elevator to go down to will call for our tickets.

"You should get them," she said, standing back away from the window.

"Okay," I replied, but didn't say more.

Inside, though, I was starting to question everything that had been going on the last day or so. My brother acting weird was one thing, but McKenzie was always a by-my-side kind of girl and she didn't shy away from these types of things. She was on her phone the whole time I stood in line to get the tickets. Once they were in hand, I headed back over to her.

"Ready?" I asked.

"Yep," she replied, then took the ticket I handed to her.

We went to the gate, showed our tickets where they scanned them, then we went inside the stadium. I began to look around, trying to figure out where we needed to go, but McKenzie pulled me to the right and around the concourse toward some concession stands.

"Food first," she said as we got into line.

"I think we get free food in the seats we're in," I said, but she just shook her head and stayed put.

Whatever. We waited in line, then grabbed some hot dogs and sodas before heading to our seats. It seemed to me that my friend actually knew where she was going, as she wasn't looking at her ticket or the signage above the crowd. Maybe Quentin had given her tickets before, so she knew where to go. That would make sense, but then he didn't mention it to me, so I wasn't sure.

By the time we got to our section, my soda was half gone, and I had to pee. Stepping down the stairs, we made it to our row. McKenzie sat in the seat on the inside, and I was going to take the aisle seat. I stuck my soda cup into the holder where my seat was, then handed the hot dog to her.

"Nature calls," I said, then turned and headed back up the stairs to find a bathroom.

It was early enough that it wasn't too crowded, and there wasn't a line at the restroom, which I was very thankful for. After I was done, I headed to the concession stand that was near there and picked up a couple of beers, one for each of us. Walking down the steps, it looked like McKenzie was talking to several of the fans around her, which wasn't super unusual. She was the friendly type, but when I got closer and heard them calling her by name, I was a bit confused.

"I think you guys make a cute couple," someone in the row next to her said.

"We haven't told anyone," she replied. "That's why I asked you guys not to say anything in front of his sister."

I was still a couple of rows up and stopped cold. What hadn't she told me? Was she dating Quentin? Did they decide I wasn't worth telling? Now it made sense that she knew where she was going. It was because she'd been coming here all season, probably. Maybe for the last couple or more years.

"McKenzie," I called, pretending I'd just gotten there.

"Hey," she said, turning quickly away from the people in the row next to us. "Beer?"

"Figured we could splurge," I said. "Hope you like this kind."

"I'm sure I will," she said, taking one of the cups from my hands.

I took a sip before sitting, just wanting to make sure I didn't spill it on me. My yellow sundress was still new, and if I could keep from having to toss it or wash it while I was here, that would be better than the alternative. The folks in the row seemed to have found something else to talk about, which I'm sure made McKenzie happy.

Trying to figure out how to confront my best friend and my brother took all my concentration, and I barely realized it was time to stand for the National Anthem. McKenzie pulled on my wrist to get me on my feet.

"They are very particular about this," she said in hushed tones, and I realized she meant that me staying seated might look bad for us, and by connection, my brother as well.

Once the song was over, we took our seats again and waited for the game to start. The announcer began giving the starting lineup, first for the visiting team, the Cascades. My heart did a little flip when I heard who the starting short stop was. Beckett Hennings. I hadn't known his name before, but it seemed to fit him. I didn't clap, but it was a difficult thing to keep from doing.

Then it hit me. I knew exactly how I could stick it to my brother. I'd sleep with his counterpart from the opposing team. The more I thought about it, the more the idea grew on me. By the time he hit a home run in the top of the second inning, I was very invested in the idea. I'd stuck the coaster with his number into my purse when I got back to the hotel room that night, so I knew I had it with me, and a plan started to formulate.

CHAPTER EIGHT

*B*eckett...

"Nice game," the sports announcer who followed our team said as we came off the field. "Beckett," she added. "Would you mind a word?"

"Sure," I replied, walking up to her.

After-game interviews were always something Coach encouraged us to do. At the beginning of the season, I didn't want anything to do with them, but as things wore on, and as I felt my teammates had my back more, I embraced being in the spotlight.

"We're here with the sole bright spot in tonight's game," she said. "Beckett, can you walk us through that at bat in the second? How did you know what was coming?"

"Film is your friend," I said. "We get scouting reports for our upcoming opponents, and we see what we can do to find a way to use the few flaws they have against them. I was lucky in that I had faced their starter before and knew what to expect."

"It seems like the bottom of that inning was your best on defense," she said. "Can you tell me what was going on and why you were having meetings with the players?"

"Can't give all the secrets away," I said, knowing that what we did was a little underhanded, but nothing compared to what Houston was doing. "Sometimes you just figure things out," I continued. "When you know what's coming, it makes things that much easier."

"Seems like you figured them out pretty well," she said.

"Tomorrow will be another challenge," I said. "But we'll rise to the occasion."

"I'm sure you will," she said, then turned back to the camera. "Let's send it back to the boys in the booth."

I watched the light go out on the camera and she looked at me.

"What did you see?" she asked, and I could tell she was asking more than just the questions she had asked on air.

"Nothing for you to worry your pretty little head about," I said. "It'll all come out in the wash, one way or another."

I walked away and stepped down into the dugout, walking slowly down the ramp to the clubhouse.

"Hennings," Coach called when I came in. "Office, now."

Doing as I was told, I followed the coach into his office.

"What the hell was going on out there?" he asked when he'd shut the door.

"They were stealing signs," I said, as if it was clear.

"Nothing wrong with that," Coach said, but I argued, "It is if they're using some cameras and other shenanigans to do so."

"You saw something?"

"Let's just say that the way their manager was acting," I began, "and the way their hitters knew exactly what was coming, it was clear."

"So," he said. "You didn't think this was something I should know?"

"Plausible deniability," I said. "You can't get into trouble for something you didn't know about."

"You knew this was happening," he said.

It wasn't a question, so I didn't answer it as such, and just waited.

"All right," he finally said. "Go get showered to head back to the hotel. I got some calls to make."

I walked out of the office, closing the door behind me, and went to my locker to pull out my stuff. My phone buzzed indicting I had a new notification, but I shoved it into my bag. It could wait until after my shower. By the time I got back to my locker, I had forgotten about it, and just got dressed to head to the bus. As I climbed onto the bus, I looked at my phone, wanting to see what the net was saying about our game and noticed I had a text.

Meet me at my room.

No name, an unknown-to-me number, and no clear indication as to who it was. I mean, I was hopeful, but who knew? I'd find out when I got to the hotel. I'd take a chance and wander down the hall a bit and knock. If she didn't answer, I would reply to the text asking for more information. For now, though, I just thought about how sweet she looked in that little yellow sundress and sandals, walking down the hall away from me. I hope she hadn't taken it off, cause I'd like to wreck it for her in the best possible way.

"Good news?" Cote asked when he plopped in the seat next to mine.

"Hopefully," I replied, but didn't elaborate.

No use giving any of these guys any ammunition to screw me over. I'd been really good about keeping my off-field activities quiet and away from the team. This would be no different. No one needed to know what I was getting up to after hours. I certainly wasn't about to tell anyone. The ride to the hotel from the stadium was much longer than it needed to be, especially since I had a fucking sex kitten waiting for me.

By the time we pulled up, I was so damn uncomfortable it wasn't funny. I hid what I could, and just ignored everyone's stares. We all walked into the hotel and the elevators filled up quickly, so I hung around in the lobby, then walked to the bar to grab a quick drink, all in an effort to delay my arrival on my floor.

"Jack and Coke," I said as I stepped up to the bar.

The bartender turned her back and poured my drink. I dropped a twenty on the bar and took the drink back to the lobby, hoping the rest of the team had taken the elevators up.

"You waiting on someone," Adams asked.

"Just the elevator," I said. "No need to rush to bed. I got time to kill."

"Want company?" Swift asked.

Those two were thick as thieves, always getting into trouble together.

"Nah," I said. "But the bar is hopping. May be able to score someone."

"Thanks for the info," Adams said, then pulled his pal in the direction of the bar.

It didn't take long until I was nearly alone in the lobby, the rest of the team having gone into the bar or headed up already. I pressed the button on the elevator and waited. When it arrived, a couple of the other guys from the team were in it, stepping out.

"Have a nice night," I said as I passed them and stepped in.

The longest elevator ride ever ensued, and finally I was at my floor. Of course, there were a handful of players in the hallway, talking about what had happened at the field, and asking what they could do about it. I raised my chin in their direction, then opened my door with my key card. Slipping inside, I set my drink on the counter next to the door and wondered how long I would have to wait before heading down to see Miss Belinsky.

"Fuck it," I said, pulling my phone from my pocket and shooting a text off to her.

Getting cockblocked by my teammates.

I waited, hoping she would answer, wondering if I'd missed her, or if she was even back yet.

Same with my bff.

Well, guess we were both fucked, and not in the good way.

How long?

Hoping it was going to be soon, I decided to ditch my jacket. It was plenty warm, and the fact that they made us wear them in this oppressive heat was ridiculous. They could let us go without the jackets when we were in the southern states during the summer at the very least.

My phone pinged as I undid my tie.

Coming in hot. Open the door.

Oh yeah, I could definitely do that. I walked to the door, turned the knob and pulled it open. She stepped in without breaking stride, turned on me and smashed her lips on mine, pushing the door shut behind me to press me against it.

Her body was soft in all the right places, and I wrapped my arms around her waist and pulled her closer, shoving my knee between hers. She let them part while simultaneously shoving her tongue into my mouth. Holy fuck, this girl was hot. Her hands went between us and began to unbutton my shirt, apparently in an attempt to get to my skin beneath. I walked her backward, moving to the bed, then shoved her down on it.

The only light that was on in the room was the one sitting on the desk. The curtains were open, so some lights from the city filtered in through the window as well. I finished unbuttoning my shirt, then pulled it off as she watched, licking her lips. She sat up, grabbing my belt buckle and pulling me closer to her. Her hands were swift, and she had my belt undone and was working on my fly when I grabbed her hands.

"Slow down, angel," I said. "We've got all night."

"Fuck that," she replied. "I want you, and I want you now."

She broke free of my grip and shoved my pants and boxer briefs down, her eyes lighting up as my cock broke free and stood at attention, waiting for her. She didn't miss a beat, plunging me into her mouth, sucking for all she was worth, and my God was it divine. Her lips were like velvet, her tongue doing everything right, and I didn't even feel the need to hold her to the task, as she was on pace and working me the way I liked.

"Fuck," I moaned and I could feel her smile around me.

One hand was on the base of my cock, stroking it in time with her mouth. The other had ahold of my balls, squeezing gently, and rolling them back and forth. Whatever she was doing, it was definitely doing the trick, and I felt that unmistakable tingle at the base of my dick, my release right there.

"Stop," I groaned, but she didn't listen. Before I had a chance to react, I was losing myself in her mouth, and by God, she swallowed every damn drop of me.

She smiled when she finally let me go, scooting up on the bed.

"My turn," she said.

Her legs dropped open, and she hitched her skirt up.

"Fuck me," I said because she wasn't wearing any panties.

I kicked myself out of my shoes, and everything else that was around my ankles, then climbed up on the bed, crawling up toward her. I kissed her shin, just above the straps of her sandal, then slid up more, kissing the side of her knee. Rolling my eyes toward her, I watched her watch me. There was something there that was just pure animal. I wanted to hear her cry out my name in ecstasy as she came apart in my arms. Kissing her thigh, she gave a shiver and her eyes became hooded, closing ever so slightly in bliss.

"You like that?" I asked, my whisper raising goose flesh on her skin.

"Oh yeah," she murmured, once again licking those luscious lips of hers.

"My name is Beckett," I said.

"I know," she replied.

"Just want you to know what to scream out," I added, laughing a little, then continued my line of kisses along her thigh.

With each movement higher, her eyes closed a little bit more, until I was near the top of her thigh, right near the junction of her legs. I smiled at the little racing stripe she had waxed in her hair, guiding me right to where she wanted me to go.

CHAPTER NINE

*F*i...

"My name is Beckett," he said, and all these words were getting in the way of what I wanted.

"I know," I replied, and tried to imply that I didn't care.

"Just want you to know what to scream out," he said, and his damn words were getting in my way.

He kept kissing up my thigh, pushing my dress up further and further. I felt his laugh against my skin as he saw my strip of hair. One of the things we did today was waxing. McKenzie didn't care that we were doing it, and just laughed at my desire to have it almost bare.

Of course, she was the reason I was in this hotel room to begin with. I mean, sure, the dude was hot, and he wasn't lying about his package, either, which was a pleasant surprise. His beard rubbing on my freshly waxed pussy was a bonus, and I shivered as he pressed his cheek against me, kissing my thigh right where it curved and joined my cunt.

Moving further along, he took a long lick up my lips, from damn near my asshole all the way to my clit, then sucked it in, giving a little nibble before releasing it. I moaned, opening my legs wider to allow him more access.

"I'm gonna wreck this dress," he said, shoving it up further.

The only thing that comment did was make me think of that fucking kid's movie from about a decade ago, and that was not at all what I wanted to be thinking about at this moment. Thankfully, he distracted me with another swipe of his tongue along my lips, sucking my clit once more. I moaned as he revved me up, and when he introduced a finger into me, I wriggled even more.

He used his other arm to bar me from moving, holding my hips to the bed so he could hold me still, I guess, and continued with his mouth, alternating sucking and biting my clit as I rose higher and higher into the stratosphere where I would find my eventual release.

Using his finger, he gave that come-hither motion and found the rough spot inside me that pushed me even further up. I fisted the bedding on either side of my hips, trying desperately to get to that perfect combination of motions to set me off. He pushed another finger inside me, filling me even more, as he kept that stroking inside until finally I fell, tumbling into the perfect fall where light and sound and reality didn't exist and it was just me and him and the way we blended.

When I came back to myself, I realized he'd stopped his ministrations and was looking at me very confused.

"Who the fuck is Ralph?" he asked.

"Excuse me, what?"

"You called out Ralph as you came," he said. "I wanna know who the fuck that is."

I couldn't help it, I started laughing. He'd already pulled his fingers out of me and pushed himself up onto his knees and was kind of giving me this glare. I just kept laughing.

"This isn't fucking funny," he barked, louder than he probably should have.

I scooted up on the bed and sat up, then threw my legs over the side and made for the door. Opening it, I stepped into the hall and looked back at him. He'd gotten up off the bed and was standing there, dumbfounded. I could hear other people in the hall, who I assumed were his teammates. Since he wanted to make this a big deal, I figured I'd give him exactly that.

"You give good head," I said. "But the rest of you is all kinds of fucked up."

I let the door close on his shocked face and walked down the hall to my own room. Sure enough, the handful of people in the hall were likely his teammates, and I honestly didn't give two fucks about it. I got to my room just as I heard him come out of his own.

"Hey," he shouted, but I stuck my keycard in the door and opened it. "What the fuck?" was the last thing I heard from him as I let the door close.

"Ralph," I said to the empty space. "What the fuck was he talking about?"

Knocking on my door stopped me just before I sat on the bed.

"Miss Bel—" he cut himself off. "Open up."

"Done for the night," I said. "Thanks, anyway."

"Not fucking funny," he called through the door.

Did I let him in or let him stew? Honestly, both seemed like good options, but my kindness overruled my petty nature and I walked back to the door.

"What do you want?" I asked as I cracked it open.

"Who, and I cannot stress this enough," he began, "the fuck is Ralph?"

"Oh my God," I said, pulling the door open further and letting him in.

Somehow, he'd grabbed one of the robes the hotel had available and made even that look sexy. It was barely belted and barely covered him. I couldn't let him stand in the hall and make an absolute fool of himself. I guess I was a softy at heart.

"You gonna answer me?" he asked, his fists on his hips.

He honestly looked like an indignant toddler standing there, which made me laugh even harder.

"I have no idea what you're talking about," I finally got out when my laughter subsided some.

"You fucking called his name," he said. "When you came, you called out Ralph."

"It's your own fucking fault," I said.

"What are you talking about?"

"You said you were gonna wreck my dress," I said, as if it explained everything. When he just stood there looking confused, I continued with, "*Wreck It Ralph.* You know, the movie?"

"Are you telling me you were thinking about a fucking cartoon?"

"Listen," I began. "You gotta understand how my brain works. If someone says something, it will trigger a memory for me. Then I associate what they said with that memory, which will probably lead to another memory, and so on, until I come to a logical conclusion that what someone said reminds me of something completely different."

"Ya lost me," he said.

"Here," I said, sitting on the bed. "I once saw a horse trailer, which made me think of the *Wizard of Oz* and their horse of a different color. That, of course, reminded me of the little people singing that song about the witch being dead, which in turn made me think of Ding Dongs, and made me hungry."

"But... wait," he began, befuddled. "I... that doesn't make any sense."

"My brain is weird," I said. "Look, you said you were gonna wreck my dress. That made me think of that movie, which is totally not what I wanted to be thinking about, but it was there. He's totally not my type, trust me. Anyway, that was the last cohesive thought I had, so that makes sense that that's the name I called out."

"Well," he said, pulling the belt from the robe. "We need to fix this right fucking now."

The robe dropped to the floor and he stalked toward me, his intentions very clear on his face. He put a hand on either side of my face, holding me where I was, then kissed me, hard. His tongue pressed against my lips until I yielded and allowed him inside. Plunging inside, I realized the true meaning of being ravaged, and it was completely fine with me. Sliding his hands down my cheeks, he ran them along my shoulders, then gripped the straps from my dress. With a swift tug, he tore them both off.

I gasped and pulled away, my dress falling to my waist.

"Didn't get to see those last time," he said, smirking. "Very nice, Miss Belinsky."

"What did you just call me?"

"It's your name," he said. "What else should I call you?"

"Fi," I replied, using the nickname my brother had given me as soon as he met me.

"Like, fee, fie, fo, fum?"

"Yeah," I said. "Exactly like that."

"Nah," he said. "I like Miss Belinsky better. Reminds me I'm fucking Quentin's sister."

"Seriously," I said.

"Oh yeah," he said. "And he's gonna hear all about it tomorrow on the diamond."

"Don't you dare," I said.

"Big brother doesn't approve of his little sister getting some?"

"He doesn't need to know about this," I begged. "You gotta believe me. It will not go well for you if you tell him."

The conversation did little to deter his enthusiasm, as displayed by his hard cock still standing there, proud as ever, right at eye level with me.

"Doesn't he know what a dirty little girl you are?" he asked, moving closer.

"Please," I whispered.

"Let's get you good and filthy," he growled, coming even closer, leaning over me, and giving me no option but to lie back on the bed. "I'm sure we can come to some sort of an agreement that will keep your dirty little secret and give me exactly what I want."

His hands were on either side of my head, his body a hairbreadth away from touching mine, and my breathing had increased to nearly hyperventilation. Then he dropped, his body pinning me to the bed. I may have been taller than him, but he definitely outweighed me, and that weight was pure muscle. He ground his cock into me. The only thing separating us was the thin fabric of my sundress, which was now in ruins around my waist and hanging down my legs.

Without realizing it, my arms had wrapped themselves around his neck, keeping him as close as I could. His own hands, which had been previously occupied with keeping him up off me, were now in motion as well. While one still held some of his weight, the other ran down my side to my hip where he began to gather the skirt of the dress, pulling it up higher and higher.

Breaking the kiss, he looked at me and asked, "Condom?"

"None," I said.

"Fuck," he replied, then pushed himself up and off me.

Reaching down to the floor, he picked up the robe and threw it around his shoulders.

"Don't move," he said, then strode to the door, opening it and throwing the little flip lock thing out so the door didn't close completely.

I heard a few catcalls from guys in the hallway, but he didn't seem like the kind of guy who cared what anyone else thought. It wasn't long before he was coming back in, flipping the lock back to shut the door completely, then locking that thing up tight.

"I brought several," he said, tossing the box on the bed next to me. "Now, where were we?"

He dropped the robe and strode over to me, grabbing my ankle and tugging me down the bed from where I'd scooted up. My skirt was shoved up, and he was on top of me in a moment, grinding his cock into my now exposed pussy. He trapped my arms above my head, holding them with one hand while his other ran down the front of me, circling his fingertips around my nipples, one after the other. I shivered at the attention.

"You like that, huh," he said.

"Mmhm," I hummed.

His hands did that dance around my breasts, circling the nipples back and forth, then he ran it down further and further, letting loose my hands as he got to my waist. Wrapping his hand on the outside of my thighs, he shoved them up, my knees bending on their own, as he raised my legs up and opened my sex to him.

"Very nice," he said. "You're still wet. What a dirty little girl."

Kneeling at the foot of the bed, he swiped his tongue up my slit from back to front, starting near my asshole and moving forward, finishing with sucking on that little bundle of nerves at the front of me.

"First," he said against my clit. "I'm gonna fuck you with my fingers until you call my name. Then I'm gonna fuck you with my cock and get you to call my name again. Finally, if you're lucky, I'm gonna fuck this little asshole here," he said, pressing his finger against my back entrance. "You'll come unglued and beg me for more."

He shoved a finger inside me, with his thumb or some other finger against my asshole, and my God, I shivered. He gave a laugh, and the rumble against me was enough to get my engines running even more. I reached down and held onto my thighs, keeping myself open for him to do with me whatever he wanted.

CHAPTER TEN

*B*eckett...

She was so responsive, and such a dirty girl, I damn near came without even getting into her. I mean, she'd come apart pretty well a few minutes earlier, but I didn't want to stop, except that one outburst. Who the fuck shouts Ralph at a climax? Fucking cartoon.

My fingers were buried inside her, my tongue on her clit, and my thumb was rubbing at her back entrance. I didn't know how experienced she was, but she seemed to know her way around a blow job pretty well, so I didn't think she was a virgin. What I did wonder, was whether she had ever been fucked in the ass. If I was lucky, I would be her first, and I wanted to make it as memorable as possible.

Unfortunately, I didn't have any lube with me, so would have to work extra hard to get her loosened up and just use her natural juices to give me what I would need. She'd pulled her legs up further than I originally pushed them, giving me even more access to her, and I took full advantage. My fingers were inside her, pumping in and out at a steady rhythm. I flipped my hand over, so I could scratch that patch at the front of her cunt and get her up and over the top of the hill I was helping her climb. Just like that, she clamped down on my fingers, moaning loudly.

"Say my name," I said against her clit, but she just kept moaning. Slowing down a bit, and pulling back, I said it again, this time with force. "Say my name."

"Oh, God," she said.

"Thank you for the compliment," I said, shoving my fingers back inside and giving her clit a nibble. "Now, say my name."

"Beckett," she hushed out, and I bit down a little harder. "Beckett," she nearly screamed, and I smiled.

"That's my good girl," I said, pulling my fingers out.

I licked them, watching her watch me, and her eyes grew wide.

"Now," I said. "I'm gonna fuck you again, but this time with my cock. I know you like it."

She was panting, and I didn't want to give her any time to recover, so I snatched the box and pulled a condom out, tearing it open and rolling it on. Her eyes never left my cock, and she smiled a bit, something I was happy to see.

Keeping her legs raised, I rubbed up and down her sex, mixing her own juices with the little bit of lube that came with the rubber. Her eyes shuddered closed, so I leaned in, not yet entering her, and grabbed one of her breasts, squeezing it to that almost painful point, then slid my thumb and first finger up to pinch her nipple, rolling it between them. She arched as best she could, me holding her nearly folded in half, pressing her tit into my hand.

"Oh yeah," I said. "We like the pain, don't we?"

She hummed, but didn't give an answer, so I pinched just a little harder until she groaned out, "Yes. Oh, God, yes."

I chuckled, releasing the pressure on her nipple and watched her shudder with the returning blood flow. My cock had never stopped sliding up and down her pussy lips, and even through the condom, I could tell she was even wetter. Oh yeah, this little girl was dirty in all the right ways.

Shifting up a bit, I used my hand to help guide me to her entrance, and I started slow, going in and out of her in small inches until she was ready for more. I'll be the first to admit I'm an asshole, but there are some lines you just don't cross. Once I'd gotten her stretched out some, I pushed the last bit in and watched her eyes open wide, a smile crossing her lips.

"Do it again," she said, and I obliged, pulling almost all the way out and shoving back in fast, bottoming out and hitting the back of her.

She shuddered as I held myself there, then pulled her hips a little bit away. I moved back at the same time, then went back in, fast and hard. With her legs up like they were, the angle was just right to run along the patch at the front that gave her all the good feels, and I was happy to keep at it as long as I could. I kept going, out slow, in fast, and watched as sweat began to bead along her brow. Even with the low light in the room, it was clearly there. She was working hard, and so was I. I was glad the air conditioner was running.

"Come on, baby," I said low and husky. "Say my name."

Her breath shuddered a bit as I picked up the pace, and then, without any notice, she clamped down on my dick and let loose with a strained, "Beckett."

She toppled over and into another climax, her body glowing in the soft light. I kept going, keeping her on that high for as long as I could. I didn't want to lose myself, so slowed down, letting her come down slowly.

"Come on," I said, pulling out of her and letting her legs down.

I helped her move higher on the bed, then turn over. I wanted to fuck her from behind and see if I could tease that asshole into something I might be able to use. I gripped her hips and pulled her up on her knees at the edge of the bed. Fuck it if I wasn't too short for this.

Patting her ass, I pushed her forward on the bed, then climbed up behind her. Now we had the right angle. I shoved into her without much resistance and stayed there, deep inside her, waiting for her shudder to pass, then I started moving in and out of her at a slow pace, working on getting her juices flowing so I could use them. I bent over her, my front against her back, and reached around to grab her tit, squeezing and massaging it, listening to her moans grow deeper and more animalistic.

Lifting, I used my thumb to glide some juices from her pussy up to her asshole, letting it rub against the opening, not quite pressing inside. Those moans that I thought were animalistic before became even more so, and I wondered if I'd hit some primal instinct inside her that made her just let go. Gently at first, I pressed just inside her hole and her eyes popped open, her head swinging to look back over her shoulder at me.

"It's okay," I said. "Just relax. I'll be gentle."

Her eyes were still wide, and I wasn't sure if she was gonna let me go forward. If it had to wait, I'd wait, because I was sure we would be doing this again. As often as I could get it, honestly.

"Want me to stop?"

She hesitated, then shook her head.

"Gonna need you to let me know," I said. "Stop or go?"

"Yes," she said. "Don't stop."

I took that and ran with it. I didn't want to push too hard, just enough to get her out of her comfort level. Easing my cock out of her, I began to get a rhythm going, in and out, slow at first, not moving my thumb in her ass at all, just leaving it there. I'd get her warmed back up before I did anything with that. While it was a little awkward the way my hand was, it wasn't so bad that it was distracting. The slow and steady pace I'd started with increased a little at a time, and it didn't take long for her breathing to speed up.

"That's it," I said in a low tone.

The sound of our flesh slapping together as I sped up mixed with her small moans and my heavy breathing was like a symphony echoing around the small hotel room. With one hand, I held her hip, keeping her from going too far forward with my thrusts, and the other had the thumb occupied. This wouldn't work for what I wanted, though, so I pulled my thumb away and she made a whimpering sound.

"Don't worry," I whispered, then dipped my finger down to gather more of her juices.

I made several passes, picking up the fluids running from her cunt and dribbled them into her asshole so I could have enough lubrication to make the insertion of my finger easier on her. Once I felt like there was enough there, I pressed my thumb against her opening again without breaking the steady in and out I was doing with my cock.

Her ass tightened as I pressed on it, but I shushed her and said, "Just relax."

She did, marginally, so I went slow. I eased my thumb in slightly, just the very tip and let it sit there while I continued to fuck her. Once I felt her relax again, I pushed a little more, and she tightened again. I stopped pressing and kept fucking, waiting for her to relax again. This went on for a while, minute movements of my thumb and her tightening and then releasing.

By the time my thumb was in to the first knuckle, she had relaxed much more and was nearly panting at my continued in and out with my cock, the little bit of pressure in her ass. Using the hand that had been holding her in place, I reached around to the front of her and started to finger her clit, trying hard to build her up to that wonderful fall I'd watched her experience several times in the last however long we'd been together.

"Oh God," she moaned. "Oh God. Oh God. Oh God."

"Say my name," I said, pressing my finger hard on the bundle of nerves at the apex of her sex.

"Beckett," she cried out. "Oh yeah."

I felt her cunt tighten around me, her asshole doing the same around the tip of my thumb, and she shuddered hard, losing her balance, and falling nearly face-first onto the bed when her arms gave out. I tried to hold her up, but I was losing my hold and had to release her body to keep from collapsing on her when I exploded inside the condom in her.

I'd pulled my thumb out of her ass, using both arms to keep myself from completely collapsing on top of her. My breathing was heavy and coming fast, and she matched it, both of us winded from the exertion we'd just experienced.

"Fuck, baby," I said. "That was fucking awesome."

She didn't answer, but likely she couldn't. I slowly pushed myself up and pulled out of her, holding the condom on myself until I was free. I pulled it off and let whatever was left just drip on the comforter on the bed. Not like it wasn't gonna get washed at some point anyway. I slid off the bed and padded to the bathroom to wash my hands, dropping the condom into a trash can there. Grabbing a washcloth, I got it wet with warm water to take back to help her get cleaned up as well.

CHAPTER ELEVEN

*F*i...

Oh. My. God.

That was one of the best experiences I'd ever had with someone. I mean, I'd had my share of hookups, but this was exceptional, to say the least. Watching him come back from the bathroom with a washcloth surprised me. He didn't strike as the type to help clean up. No, he was more the roll over and let the chick deal with the mess.

Thing was, I was a hot mess and there was no way I'd be able to figure out how to get anything taken care of until I came back to a more sensible place, like Earth.

"Hey," he said as I lay there on the bed. "Let's get you ready to sleep."

He took the cloth and wiped me, front to back, and the roughness of it, along with my sensitive bits, made me shiver. He chuckled but didn't say anything else. He wiped something off the bed, too, but I didn't really care. I was done for, and definitely needed to crash, and hard.

"Up you go," he said, pulling me to a sitting position. "Let's get this dress off you so you're more comfortable."

I had completely forgotten I was wearing anything until he

mentioned it. Once he did, though, it became constrictive around my middle. With gentle movements, he raised my arms, then reached down and shifted the dress up my torso, moving it over my breasts and pulling it off completely.

"Ralph can have your dress," he said, and I chuckled. "Let's get you into the bathroom to pee, then you can go to sleep."

I stood, with his help, and he walked me to the toilet and sat me down, stepping out of the room so I could have at least that much privacy. When I was done, wiped, flushed, and washed, I went back to the room. He had pulled the covers down on the bed for me. He reached out to me and I went to him. Pulling the covers up, he tucked me in nicely.

"Wish I could stay," he said. "Rules are I sleep in my own room, though."

He actually sounded upset about it, but I was too tired to care.

"Sleep well, Miss Belinsky," he whispered, then laid a kiss on my temple.

That was the last thing I remembered before I fell into darkness.

THE OVERTURE OF 1812 BOLTED ME OUT OF SLEEP. I DIDN'T WANT TO get up, didn't want to even open my eyes, but I did, and finally found my phone in my purse that had been left on the floor at the end of the bed. Unfortunately, whoever had been calling had gone to my voicemail.

"Fuck," I said, seeing the battery power on the phone.

I didn't plug it in the night before, but honestly, that was the last thing on my mind. My body reminded me of my extracurricular activities from last night, and I was sore in all the right places. Rummaging in my bag, I found the charger and plugged my phone in before it could die on me, then went to the bathroom to take care of my morning ritual.

When I got back to my phone, there was a voicemail and a missed call. Leaving it plugged in, I pressed my thumb to open it and pulled up the voicemail.

"*Hey, Fi,*" my brother's voice came from the devise. "*Heard there was some hubbub at the hotel and I wanted to make sure you were okay. Give me a call when you get this.*"

"Shit," I said.

The last person I wanted to talk to this morning was Quentin. I closed the voicemail app and saw there were text messages, so I pulled them up.

Last night was great. Looking forward to a repeat.

Yeah, that wasn't gonna happen. It was a one and done kind of thing, just something to do to piss my brother off. The problem was, I wasn't about to tell him what had happened. I certainly hoped that Beckett would keep that secret, but couldn't be sure, so I texted him back.

It was fun, but that was a onetime shot.

There were a couple of messages from McKenzie, too.

You okay? You were kind of in a rush to get out last night.

Yeah, well, I was in a rush because I realized that both my brother and my best friend had been lying to me. That's why I ended up with Beckett. How do I tell her I already know?

Just tired.

I decided to use that age-old jet-lag excuse. It would work for a bit, at least, and hopefully they'd both fess up to being together and we could be fine again. I didn't understand what the big deal was. They were both adults, and they made a really cute couple. I'm honestly surprised it didn't happen sooner. Or, maybe it had, and that was the reason she came to Texas in the first place.

I thought about my high school years and McKenzie was almost always at our house. Sure, she and Quentin would harass each other, but I thought it was more of a sibling kind of thing. Guess I wasn't that good of a judge on those things.

The knock at my door made me squeak, but I pulled the sheet off the bed, wrapped it around me, and made my way to the door. I looked through the peephole and saw Beckett standing there, dressed and ready to head into the ballpark.

"Fuck," I muttered, then pulled the door open just a crack.

"Morning, beautiful," he said when he saw me. "You sleep good?"

"Pretty sure I made it clear," I said. "That was a onetime deal. No need to check on me. I'm a big girl."

"Oh, no," he said. "You're not gonna push me away that easily."

"How's this," I said, then went to shut the door, but it wouldn't budge.

I looked down and his foot was between the door and the jam, effectively blocking my effort at doing anything but letting him in. He pushed the door open, just enough for him to squeeze through, then shut it behind him.

"You look good with bedhead," he said, smirking. "Wish I could have stayed."

"Yeah," I said. "Well, thanks for checking. As you can see, I'm fine. I need a shower and to get ready for my day, so…"

I let the words trail off, hoping he'd get the hint, but he was either too stubborn or too conceited to give up.

"Too bad I've already had a shower," he said. "Would have loved to join you, maybe continue our little fun we started last night."

"But you can't," I said. "So, buh-bye."

Without any warning, he snatched the sheet and pulled it away from me, leaving me standing there naked.

"Mmm," he hummed as he looked me up and down.

I didn't bother to cover myself. He'd already seen everything anyway. Instead, I just pushed past him and went into the bathroom and shut the door.

"Don't let the door hit you on your way out," I called through the closed portal.

He laughed, then said, "I'll look for you at the game. You should come down and see me during batting practice."

Ignoring him, I turned on the tap in the tub, waiting for the water to warm. I was just as stubborn as the next person, and when my mind was made up, I was very hard to budge from my position. When the water was warm, I pulled the little thing to turn the shower on, then stepped in. Letting the warm water cascade down me, I relaxed a little. Then I heard a door open, but it wasn't the door to the hall. No, it was the door to the bathroom.

"You didn't answer me," he said, poking his head around the curtain. "You gonna come see me during batting practice?"

"Didn't know it was a question," I said, tipping my head back to get my hair wet.

"You make it hard for me to leave," he said, and his register was lower than it had been just a moment before.

I glared at him, water dripping down my back from my wet hair.

"A lot of things get hard when you're around," he said, that smirk coming back.

"You can go," I said. "I won't drown."

"Say you'll come see me," he said, and the sincerity in it was enough to push me over the edge.

"Fine," I said. "Now, get out of my shower."

He raised his eyebrows a couple of times, then closed the curtain. I heard the hall door open after a minute or two, and when it closed, I blew out my breath.

This guy was something else, I'd give him that. I mean, if he wasn't such an asshole... nah, I didn't do that sort of thing. I was too young to be thinking about settling down or limiting my options when it came to men. If it happened, then whatever, but I definitely didn't want to tie myself to Beckett. Besides, he was definitely not the kind of guy to settle down.

CHAPTER TWELVE

*B*eckett...

  I dropped into my seat on the bus and pulled my phone out. Opening the text app, I pulled up Miss Belinsky's name and started typing.

"What was that last night?" Decker asked, sitting down next to me.

I locked my phone and said, "Don't know what you're talking about."

"Come on," he said. "Everyone on your floor was talking about it."

"Well," I half-shrugged. "What did they say?"

"You gonna make me beg?"

"I'm trying to figure out what you're talking about," I said, feigning ignorance. I mean, it could have been any number of things that happened last night they may have been talking about.

"That girl," he said, as if that explained what he wanted to know.

"There was a girl," I said noncommittally.

"Man," he said. "You really want me to spell it out?"

"Afraid you're gonna have to," I said. "There were just so many things going on last night."

"Word is," he began. "Girl comes off the elevator just as you open your door and she goes in, slamming the door behind her. Then, there was obviously sex in some sort of way."

"How you mean?" I asked.

"Well," he said. "Things were called out, moans and the like. Oh, why'd she call you Ralph?"

"Fucking cartoon," I mumbled under my breath.

"Then," he continued. "She came out, said something about you being fucked up or something. Of course, there was also the sighting of you walking down the hall in a robe, then walking back to your room, and back again. More sex sounds, and then the walk of shame back to your room."

"Sounds like you know a hell of a lot for not being there," I said.

I'd unlocked my phone at some point in an attempt to text her. I had written and rewritten it, but just couldn't get it right. Of course, having numb nuts jabbering in my ear wasn't helping any.

"So," he said, knocking his shoulder into me as the bus lurched forward. "Who is she?"

That question made me stop. She'd begged me not to tell her brother, but she never said anything about me telling my own teammates.

"Met her our first night in town," I said. "At the bar."

That wasn't so bad—nothing about who she actually was, just the when and where. Could have been any broad in town.

"Do you even know her name?"

"Of course I do," I said, feeling a bit offended.

"That's new." He laughed.

"I'm not a complete asshole," I countered.

"Many women around the country would beg to differ," he said.

"Oh, they beg," I said. "Trust me. They all beg."

"You gonna see her again?"

I shrugged and said, "Who knows?"

We'd arrived at the ballpark and I hadn't figured out what to text to her, which kind of pissed me off. I really wanted her to come see me at the stadium. I wanted to rub it in Quentin's face, but I didn't want to hurt her, which was an odd feeling. One I wasn't used to experiencing.

Shoving my phone back into my pocket, I got up and followed the other players off the bus and into the stadium.

Instead of worrying about what to send to Miss Belinsky, I decided to focus on the task at hand, figuring out how the hell the Dragons were stealing signs. Getting into my warm-up gear, I headed to the field, making my way out to the outfield. Somehow, they had a way of seeing the calls, and my guess was it was something in the batter's eye. The trick would be finding it.

CHAPTER THIRTEEN

*F*i...
I'd gone to the restaurant in the hotel for breakfast after my shower. I was starving, which was likely due to the lack of food last night, and the way my stress was building. McKenzie had texted me again, but I'd ignored it, along with both of my brother's additional calls. If they wanted to pretend they weren't together, that was on them, but I didn't have to buy into their story.

"Anything else?" the waitress asked.

"No thanks," I said. "Oh," I added. "Can I get my coffee to go?"

"Absolutely," she replied. "I'll just leave your tab here and will take care of it when I come back."

She left the little book thing on the table with a pen. Since my brother was a liar, I decided to charge my meal to the room. He could afford it, and it wasn't exactly that much, so he probably wouldn't even notice. The waitress came back with a large paper cup. It looked to be about the size of a venti coffee at Starbucks, and it was almost full of coffee, leaving room for me to add cream and sugar. After doctoring it up, I put the lid on and dropped my napkin on the table before leaving the restaurant.

"Fi," McKenzie said when I walked into the lobby. "I was worried."

"I'm fine," I said. "Just a little tired from the busy couple of days."

"The way you took off last night was weird," she said.

"I just didn't want you to have to sit there forever," I replied. "It was late, and I figured you'd want to get back to your guy."

I shuddered a bit, remembering that her guy was my brother.

"Oh," she said. "Well, did you want to do something today?"

"Did you have some place in mind?"

"We could go to the mall," she suggested. "There's this store in there that has the best bath bombs ever. Do you have a very big bathtub in your room?"

I thought about it and decided to throw her a bone.

"I mean," I said. "It's not huge or a jet tub or anything, but I guess it's big enough."

"Then let's go," she said. "My treat. We can get a bunch and you can take home whatever you don't use."

"Okay," I replied.

I mean, maybe I'd be able to get the truth out of her. Then again, maybe Quentin told her not to tell me. We walked out of the hotel and she grabbed her key from the valet. They hadn't even moved the car, so she hadn't been there long. The drive to the mall was quiet, neither of us making small talk.

When we got to the mall, she parked and shut the car off, then turned to look at me.

"Don't hate me," she said.

"Why would I?"

"I wanted to tell you a long time ago," she said. "But your brother said it was a bad idea. He thought you would be upset to know that we were dating."

"What would make him say that?" I asked.

"No clue," she replied. "I wanted to tell you months ago, but he was sure you would think he was taking advantage of me or something."

"Is he?"

"No," she said. "Not at all."

"Then why would he not want me to know?"

"No clue," she said.

"I did figure it out," I said. "I mean, I had a hunch he was living with someone because he wouldn't let me stay at his place. Then, when you showed up in this car, I figured you had someone who had more money than just a little extra cash. But honestly, it was when you knew exactly how to get to the park, which side streets to take, had something in your phone that you just showed in the parking garage—all those things added up. When I came back from getting us beer, though, I heard someone say you made a cute couple, and I have to agree."

"You think we make a cute couple?"

"Well," I said. "I haven't actually seen you two together, but yeah, I think it works."

"I'm so glad you're not pissed," she said, wiping a tear from under her eye.

"Why didn't you just tell me?" I asked, clearly pissed off, but more at my brother than my best friend.

"Quentin doesn't want to jinx it," she said. "He thinks if we advertise, then it's gonna go south."

"Well," I said. "He's a boy, so he's dumb."

She laughed, which was exactly what I was hoping for.

"Let's go get some girly things," she said. "And honestly, it'll be your brother's treat. You know since he's the rich one in the family."

I laughed and climbed out of the car. We walked into the mall, arms locked together, and it was just like when we were in high school. It just felt right, and I was really happy that we would become sisters at some point, even though we'd always been soul sisters.

"Okay," she said as we sat with our lunch in the mall food court. "Who's the guy?"

"I'm sorry, what?"

"Don't try to fool me," she said. "You got some last night. That's the only reason I can think of that you were texting late during the game. Not to mention why you hustled out of the car so fast when we finally got back to the hotel."

"Maybe," I said, drawing the word out.

"Was it at least good?"

"Oh, yeah," I said. "Very good."

"You gonna see him again?"

"Don't know," I said. "I mean, he is kind of a manwhore, or so I've heard."

"Don't tell me it's that dude from the Cascades," she said. "The one Quentin talks about constantly?"

"I think Quentin is jealous," I said. "Apparently, the guy is a really good short stop."

"You better not tell your brother," she said.

"Yeah," I said. "I told Beckett he couldn't say anything, so hopefully he'll keep his mouth shut on that one."

"You'll know if he blabs," she said, stuffing a bite of her General Tso chicken into her mouth.

"How so?"

"Trust me," she said. "Somehow, it will be obvious."

My phone buzzed just then, and I looked down to see a text from Quentin.

You doing okay?

"Speak of the devil," I said.

"Who?"

"My brother," I replied.

I'm fine. At the mall with McKenzie.

"He's worried about me, I think," I said. "Left me a voicemail this morning. Apparently, the baseball world is small because he knew about the ridiculousness that was last night."

"Oh," she said. "Do tell."

"You sure you want to know?"

"Girl," she said. "You better give me all the details. You know that you are so much more adventurous than I am. I mean, you gotta give me something."

"You trying to live vicariously through me?"

"Absolutely," she said. "Hey, maybe I can get some pointers and see if I can get your brother to bust out of his vanilla style."

"Eww," I cried. "Not an image I need in my head."

She laughed and took another bite of her chicken.

"Okay," I said, then told my tale.

She laughed when I told her about walking out on him, then laughed harder when he told me about my outburst.

"You seriously called out Ralph?"

"Apparently," I replied, taking a sip of my lemonade.

"Oh my God," she said, laughing even more. "We should pick up some condoms for you."

"He left the box in my room," I said.

"Sounds like he's hoping for more," she said. "Still, nothing wrong with being prepared."

"You're awful," I said, but agreed with her.

We finished our lunch, dumped our trash, and headed further around the mall.

"I need to find a new sundress," I said.

"That's right," she replied. "Forgot you got your other one wrecked."

"Never gonna live that down, am I?"

"Not a chance," she said. "Come on, I know just the place."

Leading me down the walkway, she took me to a little shop with the cutest dresses and other fun and girly outfits. It took a while, but I finally found a couple of nice options and went to try them on. I came out with the first one and McKenzie squealed.

"I'll take that as a good sign," I said, laughing.

"You're definitely getting that one," she said. "Try the other one, too."

Following her orders, I went in and switched out to the other dress, then went out to get her approval.

"That's the one you should wear to the game tonight," she said.

"You think?" I asked, turning around to look at myself in the mirror.

"Oh yeah," she said. "You do want him to see you, right?"

I shrugged but smiled. I mean, I wouldn't be upset if he noticed me.

"Good," she said. "Go change back into what you had on before so we can buy these. You have time to change before the game."

By the time we left the mall, we barely had enough time to go back to the hotel for me to change and get to the stadium.

CHAPTER FOURTEEN

*B*eckett...

"You find it?" Jonathan asked when we were changing into our uniforms.

"Nope," I said. "But it's there. It has to be. That's the only thing I can think of as to how they're stealing signs."

"Hennings," the coach called from his office.

"Coming," I replied, pulling my jersey on. "What's up?" I asked when I got to his office.

"The guys are saying something about the Dragons," he said. "I want to know what you know."

"What are they saying?" I asked.

"You know damn well," he barked. "Spill."

I explained how I saw their manager looking down the hallway to the clubhouse, then giving signs, but not until after our catcher had already thrown them down. He asked clarifying questions, then sent me on my way. Honestly, I was glad it was out in the open and not just between us players.

"Huffman," the coach called after a bit, and the man headed to the office as well.

Coach ended up talking to all of the outfield starters before we headed out for the game, so my guess was that he was letting them know to be on the lookout for anything out of the ordinary.

I'd been a bit bummed that my little sex kitten hadn't come down to find me during batting practice, but it was what it was, and I was sure I'd see her during the game. She had to be sitting in the family section, so I'd start my search there. Coach had me hitting in the number five slot, so I had at least the first inning to just look at the crowd and see if I could catch a glimpse. After our first three guys got out, I headed out to my spot on the field, but kept my eyes glancing toward the stands behind home plate.

Catch my grounder from Matsui, toss it back, look at the crowd. Wait for my turn and do it all over again. That's when I saw her. She was wearing her hair up in a high ponytail on the top of her head, that long hair cascading down and around her shoulders in waves. The dress she had on was short, even shorter than the one she wore the day before, which I really appreciated. It was bright pink with big flowers all over it, and it hugged her curves nicely.

"Hennings," Cote called. "Pay attention."

"Sorry," I said, putting little Miss Belinsky out of my thoughts.

Quentin was leading off, and he looked like he had a giant boulder on his shoulder the way he glared out at me. I simply smiled, tapped my glove a couple of times, and waited for our pitcher to throw. Kors threw the ball inside, brushing him back off the plate. He was known to crowd the plate, and it wasn't unusual for him to get plunked a time or two. We didn't want to give them any extra opportunities, so intentionally hitting him wasn't gonna be a good idea.

Next pitch was a little more out over the plate and he took a swing, sending it foul down the left field line. Too bad he was a bit early on it. Next pitch was outside for another ball.

"Come on, Kors," I said. "You got him."

With a two one count, Kors tossed a curve that dove, but didn't dive enough, and Belinsky connected with it and sent it out to left field, still early, but late enough to keep it fair. He ran to first, made the turn, but then backed up because Adams got it back in to Cameron, who tossed it to me.

"No worries," I called after tossing the ball to our pitcher. "Double play ball, right here."

Their next batter was a wiry dude who played right field. He stood just outside the batter's box, watching the third base coach giving signs. Belinsky was watching as well, then a smile crept up on his face. He was gonna try to steal.

"Time," I called, walking to the mound to grab some rosin. "Step off," I said while looking at the ground. "He's gonna steal."

I walked back to my spot on the infield, tapped my glove a couple of times, then got ready to back up Cote who was slotted to take the throw if it came. Sure enough, Kors stepped off after coming set and Belinsky was caught almost halfway to second, pulling up in that no-man's-land between the first two bases.

Kors tossed to Matsui, who ran at Belinsky, then tossed to Cote, who did the same. The pitcher caught it and did the run again, then threw to me where I tagged him out.

"Got ya," I said with a laugh, then tossed the ball to Cote.

"Stay the fuck away from my sister," he growled before turning and heading back to the first base dugout.

"She's an adult," I called out to him.

Was it the smartest thing to do? Probably not, but I honestly didn't give a single fuck. She and I had a great time, and if I was lucky, we could do it again tonight, and every night between now and when I left town.

We managed to get the next two guys out—one strike out and a pop-up foul down the left field line where Cammy caught it up against the netting along the edge of the field. Running back to the dugout, I looked up and could see that she was watching me and smiling. Yeah, she was gonna come back over again tonight, that was damn sure obvious by the look on her face.

I pulled my hat off and stuck it in my glove, swapping them out with the helmet and batting gloves in my cubby. I pulled my bat from the same place and headed up to the top step to start swinging and stretching my arms. Oh, I watched their pitcher do warm-ups, but my eyes kept wandering back to the seats behind home to a very bright pink on a very pretty girl.

Huffman got a solid hit on the second pitch, giving him a double before I headed to the plate, a couple of practice swings before digging into the batter's box with my left foot at the back of the space. Tap the plate, swing one more time, then settle in, leg ready to pull up, body coiled to swing. I kept my eyes on the pitcher, looking for any sign as to what he was gonna throw, but he was a closed book.

He nodded when he got the sign, pulled up to standing, looked back at Huffman with his average lead, then turned back to me, coming set. Wind up and throw, and it was coming right at me.

It'll drop, I kept thinking, but it didn't. As if in slow motion, it kept coming, not breaking, not diving, just dead straight at me. I turned my back and took the hit square between my shoulder blades, dropping my bat in the process.

No big deal, guys get hit all the time. Then I looked out and saw Belinsky glaring and pointing at me. Fuck that. I took off at a run, right at him. Most of the fans, and likely the rest of the players, thought I was going after the pitcher, but he was just between me and my target. He'd already dropped his glove, pulling his hands up and ready to throw a punch, but I didn't let him.

Lowering my head, I plowed right into his gut with my shoulder, knocking him down and landing on top of him. I sat up and started throwing punches with both hands, hitting his head, then his body when his hands rose. What felt like forever, with a hundred punches landed, ended up being likely just a minute or two when Huffman pulled me off Belinsky, wrapping his arms around my waist and hoisting me in the air and away from the other guy. Their third baseman was right there, too, trying to keep the short stop from coming after me.

"Stay away from my sister," he shouted.

I caught it, some of the others likely did, too, but it didn't matter. Benches cleared, umpires came in, and both of us were thrown out of the game, along with their pitcher.

"I fucking mean it," he shouted, spitting blood on the ground. "You touch my sister, I'll kill you."

"Fuck you," I shouted back. "She's mine, and you can just figure out how to live with it."

I turned and walked back to the dugout, ignoring everyone around me. A quick look up into the stands behind home plate showed me that Ophelia had her hands over her mouth, obviously concerned. The big question was whether it was me or her brother she was more worried about.

CHAPTER FIFTEEN

*F*i...

"Oh my God," McKenzie shouted.

I'd looked down at my phone for a minute and when I looked up, everyone around us was standing up and shouting. I stood up myself but couldn't see over the dude in front of me, so I stood up on the seat behind me just in time to see Beckett plow Quentin into the ground and start to pummel him.

"Oh, shit," I shouted. "What the hell happened?"

"He got hit," the dude in front of me said.

"Why is he going after Quentin?" I asked.

"You should have seen the look he gave him," the dude said, turning to look at me. "There is some serious bad blood between them, and something must have happened because he didn't even pause when he went out there."

I looked at McKenzie and said, "He knows."

"I think so," she said.

By the time the guy who was on second got to Beckett and pulled him off, the dugouts had cleared and everyone was around them. It was very clear that Quentin had gotten the brunt of Beckett's anger, but I didn't know what they were shouting at each other. They were each pointing at the other one and shouting something. When the players started to head back to their own clubhouses, I could finally see both of them, and they each had blood around their mouths and noses. My hand went to my own mouth, covering it.

"What the hell?" McKenzie asked. "They threw Quentin out, too."

I just watched as Beckett walked off the field, then looked up at me. He was questioning something, but I didn't know what. I stepped off the seat and opened my phone up, shooting a text to him.

What was that? Are you okay?

There was no way he would answer me soon, so I shoved the phone into my purse that was slung across my chest, stowing it away for now.

"I gotta go see him," I said.

"Who?" McKenzie asked, and I think she was more worried about Quentin than I was.

"Come on," I said, pulling her arm as we stepped out of the row and headed down the steps to the special club they had for family.

The security people had seen us before, and we had lanyards to indicate we were, indeed, family, and not some random fans who snuck in, so they let us pass through to the more private area within the stadium. McKenzie pulled against me and I stopped and looked at her.

"You're worried about the other guy, aren't you?"

"I'm worried about both of them," I said. "I need to know what the hell the issue is with those two."

"Okay," she said. "I can get us to Quentin, but I don't know about the other team. That's something we'll have to figure out."

She led me through a set of double doors and down a hallway into the bowels of the stadium. After what seemed like an eternity, we arrived at a space just outside another set of double doors.

"He'll come out here," she said.

"So," I replied. "We just stand here and wait?"

"Pretty much," she replied and leaned up against the wall.

I was nowhere near relaxed enough to just stand there, so I paced back and forth in front of the doorway that led to what I assumed was the locker room. If it weren't a concrete floor, I likely would have worn a path in it. The door burst open after what felt like forever and Quentin came out.

"What the hell was that?" I shouted.

"That was what he got for screwing around with you," he barked back.

"I am a fucking adult," I screamed. "You can't tell me who I can and who I can't see. You may be my older brother, but you are not the boss of me."

"He's bad news," my brother said. "Whoever he's been screwing around with is usually only there for the series, not long term. I don't want you to have to deal with that."

"And who says I'm looking for long term?" I asked. "Did you ever think that I just wanted to fuck around for a while? Maybe I screw them and leave them, too. You don't know my life and have no say in what I do and don't do."

"Fi—" he tried, but I interrupted him.

"No," I shouted. "You and McKenzie have been playing house for a while now and you didn't even bother to tell me. She didn't even want to tell me because you got it into her head that I was gonna be pissed. So, you can take all your relationship advice and shove it where the sun don't shine."

"Fi, wait," he said, but I'd already turned to walk away.

"Leave me alone," I called over my shoulder, stomping away from both of them.

I felt my phone buzz in my purse and I pulled it out.

Your brother is an asshole.

"Tell me about it," I muttered.

Where can I meet you? I'm by the Dragons' locker room.

Once I was around a corner, far enough that neither my brother nor my best friend could see me, I stopped and leaned against the wall.

Don't move. I'll be right there.

I took a picture of what was around me so he'd know where I was and sent it to him, then waited. It took forever, but finally I spotted him coming from the opposite direction as the home team's locker room, and I was thankful he hadn't had to walk past my brother.

"Hey," he said when he was close.

His eye looked like it was gonna be black pretty soon, but at least the blood had been removed from his face. There was still some dried blood at the corner of his mouth, though, and I reached up to touch it.

"Are you okay?" I asked.

"You should see the other guy," he said, but winced when he laughed.

"Should you see a doctor?"

"Team doc said I was fine," he said, closing the distance between us and pressing a tender kiss against my lips. "Now that you're here, you can make me feel all better."

"I'm serious," I said. "If you need to see a doctor, you should."

"Like I said," he reiterated. "Doc said I was fine to go back to the hotel. I've got an Uber coming to get me. Want a lift?"

"Uh, yeah," I said. "I came with McKenzie, but she's with Quentin, and I don't want to be around him right now. What happened?"

"I think he found out," he said. "Had the pitcher throw at me."

"Did you tell him?"

"You asked me not to," he said, sounding hurt.

"Just making sure," I replied.

"Uber's almost here," he said. "Let's go."

He grabbed my hand and pulled me to him, wrapping his arm around me, then winced with the stretch.

"You sure you're okay?"

"I'm fine," he said. "Trust me. Nothing is gonna keep me from you."

We walked down the hallway and out a side door where a security guard was standing.

"Goodnight, folks," he said as we stepped out the door.

Beckett walked me around the end of the building where there was a driveway of sorts and pulled out his phone, unlocking it with a swipe of his thumb and pulling up his Uber app.

"Should be here in a minute," he said, showing me his phone.

Sure enough, we turned to look at the entrance and the car indicated on the app was pulling in and stopped in front of us. Beckett opened the back door and let me slide in, then climbed in behind me as I slid across the bench seat in the back of the SUV.

"Hello," the driver said.

"Hey," I said.

He pulled out and drove us out of the parking lot and onto the side streets of the city. Since the game was still near the beginning, the traffic around the stadium was pretty light, and we made good time getting to the hotel. When we pulled up in front, Beckett opened the door and slid out, holding it open for me to follow.

"Thank you," I said before setting my feet on the ground.

Beckett took my hand after he shut the door behind me, and we walked up to the automatic doors as they hushed open. Crossing the lobby, I could hear the sounds from the bar echoing out into the space but ignored it. He pressed the button on the elevator and we waited for it to come down. I stood right next to him, our fingers intertwined between us, and I'd never felt more at home than I did in that moment.

"Ophelia," I heard from the door just as the elevator arrived.

We stepped in and I turned to see my brother standing there in the lobby, looking at me. I just shook my head as the doors to the elevator shut and we began our ascent.

"He's gonna be pissed," Beckett said.

"I don't care," I said. "He had no right to tell me who I could be with."

"He's just looking out for you," he said. "I would think you would appreciate that."

"My brother has always been about making sure that I didn't get into things," I explained. "But that came at a price. I never got to make mistakes when we were in the same school, so when I went out on my own, I didn't have the limits I'd found out by myself. Things kind of went crazy when I was in college."

"You saying you were one of those girls gone wild?"

"Not exactly," I replied. "I just had to find my own way. He thinks that he still has that power over me, but I've been doing just fine by myself. If he'd been in touch with me or made an effort to actually learn what I've been doing, I might listen to him."

"So," he said as the elevator came to a stop at our floor. "I'm just a way to say screw you to your brother?"

"Not gonna lie," I said as we stepped out of the elevator. "That's what it started as."

"And now?"

We were walking down the hallway and got to his door. He paused.

"I kinda like you," I said, but didn't look at him.

"You do?"

"Don't sound so surprised," I said, laughing.

"I mean..." he said but paused long enough to get me to look at him. "Check me out. I am a fine specimen of the human male species. You would be an idiot to not like me."

Was what he said cocky? Absolutely. But he said it with a smile and it seemed a bit more self-deprecating than anything else. I heard the elevator ding and turned around to look at it. Quentin was getting out and McKenzie was right behind him.

"Ophelia," he said.

"Quentin," I replied coldly.

Beckett was still holding my hand, and I didn't even try to hide it.

"I'm sorry," he said, but he was only looking at me.

"For what?" I asked.

"Can you give us a minute?" he said to Beckett.

"He can stay," I said, keeping my hand firmly in his.

"Seriously?"

"Look," I said. "I'm an adult. You may still think of me as your little sister, but I have my own life I'm living. I know who I am, what I want to do, and more importantly, who I want to do it with. I know you think you're looking out for me, but you did that my whole life. It's time for you to let me be who I am meant to be."

"I just—"

"No," I said, cutting him off. "You can live your life, but you also need to let me live mine. If you can't trust me with the fact that you're living with my best friend, then I don't think you have a leg to stand on when it comes to who I hang out with."

He started to say something, but McKenzie grabbed his arm.

"She's right," she said. "You know it, too."

"Don't hurt her," he said, looking right at Beckett.

"Only if she asks me to," he said, giving my hand a squeeze.

Quentin waited for a moment, maybe figuring out whether I was okay with what Beckett had said or something, but then turned on his heel and walked back down the hallway.

"I'll keep him in check," McKenzie said before giving me a hug. She then followed my brother down the hall and they got into the elevator.

CHAPTER SIXTEEN

*B*eckett...

"Your place or mine?" I asked.

"Either one is good," she replied.

"The condoms are in your room," I said.

She smiled and pulled a box out of her purse.

"If I didn't know any better," I said. "I'd think you were a Boy Scout, prepared as you are."

"Nope," she said, popping the p. "Definitely not a Boy Scout."

I pressed the key card against the reader on my door and heard the click of the lock disengaging. Opening the door, I pulled her in. Tonight, I wanted to take things a little slower and actually get to know her body in every minute detail. The door closed behind her and she flipped the extra lock at the top. Closing the space between us, I pressed her back against the door, grabbing both hands and raising them slowly above her head where I held them with one hand, the other sliding down her arm, wrapping around the front of her neck.

She inhaled quickly, but I wasn't gonna press it, just hold her where I wanted her. My body was flush against hers, our height nearly identical, which was just perfect because it let my cock sit right against her pelvis. There was no way she didn't know how turned on I was, but I ground against her just to prove the point.

"You feel what you do to me?"

"Mmhm," she hummed back, her eyes holding mine.

"You don't sound very enthusiastic about it," I said, pressing against her even harder.

"Had some pretty good sex last night," she said, her voice low. "Not sure how you're gonna top it, to be honest."

The smile that played across her lips told me she was fucking with me, but it didn't matter. I was planning to blow her mind tonight. The fact that we were here well before the rest of the team was just a bonus. I squeezed a little more on her throat and her eyes widened a bit, but that smile never left her lips.

"You like it rough?" I asked.

She nodded, the smile still there. I stuck my knee between hers, spreading her legs apart so I had access to her. Sliding my hand away from her throat, I dipped it between her tits, but stayed above the fabric. I'd already ruined one of her dresses, no need to ruin more. Instead, I kept its route south, slowly inching down as she was pinned to the door. Pressing my hand between us, I gripped her cunt, rubbing back and forth as her eyes slipped closed and she sighed. Oh yeah, she likes to play hard.

Instead of pulling the dress away, I found her slit and shoved my finger inside her with the material wrapped around it. Hard, fast, and not giving her time to recover, I slid it out and shoved it back in. Her eyes popped open and she looked at me, but not in anger or anything like that. No, it was a look of surprise, like she hadn't thought this would feel as good as it did. Her hips bucked against my hand and I continued to finger fuck her, the rough material doing things she likely hadn't experienced before.

"Oh," I said. "You like that, don't you?"

"Mmhm," she hummed out.

"Don't you?" I said with more force.

"Yes," she said, letting it out on a sigh.

"Good girl," I said. "I'm gonna fuck you like this until you call my name. Then we'll see what else we can do."

She let her eyes slip closed and I could tell she was just experiencing the moment, feeling all the things and letting go of herself. I had to shift my hand a bit, her dress becoming bunched more than I wanted, but I got right back at it and kept fucking her through her dress with my fingers. I watched as she climbed that metaphorical hill and when she plummeted down the other side, she called my name repeatedly.

"Oh yeah, baby," I said as she came back to herself. "Can you stand?"

She took a big breath, then nodded, so I pulled my fingers out of her and she shuddered, getting that bonus feel from the removal. I released her hands, and she instantly wrapped them around my neck, pulling me against her, pressing her lips to mine in a soft kiss before releasing me.

"Come on," I said, stepping into the bathroom. "I wanna fuck you in the shower."

"That sounds like a good time," she said, pulling her purse over her head and dropping it on the counter in the bathroom.

When she started to pull her dress up, though, I stilled her hands and shook my head.

"Not so fast," I said. "You're a gift I wanna unwrap myself."

"Then I get to do the same," she said, reaching for my tie and pulling the knot away from my throat.

She was slow and methodical, almost as if she was trying to see how slow she could go before I gave up and just did it myself. Obviously, she didn't realize I had immeasurable patience, and so I stood there, letting her first undo my tie, which she slung over her shoulder. Then she unbuttoned my shirt. With each piece she removed, the harder I got, almost to the point of being painful.

Next were my pants, which started with her unbuckling the belt and pulling it free, slinging it over her other shoulder. Not sure how I should feel about it, but I let it go and allowed her to undress me painstakingly slow. She undid my pants and slowly slid them down my legs, squatting to pull my shoes and socks off before the pants followed. I was left standing in my boxer briefs, rock hard, and at her mercy.

"Fancy a little payback?" she asked.

"Not sure what you mean," I replied.

She made a loop of the tie, then walked around behind me, grabbing first one, then the other arm, and stuck my hands in the makeshift restraint before pulling it tight and tucking the end between my hands.

"My turn," she said, coming back in front of me.

Ever so slowly, she started to lay kisses down my body. First, it was the lips, slow and sensual, then she moved down and kissed my neck just below where my beard stopped. Along my collarbone until she reached the edge of my tattoo, then following the swirls and lines down to my nipple where she licked around it and sucking on it. I didn't realize what that kind of shit did to a body. I let my head fall back and just enjoyed the feel.

Continuing her cruise, she kissed and nipped along my ribcage just below my peck, moving slowly down and further down until she came to the edge of the word written around my lower torso.

"Relentless," she whispered, her breath causing goose flesh to rise. "Is that more to do with baseball or something else?"

"I'm relentless in everything," I said, looking down at her.

Without another word, she continued with her trail of kisses and nibbles. When she got to the top of my boxer briefs, she paused only for a moment, then skipped right over them and kissed my thigh right below where they landed.

"You're killing me," I groaned, watching her be so damn close to where I wanted her mouth, yet not hitting the mark at all.

"Patience," she said, smiling.

Her hands hadn't touched me once she tied my own, but now they grabbed my ankles, pushing them apart slightly. I was able to move them little bits at a time and still stay standing. What she was going to do to me, I didn't know, but the buildup was very exciting. She trailed her fingers up my legs with barely there touches and I shivered from the sensation. When she got to my hips, skipping over my briefs once again, she was standing up again, and she looked into my eyes.

"Do you trust me?" she asked.

"You haven't shown me any reason not to," I replied.

"Good," she said, then swiftly pushed my briefs down, so they were just below my cock and balls.

They couldn't go further because of the way my legs were, and with my hands tied behind me, I couldn't push them further. She stepped back and smiled, looking me up and down. Grabbing a towel and licking her lips, she laid the towel on the floor, then kneeled in front of me, her eyes cast upward, and slowly ran her tongue from the base of my cock all the way up to the tip, swirling it around the head.

"God," I groaned, not taking my eyes off her.

"You like?"

"Very much," I said. "Do it again."

"Now, now," she admonished. "I'm in charge right now, so what I say goes."

Without hesitation, she took my entire length into her mouth, bumping the head at the back of her throat, then with her teeth set against me, she pulled back, sending shock waves through me.

"Oh, God," I said, barely able to control myself.

She wrapped her arms around my thighs, holding me still, as she took me back into her mouth and sucked. I shuddered, convulsing inside her mouth, holding onto my control as much as possible, but she was going to be the end of me, and I didn't even care.

"I want to feel you come in my mouth," she said with a wicked grin, then sucked again.

As much as I would like to say I had control in that moment, she was definitely the one in charge. She played me like I was a two-buck whore, making me come in record time, and she didn't disappoint, swallowing every drop down. When I was done, I was having a hard time keeping myself upright, so she took pity on me and untied my hands. I shoved my shorts the rest of the way off, then pulled her to me, kissing her fiercely, pulling her dress up in the back, then pulling it over her head.

"Damn," I said, drawing out the word. "You are just about the most beautiful thing there is in Houston."

"I believe you promised to fuck me in the shower," she said, pulling away and walking to the tub.

She bent over to turn the tap on, and I couldn't help but walk up behind her and rub my softening cock against her ass. It responded like it should, growing hard once again.

"Grab the condoms," she said, then stepped into the tub.

I took the couple of steps to the counter and grabbed the box, ripping it open and pulling out the foil packets, setting them on the edge of the tub. I also grabbed a couple of towels and set them on top of the toilet so they were within easy reach.

By the time I was ready to step into the tub, she had the shower going and was under the spray, wetting her hair. I watched the water run down her tits, over her nipples, and I couldn't help but lean in and pull one into my mouth, sucking it hard. Tonight was going to be a very good night.

CHAPTER SEVENTEEN

*F*i...

His hands were like magic, the way they moved on my body, the way he rubbed me in all the right places. I could get used to being around him, really used to it. It was as if he knew me better than I knew myself, and it was fucking amazing. When he got into the shower and sucked on my tit, it made my knees weak and I had to put my hand on the bar to keep from falling over. Once I was good and wet, both from the shower and his ministrations, he turned me around and pressed my upper body forward, pulling my hands up to press against the wall.

"Stay there, baby," he said, and I heard him tear the foil wrapper from the condom.

Looking over my shoulder, I watched as he stroked his cock, then rolled the condom down the length of it. Something about watching a man get himself ready to fuck me did things to me, and I wasn't ashamed at all to let him catch me watching.

"You like what you see?" he asked.

"Not yet," I said.

"What's that's supposed to mean?"

"You're not fucking me yet," I explained. "Then I'll like it."

He swatted my ass enough to make it sting and I let out a little yip, but he was up against me already, shoving his cock inside me and all that went out the window. His strokes were short and fast, working me up into a frenzy until I lost myself and crashed through the glass ceiling of my own euphoria, calling his name over and over as the waves washed me back and forth in ecstasy.

"God, I love that sound," he said as I came back to myself.

When I was steadier, he slowed his pace, sliding in and out of me, slow and steady, holding my hips to keep me where I was. My legs were parted just a bit, and he reached one hand around and in front of me, fingering my clit in quick little motions, building me up once again. Panting, I felt that building pulse deep inside and I relaxed into it, letting it fill me up and push me over the edge again. He pulled me up to standing in front of him, his cock sliding out of me, and I shivered with the release.

"Let's take this somewhere easier," he said, turning the tap off and pulling the curtain back.

He picked up a towel, and wrapped it around me, rubbing the soft fabric on my skin, then he helped me step out of the tub, picked up the other towel and dried himself off. I stood there as he did this and just kind of looked at him. What he did to me flipped my switch, and it was hot as hell. But he was a manwhore, according to my brother, and I wasn't sure if he was interested in a long-term kind of thing.

"So serious," he said, and I realized that I'd been staring at him.

"Sorry," I said.

"Don't worry about it," he said. "I'm sure I can find something to get you out of that little head of yours and forget everything for a little while."

Snagging the towel, he pulled it off me and dropped it on the floor, then took the step needed to be right up against me, reached around and grabbed my ass with both hands, planting a kiss hard on my lips, where his tongue insisted I let it in. His cock was hard against me, and he ground it into me just to make a point. Using his body as leverage, he walked me backward out of the bathroom and into the rest of the hotel suite, promptly shoving me down onto the bed when my legs backed up against it.

I let out a gasp and a giggle combination and just stared at him. He was primal. A feral look crossed his face and he damn near pounced on me, pressing me back into the bed with his body and kissing me once again. The way he was lying on me, though, was awkward at best, and my legs felt uncomfortable trapped between his thighs. I wriggled a little, but he growled, his arms trapping mine at my side.

"You're all mine," he said low in his throat, and the look he gave me was almost alarming.

Maybe he realized what he said was a little off-putting, because it was like a light went on inside him and he pressed himself up on his arms, giving me room to move again. Shifting his hips, he slid one hand down my body, slipping it between my thighs and pressing them apart so he had access to my center. I moved my leg to open to him and he slid his hand down and onto my sex, stroking with slow and even movements, then he slipped his fingers inside me, ramping that motion up to a faster pace.

His leg went between mine, then he shifted the other there as well, placing him in the perfect position to enter me. The hand that had been stroking in and out of me pulled out and shifted to push my leg up higher, allowing him a better angle to slide inside, which he did at a slow and methodical pace. In and out, small strokes at first, getting deeper with each movement.

I felt him hit my cervix when he pressed in tight, his hips meeting mine, and he paused. When he pulled out again, he was nearly all the way out, and then swiftly plunged deep again, hitting the back wall one more time. I winced a bit, but the pain was gone in an instant.

"You good?" he asked, and I nodded. "Should I keep going?"

"Don't stop," I said, and he chuckled a bit, but did as I asked and kept moving.

That slow and steady pace was ramping me up again, and he pushed my leg higher, raising it up onto his shoulder and good God, that did things to me I didn't know I needed. He quickened his movements, going faster and faster, hitting the end of me with each stroke, and rubbing just right on the inside of me. Over I went, sparks flying, lights flashing, my body exploding into a million pieces. I barely registered him having his own release as I clenched around his cock buried inside me.

I could tell it was an effort for him to stay upright and hold my leg where it was, so I pulled it down, sliding along his arm and to the bed. He collapsed on top of me, panting with exertion. We lay there, both of us collecting our breaths as our bodies cooled in the air-conditioned room.

"Holy fuck," he said. "That was intense."

"Very," I agreed.

He pulled out of me, holding the condom at the base of his cock, and the release made me shudder. He chuckled. Leaning over, he pulled the condom off, then dropped it onto the floor next to the bed.

"Eww," I said. "Please tell me you don't just leave those things lying around."

"That's what the cleaning crew gets paid for," he countered.

"No," I said, looking at him. "That is disgusting. No one wants to go around cleaning up used condoms, no matter how well they're paid."

His eyes searched my face, and he realized I was right. He mumbled an apology and scooped it up off the floor and tossed it into the trash can that was next to the bed.

"That wasn't that hard, now was it?" I asked.

"I guess not," he said, but seemed a bit mad about it.

"Shall I leave you to mope around?"

"What?"

"You seem a little cranky," I said.

"Considering you just scolded me like I was a petulant child," he said. "I feel like I deserve to have a few emotions."

"Sorry," I said, sitting up and pushing him off me. "I'll just go."

"Hey," he said, grabbing my arm. "You don't have to."

"No," I said. "It's fine."

I climbed off the bed, walked into the bathroom, and picked up my dress. I pulled it over my head and settled it around me, then picked up my shoes. I took a quick look in the mirror and realized that I had seriously messed up my makeup and hair. Didn't really matter, though, cause I was just going to walk down to my room and crash.

Snatching my purse off the counter, I walked out of the bathroom and looked over to the bed where I'd left him. He was sitting on the end of the bed, his head in his hands, and looking… I'm not sure what —maybe upset, embarrassed, something. Whatever it was, it wasn't my issue.

"Thanks," I said, flipping the latch at the top of the door open. "See ya," I added when I opened the door.

He didn't look up, didn't acknowledge me at all. I let the door close behind me and walked down the hall, opening my own room with my key. I stepped inside and flipped the latch at the top of the door. I wasn't really sure what to make of his reaction, but I was tired and simply threw my purse on the counter by the door, dropped my shoes, and fell into bed.

CHAPTER EIGHTEEN

*B*eckett...

She left, and I didn't know how I felt about what just happened. I mean, the sex was fucking hot, and I loved the feel of her body, but that whole thing with the condom was a little over the top. It was one thing to be conscientious of those around you, but it felt like I was back at home with my mom nagging me to pick up my bedroom, do the dishes, do every fucking thing around the house while she couldn't be bothered to lift a finger to help.

No, she would use things, leave them lying around, then bitch at me that the house was a mess. Add in her chain smoking, beer and booze drinking, and the revolving door for the guys who came through the house screwing her, and it was no wonder the place was trashed. If it weren't for that one fucker who gave us so much money, I never would have gotten out of that shit town I grew up in.

She was gone more than she was home, and the fact that she still managed to make the house look horrible was just something else. Of course, she would always say it was my fault the house was a mess because I was the one home, so obviously it was my doing.

"Fuck," I said to the empty room.

I got up and went into the bathroom, took a piss, then climbed back into the shower. I had to get the smell of her off me—not Belinsky's sister, but my mom. God, it was like I could still smell that fucking house, as if I'd never left, and I couldn't stand it. I stayed in there until I could no longer imagine the stench of my upbringing permeating my entire being. By then, I could hear the guys coming back from the game, so I hurried and dried off, threw on a pair of lounge pants and pulled the door open.

"We win?" I asked Decker when he stepped out of the elevator.

"No," he said. "And Coach is pissed you left the stadium, too."

"Why should I stay?"

"The fuck should I know," he replied, then walked down the hall.

Well, this was just fan-fucking-tastic. I'd likely get chewed out when I got in the next morning, but what else was new. I was the team fuckup, although I thought I'd gotten out of that role. Guess I just kept putting myself into it every fucking day.

"Hennings," Coach bellowed when he saw me walking into the clubhouse. "My office. Now."

The teammates around me kind of kept their eyes to the floor, not wanting to look like they were thankful that they weren't the ones walking into the coach's office to get their ass chewed out. Whatever, I could take a chewing out, then show myself to be the team player I was when I got between the lines.

"What the fuck is your beef with Belinsky?" he asked before I had even stepped into the office.

"He's got a sister…"

The look he shot me told me what he thought of my lifestyle and extracurricular activities.

"You need to keep it in your pants," he said. "Baseball is a family, even if it's another team. We don't fuck with family. Got it?"

"Yeah," I said, dropping my head.

"From now on," Coach began. "You're on a short leash. You fuck up, you're riding pine. You start shit, you're riding pine. You spit funny, you're riding pine. Got it?"

"Yeah," I muttered.

"Good," he said. "You're not in the lineup tonight. You need to keep your head down, show me you can be a team player, and not fuck up. Maybe, if you're lucky, I'll let you play tomorrow before we head out. Now, get the fuck out of my office."

I turned around and walked back to my locker to get into my warm-up gear. No one talked to me, which I expected. It was like I was contagious and they didn't want to catch whatever the fuck I had, not that I blamed them. I wouldn't want to be around me if I were them.

The walk to the field was lonely, but I just pushed everything down. I went out into the outfield to catch some fly balls, just to keep myself occupied. I stood away from everyone, snagged balls and threw them back to the bat boy behind second, and just did whatever the fuck I wanted. I also thought about what it was that flipped my interactions with Ophelia from what we had the last day or so to whatever the fuck happened last night.

Nothing I could remember switched things like that, and it was fucking infuriating. The more I thought about it, the more I just got pissed. Her brother was an asshole, but I thought she was at least decent. Turns out, she's just a nagging bitch who wants it her way, and apparently, I couldn't do that for her.

Guess I'd just have to pick up some rando and take her back to the hotel with me, fuck her 'til I forgot about my girl, and then kick her to the curb the way Ophelia did to me. By the time batting practice wound down, I was good and pissed at the whole fucking world, and I didn't bother to try to keep it off my face.

The entire game, even when we got a couple good hits and scored some runs, I just fucking sat by myself at the end of the bench, chewing sunflower seeds and spitting the husks on the ground. Fuck whoever had to clean up after us. I was done being nice.

CHAPTER NINETEEN

F i...

"But you gotta go," McKenzie pleaded.

"My flight leaves at the ass crack of dawn," I complained. "And that means I have to be there two hours before that, which means a late night just isn't gonna work for me. I mean, I can go to the game, but I have to leave by the fourth or fifth inning."

"I'll take it," she said, hugging me.

She'd come to my hotel that morning—the morning after whatever the fuck it was that had gone on with Beckett—and said she was sorry that she hadn't told me sooner about her and Quentin. That she wouldn't keep me out of the loop anymore, promising that I would be the first one to know anything from then on.

The day ended up being all about finding things she wanted to look at for when she finally got my brother to ask that all-important question. She wanted to look at bridal gowns, bridesmaid dresses, and the whole thing. Honestly, though, I thought it was a bit premature, but to each their own.

By about two, we were both starving, so we headed to the same place we had brunch that first morning. Instead of getting two meals, though, we shared one, and left the stuff we didn't eat there. No need to leave it in my hotel refrigerator when I wouldn't be able to take it with me. I opted for shorts and my Dragons' jersey for the game, knowing that it would still be warm by the time I left, and wanting to have everything else packed except what I needed first thing in the morning.

We arrived at the stadium, her pulling out her phone to allow us to pull up to the level where players and their families parked. We walked through the garage and down to the entrance, placing our lanyards around our neck to show us as family. When we made it to our seats, McKenzie introduced me to the people around, letting them know who I was, and that we'd been friends for years. They were all very nice and said nice things about my brother.

The game started, and I noticed that Beckett wasn't playing, and neither was Quentin. I thought it was odd, but figured it had to do with the fight they had the night before. Whatever the reason, the Dragons were struggling, but they managed to at least get some players on base. It was around the third inning that my phone buzzed. I pulled it out of my purse and was a bit shocked at the message.

"What's up?" McKenzie asked when she saw me looking at my phone.

"Nothing," I said. "I gotta run to the bathroom. I'll be right back."

"Okay," she said. "You sure you're okay?"

"I'm fine," I said, standing and making my way down the stairs to the family area under the seats.

I dialed Beckett back, but he didn't answer. I was doubtful that he actually had his phone with him in the dugout, but maybe he had left early. I looked at the text again.

Forget you ever met me.

Why was he being like this? What had I done to piss him off so much that he was basically breaking up with me? It wasn't like we were actually dating or anything, just having a good time while we were both in town. Except this hurt more than it should. I sent a text back to him and hoped he'd see it.

I'm sorry. I don't know what I did, but I don't want it to end like this.

Shoving the phone back into my purse, I went back up to the seats and sat down. It was only the third inning, but I was already done with it. I waited a little while longer, then told McKenzie I wanted to go.

"You sure?"

"Yeah," I lied. "I'm kind of tired already, and knowing I have to be up and out so early is just putting more pressure on me. I think I need to go to sleep."

"I can go with you," she suggested.

"Nah," I said, begging off. "I'll call an Uber and get a ride back."

"Text me the image of the car," she said. "And a picture of the driver. Let me know when you get to the hotel, too. I don't want you to go missing and it be my fault."

"I'm not gonna go missing," I said. "But I'll be sure to send you all the information."

"Thanks," she said, then stood up with me and hugged me. "I miss you. You need to come back again when we can spend more time together."

"I'm gonna have work," I said. "Besides, you'll have plenty of things to do, especially if my brother gets his head out of his ass and does what he probably should have done a while ago."

"I'll let you know if he does," she said, then giggled.

"Okay," I said. "I'll text you when I get home, too, just so you know."

"Bye," she said, and several of the people around us also said goodbye.

I waved, then walked back down the stairs and into the family area, pulling up the ride share app on my phone and ordering a car. No text from Beckett, but then again, I didn't expect one. Oh well. If I never saw him again, I guess it was fun while it lasted.

CHAPTER TWENTY

*B*eckett...

About halfway through the game, I headed into the clubhouse and down the hallway. This whole day had gone to shit, and I was just about done with everything. Honestly, all I wanted to do was head back to the hotel and either punch someone or fuck someone. Those thoughts of course led me to thinking about Miss Belinsky and how much I wanted to fuck her again.

"No," I mumbled to myself, and walked to my locker.

Pulling my phone out, I sent her a text. telling her to forget she ever met me. Hopefully, I could do the same, but it wasn't something that was happening right now. I shoved the phone back into my bag and hit the head, grabbed a cup of water, and headed back out to the dugout to ride the pine like the good little soldier I was.

"Hey," Jonathan said when he saw me. "How you holding up?"

"Fine," I lied, then sat down at the end of the bench.

"You know he'll let you play tomorrow, right?" he asked.

"Sure," I said, but just kept looking at the ground in front of me.

"Okay," he said, then walked away.

The rest of the game went about the same, most of the players staying away from me. We won, so there was that, and at least no one was pissed that I wasn't in and screwing things up. After the game, I changed into my street clothes and waited for everyone else to shower and do their shit until finally we were able to board the bus and head back to the hotel. Everyone was all cheers and happy, but I just didn't feel it.

I hit the bar as soon as we got off the bus, hoping to find someone who might be willing to take my mind off my problems, but none of the women there held my interest, which just pissed me off even more. Instead of going out looking, I headed up to my room to see if I could just pass the fuck out and forget. When the elevator opened, the hallway was empty, which just meant that I'd spent more time in the bar than I thought I had.

Instead of going to my room, my feet took me further down the hall until I was standing in front of her door. I fought myself for entirely too long until I finally just knocked. If she wasn't interested, I'd take the short walk back to my room and call it a night.

"Hey," she said through the crack in the door. "I thought you were mad at me."

"So did I," I replied. "Do you mind?"

She pulled the door further open and let me into the darkened space. The curtains were cracked just enough to let the light from the city in so that it wasn't quite pitch black.

"You win?" she asked.

"Didn't you stay?"

"I have to fly out really early tomorrow," she replied. "I left after the third inning."

"I should go," I said, turning to head back out the door.

"Please," she said, placing her hand on my arm, but not holding me back.

"You sure?"

She nodded and I crumbled, turning and taking her in my arms, kissing her fiercely and passionately. She returned it with enthusiasm, wrapping her arms around my neck, pulling me back with her to the bed where she broke the kiss and sat on the edge. Her hand had skimmed down my chest and was now at my belt, working it loose.

Once she had the belt undone, she unbuttoned my pants, pulling the zipper down and shoving them down below my ass as my cock popped out of the boxer briefs she'd shoved down as well. I wasn't hard, at least not hard enough to fuck her, but she sucked me into her mouth anyway, and that was pure heaven. Between her tongue and lips, my dick grew harder with each suck and stroke, and her hand around my balls was just enough pressure to tighten them up as well.

"God, yeah," I whispered and felt her smile.

I might be addicted to her, and I'd only known her for a couple of days. What this meant for our future, I didn't know, but it wasn't something I needed to think about right now. No, now was the time to enjoy her, because soon she'd be gone and I would be flying off to another city with a whole other set of fans.

"Let me fuck you," I said, pulling back, so she had to release me.

She scooted up on the bed, turning on the lamp next to the headboard and picked up the box of condoms I'd left here the last time I was in this room. I kicked off my shoes, shoved my pants the rest of the way down and walked out of them and my socks while unbuttoning my shirt and dropping it into the pile on the floor.

Watching me, she pulled one of the foil packets out of the box, placing it in her teeth at the edge. I crawled up toward her and was glad she had on very little. It looked like just a tee shirt and panties, which could easily be worked around. Settling myself between her legs, I pushed her shirt up, smiling that the light was on and I could see her beautiful tits, their pink nipples clear against her light skin. I took the foil packet from her teeth and set it aside for now, bending down to take one of her nipples into my mouth. She gasped, arching her back and pressing herself into me.

I lavished her with my tongue and teeth, blending that pain and pleasure connection, listening to her breath become faster and shallower. One hand held me up, but I used the other to run down between her legs, shoving her panties to the side and sliding up and down her folds. She was already wet, which was a pleasant surprise, so I used one finger to slide inside her, stroking in and out, scratching that little patch at the top inside her. Her hands fisted in the sheets on either side of her, clenching and gathering the material.

"That's it, baby," I said, breathing on her wet breast.

"Oh, God, Beckett," she said, and I watched her let go and give in to the passionate pleasure that was running through her.

I sat back, my fingers still working in and out of her, and picked up the condom, using my teeth to open the pack, then sliding it on. Pulling my fingers out, I lined myself up and pressed into her. She gasped at the quickness of it, but her hips rose to meet mine. I held myself there for a moment, letting her get comfortable, then began to move, sliding in and out of her in slow, methodical strokes. It was a bit awkward with her panties shoved to one side, but I made it work.

Increasing my speed, I pounded her harder and harder, her head nearly hitting the wall behind her a few times until she put her hands above her to keep it from happening. Faster and faster, harder and harder, I thought about how much I wanted her to remember me, to never forget this long weekend she came to see her brother and got fucked so good she had a hard time walking after.

"Oh God," she said, breathing heavy.

"Come on, baby," I said, feeling my own impending explosion coming as well.

"Beckett," she called out, and I lost it in that moment, shooting my load into the condom that was inside her.

Shaking as I finished my release, I collapsed on top of her, landing a little harder than I probably should have, but I didn't really give a fuck.

"Can't breathe," she said, shoving my shoulder.

I shifted off her, pulling out at the same time, and the condom just kind of slid off onto her thigh. I rolled on my back, not bothering to clean her up, trying to slow my own breathing. When I had more control, I sat up, looking over at her. She had a sheen of sweat on her chest, her shirt shoved up to her armpits, and her breathing was still heavy, though was slowing down.

"Now you won't forget me," I said, then stood up, picked up my clothes and walked to the bathroom to piss and dress.

When I came out, she was sitting on the end of the bed, watching me.

"See ya," I said, then walked out the door and down to my own room.

CHAPTER TWENTY-ONE

F i...

"What the fuck?" I muttered as the door shut behind him.

I mean, yeah, it was good, but he just left everything for me to take care of. God, he was such an asshole. Maybe my brother was right and I shouldn't have gotten involved with him. But then again, my brother would probably just say something about having told me so if I said anything to him. I couldn't tell McKenzie, 'cause she'd just tell Quentin, and I didn't need him even knowing. It was bad enough what had already happened, but yeah, he so didn't need to hear this little tale.

Grabbing the condom by the opening, I carried it to the bathroom and tossed it in the trash, then sat down to pee. He didn't even bother to put the seat down after he was in here, and he peed all over the floor, too. Good God, what was it with this guy?

"Fuck it," I said, and finished peeing, washed my hands, and turned out the light.

Climbing into bed, I was sure I was gonna be sore in the morning. The clock said it was almost one, which meant that I was only gonna get another hour and a half or so of sleep, and I debated on whether it would be worth it or not.

I didn't even realize I dozed off until my alarm on the phone started going off. I shut it off and rolled up to sit on the edge of the bed. Yep, I was definitely sore. I got up and went to the bathroom, ran a brush through my hair, then pulled it all up into a messy bun on the top of my head, before shoving my brush into my bag. I pulled on the lounge pants I'd had out, then my socks and sneakers. Forgoing the bra, I pulled on a sweatshirt before checking the room for any leftovers that I might have forgotten.

Rolling my bag out the door, I let it close, then headed to the elevator. I paused outside his door, thinking that I should maybe knock. I almost did, but then remembered the way he'd left the night before, or rather earlier that morning, and just continued to the elevator.

"Good morning," the man at the front desk said.

"Hi," I said. "I'm checking out."

"Room number," he said, and I told him. "Looks like you're all good. Do you have the room key?"

I handed it over to him, then asked, "What time is the shuttle to the airport?"

"We have one leaving in about fifteen minutes," he said. "What airline?"

I gave him the name of the airline and he said that wouldn't be a problem, then suggested I wait near the entrance. Walking over to the seats near the front door, I pulled my bag in front of me and sat in one of the chairs and waited. I was so tired, with broken sleep, but I was almost on the way home. Once I got there, I could shower and crash for the rest of the day.

I'D LEFT MY CAR IN ONE OF THOSE CAR-PARK PLACES WHERE THEY shuttle you to the airport and you pay for the time you were parked there. I got off the plane, picked up the shuttle, and got to my car without much fuss. By the time I got home, McKenzie had texted me a couple of times. After throwing my car in park, I sent a text back, saying I landed, and that I was going in to shower and sleep, and that's just what I did.

When I woke up, I was disoriented because it was almost dark. Looking at the clock, I realized I had slept for a good four hours. I was still tired, but I needed to put food in my face and figure out the rest of the evening so I could head into my new job first thing tomorrow morning. Heading to the kitchen, I opened the fridge to find something to make for dinner, but it was pretty sparse pickings. Instead, I went in search of my phone to order some takeout to be delivered. God bless technology for my lazy ass.

My apartment was pretty small, but it had more than enough room for what I needed. My bedroom was just that, big enough for my bed and the small nightstand next to it and not much else. My dresser ended up in the closet on one side, with the other open for longer items like my dresses and jackets. The kitchen slash living room slash dining room was the rest of the place, minus the small bathroom off to the side next to the bedroom.

Rummaging through my closet, I found a decent dress to wear on my first day, so I set it out, along with a slip and camisole to wear underneath. Leftovers from my dinner would be sufficient for lunch tomorrow, and I could pick up some groceries on the way home. I found shoes that worked with the dress, and my all-purpose purse that I had used for pretty much forever would work nicely and wouldn't look out of place.

The phone buzzed and let me know my food was on the way and would be there shortly, so I went back into the main area of the house to see if I could find something to drink. When my phone buzzed a second time, though, I thought it was pretty quick for my delivery, so I picked it up to see a text.

How are you doing?

Quentin didn't know when to quit. I'd told McKenzie I'd landed, and that I was coming home to crash. This sounded somehow different, though.

What do you mean?

Either he'd let me know what he was asking about, or he'd call me or ask me to call him. Sure enough, my phone rang, and I answered it.

"Hey," I said.

"How are you?"

"Fine," I replied. "I landed earlier and let McKenzie know. I figured she'd tell you."

"Yeah," he said. "She did. I just wanted to make sure you were doing okay after this weekend."

"I'm fine," I replied. "Just getting things ready for my first day on the job tomorrow and getting some dinner."

"Just wanted to make sure you weren't mad at me," he said.

I paused. Was I mad at him? Honestly, I couldn't answer that.

"I'm not mad," I said. "But you do need to remember that I am an adult and capable of making my own decisions. I don't need you to run interference for me. I'm not fragile or breakable."

"It's just that Hennings—" he began.

"It's over," I said. "It was a weekend thing and we're done."

"Oh," he said, sounding surprised. "Well, good."

A knock came from the door and I walked that way.

"Gotta go," I said. "Food's here. I'll talk to you later, okay?"

"Um," he hemmed. "Sure. Have a good first day."

"Thanks," I said, then disconnected the call.

I opened the door to my food right in front, the delivery driver already gone. I sent a tip in the app and picked up my dinner, closing and locking my door to settle in for the evening.

CHAPTER TWENTY-TWO

*B*eckett...

Another day on the bench, and word came in that both Belinsky and I were gonna be suspended for one game and each fined fifteen thousand dollars. Not a big chunk of change, but it was enough to make me realize that I needed to make sure my off-field activities didn't screw with the ones on the field. I was going to serve my suspension on the first game in Dallas. It would mean three days off in a row, but it would all work out. They'd pull the fee directly from my pay, so it would be as if I never saw it.

After the three games in Dallas, we were heading to Indigo City to play the Anglers, who had been playing beyond exceptional ball all season. They were the number one team in all the American league, not just the eastern division. For some reason, though, when they came to Seattle in May, we had been able to handle them easily, winning all three games. This trip would be four games, and they were now in mid-season form after sending five players to the all-star game this season.

I tried to forget little Miss Ophelia Belinsky, but she was almost always on my mind. The shit I pulled that last night was something I would regret for a while. It was callous, cruel, and honestly even disgusted me, which is saying quite a bit. Problem was, I was more than just a little horny, and Dallas had some beautiful babes all around. I concentrated on keeping my eyes down, not looking around, but it was very hard, and I mean *very* hard to not notice the barely there tops and super short shorts.

It was like I needed a fucking sponsor to keep me on the straight and narrow. While it was difficult, I managed to get out of Dallas without banging any of the bullpen bunnies that were hanging around our hotel. The flight to Indigo City was long, and we landed late after the day game on Wednesday. A bus ride to the hotel, then to our rooms where we all pretty much crashed for the night. Thursday morning was another story, though.

"It's him," a young girl shouted, pointing at me.

Her friend was smiling damn near as bright as the sun, nodding along with the other one. They looked like they were maybe fifteen, which was definitely a no-go in my book, even if I was a pervert and an asshole. I was not at all interested in getting caught with an underage girl. That was a lesson I never had to be taught. It was instinctual, given my history. I just waved at them, then turned and headed to the bus with the rest of the team.

"Got a couple of admirers," Decker said.

"Too young," I replied, throwing my sunglasses on once we stepped outside the hotel lobby.

"There are rules you follow?" he asked mockingly.

"I'm an asshole," I said. "But I'm a smart asshole."

"Didn't seem that smart in Houston," he returned.

"Fuck you," I said, but laughed to soften the blow.

We climbed the steps onto the bus and found our seats, sitting with our headphones in, waiting for the ride to the stadium. By the time we were out on the field for batting practice, I had my head in the game, concentrating on the plan of attack against their starting pitcher, Crawford, who was a hard-throwing right-handed pitcher who had a nasty habit of plunking batters who crowded the plate.

I worked with our infield coach on fielding grounders and doing the exchange for tosses from both the third baseman and the second baseman, especially that catch and quick throw, even working on the barehanded catch and toss. Honestly, it was good to do the work, and I felt pretty good about how I handled it. I was looking forward to putting my practice into play when the game started. They'd opted to take the day I had off the previous day as my suspension game, so I was going to be able to play the whole series in Indigo City.

Speaking of the game, it started with a bang, Matsui hitting the first pitch out to center field and over the fence, and it just kept getting better the rest of the way. We were only in the third inning and were already in double digits and had chased their starter and their long relief guy. If they didn't end up using position players to pitch, it would be a miracle.

My third at bat began with two foul balls, then three pitches in the dirt. I kept fouling off pitch after pitch, losing count of how many times I'd just gotten a piece of the ball to stay alive. Finally, their pitcher threw a slow curve that had the bottom dropping out of it. I could somehow tell it wasn't gonna drop all the way, so I readied myself and swung, hitting it high and far, going the other way over their short porch in left field. Home runs were fun, but grand slams were even more so.

Rounding the bases, I gave high fives to the first base coach and the third base coach before coming to home to be pummeled by the rest of the players who were on the basepaths, then into the dugout for more congratulations.

"Looks like you've figured out whatever it was that was bugging you," Bridge said.

"Looks like," I replied, dropping my helmet and gloves into my slot in the small space.

By the time all was said and done, we ended up winning eighteen to three, going through damn near everyone in their bullpen. It was a very rowdy and happy bus ride back to the hotel. Some of the guys wanted to hit the bar, but I kind of wanted to just be alone, so I rode the elevator up with Bridge and Strawberry, who were both family guys and weren't into that whole scene.

"Goodnight," I said as I passed them both to my room at the end of the hall.

My keycard let me into the space, but I stopped before I even stepped in. Candles were lit, and the space had a low-light glow all around.

"Hey there," the girl from earlier said as she stepped out of the bathroom.

"Who the fuck are you?" I asked.

"I'm your prize for the good game you played," she purred, licking her lips.

I held the door open and glared at her, unsure what the hell I was supposed to do. Finally, my brain kicked into gear and I realized this was so not something I needed to have happen right now.

"Out," I said, giving her plenty of space to leave without touching me.

"What?" she asked.

"Out," I said a little louder. "You are not here on my request. You do not belong here, and you need to leave. Now."

I shouted the last word and something clicked in her. She gave me a sneer that sent shivers down my spine.

"You'll pay for this," she said, then stepped out, holding the sheet she'd been wrapped in around her, walking down the hall toward the elevators.

"And don't come back," I yelled.

"What's up?" Bridge said as he stuck his head out into the hall.

"Help me," the girl pleaded, pouring on the waterworks. "He tried to rape me."

"The fuck I did," I shouted. "I just got here and you were in my room. I didn't invite you at all."

"He's lying," she cried, starting to sob and hyperventilate.

"Sit down," Bridge said, ushering her to a chair that was at the end of the hallway.

I didn't enter my room. No need for me to know what was going on in there at all, especially since this bitch was accusing me of raping her. Just then the elevator opened and a couple of police officers stepped out.

"There," she cried, pointing at me. "He tried to rape me."

"The fuck I did," I reiterated. "I just got here, opened my door, and she was in there."

"Sir," one of the officers said, coming down the hall. "Please stay calm."

"I am calm," I replied. "But I did not, nor would I ever, rape anyone or even attempt it. Ask the guys," I continued. "They came up the elevator with me, so they know what time we got here, which was like five minutes ago."

The other cop was down there talking to the girl, Bridge standing near her and looking at me in some type of way I wasn't sure I liked.

"Which room is yours?" the officer asked, bringing my attention back to him.

"Right here," I said, pointing.

"Your keycard," the officer said, and I handed it over. "Please stay right here."

"No problem," I said, stepping across the hall to lean against the wall.

The cop opened my door and saw exactly what I saw when I first opened it.

"Is there a reason there are candles lit everywhere?" he asked.

"Ask her," I said, pointing down the hall. "I just got here."

"All right," he said, flipping the little lock thing so he could go in without the door shutting all the way. "I'm going to blow the candles out, just so you know."

"Knock yourself out," I said. "I didn't light them and didn't even bring them, so…"

I had no idea what he was gonna find in that room, but I was sure I wasn't gonna like it, that's for damn sure. It took longer than I would have expected, but he stepped out of the room, the lights on and the candles already out and kind of gave me a look.

"When I left for the game today," I began. "My suitcase was packed, aside from my bathroom kit, which was on the sink. I have been at the stadium since we left around two or so."

He nodded at me, then keyed his microphone on his shoulder.

"I'm going to need forensics at my location," he said.

"*Copy*," came the response through the crackling radio.

"I assume I can't go in there," I said.

"Nope," he replied. "And you might want to call a lawyer."

"Fuck," I muttered, and he just nodded.

I pulled out my phone and dialed the number we all had saved in our contacts for the team's legal help and waited for an answer.

"Seattle Cascades," the woman who answered the phone said.

How the hell she managed to sound chipper and awake at this time of night was beyond me.

"I'm Beckett Hennings," I said. "We're in Indigo City and the cops are recommending I call an attorney."

"No problem," she said, and I heard some clicking on a keyboard. "I will have someone call you in about five minutes."

"What if they take my phone?" I asked.

"Coach Johnson will also be notified," she said. "He should meet you either at your hotel or the police station, whichever is closest."

"I'm still at the hotel," I said. "Standing outside my room right now, in fact. He can come up here."

"I'll let him know," she said, then disconnected the call.

"Fuck," I muttered and looked at my phone.

It was almost midnight here, but that meant it was only nine in Seattle.

"Fuck it," I said, then dialed her number.

"Hello?"

"Hey," I said. "I just wanted to let you know not to believe anything you might see in the papers or on the news in the next couple of days."

"What are you talking about?"

"Some bitch broke into my room in Indigo City," I explained. "I told her to get out, and she's accusing me of attempting to rape her."

"Did you?"

The fact that she asked me really hurt, but I was honest with her.

"Not a chance," I said. "I don't do that. Besides, she looks like she's about fifteen or so."

"Why would someone do this?"

116

"Fi," I said, using the term she'd given me just a few days ago. "I have a reputation for being a player. I don't do underage girls, and I never let them into my hotel room to wait for me. Someone is setting me up."

"Beckett," she said. "Why did you call me?"

"Because I don't want you to believe the lies," I said.

"But why?" she asked, implying more than just what we were talking about.

"I was an asshole," I said. "I'm sorry I fucked it all up. I understand if you never want to see me again, but I don't want you to think worse of me than you already do."

"Okay," she said. "Not sure what else I can say, really."

"Thank you for answering," I said.

"K, bye," she said, then disconnected the call.

The elevator dinged and my manager walked out and headed straight for me.

"Don't talk to anyone," he said. "Don't make a statement, and do not under any circumstances let them into your room."

"Too late on that last one," I replied, pointing to the open door.

"Fuck," he said. "Okay. That stops now. Remember, they can't ask you anything once you invoke attorney privileges, so do not say anything. Give me your phone, too."

"Why?"

"If it's in your possession, they will take it for evidence," he said. "We don't let them do that. Hand everything over to me right now."

Doing as he said, I emptied my pockets into his hands just as the officer who went into my room came back down the hall.

"We've got a team that will be here in a minute to go over the room," he said.

"That's actually not going to happen without a warrant," my manager said. "Until then, the room is off-limits."

"I've already searched it," the officer said.

"You're done, now," my manager replied.

"All right," he said. "But I am going to have to put this man under arrest."

"Charges?" the manager asked.

"Attempted rape for now," the cop said. "The rest will come later."

"I want a lawyer," I said, not even giving him time to read me my rights.

"Absolutely," the officer said. "I'm going to have to search you first, cuff you, then we'll head to the station."

"Wait for the attorney," Coach said.

I just nodded. This was not how I wanted to spend my night. Not at all.

CHAPTER TWENTY-THREE

*F*i...

Don't believe anything I hear?

Is he kidding me with this right now? The way we left it was that neither of us wanted to see each other again, and now he's calling me late at night to tell me he's gonna be accused of raping a girl? Where does he think he gets off telling me what to believe?

Instead of just ignoring it and going to bed, I pull out my phone and go to the team's website to see where they are. Indigo City is somewhere on the East Coast, so it must be close to midnight there. Maybe there wouldn't be anything about it online yet, but I do a search just to see. The only thing I could see about the team is that they won tonight, which, good for them, but nothing about Beckett or anything like that.

For some reason, though, I just couldn't let it go, so I sent a text to McKenzie to see if she or Quentin had heard anything I might not have seen.

Seen anything on the Cascades for what may have happened after the game tonight?

Since it was Thursday, she was probably already asleep, so I was surprised when my phone vibrates.

Nothing I know of. What's up?

Did I tell her? No, I didn't want to start rumors, or make my brother even angrier about me having hooked up with him.

Just a strange phone call.

I put my phone on the nightstand and plugged it in, then went into the bathroom to get ready for bed. Maybe he was just fucking with me and trying to make himself out to be a bigger asshole than I already knew he was. Except, there was something in his voice that made me wonder whether he really was in trouble. I sent a text to his phone, just to ask him to tell me what happened but didn't expect a text back.

Climbing into bed, I turned the light out and tried to go to sleep, but my mind just kept wandering back to the man I shared a bed, well, and shower and door, with. I didn't think he was capable of rape, but I had only known him for a couple of days, so who knows? Turning over, I closed my eyes, willing my mind to shut off and let me sleep, but it just wouldn't listen. By the time I finally fell asleep, my alarm was waking me up.

"Ugh," I groaned, flipping over to turn it off. "At least it's Friday," I said to no one.

I rolled out of bed and padded into the bathroom to get my morning started. Showered and changed, I picked up my phone and saw I had text messages and at least one voicemail. I slipped into my shoes and made my way to my kitchen to get some coffee before I tried to look at what was going on. Once the machine was going, I pulled out the milk to add to my drink, then opened my phone.

Holy shit! Call me!

McKenzie was known to be dramatic, but this felt off. I pulled up the voicemail and listened to my brother's voice.

"You need to never contact him again," he said. *"I don't want this to screw your life up, so please do me this favor and avoid him like the plague. He's bad news, which I already told you. Just look up what he's done and tell me I'm wrong for worrying about you."*

Well, shit. Guess I better do a search to see what was happening, but not before coffee. I pulled my cup from beneath the spout, popping the little disposable cup from the machine and tossing it in the trash. I added milk and stirred it up, taking a sip and savoring the flavor before I had to do a deep dive into whatever it was that had happened.

Cascades Player Arrested read one headline. *Playboy Gets Nabbed* was another. I pulled up the team's website to see if there was any official notice there, but it wasn't mentioned. I went back to my search and clicked on the first article and read it.

There was a sixteen-year-old girl who had been kicked out of his room and sent packing in nothing but a sheet. She was saying that he invited her up to his room for an autograph, then attempted to rape her but she was able to escape. There had been no statement from the team or the police, just that he had been taken in for questioning. She had gone to the hospital for an exam, but nothing had been released yet. They were also not releasing her name, citing her age and the fact that she was a victim of a crime.

"Shit," I muttered. "Shit, shit, shit. What the fuck did you do?"

Nothing could be done from here, and I honestly didn't even know if he wanted me to try to do anything, so I just replied to McKenzie's text and ignored my brother's voicemail.

I saw what happened. On the way to work. Can't talk right now.

Hopefully that would keep her off my case, at least for a while. I stuck the lid onto my travel mug, grabbed my purse and keys and headed out to work. Sitting in an office all day might be boring to some, but it was exactly the distraction I needed.

"HAVE YOU SEEN THE NEWS?" CAROL, THE OFFICE GOSSIP, ASKED when I went into the break room around ten.

"I've been too busy working," I replied.

While she was a nice enough woman, she was of that school of thought that whoever told the story first told the truth, and anything that came after it was part of a coverup. The thing was, she usually had the wrong information, and then would never correct herself, just explain it away as being fed to her by wrong sources.

"That one player for the Seattle baseball team," she continued, even though I was obviously not interested. "The one that got into so much trouble at the beginning of last year. He was arrested for raping a child. The team is going to let him go and they are cutting ties with him altogether."

"Whatever," I said, but she'd piqued my interest.

I went back to my desk and pulled out my phone, doing a search again, just to see if any new information had been posted. Sure as shit, there was an article with a picture of him in his jersey and the words, *Child Rapist*, in bold letters at the top.

"See," she said, creepily standing behind me in my cubicle. "He's gonna be shoved in jail and won't see the light of day for years. Good thing, too. He's a creep."

"You've met him?" I asked.

"Well, no," she said. "But just look at him. He has the look of an absolute monster."

"Do you know anyone who has met him?"

"Of course not," she said, sounding indignant.

"So," I began. "You've decided that he is guilty of this charge, without having met the man, without having heard any evidence, just because he looks like a monster?"

"I mean…" she stammered.

"How about you let the cops do their job," I suggested. "Maybe, when they've looked at the evidence, and spoken to the actual people who were involved, then they will be able to tell us what exactly happened."

"Humph," she grumbled and walked away.

"Nice job," Jean said, peeking over the short wall that separated our desks. "She is always going on and on about shit she doesn't know anything about. Honestly, I'm surprised she hasn't gotten into trouble for the lies she's told."

"She actually did lie," I said. "I know him. In fact, he called me last night and told me not to believe anything I saw."

"Wait," she said, her eyes huge. "You met him? He's so hot."

"My brother plays for the Dragons," I said, standing so my voice wouldn't carry. "I was down in Houston last weekend and that's when I met him."

"Is he as hot in person as he is on the screen?"

"Sure," I said, trying to come off noncommittal. "I mean, he's short, so there's that."

"How tall is he?"

"About my height," I said, and she looked even more shocked. "What?"

"I never knew he was that short," she said. "But why did you meet him?"

"Players know each other," I said. "I met him when I was out with my brother."

I really didn't want to get into this whole thing with my coworker, but at least she was the kind that listened to what I said instead of trying to figure out how to screw me over. My phone buzzed just then, so I turned around to grab it.

Can you talk?

"I gotta go to the bathroom," I said, turning and walking straight to the elevator to take me to a lower floor so I could have a little more privacy.

When I got to a floor or three below me, I went into the restroom that was farthest away from any of the offices and dialed his number.

"Hey," he said.

"You okay?"

"Been better," he said. "Have you seen the news?"

"Yeah," I said. "One of my coworkers has already gotten you convicted and sentenced to life."

"They're not charging me," he said.

"Really?" I asked, then added, "I mean, that's good, right?"

"Very," he began. "Apparently, the girl's friend ratted her out. The friend's mom works at the hotel, so that's why they were in the lobby when we left for the game. They figured out what room I was in using the mom's log-in information, then swiped a pass key and set the room up. Once it was all ready, the friend took the key and left and the girl finished setting up and getting ready for me to come back."

"She did all that?" I asked. "Why?"

"I guess I was supposed to be her boyfriend," he said. "She'd told all of her friends that we were sleeping together, that I invited her to the hotel and gave her a key, and that we were gonna convince her parents to let us get married."

"That's a wild story," I said. "What's going to happen?"

"She'll probably face some time in juvie," he said. "Her friend is also in trouble and will probably get probation and community service. The mom got fired and won't be able to work at any hotel for at least a few years, if ever again."

"Good God," I said. "What about the press? Anything happening there?"

"The team is going to put out a statement," he said. "The police are going to make a statement as well. Even so," he continued, sounding frustrated. "My life is about to get a whole lot more complicated."

"I'm sure it is," I said.

"Anyway," he said after a pause. "Thanks for taking my call last night and for calling me when I asked this morning."

"Sure," I said. "I'm glad you got it all worked out."

"Me, too," he said.

The silence stood between us. I didn't know what else to say, and I wasn't sure if he did, either. We weren't really in a relationship, at least not a real one. But apparently he trusted me enough to tell me the truth and wanted to make sure I knew what really went on.

"I gotta go," I said when I heard the door to the restroom open.

"Okay," he said. "Thanks again."

"Sure thing," I replied, then disconnected the call.

"Why are you hiding?" Carol asked when she saw me.

"Not hiding," I said. "Just needed a little bit of privacy."

"We're not supposed to take calls during office hours," she said, and I could hear the warning in her voice.

"It was a family emergency," I said. "Those are allowed."

She sneered at me, then turned around and walked back out. I guess she had been searching for me while I was gone. Heading back to my desk, I sighed because I really didn't need to get into trouble in my first week on the job.

CHAPTER TWENTY-FOUR

*B*eckett...

I don't know why I needed her to believe I didn't do anything, but it was definitely there, lingering in the back of my brain. She needed to know that I wouldn't do what I had been accused of, and she believed me, which was a huge weight off my shoulders. The next few days, hell, maybe even the next few weeks, were going to be a struggle. I had to keep my head down and just do my job, not let everything going on around me get to me.

When we headed out of the hotel, they had told me to make sure I had at least two other players with me, and to not linger or talk to anyone. It wasn't just me the world was watching, but the entire team. Anything we did right now could be taken as something it wasn't, whether it was them shielding me from justice or trying to minimize what happened. A hard knock fell on my door and I opened it.

"You ready?" Bridge asked.

"Yeah," I said.

"We got you," he said, and I saw that Cote was with him.

Figures that it was the two guys who were family men, with steady relationships and kids, who they wanted me to be teamed up with.

"Let's go," I said, stepping into the hall.

The ride in the elevator was quiet, just the piped-in music keeping us company. When the doors opened to the lobby, though, it was a whole other world. Reporters had filled in the space just outside the doors on the sidewalk, but there were several regular folks standing around inside. I could feel their eyes on me, but I held my head up. Adams, Huffman, and Cameron had met us when we stepped out, and created a human fence, with me in the middle of all their larger bodies. Maybe there was a benefit to being short, as my teammates effectively blocked me from those around.

When we got to the automatic doors, they hushed open and I could hear all the reporters shouting questions and see the flashing of the cameras as we stepped onto the bus. Good God, I would be glad when this whole thing was over, or when we left town, which I had a feeling would come much sooner than the other.

Once we were all on the bus, the doors shut and the sound was muffled. We pulled out of the lot and headed toward the stadium.

"You doing okay?" Decker asked on the ride.

"This fucking blows," I said, honestly. "I just don't understand how they can print all the garbage they did before anything even gets going. Like, can't they wait until I actually get charged before they go saying I'm guilty?"

"What can I say," he replied. "Sex sells, especially if it's of the not-so-traditional manner."

"That's the thing," I replied. "There literally was no sex. None, zip, nada."

"But that girl wanted there to be," he said. "She was all set to go all the way with you, and when you rejected her, she had to figure out a way out of what she started."

"It's just such fucking bullshit," I said. "Fuck my life right now."

"Got anyone you can lean on?" he asked.

"Like, what do you mean?"

"Do you have anyone you can talk to?" he asked. "Someone you can bitch to, share your shit with, dump on."

"I've got the team," I said.

"I mean someone closer," he said. "Family, a good friend, something like that."

"Nah," I said. "No family left at all."

"Don't you have parents?"

"My dad took off before I was born," I said.

"What about your mom?"

"Yeah," I said. "She's a lost cause. Haven't talked to her in years. Wouldn't even know how to find her if I wanted to."

"That bad," he said, but the question was there.

"Worse," I said, but didn't elaborate.

No one needed to hear my shit history. I didn't need that kind of pity. I did my job, played well, and the rest just didn't matter.

"You should find someone," he said. "I mean, my brother is my best friend and we share all our shit. It's great to have someone to lean on when you can't carry the load yourself."

"I ain't got one," I replied. "Don't really need one, either."

"Suit yourself," he said. "But, if you wanna talk, feel free to shoot the shit with me. I'm a good listener."

"Thanks," I said.

Thing is, that was just what I had done this morning with Miss Belinsky, Ophelia, Fi. God, what did I even want to call her? I mean, did I want to keep connected? She was probably just nice today because she'd been trained to be that way. My guess, though, was that she really didn't even care. Who did? Certainly not anyone that mattered.

～

THE REST OF THE WEEKEND WAS FAIRLY UNEVENTFUL. OH, THE reporters kept asking Coach about what happened, where I was, wanting to talk directly to me, but he kept them at bay, reminding them that they were there to cover the game, and anything outside of play on the field could be directed to the press office with the team. He was a good guy and kept me out of the limelight as much as he could.

My play, and that of my teammates, was beyond stellar. We were hitting at an all-time high rate, fielding was perfection, and our starting pitchers, as well as the bullpen, were doing everything right. After the games, we would go straight back to the hotel, no stopping in at a bar or hitting up a restaurant, or anything we normally would do while in town. If we weren't in our rooms, we were at the field. Nothing else was happening for us. I knew there were some of the guys who were a bit pissed about it, but it wasn't my fault this time. No, this time, I had been the victim, odd as that was.

By the time we were boarding the plane to head back home on Sunday evening, I was exhausted. I slept the whole way home, then took my car and headed back to my apartment in Bell Town, parking under the building. These were the times I was thankful that no one knew where I lived. I just drove an average car to an average apartment —nothing flashy or extravagant for me. Oh, I thought about it, believe me, but I knew that people would notice the fancy things, but tended to forget the ordinary.

It was after midnight, which meant that the city was already asleep, getting ready for the work week to come. I absently wondered whether she was up, but figured it was too late to even think about it. Besides, I had no idea where she lived, or if she was even in Washington. Even if she was, it was far too late to be worrying her or asking for her shoulder to cry on. No, I just needed to go to bed and sleep it off.

Maybe tomorrow would be a better day, with the fact that both the team and the police in Indigo City were making their announcements about what happened. They initially did small announcements but were going to make a point to be louder with the fact that I was not, in fact, in any way, shape, or form, involved with an underage girl. Hopefully that would garner enough attention that everything else would fall away and I could get back to just playing baseball.

Coming off the elevator, I could see something sticking on the door of my apartment. As I got closer, I could see that it was one of those delivery notifications saying they missed me. Looked like it was just from the weekend, so I would just pick it up tomorrow when I got up. I unlocked the door and stepped inside, closing and locking the door behind me.

My space, small as it was, held everything I needed. There was a kitchen just to the left of the front door with a breakfast bar on one side. Past that was a living room where I had my leather reclining sofa and a coffee table, the big screen television on the wall with a gaming console and DVD player underneath it. To the right, just behind the front door, was a closet for my coats and shit, and then the small hall that went past the bathroom to the bedroom.

I headed down the hall to my bedroom and set my bag down by the closet, pulling my laptop and its cord out to plug it in on the desk I had in the corner of the room. Once that was done, I undressed and threw my clothes on top of my bag. Even though I slept on the plane, I was still somehow exhausted, so I climbed into bed to crash for the night. Tomorrow would have enough worries for itself that I didn't need to dwell on them tonight.

CHAPTER TWENTY-FIVE

*F*i...

"Ophelia," Mr. Jackson said as he stepped up to my desk.

"Hi," I said.

"Someone is here to see you," he said.

"There is?" I asked.

"We would prefer that social calls happen outside office hours," he said, and I could tell he was not at all happy about this.

"Of course," I said. "I had no idea anyone was coming. I'm sorry. I'll ask them to leave."

"That would be best," he said, then turned and walked away.

"Who is it?" Jean asked as she popped her head up over the small wall between our desks and looked at me.

"No clue," I replied, then picked up my phone and walked over to the elevators to go to the lobby of the building.

When I walked by her desk, Carol glared at me. I mean, I knew she didn't like me, but was the glaring necessary? Couldn't she just ignore me instead? I stood waiting for the elevator, wishing it to come faster. The last thing I needed was to get fired after only a week on the job, so whoever it was that came to see me at work was going to get an earful, that was for sure.

I stepped out of the elevator and made the turn into the main lobby of the building. My fucking mom was standing there, talking to the security dude at the desk.

"Mom?"

"Hey," she called, turning to me. "There's my little working girl."

"Okay, first," I began. "That is not a term you should use. Second, what are you doing here?"

"I wanted to take you to lunch," she said.

"Mom," I countered. "It's ten in the morning. I don't go to lunch this early."

"Can't you just this one time?"

"No," I said. "And you can't come to see me at my office. I got into trouble for having someone come to see me. Do you want to get me fired?"

"Oh," she said, clearly not realizing what she'd done.

"Yeah," I said. "Next time you want to go to lunch with me, send me a text and we'll work out a day that will work. Until then, though, I have to go back to work."

"But," she began.

"No," I said. "I have a job and you have to leave. I love you, but you can't do this again."

"Okay," she said. "I'll just go home then."

I could tell she was upset, but this was not okay. Instead of succumbing to her personal pity party, I turned around and headed back up the elevators to my office.

"That was short," Carol said as I stepped off the elevator. It was like she was waiting for me in order to pounce as soon as I came back up.

"It was," I replied, then tried to ignore her.

"You're lucky you didn't come back to your desk packed," she said. "That's what usually happens when something like this takes place."

"Carol," Mr. Jackson said as we got to the office area.

"He's probably going to ask me to get you to leave," she whispered, then beamed at my boss.

I blew out a breath and sat down at my desk, picking up the task that I had been previously working on. It didn't take long for me to forget everything else and just dive right into the numbers on my screens. I'd always been good at math, and it was logical that I got into the accounting field. While this wasn't my ideal job, it was definitely a great one to get first thing out of college. To find one relatively close to home was more than a blessing.

By the time lunch rolled around, I was starving, and also wondering what was going on with Beckett. I'd be lying if I said I wasn't curious as to what happened. The question was whether I was just curious about what happened or concerned for him and the ramifications it might have on his life going forward.

"You're deep in thought," Jean said when she peeked over the wall.

"Oh," I said, a little surprised at her appearance. "I was just thinking over these numbers."

"That look had nothing to do with numbers," she said, a devilish smile on her lips. "Let's do lunch and you can fill me in."

"Well," I hesitated.

"We can go out," she said, pointedly looking over to where Carol sat. "That way we can talk freely without prying ears."

"Sign me up," I said.

After locking my computer, I picked up my purse from the back of my chair as I stood. We walked past Carol's desk, but she wasn't there. Not that it mattered, but it was nice to not be watched every moment of my day. We walked down the street to the bistro that was in the basement of the Post Office building. They had sandwiches and salads and the like, so it was an easy option for us. After we ordered, we sat in the little space they had there for patrons and waited for our names to be called.

"Who came to see you?" she asked once we'd settled.

"My mom," I said, sighing. "She thought I could just go to lunch any time I wanted."

"Does she work?"

"No," I said. "And she hasn't since my brother was born, so it's been forever since she did. You would think she'd remember that office people have schedules, because my dad worked in an office and she had it all figured out then."

"She also had a couple of kids to deal with," Jean said. "Maybe she just needs to find a good group of women to hang out with. You know, like the sewing bees they had in the pioneer days?"

"Yeah," I said. "If only I could find something for her to be involved in that kept her out of my hair. I mean, I love her to death, don't get me wrong, but she's kind of just a bit much sometimes."

Our names were called then, so I got up and grabbed both our lunches, coming back to the table to sit again. We ate in relative quiet, but it didn't take long for Jean's mind to circle back to the topic of last week.

"Tell me about the ball player," she said.

"I'm sorry, what?"

"You know," she said, winking at me. "Tell me all about your trip to Houston and the shenanigans you got up to. My life is boring, so I need to live vicariously through my friends, and you've got the most interesting life of any of them, so dish."

"Well," I said.

"Please," she begged. "I won't tell anyone, I promise, but I need to know all the details."

"You're worse than my best friend," I said. "And she was there all weekend."

"Did she get the details?" she asked. "Because, if so, I need them, too."

Her eyebrows bounced up and down. It was so ridiculous that I couldn't help but laugh at her.

"Fine," I said. "I'll let you know some of the things. I mean, it was kinda hot, actually."

"Oh," she said, setting her sandwich down and giving me her full attention. "I'm all ears."

I spilled. Not everything, but enough to keep her satisfied yet not enough to get me into trouble. Basically, it was the vanilla version of events over that weekend.

"Holy damn," she said, her eyes wide, even from the tamed-down version I'd shared.

"Definitely," I said.

"Are you guys like, together?"

"No," I said. "It was a weekend fling, nothing more."

"Can you introduce me?"

I laughed because I didn't think her husband would appreciate that. We'd known each other only a week, and we were best work friends from the beginning, commiserating over our shared disdain for Carol, the office snitch and gossip. Jean had been the one to let me know that whatever I did, I shouldn't share any information with Carol that I didn't want spread throughout the entire office. It was the reason she didn't know I knew Beckett, and never would if I could keep it that way.

We finished our lunch and headed back to the office, which was just across the street and down one block. The security guard waved to us as we passed his desk and got into the elevator to ride it up to the boring institution we slaved for, chatting about finding a day to go to one of the games when my brother's team was in town. It was a couple of weeks out, but I promised her that I would see if I could get us some family seats for either the Saturday or Sunday game. She wanted to bring her husband, which I told her was fine as well.

"He's gonna flip," she said as we got off the elevator.

"Who?" Carol asked.

"Who what?" Jean replied.

"Who is gonna flip?" she asked pointedly.

"None of your damn business," Jean deflected. "This conversation has nothing to do with you. Contrary to what you may believe, you do not need to know every detail of all our lives simply because you work here."

"There's no need to be rude," she replied. "I was just being friendly."

"No one wants to be friends with you, Carol," Jean said. "You're a gossip, an eavesdropper and an all-around busy body. Now, if you're finished interrogating us about things you don't need to know, we have work to do."

She grabbed my elbow and steered us back to our desks. I was holding my stomach, trying desperately not to burst out laughing. My shoulders started to shake as we got closer to our desks.

"Don't let it out," she mumbled under her breath.

I snorted but tried to cover it with a cough. When we sat down, I pulled my sweater from the back of my chair and shoved it against my mouth, letting the giggles out as quietly as I could. Finally, after entirely too long, I got control of myself and was able to get back to work.

By the time I was done with my work and heading out, I was well under control. I texted my brother in the elevator, pressing send as soon as I hit the lobby. He probably wouldn't see the text, what with the two-hour time difference, but I wanted him to have time to get tickets for the game coming up. Hopefully it wouldn't be too hard for him to get them, but time would tell.

CHAPTER TWENTY-SIX

*B*eckett...
"I got this on my door," I said when I stepped up to the counter at the Post Office.

"Let me see," the gal behind the counter said. She scanned the bar code on the notice and then asked, "Can I see your ID?"

"Sure," I said, pulling my license out of my wallet.

She looked at it and compared it to whatever was on her screen, then said, "I'll be right back."

She walked to the back of the building through a small door and disappeared. After a couple of minutes, she came back with a small box.

"Here we go," she said, scanning another bar code from the box. "Just need your signature and you're good to go."

I signed the little card reader thing mounted to the counter, then she handed the box to me. There was signage on the box about it being human remains, so I asked her about it.

"They are legal to ship," she said.

"But who sent them?" I asked.

"Looks like they came from a funeral home," she said. "Probably a family member."

"I don't have family," I said.

"Well," she said. "They were shipped legally, so maybe there is something inside to indicate more information."

"Okay," I said, feeling a little skeeved out about it, but I took my dead person and walked away.

I got to my car and set the box in the passenger seat. I didn't want to open this in my car, didn't really want to open it at all, but I figured that someone wanted me to have them, so I should at least figure out who it was. The drive home was short, but uncomfortable. When I got to my apartment and got inside, I set the box on my kitchen counter.

"Dead people in my apartment," I mumbled as I grabbed the scissors from the junk drawer.

I slit the tape that was holding the box closed and opened it up. Inside was a plastic bag around some bubble wrap. The bag was sealed as well. Maybe they didn't want dead people falling out or something. I cut the bag open wide enough to pull back the bubble wrap that was around a small, wooden crate type thing. When I pulled that out, I found a letter in an envelope, so I grabbed that, setting the box back into the cardboard container it came out of.

Mr. Hennings,
Please accept our condolences on the death of your mother. Per
her wishes, we have cremated her remains and sent the ashes to
you. If you wish to obtain an urn to keep her in, we can recom-
mend some funeral homes that you can visit to find just the
right one for your loved one.
Again, please accept our condolences on your loss.
Sincerely yours,
Wayne Curtis
Senior Director
Standing Rock Funeral Home

"What the actual fuck?" I asked, looking back at the box on my counter.

I reread the letter three times, confused as to what the hell was happening. I mean, obviously my egg donor had finally kicked it, but where did she get off sending me her remains? Never had I agreed to this, didn't want it, and honestly was totally grossed out about the whole thing. Unfortunately, it was already pretty late in the day, and I had a job to get to, so it wasn't something I could deal with any further at that moment. Instead, I did what I almost always did when it came to dealing with her shit. I shoved the letter back into the box and stuck it into the closet by the front door.

Grabbing my bag, I left the apartment and headed to the stadium. Maybe being between the lines would get me out of my head enough to wrap my brain around what I had to do next. When I walked in, the rest of the guys were there, so I changed and headed to the batting cages that were under the stadium. Hitting the shit out of some balls would probably do me good, and it wasn't like I couldn't use the practice.

By the time I ended up on the field for batting practice officially, I was already sweaty and my muscles were wound tight. I headed to the outfield to stretch and shag some balls, finding a place that wasn't near any of the other players. Between the running from side to side and stretching out to catch fly balls, I felt pretty good about myself and was ready to start the game at my position on the infield. We were playing pretty well this season, just outside of first behind Houston, and it was my goal to beat Quentin Belinsky for the division championship if at all possible. That desire was fueling my play, especially in the last couple of weeks.

While it wasn't Houston we were playing against tonight, I still couldn't help but feel smug for the fact that we'd beaten the Anglers, on their home turf, and soundly. Oh sure, there was other shit we had to deal with there, but baseball wise we were good. With Boston in town, there were sure to be plenty of fans rooting for the visiting team, but we usually didn't pay too much mind to the fans, so it would likely be just another game for us.

"Hennings," Coach called from his office when we were all nearly changed.

I walked that way while buttoning up my jersey.

"What's up?" I asked.

"Got a letter for you," he said, handing me an envelope.

I took it and looked it over, but I didn't recognize the printing, and the law firm name wasn't familiar to me. Then I saw that the address was in Santa Fe and my blood ran cold.

"Aren't you gonna open it?" he asked.

Fuck. This was all I needed today. Not like it hadn't been a shit-show already, but did I really want to add fuel to the fire that was my burning psyche? I tore the envelope open, pulling out a piece of paper. I unfolded it and a check fell to the floor. Looking down at it, I shuddered, then picked it up. No, now was not the time to deal with this. I folded the letter back up and shoved both it and the check back into the envelope.

"Thanks," I said, though there was no emotion behind it.

Leaving his office, I went back to my locker and shoved the envelope into my bag, then headed to the dugout, tucking my shirt in along the way.

"Hey," Huffman said when I met came out of the tunnel. "You okay?"

"Not at all," I said.

"Well," he said. "Take it out on the damn Shamrocks."

"Will do," I replied and headed to the top step of the dugout.

We were all there, waiting for the pregame festivities to finish up. The anthem had already been sung. They were just doing the final fancy things like ceremonial first pitch, then it was our turn to take the field and get things going.

"And now," the announcer said. "Let's hear it for your Seattle Cascades."

That was our cue, and we all trotted out to our positions, Matsui throwing the ball on the ground to Cote, and the game began. Maybe, just maybe, I could get through tonight and not have to deal with all the other bullshit. If I kept my head in the game, the rest would just fade away.

～

"Let's go, let's go," I shouted from my position on the field.

We were up a couple of runs and it was the top of the fifth inning. Wolfe was on fire, pitching like we hadn't seen him all season. First pitch and their third baseman hit it out to short right field, over Cote's head, but in front of Adams, who had to play it on a short hop.

"Okay," I shouted. "Let's get two."

"Ground ball, my man," Cote called to the pitcher. "We'll pick you up."

Our pitcher nodded at us, then got to the top of the mound, settling himself in front of the rubber. Decker threw down the sign for a fastball, low and inside. Wolfe nodded, checked the runner at first, then set for the pitch. As soon as he kicked, their third baseman bolted straight for second, trying to steal. Pitch went home, and Decker popped up and threw it down to me, but it was a bit high. I jumped to catch it, then dropped to swipe a tag. All of a sudden, I was on my back, the wind knocked out of me.

"Safe," the ump called, and I looked around.

I had the ball in my mitt. I know I tagged him, and somehow me ending up on the ground made him safe?

"The fuck he is," I shouted as I got up.

"It's all good," Cote said, getting between me and the umpire. "Walk it off."

"Nah, man," I barked. "It's bullshit. That was an intentional spiking slide, and he knows it."

I spit on the ground, glaring at the umpire, but he just turned his back and walked away.

"Come back here, Blue," I shouted. "Or are you too much of a pansy to take it like a man?"

"Beckett," Cote said, shoving my shoulders back to get my attention. "Let it go."

There was a warning in his voice, something he didn't show unless he was well and truly pissed off. Something in his eye told me that there was more here than what I saw, felt and experienced. This wasn't right, though, and he knew it.

"Come on," he said, patting my shoulder. "Let's get two."

I looked at him, completely baffled by his willingness to let whatever this was slide. Had I read it wrong? Was the slide good? No, I knew what happened, and there was no way I was gonna let it go. I sidestepped, trying to get around my teammate, but he grabbed my arm, holding it tight. When I turned my eyes up to the big screen, I watched as they replayed the play. Kick by Wolfe, throw by Decker, my catch and swipe. I missed him. The slide was good. What the hell?

I slapped the ball into Cote's glove, then started walking off the field. Something was up, but I wasn't sure what it was. Only thing I knew was that I needed to get out of here and figure my shit out. My teammates were calling my name, but I ignored them all. Coach tried to stop me from stepping off the field, but I glared into his eyes, which were right even with mine because he was standing on the first step of the dugout. Whatever he saw made him realize that this was not something he could talk me out of, so he stepped aside.

"Bridge," he called, but I didn't hear the rest.

The tunnel to the clubhouse was the longest it had ever been, and it took forever for me to get to my locker.

"Meet me at Fadó Irish Pub," I said when she answered.

"What just happened?" she asked.

"Just," I said, then swallowed hard. "Please, just meet me."

"It'll take me a while to get there," she replied.

"Don't care," I said. "I need you."

I disconnected the call and kicked my cleats off, ripped my jersey off, and shoved my pants and cup down and off as well. Everything ended up in a pile as I pulled my street clothes on. The damn envelope that Coach had given me before the game fell to the ground and I growled as I picked it up, shoving it into my bag. I shoved my phone into my back pocket, took my bag and headed to the parking garage where I stuffed everything into the trunk of my car, then started the short walk to the bar. I didn't need my car and didn't want to risk losing anything inside by leaving it on the streets of Seattle.

CHAPTER TWENTY-SEVEN

F i...

My normal twenty-five-minute drive home took almost an hour and a half because of an accident on the freeway. If I had known about it early enough, I would have altered my route and missed it completely, but I tended to listen to podcasts instead of live radio when I drove, so there was no way for me to know. This meant that I had barely enough time to throw some leftovers into the microwave before the game started.

Used to be, I would only watch a Cascades game if they were playing the Dragons, but that all changed when I left Houston. I found myself watching more and more of the home team games and enjoying it quite a bit. When the microwave dinged, I grabbed a hot pad and fork and sat down on my couch to watch the game.

The announcers mentioned the amount of green in the stands, indicating that Boston had brought a big fan base with them. It wasn't surprising, though. Their team always had lots of fans from all over, and they showed up in droves wherever they went. A lot of that had to do with the fact that the team had been around for over a hundred years, so I guess it made sense.

After the first couple of innings, the game got a little rough, with

Boston getting three guys on base before the pitcher figured it out and got the final out by strike out. I took my dishes into the kitchen, rinsed them off and stuck them into the tiny dishwasher I had. I heard the roar of the crowd and the announcers were excited with the home run we hit after a walk. At least we were winning.

Hold up. I think I just changed from a Dragons' fan to a Cascades' fan in the span of a moment and I wasn't sure exactly how I felt about it. I got back to the couch in time to see Beckett strike out for the second time tonight. He was off, but it wasn't just baseball. There was a look of some sort on his face, and I couldn't place it. It was probably all in my imagination anyway, so I just forgot about it and watched as the game continued.

The top of the fifth inning started with their third baseman hitting a single to right field. Nothing unusual about that, and I could see the players cheering each other on, probably telling the pitcher to throw something low so they could get a ground ball and get two outs. The pitcher got set on the mound and looked in for the sign, checked the runner, then threw the pitch.

Their player took off from first on the first move, which was ballsy considering how good of a pick-off move Wolfe had, according to the announcers, but he had already started toward home. The catcher caught the ball and threw it in one fluid motion, but the ball carried up, well above Beckett's head. He had to jump to catch it and landed on top of the runner, never getting the tag down. The ump called him safe, which was the right call, and they played a slow-motion replay of the throw and miss. When they went back to live action, Beckett was shouting at someone, likely the umpire, but the second baseman was between them, holding him back.

When they changed the camera view, it showed Beckett shouting, and the commentators were talking about the call being good, just a bad throw by the catcher. He wasn't having any of whatever his team-mate was saying to him. Then a look came across his face, something I'd never seen before. He was hurting, but not in a physical way. No, this was a deep hurt that went clear to the center of his soul.

All of a sudden, he took the baseball and shoved it into the second baseman's glove and walked off the field. He paused at the top of the dugout, his coach standing there, but neither of them spoke, at least not that I could see. The coach moved back, and he went down the steps and away from the cameras and prying eyes.

The commentators were talking about how they'd never seen anything like that and were wondering whether he had been injured in the landing and fall. My phone rang just then and I jumped. I answered it without looking to see who was calling.

"Hello?"

"Meet me at Fadó Irish Pub," he said.

"What just happened?" I asked.

"Just," he said, then paused. "Please, just meet me."

"It'll take me a while to get there," I replied.

"Don't care," he said. "I need you."

He disconnected the call. I stared at my phone for a heartbeat, then stood up and shut the television off, rushing to my room to throw on some jeans and shoes. I had already taken my bra off and was wearing an oversized tee shirt with a tank top underneath. It would have to be enough, but I was a little subconscious because I had no idea what this bar he mentioned was like. I'd hate to show up in jeans and a tee shirt and have it be a more upscale kind of place.

"Fuck it," I said to myself and shoved the phone into my purse.

I headed out the door, locking it behind me, and took the stairs down the two flights to the ground floor. Pulling out my keys, I opened my car door and threw my purse in the passenger seat. When I got in, I took my phone out and did a quick search for the bar he'd mentioned, forgetting what it was actually called. Finally, I found it and asked my phone to get me there via the GPS installed in it.

Starting the car, I pulled out and headed to the freeway. The map said it would take me at least forty-five minutes to get there. I just hoped he didn't do anything stupid before I did. At least most of the rush-hour traffic had subsided, being it was already after eight. Thankfully, being it was late July, the sun was still up and it wasn't raining, neither of which I wanted to try to deal with while trying to figure out where the hell I was going, especially in downtown Seattle.

~

IT WAS JUST AFTER NINE WHEN I FINALLY FOUND A PARKING PLACE near the bar he'd mentioned. I was a little hesitant to leave it there, but there were plenty of people still around, and it didn't exactly look like a sketchy part of town. I checked the meter, and it was late enough that I didn't have to pay to park. Instead, I locked the car and walked down the block to the bar.

The building was beautiful with its dark green marble surrounding the gilded gold in the doorway. As I stepped through the portal, I had to stop and let my eyes adjust to the dimness. A dark bar was across the side of the space with stools next to it, and there were a handful of tables scattered around. There was a set of a couple steps just to the left and that's where I saw him.

I climbed the steps and walked over to him, sitting down at his table. From the looks of it, he'd spent the entire time I was driving, drinking, and it wasn't just beers. It appeared to be a combination of that, plus mixed drinks and perhaps some shots as well.

"Oh," he said, looking at me. "You made it."

"Yeah," I said. "How you doing?"

"Fine," he said, drawing the word out.

He was definitely feeling the booze he'd ingested.

"You're pretty," he said.

"And you're drunk," I replied.

"Yeah," he said. "C'mere."

He kind of waved me toward him, but he was definitely over his limit.

"Let's get you home," I said, waving over the waitress. "Can we get his tab?"

"I'll charge the card he left," she said. "Be right back."

"But I wanna drink more," he whined.

"They won't let you," I said. "When she brings the card back, you need to sign it and then I will take you to your place. Okay?"

"Oh," he said. "You just wanna get me into bed, don't you?"

"Sure," I said, humoring him.

I'd do whatever I could to get him out of here and back to his place. I didn't want to try to drive him all the way to my place. Besides, I wasn't sure how he'd get home tomorrow if I did. No, probably better to get him to his place and into bed.

"Here you go," the waitress said, handing me one of those folder things with his card and a pen.

I looked at him and he was in no shape to sign, so I added a tip, and a big one, then signed it and handed the folder back to her, putting his card in my pocket.

"Okay," I said, pulling on his arm, trying to get him on his feet.

He swayed a little, but then seemed to be solid. Leaning on me, his arm across my shoulder, I walked him toward the door, taking care going down the steps. He only stumbled a little when we went out the door, but I caught him before he fell. I was very thankful that I was only a little way down the block and was able to steer him easily to my car. Clicking my key fob, the car unlocked and he looked at it, eyes wide.

"Come on," I said, pulling the door open. "Get in."

"Bossy, ain't ya?" he said, but he did what I asked.

I shut the door behind him, then went around the front of the car and got into the driver's side.

"What's your address?" I asked him and he looked at me very confused. "Do you know where you live?"

"I usually know how to get there," he said, but it was clear that these questions were well outside what he could handle.

"Give me your ID," I said.

He just blinked at me, very confused.

"Your phone?" I asked.

That one he did, but it had a lock on it, so I turned it to him. It took him a couple of tries, but he finally unlocked it. I pulled up his maps feature and sure enough, he had his home address saved. That made things much easier. I plugged the address into my own GPS and saved it as his place, then handed his phone back to him. I started the car, then pushed the go button on the map and the lady inside my phone gave the first direction.

"She's talking funny," he said, still slurring his words.

This could be a long night. After a short time, we arrived at an apartment complex that had an underground parking garage.

"Do you have a pass for this?" I asked, but he was out.

I put the car in park and rummaged through his pockets, finally finding his wallet. Instead of trying to figure out which card worked the door, I just stuck the whole wallet next to the reader, and the gate began to rise. I dropped his wallet into my lap, put the car in drive, and headed in. Fortunately, the parking spaces had the number of the apartment on the wall, so I was able to figure out where to park. Once I did, I shut the car off and turned to Beckett.

This was going to either be very easy or extremely difficult, and I wasn't sure which option I thought would be better. Oh well, no time to wait. Tomorrow was gonna suck, but maybe I could get him inside, in bed, and then head home.

"Come on, babe," I said. "Let's get you inside."

"No, Mom," he said, his eyes closed. "I don't wanna go. Let me sleep in."

"I'm not your mom," I said, but he was still not fully awake. "You wanna go have some fun?"

Maybe, if I appealed to his sexual appetite, he would get out of my car and I could get him into his apartment. He blinked a couple of times, looking at me, clearly confused.

"When did you get here?" he asked.

"I came because you called," I said.

"That was nice of you," he said. "We should go fuck around a bit."

"Yeah," I said, playing into his delusions. "But first, we need to get to your apartment."

He looked at me, then looked around and said, "Oh, hey. We're here. That was fast."

"Sure was," I said. "Can you walk?"

"I can do a whole fuck ton more than walking, baby," he said, smiling.

"Then let's get to it," I said, opening my door.

I walked around the back of the car and opened his door, reaching in to help get him out. He swatted my hand away and shifted so his feet were on the concrete floor of the garage. His eyes went wide, and he swayed a bit with the rapid movement, but he steadied himself eventually.

"Come on," I said, stepping back to give him room to get out.

It took four or five attempts, but he was finally on his feet and outside the car. After he got his balance, I stepped close to him and he kissed me, full on leaning on me.

"Okay," I said, pulling back a bit. "Let's save that for upstairs."

"Oh yeah," he said, his arms still around my neck. "We should go up and fuck."

"Can't do that standing here," I replied.

He moved his feet, shuffling away from the car, and I was finally able to close the door and click my fob to lock it. I guided him to the elevator that I'd seen on my way down into the parking garage.

"What floor?" I asked when it arrived.

"Three," he said. "No, wait."

He paused, and I waited for him to figure out whether he was right or not. When he didn't answer, I got worried that I wouldn't be able to figure it out.

"Well…" I said, waiting for him to remember.

"Yeah," he said. "Definitely three."

"Okay," I said as we got into the elevator.

I pressed the button for the third floor and the doors hushed shut. There wasn't any music, but he was swaying back and forth as if he heard something no one else did. When the elevator jolted at the floor, he nearly toppled over, but I caught him. Picking him up from the ground would not be easy, especially in this enclosed space.

"Come on," I said. "Let's get you to bed."

He seemed to be on autopilot as he steered us down the hall and right to a door. He fumbled a few times, trying to get into his pocket, but was unsuccessful. I shoved my hand into it and pulled out his keys.

"You should see what else you can find in there," he said. I think he tried to wink but was completely ridiculous with it.

I tried a couple of keys before I got to the right one and got the door open.

"Welcome home," he said. "Let's go fuck."

"Let's get you changed, first," I said.

Honestly, while he was still sexy, this was not the time to be doing anything that he may regret in the morning. I locked the door behind me and he hung on my shoulder, smiling up at me with this little boy smile that was kind of endearing.

"Let's get you in bed," I said.

"Been trying all night," he replied, then kind of pulled me further into the apartment.

There was a light on over the stove in the kitchen, but the rest of the place was pretty dark. We walked, slowly, with him stumbling, to the bedroom, and I was surprised to see how big the bed was. I mean, I only had a full bed, and it was plenty big enough for me, and to share if needed. This thing was massive. The covers were a mess, but that wasn't that big of a deal.

"Okay," I said, guiding us to the edge of the bed. "Sit down and I'll help you get undressed."

"I wanna undress you," he said. "You're pretty."

"Let's start with you," I countered and got him to sit down.

I kneeled in front of him and pulled off his shoes and socks. Then I stood up and started unbuttoning his shirt. He almost fell over, and it was very clear that he was just gonna pass out, so I tried to hurry. I got the shirt off and was attempting to undo the belt when he fell over sideways onto the pillow. Shaking my head, I worked to get his pants undone, then pulled them down while shoving his legs up onto the bed.

"Uh oh," he said, then began to gag.

I looked around and found a trash can that had a bag in it, but it was damn near full. I pulled the bag out and stuck the can under his head just as he hurled. Now don't get me wrong, I know it wasn't his fault, but good God, I hated the smell and the sound of vomit. It was all I could do to keep my dinner down while he lost whatever he'd had that night into the can. Once he'd finished, and I felt like he wasn't in imminent danger of tossing his cookies again, I took the can into the bathroom and poured the contents into the toilet, flushing it. Then, I stuck it under the faucet in the tub and filled it halfway with water to rinse it out, flushing that down as well.

Turning around, I saw he was out, his eyes closed and his face slack with sleep. He was kind of adorable, and I would put money on the fact that he only had a beard to keep from looking like he was twelve. Normally, I probably would have just headed home right then, but the fact that he threw up and was now out cold gave me a little bit of concern. I didn't want him to throw up again and not be able to roll himself over if he was lying on his back. Despite my hesitancy, I decided that I should probably spend the night, just to be safe.

I put the washed-out trash can next to the bed, clicked off the light in the bathroom, then pulled my shoes and jeans off and climbed into the other side of his bed. It felt like I had to travel miles to get to where he was at the edge, but I wanted to be close enough to feel him if he was in distress. At least it was early enough that I would likely get some good sleep and still be able to make it home in time to put on some different clothes and make it in to work on time. I sighed deeply, then closed my eyes, hoping to be able to sleep.

CHAPTER TWENTY-EIGHT

*B*eckett...

My dick twitched next to her ass, and my God did I want to bury myself inside her. She was warm and soft in all the right places. I smoothed my hand up under her shirt and palmed her tit, her nipple responding to my touch. Grinding into her ass, I nuzzled her neck, biting on her earlobe.

"Ouch," she said.

She tried to turn toward me, her hand pushing mine away from her, but I held her tight. My other arm was under my head, so I shifted to put it around her as well, underneath her own head and crossing her chest to hold her firmly against me.

"I want you so fucking bad," I whispered, biting her earlobe once again.

"Beckett," she said, and her voice was stern.

"Yeah, baby," I said. "You want me, too. I can feel it. You are wound so tight, but I know just how to loosen you up."

Again, I ground my hard cock into her ass.

"Just stop," she said and I stilled. "Thank you."

"Anything for you," I said.

She was still against me, and I could feel her heat, as if it were a siren calling to me, begging me to plunge over the side of a ship to the depths below and die in her arms.

"Can we talk about last night?" she asked.

It was still dark, and I could still feel some of the effects of the booze I'd drunk earlier, but what she was asking was not something I wanted to talk about.

"Let's not," I said, grinding again.

"Beckett," she barked and I stilled again. She shifted in the quiet space and turned to face me. "What happened last night?"

"I don't want to talk about that," I said.

"Why did you walk off the field?"

"I said," I growled. "I don't want to talk about that."

"So," she replied. "You get to call me up after I watch you walk off the field and demand that I meet you at some bar. Then, when I get there, you are beyond drunk, to the point of falling over. And when I get you home, you hurl your guts out, which I cleaned up, thank you very much, and then pass the fuck out. Now, after staying because I didn't want you to die, you seem to think that sex is a good idea?"

"Fucking is always a good idea," I said.

"I am not just some safety net you can call on when shit goes sideways," she said. "Something happened yesterday. I could tell the whole game. Then, you basically left your job without a backward glance, called me up, and demanded I take care of you. How do you not see that this is totally not cool?"

I pulled my arms away, rolling onto my back, and sighed.

"Fine," I said. "Just fucking leave."

"No," she said, and it was fierce.

"What?"

"I said, no," she replied. "Not until you tell me what the fuck is going on with you. I mean, I get that you had a shitty situation when you were across the country, but that shouldn't have anything to do with last night's game. What happened there was dealt with, so what changed?"

I ran a hand down my face and sighed. Fuck. I did not want to have this conversation, and least of all with her.

"You know what," she said. "Forget it. I have to work in a bit, and I need to get home so I can take a shower and get dressed. I don't want to smell like puke all day. It's a bad look."

I felt her shift on the bed and she climbed off, the bed lifting with the absence of her weight. Closing my eyes, I wondered whether I should just tell her what happened or if it was too late for that. Did she need to know? Fuck, I didn't know what to do. She, however, knew exactly what to do. She was dressed and walking out of my room while I just lay there trying to get my shit together. And I let her go, let her walk right out of my room, my apartment, and maybe even my life.

"Fuck you, Mom," I shouted.

"HENNINGS," COACH CALLED WHEN I WALKED INTO THE LOCKER ROOM. "Get in here. Now."

"Shit," I mumbled, walking in that direction.

"Sit," he said, pointing to one of the chairs across the desk from his.

Normally, I didn't go for someone treating me like a dog and demanding I do shit, but this was something I was expecting. He slammed the door, then stalked to his own chair, but didn't sit. He glared at me, and I knew I was about to be chewed out at best.

"What the fuck was up last night?" he asked.

"Umm," I hesitated.

"Doesn't matter," he barked. "Whatever the fuck is in your head, you need to figure it the fuck out. I'm putting you on the injured list and I don't want to see you for a week. Effective immediately. Now, get the fuck out of my office and my clubhouse and don't come back until next week. When you do, you sure as shit better have a good explanation for whatever the fuck you have going on in your head. If you don't, then expect to be heading south to the Shoremen, because I don't need someone who isn't a team player in my clubhouse."

"Yes, sir," I said.

"Glad you understand," he said, softening a bit. "Now, get out."

He hadn't sat down at all, just stood behind his desk, looming over me. I mean, he had a good eight inches on me, but with me sitting, it felt like I was that little boy once again, sitting in the principal's office in trouble for something or other. I got up and opened the door, walking out of the office and back to my locker. The only thing I'd brought in was my phone, and I picked that up and headed out to the parking structure.

"Where you going?" Decker asked as I passed him on my way to the car.

"Taking time," I said.

"For what?"

I didn't answer, just climbed into my car, and shut the rest of the world out. I started it up and put it in gear, heading out to go back to my apartment. Once I pulled into the garage and parked, I headed back upstairs. There were so many things that went wrong yesterday and into this morning, and I honestly wasn't sure exactly what I wanted to do. Maybe this week would give me time to figure my shit out.

Walking into my apartment, I tossed my bag from the trunk onto the couch, then headed into the bedroom, flopping onto the bed. Her scent wafted up from the pillow she used and I closed my eyes, remembering the feel of her body next to mine.

"You are an absolute idiot," I said to myself.

It was true. She was fucking beautiful, amazing in bed, and came and saved my ass last night. I didn't know anyone who would do that for me. Certainly not my mother. No, she left me to fend for myself, so long as she could drink and fuck. The fact that I was out of her hair for hours on end was just what she wanted. Instead of helping me deal with my demons after that fucker, she left me to fend for myself. She was shocked when I bounced the moment I got the chance.

Now, though, I felt the need to connect. Never before had I needed anyone else. I prided myself on my self-sufficiency but having Fi in my bed when I woke up was something that felt right. Obviously, I felt comfortable with her, comfortable enough to call her when I was vulnerable, in need, and she came, which said a hell of a lot for her, too. I definitely needed to fix whatever it was between us, because I didn't want to try to do this without her.

Grabbing my phone, I pulled up my texts and shot one off to her. She said she was going to work, so calling was probably not a good idea.

I'm sorry. Can we talk?

I wasn't sure whether she would respond, but I hoped she would.

CHAPTER TWENTY-NINE

F i...

"You okay?" Jean asked when I sat down.

"Just really tired," I said. "It was a long night."

"Good long?" she asked. "Or bad long?"

"Bad," I said. "Lots of drama, but nothing I really want to talk about."

"Well," she said. "I have just the thing to take your mind off your worries."

"Oh yeah?"

"Definitely," she said. "There's this mead shop up by the mall in Tukwila and they have some of the best I've ever had."

"What's mead?"

"It's made from honey," she said. "Doesn't matter because it tastes amazing. Anyway, the guy that runs it is like this Viking or something and he makes all these crazy flavors and stuff. Things you wouldn't think would work, but they do. Well, he's got this new one coming out tonight and they have all these taco trucks there to help celebrate it."

"Like a Taco Tuesday kind of thing?"

"Exactly," she said. "His new mead is called Taco Meat."

"Should I be worried?"

"I wasn't sure about some of the ones I first tried until I tasted them," she explained. "It's like he's got some kind of magic wand or something that just makes everything taste perfect. We should go."

"Okay," I said. "I mean, sounds fun, and I love tacos."

"Oh yeah," she said. "And taco trucks make the best kind. Like, I gain weight just looking at them, but that's a whole other story."

"That's probably just what I need," I said. "Maybe it'll get me out of my funk."

The day drug on after that, just putting my numbers into my spreadsheets. I was heading to the break room when my phone buzzed.

I'm sorry. Can we talk?

What did I say? I mean, he kind of pissed me off last night, more so this morning. He looked off, though, so maybe it was just a bad night. Not that it excused what he did, but maybe giving him a chance would lead somewhere.

Meet me tonight.

I walked back to my desk, but Jean wasn't there.

Where?

I went back to the break room to grab the lunch I forgot and ran into Jean.

"Hey," I said. "What's the name of that place we're going to?"

"Let me look it up and show you," she said. "It's got a funky name."

She pulled her phone out and did a search, pulling the name up.

"How do you even say that?" I asked, looking at it.

"Not exactly sure," she replied.

"Okay," I said, looking at her phone again. "I'll just text him the name and he can do the search."

Oppegaard Meadery.

He'd be able to figure it out.

"What time do you want to meet there?" I asked Jean.

"We can go straight from here," she said.

"Sounds good," I replied, then sent another text.

Will probably get there about 6:30.

"You inviting someone?" she asked.

"You don't mind, do you?" I asked.

"Oh, no," she said. "My hubby has a work thing, so I'm going solo, but no need for you to if you don't have to."

"Great," I said, taking my lunch back to my desk.

When I sat down, I pulled up the baseball app and looked at the team's schedule. They were playing tonight, so how was he going to be able to meet me?

You sure you can come?

Better to ask than to expect and be stood up, but at this point, I wouldn't put it past him. When he didn't answer right away, I got a little pissed, but figured he was trying to find a way to explain whatever excuse he was gonna come up with.

Coach wants me to take some time.

That was not the response I expected, but whatever. If Coach told him to take time, I guess he could do whatever he wanted instead of going to work. Must be nice to be able to blow it off like that.

About half an hour before we were gonna leave, Jean popped over the wall.

"Bad news," she said.

"What's up?"

"Apparently I'm supposed to go with hubby to this thing tonight," she said. "That means no Taco Meat mead for me."

"Oh, man," I said. "I was looking forward to hanging out."

"You can still go," she said. "Maybe get a bottle and bring it in tomorrow. We'll have it in our coffee cups throughout the day."

I laughed. "Not a good idea," I said. "But I am still gonna go."

"Great," she said. "You'll have a good time. Maybe make up for your bad time last night."

"I hope so," I said, but wasn't feeling it.

"Here," she said, handing me some cash. "Get me a bottle of the Taco Meat mead. I gotta try it and don't want to miss the run. If you like it, you better get your own bottle. He sells out of his stuff pretty quick, so if you like it, get it."

"Sounds good," I said, putting her cash into my purse.

I finished up my spreadsheet, saving it and shutting down my computer. Our office dress code was business casual, so I was dressed nice enough to go out on the town, and not overly dressed to look it. I was actually wearing one of the sun dresses that I got while I was in Houston. The one Beckett ruined was still sitting in my suitcase. It was one of my favorite ones, so I wanted to see if I could fix it but hadn't had the time to try. Once everything was shut down, I hung my purse over my shoulder and headed to the elevators.

"You look like you're in a hurry," Carol said as she came up to wait with me.

"Just done with work and ready to change gears," I said.

I didn't want to alienate her, but she had no business in knowing what I was doing or where I was going. When I was off the clock, my time was not up for discussion.

"Probably gonna go work first avenue," she mumbled, but I just ignored her.

Nothing pissed her off more than people ignoring her. I didn't even look at her when we went to enter the elevator, her shoving in front of me to get in first. Whatever, it wasn't a race. We'd all get to the ground floor at the same time. I stepped in and went to the opposite side as her, waiting with the couple other people who had gotten in as well. The ride was quiet, stopping a couple of times to add more workers into the space, all on our way out of the salt mines and into the wild free world.

I snickered at my musings, wondering why that imagery came to me, but it was there. I just imagined us all covered in salt, wielding some sort of weapon to get the salt out of the mines, then escaping into some jungle or something. Ridiculous and silly, but actually helpful to lift my mood. The doors opened in the garage and we all shuffled our way out, Carol pushing to be the first to exit, as usual.

Walking to my car, I pulled up my GPS and put in the name of the meadery so I could get there without having to think about it. I plugged my phone into my car stereo system, then pulled up one of my favorite true crime podcasts and got things started. The drive was tough, slogging through the rush-hour mess with everyone else, but I did make it a little early, which was nice. Maybe I would get a chance to get my bearings before having to deal with Beckett.

Jean was right about the Taco Tuesday thing because there were four trucks parked strategically around the parking lot. I also noticed several motorcycles parked near the building. Who knows, maybe bikers really liked tacos. I was not one to judge, cause I freaking loved them. I found a spot a bit down the way from the shop itself, which was located in this industrial-type center, then got out with my purse slung across my chest and locked my car. I walked over to the place where there were several people milling around and looked at what kind of food was being offered.

Not all taco trucks were the same, and these four had such an amazing variety of options I didn't even know where to start.

I wish I could have come.

Jean's text startled me a bit when my phone went off, but I replied quickly.

This is madness. There are a ton of people here.

I followed the text up with a picture of the crowd that had gathered.

"Hey," some guy with a leather vest on said to me.

"Can I help you?" I asked.

"No photos of the club," he said.

"I was taking pictures of the trucks," I countered.

"Just make sure you don't take photos of the brothers," he said.

"Sure thing," I replied.

He didn't need to be so rude, though. I mean, you're in public, why can't I take a picture? Whatever, I did my best to make sure that I never had a picture of any of the guys who were wearing the vests. They all looked a bit mean, but there were a bunch of girls that seemed to be with them, so maybe they weren't. Whatever. My phone buzzed again.

Yeah. That's what it's like every time a new flavor comes out.

My phone buzzed again while I was reading her message, and it was Beckett.

You sure about this place?

I rolled my eyes. Was he really this much of a pussy?

I'm here and it's fine.

It didn't take long before I saw him walking between a couple of the trucks, glaring around at the crowd of people. The bikers were the most interesting group, but there were hipsters and yuppies and damn near every other kind of person in the crowd.

"You made it," I said.

"Yeah," he said, sounding angry. "I kind of wanted a little privacy to have this conversation."

"And I want tacos," I replied.

I walked up to one of the trucks, the one that looked like it had the biggest selection and ordered a set of six street tacos. I paid then took my little ticket so they could call me when it was ready. Beckett had wandered over to a different truck to make his order, then came back to me.

"Do we sit out here?" he asked.

"I think we wait until our food is ready, then head inside to get some mead," I said. "This is my first time."

"Then why here?"

"I was supposed to come with a work friend, but she had a last-minute change of plans," I replied. "It sounded good, so I wanted to come anyway."

"It just looks like a seedy place," he said. "I mean, who opens this kind of place in an industrial park?"

"Probably cheaper rent than the mall," I replied. "Besides, if the food is good and the mead is good, does it really matter?"

He didn't argue, but I could see he wasn't happy about it. Tonight might end up just as bad as last night, but only time would tell.

CHAPTER THIRTY

$\mathcal{B}$eckett...

     We got our food, and she headed into the building. I wondered whether she knew all these bikers were gonna be here. Maybe she felt threatened by me or something, but that didn't seem right. She was ballsy and had shown absolutely no fear during any of our interactions. Whatever her reasoning, I was just gonna go with it. Hopefully there was some quiet space inside so that we could actually talk.

The interior was dim compared to the bright summer sun outside, so it took a minute for my eyes to adjust. When they did, I looked around and was actually impressed. This dude had made what appeared to be a Viking man cave out of an industrial space. The walls were wood with pictures and axes and a bunch of shit I didn't even have a name for all over them. The little counter across from the main door had a kiosk type thing on top, which I assumed was where you paid for your booze.

I saw three biker guys inside talking to another guy who was tall and had this super long red beard. I assumed he was the owner, but could be totally wrong, too. He seemed just fine with the bikers, though, so maybe he was part of their gang or club or whatever.

"Welcome in," he said over their shoulders, and the others turned to look at us.

"Thanks," Fi said, smiling at all of it.

"You comfortable?" I whispered.

"Grow up," she said, then walked up to the counter.

"Hey," the girl behind the counter said. "Can I see some ID?"

"Sure," Fi said, setting her little takeout container on the counter and pulling her wallet out of her purse and showing the girl her license.

"You, too," the clerk said to me.

I shifted and pulled my wallet out, flipping it open to my ID.

"Great," she said. "What can I get you guys?"

"My friend said you were releasing a taco mead," Fi said. "I need to buy a bottle for her, but I'd like to try it, too."

"Taco?" I asked.

"Don't knock it till you try it," the bearded guy from the other side of the room said. "It's pretty good, even if I do say so myself."

"Did you want to pay for the bottle separate?" the girl behind the counter asked Fi.

"Yeah," she said. "I have cash for that. How much is the tasting of it?"

"Free," the man said as he went behind the counter and pulled a bottle out of the little fridge I hadn't seen was there.

He set up a couple of small glasses on the counter and poured a little bit of the wine into them, then gave a kind of head nod to us. Fi picked one up and took a little sip. I watched as her eyes went wide and she smiled.

"This is really good," she said.

"Really?" I asked.

"Try it," she said, using her cup to indicate the other small glass.

"When in Rome," I said and picked it up, taking a small sip.

It was sweet, but not overly so, and there were definitely some spices in it that I wasn't sure exactly what they were, but it all blended together pretty nice. I swallowed it and understood the taco reference. After a moment, though, it was as if I had already eaten my burrito, sour cream and all, and it was a little freaky.

"Well?" Fi asked.

"Not bad," I said.

"Told ya," the bearded guy said. "Do you want a full glass of this, or did you want to try something else?"

"I think I want a full glass," Fi said. "Can I buy a bottle and drink it here? Then take home what I don't drink?"

"We don't let you leave with a partial bottle," he said. "I can sell you the bottle and you drink it all, or I can sell you the bottle to take home, then sell you a glass to drink here."

"That works," Fi said.

"You want this, too?" the guy asked me.

"Sure," I said.

"I'd suggest you only have a glass or two," the guy said, pouring some out for me. "The thing about mead is it has a higher alcohol content, so it hits a bit harder. Add to that the sweetness, and you can end up done in before you know it."

"One glass it is," Fi said, taking hers.

"Same," I added. "I'm buying."

I pulled out my card, which I'd found sitting on the counter in my kitchen and waited for the girl to input everything into her kiosk. Fi took her glass and headed over to where there was a little alcove off to the left and back a bit. The girl gave me my total, and I stuck my card in their reader, then added a decent tip before signing for the purchase. I stuck the card back in my wallet and shoved it into my pocket, picking up the glass that was poured for me.

When I got to where she was sitting, I saw that there were small shelves around the alcove with all sorts of little things on them. Some books, some trinkets, and on the wall there were more axes and some swords hanging around, as well as more paintings that were clearly in the Viking theme that they had going on in here. The guy had set the two bags down next to Fi so she wouldn't forget them when we left.

"You must be hungry," I said, sitting down across the table from her.

"No reason to wait," she replied, taking another bite of her street taco.

I dug into my burrito, enjoying the flavors, washing it down with some of the mead in my glass. We ate in comfortable silence, well as silent as a place can be with a handful of people in the small space we occupied.

"So," she said after we'd eaten most of our food. "What was up last night?"

"Personal shit," I said.

She stared at me, like she was waiting for me to say more.

"Personal shit?" she asked after a while.

"Yeah," I replied. "Not something you need to worry your pretty little head about."

"Excuse me, what?"

"It doesn't matter," I said.

"Oh, I see," she said, setting what was left of her last taco down in her box. "You walk off the field, call me up and tell me to meet you, drink yourself into oblivion, expect me to pick you up and take care of you, then you try to fuck me, and it doesn't matter?"

"It really doesn't matter," I said, because it didn't.

"Yeah, no," she said. "What doesn't matter is the fact that you're an asshole and I should have just let you figure your own shit out last night. This is obviously not gonna work."

She stood up, picked up her two little bags and her box with the tacos in it and walked away. I sat there, kind of stunned, and waited. I figured she'd throw her food out and come back, but when she just walked out the door, I knew I fucked up. I got up and headed out the door shortly after her. She was already almost to her car, so I picked up my pace.

"Fi," I shouted, but she ignored me. "Ophelia," I tried again, but she just climbed into her car. "Wait," I called, but she started her car and pulled out, not even looking back at me.

This was not how this was supposed to go, and I had no idea what the fuck I was supposed to do about it. Why did I keep fucking things up? If I wanted to make things work, something had to change, but I wasn't exactly sure what that was supposed to be.

"Fuck me," I said, shaking my head.

CHAPTER THIRTY-ONE

F i...

He'd said it didn't matter, but that was the furthest thing from the truth. It all mattered because whatever it was that happened, personal or not, it affected everything else. I heard him calling my name, but I wasn't in the mood to deal with his shit anymore. Best to just cut it all off and walk away now before I got even more involved than I already was.

I drove away, trying to remember exactly how I'd gotten to the mead store, and finally found myself on a street I recognized. Hopping on I-5, I headed south, toward home. I didn't even turn on the radio or a podcast, just let the silence surround me. I probably needed to think about where everything fell apart, but that wasn't something I could control. No, he was the one who was fucking things up, and I was not about to baby him 'til he figured his shit out.

My autopilot skills were on fire because I didn't even realize I was almost home until I was pulling into my parking lot. Once my car was in its spot, I climbed out, taking both bottles of mead I'd picked up with me. I keyed into my apartment and set them on the kitchen counter, then headed to my room. It was late enough to be getting dark, but it was much earlier than I normally went to sleep.

Kicking my shoes off, I flopped on my bed, pulled my phone out, opened the texts and shot a message to McKenzie.

I need girl talk. Can you call me?

It was sort of late there, but not overly so. I got up and changed into some comfy pajamas and went to the kitchen to get some water and chocolate. When I opened the freezer, I saw a small tub of salted caramel toffee ice cream and decided that was what I actually needed, so pulled it out and grabbed a spoon, along with a wash rag to hold the cold container in. Dropping onto the couch, I turned the television on and waited for the image to come into view. My phone buzzed and I looked at it.

I'm sorry. I fucked up. Let me make it up to you.

This guy didn't know how to take a hint. I wondered if I should block him, or just ignore his texts. My phone began to play its ring tone, and I saw it was McKenzie.

"Hey," I said when I answered.

"You okay?" she asked.

"I don't know," I replied.

"Talk it out," she said. "That's the best way to start."

I sighed, then looked at the television. It was on the local sports station that played the games, and the Cascades were on and up in the second inning.

"Beckett called me," I said. "He wanted to meet, but he was kind of bossy about it. He basically said to meet him at this bar in Seattle, then hung up like he expected me to go."

"Did you?"

"Yeah," I said. "Maybe I shouldn't have, but he sounded like something was wrong. Besides that, he had just walked off the field."

"In the middle of a game?"

"Yup," I said. "He tried to tag a player who was stealing second and got upended and missed the tag. When he got up, he just walked off."

"Was he hurt?" she asked. "Did he need to be seen?"

"I don't think so," I said. "He just seemed... off, I guess."

"How so?"

"Well," I said, then paused.

"Never mind," she said after I'd been quiet for a while. "What happened next?"

"That's when he called me," I said. "He told me to meet him at some bar, then hung up. I sat there for a minute, trying to figure out exactly what was going on, but then I just got dressed and headed to Seattle."

"From your place?"

"Yeah," I said. "It took almost an hour to get there, too. By the time I did, he was drunk off his ass. Got his check and used his card to pay it, then took him to his apartment."

"Tell me it was trashed," she said.

"Actually, it was really neat," I replied. "I mean, I didn't trip over anything walking him to his bed. I got him out of his clothes and he hurled into a trash can next to his bed, so I cleaned that up, too. He passed out, but I was worried he'd choke if I didn't at least stay near to make sure he lived through the night. I wouldn't have been able to live with myself if that had happened."

"I get it," she said.

"Of course, he wakes up in the middle of the night and gets handsy," I added. "Not that I would expect anything less from him, though. When I asked him what happened, he just blew me off, so I got up and left."

"Good for you," she said. "He sounds like he's more drama than he's worth."

"Except I feel bad," I said.

"Why?"

"I don't know," I said. "He texted me today and said he was sorry and asked if he could talk to me."

"He does know you have a job, right?"

"That was what was weird," I said. "We met tonight, even though the team has a game. He said he was taking time off or something."

"Did he explain what happened?"

"He said it was personal shit," I replied. "Like, literally, word for word, personal shit."

"And…"

"That's it," I said. "I waited, asked what he meant, and he said it was nothing for me to worry about."

"Please tell me you ripped him for that," she said.

"Oh, yeah," I replied. "Then I got up and left."

"What do you want me to do?"

"Nothing," I said. "I mean, there really isn't anything you can do. I guess I just need to learn to say no to him, or ignore him—"

"Or block him," she suggested.

"I could," I replied.

"But you won't," she said. "You're too nice sometimes."

"I guess," I said. "What do you think I should do?"

"What I think doesn't matter," she said. "And that's completely different from his it doesn't matter shit. My opinion is to drop him like he's not hot, let him go and figure his shit out. Once he does that, if he can, then maybe he'll be able to have an actual relationship."

"I just don't know if I want that," I said. "Like, I have a job right now, and I kind of need to concentrate on it. If he decides to go off the deep end like this again, I can't go bail him out. It was too hard to work today while thinking about him and wondering what was going on and shit. I can't do that. I can't be his mom and rescue him every time he goes off the deep end."

"You shouldn't have to," she said.

I sat there, letting my thoughts run, trying to understand why I felt the need to pick up his pieces when all he did was screw me over. I mean, sex could only get you so far in a relationship. What mattered more were the little things, like taking care of each other, but not using the other person in any way.

"You decided something," she said.

"I think I'm just gonna ignore him," I replied. "It isn't exactly a decision, but a way to keep myself sane. At least until he's ready to own up to whatever the fuck is going on with him and decides to deal with it. Obviously, he has demons, but I can't be the one to deal with them. That's on him."

"Anything I can do to help?" she asked.

"I think you just did," I said. "Maybe I'll need to call again, but hopefully it won't be for a while."

"Good," she said.

"I should probably let you go," I said.

"Yeah," she said. "I've got work tomorrow, so need to crash. I'm glad I was here for you."

"You're the best," I said. "Love you."

"Love you, too," she said. "Goodnight."

"Night," I replied, then disconnected the call.

I turned off the television, picked up the ice cream I'd forgotten, and stuck it back in the freezer, then headed to bed. Maybe sleep would help me figure things out.

CHAPTER THIRTY-TWO

*B*eckett...

   I'd texted her and waited for a response. She read it, I could tell, but she didn't respond. Now, it was close to midnight, and she was probably asleep. That meant no answer tonight. I didn't want to wake her up, so didn't try to call, but I needed to do something.

   Lying in my bed, I stared at the ceiling, wondering how badly I fucked it up. I fucked almost everything in my life up at some point or another, so it shouldn't have been a surprise that I fucked this up as well. But this felt different somehow. This felt like I had really screwed my entire future up, like she was the one that was supposed to get me, to understand my crazy, and to keep me safe from the demons that ran through my head on the regular.

   There was no reason why I should think this, though. Usually, I just shoved the demons further back into the recesses of my brain, back in the dark where they belonged. But they'd been coming to the forefront much more frequently, and I didn't like that one bit. No, I needed them to stay away, stay buried, live in the darkness where no one looked. That's where they absolutely had to remain in order for me to function.

   Except, I wasn't functioning. I was screwing up and doing things that I hadn't done in years. The letter at the beginning of the season was bad enough, but Mom sending her ashes to me? No, that was not okay at all. Somehow, in the midst of my thoughts, I went to sleep, still battling my demons.

When I woke up, the demons were still there, and if possible, even larger than before. She hadn't texted me back, so I sent another one, just letting her know that I knew everything was my fault, and that if she didn't want to have anything to do with me, to just let me know. I just hoped she didn't take me up on that, because I didn't know what I'd do if she wasn't around any longer.

Instead of just wallowing in my own pity party, I decided that I had to figure something out. My plan was to contact her brother and ask for his help. Whether he would do that was another question, but I needed to try. Maybe I could get her friend to help me out, too. I looked up the Dragons' schedule, and they were in Houston through the weekend, once they got home from Florida. I had enough time to get down there and have a sit-down with them. I just had to convince him to meet me.

I booked a flight and a hotel, then packed a bag, hoping I could meet him the next day. I knew he'd be back that same night but wanted to ensure I had plenty of time to meet with him. Now, I needed to find a way to get in touch with him. I did a search through social media, then it dawned on me to just email the team from my own team email address. I shot off an email, telling them I needed to meet with Quentin and left it at that. Hopefully it would be enough, but we'd find out by the time I got down there.

I FUCKING HATED TEXAS. IT WAS TOO HOT, TOO HUMID, AND THERE were entirely too many cowboy hats and boots for my liking. When I turned my phone back on after landing, I saw there was an email from the Dragons. I waited until I was off the plane with my bag in hand and headed to the ground transportation section of the airport before opening it up.

Mr. Hennings,

Mr. Belinsky is amiable to meeting with you in a public location.

Please contact the clubhouse when you have landed and we will arrange a time and place for the meeting to happen. We are hopeful that this will ease the conflict that has arisen between the two of you over the last couple of weeks.

Sincerely yours,

Helen Waverly

Team Communications Coordinator

I hoped it would lead to more than just easing the conflict between us, but that wasn't something I needed to tell this woman. I dialed the number in the email and it rang once before being answered.

"Houston Dragons," the woman said. "How can I direct your call?"

"My name is Beckett Hennings," I said. "I have been emailing with Ms. Waverly to set up a meeting between myself and Quentin Belinsky."

"Yes, Mr. Hennings," the woman said. "Please hold."

I heard some play-by-play of an old game through the receiver as I sat on one of the chairs set up in the luggage claim area, waiting for someone to answer.

"Mr. Hennings," another woman said.

"That's me," I replied.

"Thank you for reaching out," she said. "Mr. Belinsky is eager to bury the hatchet, so to speak, with you and was pleased that you reached out."

"I am as well," I replied.

"Are you in Houston?"

"I just landed," I said. "I am on the IL for a few days, so had time to make this trip happen."

"Perfect," she replied. "Do you need a car service or have you arranged something?"

"I was just going to use the shuttle service to my hotel," I said. "Is the location where we will meet close?"

"I haven't arranged it, yet," she said. "I wanted to see when you would be in town, and where you would be staying before I got anything set up. If you are comfortable with it," she continued, "we can set it up in the restaurant in your hotel for convenience."

"That would work," I replied, then gave her the name of my hotel.

"I'll get something set up," she said. "I'll ask the hotel if they have a small conference room where you can meet with him."

"There's no need for that," I replied. "I kind of want to keep this out of the press if possible. There are some personal matters that I need to discuss with him, so would…"

I stopped. If they were willing to set up a room, we could actually talk about everything and not have to worry about someone over-hearing us. That might actually be better.

"Are you there?" she asked.

"Yeah, sorry," I said. "If you want to set up a small room, that's fine. Do you have my number?"

"I don't," she said. "Is it in your email?"

"No," I replied, then rattled off the number for her, repeating it a couple more times.

"Thank you," she said. "Why don't you go get settled in at your hotel and I'll call once I have something set up."

"Would you mind giving me Quentin's phone number?" I asked.

"I'll have to ask him if he's comfortable with that," she said.

"Thanks," I replied.

"I will call when I get it set up," she added. "Until then, have an enjoyable stay in Houston."

"Thanks," I said, then disconnected the call.

I looked up the hotel's shuttle information on the reader board they had, then headed out into the unbearable heat to catch it. Hopefully this would be a good visit, and I'd be able to actually make some headway. Maybe, just maybe, I could salvage what I had with Ophelia. I certainly hoped so.

CHAPTER THIRTY-THREE

*F*i...
He'd texted me Tuesday night saying he fucked up and wanted to make it up to me. Well, he fucked up for sure, but I wasn't sure whether I wanted him to make it up to me. I had chosen the ignore method for dealing with it, and had tried desperately to put it behind me, or in the corner, or something, but it was a struggle to say the least.

"How was it?" Jean asked when I handed her the Taco Meat mead.

"It was okay," I said.

"What happened?"

"Remember that guy?" I asked. She nodded, so I continued, "He came to meet me. I tried to figure out what was going on with him, but he kind of just blew me off, so I left."

"Wow," she said.

"There's more," I said, nodding my head behind her. "But not the time or place for that conversation."

Jean turned to see that Carol was standing behind her. When she saw Jean look, she turned and walked away.

"Yeah," she said, then sat down at her desk.

I had already turned my computer on, so I sat and began on the project of the day. With it coming up on month end, I knew that my duties were going to ramp up for closing. I wanted to be ahead of the game as much as possible. Sure, I was only a week and change into this, but I had studied economics and accounting and knew that many things happened in rapid succession at month end. Besides that, I had a calendar full of all the tasks that would need to be done, and what days they were required to be finished. I was in the work zone, so jumped when Jean tapped my shoulder.

"Hey," she said. "It's noon. Wanna grab some lunch?"

"Already?" I asked, then looked at my computer. "Wow, yeah, let me save this last thing here and I'll be ready to go."

"Great," she replied, then waited.

We walked to the elevator after I grabbed my purse and phone and headed out to pick something up for lunch. Once we had something to eat, we sat at the outside tables to enjoy the sun and catch up.

"How was your thing last night?" I asked.

"Boring," she said. "Honestly, I wish I'd have been able to skip it. Some big wig is retiring, and they had to have everyone get together to send him off. Of course, can't just do a lunch in the office. Oh, no, they have to go big and rent out a hotel ballroom for it. Dinner, drinks, cake, speeches, the whole nine yards. And the booze wasn't even free. We had to pay for it."

"Sounds like a nightmare," I said, taking a bite of my salad.

"For sure," she replied. "The worst part is, Paul didn't even know the guy. I mean, he's been there a while, sure, and he probably saw him in passing at least a couple of times, but he didn't work directly with him. Not even in the same department. But it was a mandatory party, spouses required, and don't you dare try to leave early. Ugh, that's four hours I'll never get back."

"That's nuts," I said. "Did they pay anything for it?"

"They paid for dinner," she said. "If you can call dry chicken in a paste that's supposed to be a sauce of some sort, wilted veggies, and potatoes that looked like they'd been sitting under one of those warming lamps for entirely too long a dinner."

"Eww," I said.

"Exactly," she replied.

"Please tell me your husband let you drink," I said.

"Only one drink," she replied. "And that was ten bucks."

"Glad I brought you mead, then," I said. "At least you'll have something tonight."

"You better believe he's gonna make it up to me tonight," she said, then winked at me.

"Oh," I said. "That's how it is. Nice."

"For sure," she replied. "He knows he's in the doghouse, so is going to give me lots of attention tonight, then has said I can do whatever I want this weekend, no strings."

"You should definitely take advantage of that," I replied.

"Speaking of the weekend," she said. "What are you doing?"

"Not really sure," I said. "I'll probably just spend it cleaning my apartment and getting caught up on the regular adult-type things like laundry and such."

"You should come to the spa with me," she said. "I can convince Paul to pay for both of us, 'cause I need moral support. It'll be great."

"I mean…" I paused, unsure whether I really wanted to do this or not.

"Invitation is open," she said, clearly sensing my hesitancy. "Just let me know."

"Okay," I replied.

We finished our lunch and headed back to the office and the grind of working. I checked my phone about a dozen times in the afternoon, and nothing came in from Beckett. Maybe he took my silence to mean that I was completely done with him. More likely, though, he was just mad and didn't want to give in. As I was leaving, though, I sent a text to McKenzie.

Hey, can I call you? I need more girl time.

The elevator wouldn't let me receive anything, so once I got to the ground floor and stepped out, I looked to see if there was a message, but nothing. That was odd. She was usually pretty good about replying right away. Maybe she was busy or something. I headed home, figuring

I'd have to get to bed early. The last few nights were unbearable, and I hadn't slept well at all. In fact, I would probably pass out as soon as my head hit the pillow.

CHAPTER THIRTY-FOUR

*B*eckett...
    Considering it was already early afternoon, I knew the meeting with Quentin wouldn't happen today. So, I just hung out at the hotel, ordered room service, and tried to be patient in waiting for things to move in my direction. Patience was never something I was good at. I also tried to wrap my head around what had happened between Ophelia and me. I mean, we were fucking amazing in bed, but the other shit just seemed to not want to work, and I wasn't sure why.

Maybe I wasn't cut out to have that one person. My life was shit to begin with, so it made sense that I was just dealt a crap hand that I had to live with. Add in all the other shit I had dumped on me and done to me and it just fucked everything up. By the time I got to a point where I could determine my own life, I had to figure everything out on my own, and I had never been taught. I guess that's why I was the way I was, fucking whoever I wanted without thinking of the future.

Except, Ophelia made me want to look beyond just the hookup. Oh, don't get me wrong, that first one was all about the sex, and sticking it to her brother. But there was something more that I wanted from her. Something I couldn't put my finger on. My phone dinged indicating a notification, so I picked it up and checked. It was an email, but instead of opening it on my phone, I pulled out my laptop and got it booted up. It would give me something to do.

After what seemed like forever, the laptop had the lock screen, asking me to enter my password. Once that was done, I hooked it up to the hotel Wi-Fi and pulled up my email.

Mr. Hennings,

We have scheduled a meeting for noon Friday in the Galveston Room. Lunch will be catered, but they would like to have your request tonight. Please respond to this email with your choice from the list below with your selection. Additionally, Mr. Belinsky has requested that his partner, Ms. Foster, be in attendance at this meeting as well. If you are not comfortable with that, please let me know as soon as possible. I look forward to hearing from you soon.

Sincerely yours,

Helen Waverly

Team Communications Coordinator

Well, I'll be damned. Looked like I didn't have to try to figure out a way to get her friend to the meeting, which was extremely helpful. I responded, selecting my food from their list, and let them know that the girl could come with, and that I was pleased she would be there. They didn't need to know that I had questions for her as well. That would happen after the burying of the hatchet, which hopefully didn't end up with it being in my back.

What I wasn't sure of was whether there would be a mediator of some sort at the meeting as well. That wouldn't do for what I really wanted to talk to him about. I guess I would just have to wait and see what happened in a couple of days. Until then, though, I thought I'd do a little snooping and see if I could find my own little Miss Belinsky on social media.

It took me forever, but I finally found her on Instagram, and she was not at all shy about showing her body. I was also surprised to see the number of followers she had. There were a ton of pictures from her college days on the softball field, which was pretty awesome. She played short stop as well as second base, and from the looks of it, she was damn good. Instead of continuing to scope around on her social media, I figured I'd look her up on her school's website to see her stats and such. I wanted to know as much about her as I could, and this was the best time to do that.

CHAPTER THIRTY-FIVE

$\mathcal{F}$i...

McKenzie hadn't texted me at all on Wednesday evening, and I didn't hear from her on Thursday, either. If I didn't know better, I'd think she was ignoring me, but she had a habit of reading a message, thinking of a response, then completely forgetting that she hadn't actually sent it. She'd been that way all through high school and even into college, so I didn't worry. When Friday rolled around, though, I thought I'd send a text to my brother and see what he was doing. I'd seriously considered taking Jean up on the weekend spa thing but didn't want to be neck deep in a mud bath and have her call me.

I texted McKenzie on Wednesday. You guys busy?

It was still early in the day, but he was a couple hours ahead of me, so it was late morning for him. Honestly, though, he was probably still asleep. He'd never really been a morning person, even when we were little. Now, though, it was even worse with his work schedule.

"You think about this weekend?" Jean asked at lunch.

"I think I should go," I said. "Not like the laundry will do itself, but I could use a little bit of pampering after the last week or so."

"Everyone could use some pampering," she said, then kind of wiggled her eyebrows in the general direction of Carol's desk.

"Some people need it more than others," I agreed.

She pulled up the spa's website, and we looked at all the amenities they had available, planning our Saturday. I asked several times whether she was sure she didn't want me to pay for my own stuff, but she insisted her husband owed her. Apparently, he'd paid some of the debt off the last couple of nights, which she thankfully didn't give too many details about, but was sure to tell me he had been *very* accommodating to her desires.

By the time our lunch break was over, we had planned for manicures, pedicures, and facials, along with a hot stone massage, something I'd never experienced before. I was actually looking forward to the day, so when Carol came over to tell us that we may need to work on Saturday, we were both annoyed and said we had plans that couldn't be changed.

"Sorry," she said. "The boss said it's all-hands-on-deck, so all weekend plans will need to be canceled."

"When we receive the notice from our supervisor, we'll be sure to ask about our previously planned events," Jean replied.

"Don't plan on making them," Carol said. "We're a team, and everyone needs to pull their own weight."

"Well, we're also humans who have lives outside the office," Jean said. "Sometimes we aren't available, and if we had known there was a possibility of working this weekend, we likely would have altered our plans. I'll ask Greg about it and let him know we have plans already and see what he says. Thanks for the heads-up."

Jean had the best way of saying "go fuck yourself" without actually using those words. It was like that southern saying of "bless your heart" when that's actually not at all what you meant. I just put my head down and continued to work, knowing that if I could get the tasks that were due done, I'd be less likely to be asked to work on Saturday. I didn't want there to be any reason why it would be mandatory for me.

When quitting time was rolling around, Jean was peeking her head over the cubical wall and giving me that *pst pst pst* noise.

"What's up?" I asked.

"I talked to Greg," she said. "We're good to be off all weekend."

"I thought…"

"We don't have anything that is pressing that won't wait," she said. "The accountants have stuff, but we don't. We're actually well ahead of where we need to be for month end."

"So, what you're saying is Carol has to work this weekend and we don't," I said.

"Exactly," she replied.

"Karma can be fun," I said, laughing.

CHAPTER THIRTY-SIX

*B*eckett...

By the time Friday morning rolled around, I had done as much searching as I could on my little Miss Ophelia Belinsky. I wasn't going to use all of it, but I did want to go into this meeting with her brother and best friend with the hopes of figuring out a way to fix the damage I'd caused. I knew I was the one to break it, and I knew I was also the one who had to fix it, but I didn't know how.

I arrived at the room just before noon, and there was a table set for the meal. There were only three spots at the table, which meant that we were not going to have a mediator, or at least not one who would be eating with us. The room was pretty small, not actually a conference room like I had imagined, but more like an oversized office space, just long and narrow.

"This is for a private meeting," the man who was setting up said.

"I'm one of the ones in the meeting," I replied.

"Oh," he replied. "They said the people were arriving at noon."

"I'm just early," I said. "Do you want me to wait outside?"

Just then, Quentin and his girl showed up.

"This is a private meeting," the man said to them.

"They're the rest of the party," I said.

"I guess we'll get things going," he replied. "Please take a seat. I'll be in shortly with your food."

"Thanks," I said, taking one of the seats at the table.

Quentin and the girl sat as well, but neither of them said anything. He looked mad, but not as mad as he had before, so I would take that as a good sign.

"I'm McKenzie," the girl said, sticking her hand out to me.

"I'm Beckett," I replied. "Beckett Hennings."

"Glad to officially meet you," she replied.

Just then the guy who had been in there earlier walked back in with a cart. He had plates covered with those metal lids like they use for room service, as well as a carafe of water.

"I'm not sure who ordered what," he said after putting the water on the table.

We each told him what we ordered, which was interesting in that both Quentin and I had ordered almost identical meals. Once he'd placed them in front of us, he asked if there was anything else we needed. When we said we were good, he took his cart and walked back out. I looked at Quentin and he looked back at me. I decided that since I was the one to call the meeting, I should be the one to start it off.

"I'm sorry," I said, and it took everything I had not to add something about his feelings being hurt. "I was rude to you. I caused you issues with your club, and it was completely unprofessional."

"Damn right it was," he said, and I could hear the anger in his voice. "That's my baby sister you're fucking around with."

"Who's an adult," McKenzie interjected.

Quentin looked at her and it was one of those "if looks could kill" kind of stares.

"What?" she asked. "She's an adult, just like me. She didn't get all bent out of shape at the fact that we're together. Well, actually she did, but only because you demanded that I keep it a secret from her. Otherwise, she was totally fine with us being together. In fact, she said she was surprised it took so long."

"She did?" he asked.

"Yeah," she confirmed. "So, you kind of don't have a leg to stand on when it comes to who she dates or what she does. You probably didn't realize that I knew all about all her hookups in high school and college. Sorry," she said, looking at me.

"No problem," I replied, enjoying seeing Quentin handed his ass by a chick. Besides, I knew she wasn't a virgin, and assumed she had plenty of experience with the way she handled our sexual interactions.

Quentin sighed, rubbing his head with the palm of his hand.

"I guess you're right," he said, then looked at me. "I should have trusted my sister. I just don't want her to get hurt."

"That's why I'm here," I said. "I fucked up, bad, and I need your help to fix this."

"Why would I help you?" he asked.

"You just said you don't want to see her hurt," I explained. "Well, I don't either, but I did hurt her, and I'm trying to figure out a way to make it up to her."

He stared at me and I couldn't tell if he was confused at what I was saying, unsure of my actual needs, or just trying to not come across the table and punch me.

"What did you do?" McKenzie asked.

I took a deep breath, then said, "I got bad news Monday morning. At the game, I kind of just lost it and walked off the field. I called her and asked her to meet me somewhere, and by the time she got there, I was already three sheets to the wind. She took me home, to my place, and cleaned me up after I got sick, then stayed with me to make sure I didn't die. I didn't want to talk about what happened to cause me to go off the rails, so I just kind of brushed her off, and she left without a backward glance.

"I met up with her Tuesday night to try to talk it out," I continued. "But she wanted answers I wasn't ready to share. I told her it wasn't something she needed to worry about, but she didn't want a brush off, she wanted a conversation. I wasn't in a position to do that then, but I think I am now."

"What was the news?" McKenzie asked.

I swallowed hard and said, "My mom died."

"I'm so sorry," she said, but I replied, "Don't be. She wasn't worth it."

Quentin blinked, like something just occurred to him. Some little thing I'd said made things make sense to him or something, which was odd because nothing made sense to me.

"She likes to take care of people," he said.

I waited, but he didn't elaborate.

"She's good at it," I finally said after a long pause.

I couldn't tell if he was still trying to figure out what to say, or if he was trying to not say something that would help me. Honestly, I get him not being happy about me banging his sister. But if I was going to make this work with her, and I really wanted it to, I kind of needed his blessing, or at least not have him fighting against me.

"Can I ask you some questions?" McKenzie asked.

"Shoot," I replied, finally taking a bite of my meal.

Quentin followed suit, picking up his fork and taking in a bite of the veggies.

"Was the bad news that your mom died?" she asked. "Or was it that you found out in a way that was hard to deal with?"

"My mom has kind of been dead to me for a while," I said. "She wasn't exactly mom of the year, or even mom of the day, to be honest. She made sure I had a roof over my head, and that I had food, but the emotional support was beyond lacking. I had some shit go down, and she was madder with me for making it stop than she was about what happened. And no," I continued, seeing the question she wanted to ask. "I am not going to tell you what happened."

"Fair enough," she said. "So, your mom died. How did you find out?"

"The team got a letter right at the beginning of the year," I said. "It said she had cancer, and that it wasn't looking good. I didn't do anything with the letter, or even let her know I got it. When I came home from Indigo City Sunday night, there was a note on my door that said I had a package to pick up at the Post Office. I went on Monday morning and the package was the remains of my mother. She had it set up with the funeral home to have herself cremated and the remains sent to me."

"That's fucked up," Quentin said, and I was a little surprised by the anger I heard in that small statement.

"Definitely," I agreed.

"What about your dad?" McKenzie asked.

"Never had one," I replied. "The moment my mom told him she was pregnant, he bounced. I honestly don't even know who he is."

"Wow," McKenzie said. "I feel like I've lived a privileged life now."

"It's all worked out," I said.

"Except it hasn't," Quentin said.

"How do you mean?" I asked.

"Look," he said, setting his fork down. "My sister obviously means something to you. I don't get it, but whatever. I guess I can't run her life. But, if you're gonna be with her, you need to figure your shit out. She can't become your emotional support human. She deserves more than that. If all you want is someone to cry on, then go to a therapist. But, if you want a relationship, like a real honest-to-goodness partnership, then you have to put in the work. You have to tell her when you're having a shit day, when things aren't going well, when you need her. You also have to be willing to be there for her when she needs it, too. First step is to figure your own shit out. Once you've done that, then you can look for the relationship you want."

I blinked at him in surprise. What he said made a lot of sense, and I hadn't seen it from that perspective before. I really was using her, and not in the best of ways, either. When I looked at McKenzie, she was looking at him with an absolutely confused look as well.

"What can I do?" I asked.

"Therapy," he said.

"I meant with her," I said.

"Show her that you aren't the guy you first portrayed," he said. "If you can be a stand-up dude, give her what she needs, and be honest with her, you may get somewhere."

"You should also apologize," McKenzie added. "Her favorite flowers are daffodils."

"But don't just send them to her with a note," he said.

"Give them to her in person," McKenzie said. "I can give you her address and her work address if you want."

"Umm," Quentin hedged.

"It'll be fine," McKenzie said, obviously knowing her friend better than he knew his sister. Honestly, I was really glad she was there because I trusted her judgment.

"But first," Quentin said. "You need to get right with the team, with yourself and your own demons. You can't expect her to fight them with you if you haven't started the work already."

"You're right," I said.

"Team should have someone they can recommend you to," he said. "Find someone who works for you, so ask for a couple of names to try out. Meet with them, ask them questions, see who you're comfortable with. Once you know that, you can actually get the work done."

"Sounds like you know a thing or two about this," I said.

"Let's just say, I've been around the block a time or two," he said.

"Okay," I said, looking down at my plate.

"Hey," McKenzie said. "It'll all work out. You just have to do the work. If you're anything like Quentin, you can get it done."

"Please don't compare me to him," Quentin said.

"Only because you pale in comparison," I said, ensuring there was laughter in my voice.

"You're both hard workers," she said. "You both want what's best for Fi, and for that, you might as well be the same. I mean, you're on the same team on this, right? You want what's best for Fi, right?"

"I know I do," I said.

"So do I," Quentin agreed.

"Good," McKenzie said. "It's settled."

The conversation lagged, then, but it was comfortable in the silence.

"So," McKenzie said after a time. "Which one of you is the better short stop?"

Both Quentin and I said, "Me," then laughed, and the mood was lightened. I guess we could report to our teams that our hatchet had officially been buried when it came to the beef between us. I'm sure both the Dragons and the Cascades would be happy about that.

CHAPTER THIRTY-SEVEN

$\mathcal{F}$i...
Saturday morning, I threw on some leggings and an oversized shirt with a bag that had my flip-flops in it, as well as a change of clothes, then headed out to meet Jean at the spa. She'd texted me the address and the time of our first appointments. When I pulled up, I was a bit nervous as to how much money her husband was spending on this little day of pampering.

"Hey," she said when I stepped in the door.

"Hey, yourself," I replied.

The place smelled amazing, with floral and earthy tones running through the air. I looked at the chairs that were in the lobby and thought about how much they must have cost with their plush cushions and leather covering.

"First stop is the massage," Jean said, drawing my attention to her from the surroundings. "Then we'll do the facials, followed by manicures and pedicures at the same time."

"Nice," I said, taking the seat next to her.

"You ready?" a woman asked as she came out from a curtained back area.

"Yep," Jean said. "We're both here and ready for our pampering."

"If you'll follow me," she said, holding the curtain back so we could step to the back area.

I saw several doors along one side of the hallway, and the other was open with those chairs with the foot bath things in them. A couple of women sat in them, but the space was otherwise unoccupied. We followed our guide down the hallway to a door near the end.

"One in here," she said, opening the door. "The other can go in here," she said, indicating the next door down the way.

"Are they both hot stone?" Jean asked.

"Yes," the woman said.

"Well?" Jean asked, looking at me, but I just shrugged. "You go in there," she said, pointing to the doorway further down. "See you soon."

"See you soon," I said, stepping past her door to the next one.

The room was dim with the massage table in the center, its hole at the head where your face went through. There was a waterfall machine of some sort that gave off that bubbling water sound which was almost always relaxing. I could also hear soft music playing, just instruments and no voices. Almost immediately, I felt relaxed. There was a standing divider in the corner with a chair behind it, that I assumed was where I could leave my clothes for the massage. Before I made it over there, though, there was a knock, the door opened, and a young man stepped in.

"Hello," he said, sticking his hand out. "My name is Lee and I will be doing your massage today."

"Good to meet you," I said.

"You can undress as much as you're comfortable with," he said. "Your clothes can go there," he continued, indicting where I had thought they would go. "We do like to have the whole top off, though. It gives us plenty of room to work the stones without being hindered by the clothing. I'll leave you to get changed and be back in about five minutes unless you need more time."

"That should work," I said.

"Perfect," he replied, then stepped out of the room, closing the door behind him.

I'd had a handful of massages before, but every single time, it was with a woman. I wasn't sure what to think about a man rubbing all over me, but I decided to just go with the flow. He was a professional, and I was a customer, so this would all work out just fine. Getting undressed, I put my clothes into my bag, only leaving my panties on. I just wasn't quite comfortable with taking those off. I climbed up on the table, which was warm, and settled myself under the sheet and blanket that were on top, pulling them around my body to cover me, dropping my head into the open space in the head rest.

I heard a knock on the door, and it cracked open a bit.

"All ready?" Lee asked.

"Yes," I said, and he stepped in, barely opening the door enough to slide through.

Closing my eyes, I vowed to just enjoy the sensation, hoping it wouldn't get awkward. Of course, usually, you heard about those "happy endings" in massages that catered to men. I didn't think anything like that would happen here, but you never knew.

"I'm going to place the first stone on your upper back, near your left shoulder," Lee said. "Let me know if it's too warm."

I felt his hand, then the weight of the stone, and it was warm, but not overly so.

"Doing all right?"

"Yeah," I said.

"Good," he replied. "Do you want me to tell you with each stone I place?"

"If it isn't too much trouble," I replied.

"No trouble at all," he said. "I want you to be comfortable and use this time to relax. Placing another stone on your right shoulder."

He continued telling me the placement of each stone, also adding in some information about how the stones worked, how they helped to heal the body, and why the stones were warm. It was an interesting procedure, something I hadn't ever experienced before, so it was also a learning moment for me. Once he'd placed all the stones, he let them sit for a bit, then began moving them around. Between the warmth of the stones, and the pressure he was putting on my body, it was more relaxing than I thought it would be.

By the time the massage was done, I was so relaxed I could have probably gone to sleep right there. He left the room to allow me to get dressed, which I did as quickly as my mellow body would allow. I stepped out of the room just as Jean stepped out of hers.

"Ready for the next thing?" she asked.

"Sure," I replied.

We walked down the hall back toward the front, but the gal who brought us back caught us before we made it all the way out.

"Let's get you into the facial room," she said, turning us back the way we had just come from.

A little further down the hallway, the space opened up some and there were a handful of chairs placed around. They looked like dentist chairs, but without the little tray and implements for working on teeth. We each took one, setting our things on our laps. When the two young women came in, they introduced themselves and gave us a rundown on what options were available for facials. Once we'd made our choices, they got to work rubbing, exfoliating, adding masks, and all other manner of pampering. It felt like they scrubbed off several layers of dirt and grime, and I was sure my face was going to be glowing with how fresh it felt.

We were then sent to the manicure and pedicure stations, where we picked out colors and were again treated to a massage on our lower legs and arms, as well as our feet and hands, after which we were painted and polished and shined up. When we walked out the door, I felt as if I were a whole new person, the old having been removed with every bit of the day's treatments.

"This was amazing," I said. "Thank you so much for allowing me to come with you."

"Are you kidding?" she asked. "I wanted you here. You looked like you had been having a hard time the last few days, so I was sure this was just what the doctor ordered. A day of pampering where you don't have to make any decisions other than what color of polish goes on your nails."

"Well, it was truly wonderful," I said.

"Now, go find your happy," she said, giving me a hug. "I know you're dealing with some crappy things with that guy, but if he's gonna cause you heartache, then maybe you should cut him out of your life."

"Yeah, I know," I replied. "I just have to figure out if he's gonna get his act together or if I'm always going to be running to his rescue."

"Girl, that's no way to have a relationship," she said.

"Don't I know it," I agreed.

"See you Monday," she said with a wave, then headed to her car.

I walked to mine as well, climbing in and plugging my phone into the charger, hoping to listen to my podcast on the way home. Before I even got the car started, it began to ring, and my best friend's face showed up on the screen.

"Hey," I said when I answered it.

"Hey yourself," she replied. "Got a minute?"

"Sort of," I said. "I'm just heading home from the spa."

"I love a good spa day," she said. "Do you think you can drive and hear big things? Or do you wanna call me back when you get home?"

"You getting married?" I asked.

"What? No," she said.

"Kicking Quentin to the curb?"

"No," she said, laughing.

"Sounds like it's probably too big for a quick conversation, then," I said.

"Oh yeah, it's not gonna be quick," she confirmed.

"While my curiosity is piqued, I think I'll call you back when I get home," I said.

"Okay," she said. "About how long?"

"Maybe half an hour," I said. "I'm in Tacoma."

"Great," she said. "Talk to you soon."

"Talk soon," I agreed, then ended the call.

The drive home would probably be much longer than normal, but just because I knew there was going to be an interesting conversation by the time I got there.

CHAPTER THIRTY-EIGHT

*B*eckett...
    I caught a late flight home on Friday night, and by the time I made it to my place it was late evening. I wanted to talk to her, but I figured she'd probably be in bed, and didn't want to wake her up. The waiting was excruciating, but I decided to do something about it.

Pulling the box that had my mother in it from the closet, I set it on the coffee table and opened it up, taking care to pull out just the letter that was at the top. I recognized my mother's handwriting, even if it had been a while.

My baby boy,
I know that we have not spoken in years, and I am to blame for
that. When you were growing up, I only wanted what was best
for you, but I also had to live my own life as well. I realize now
that it was selfish of me to not do what was needed to keep you
safe. I regret that more than you could ever know. I'm so proud
of you and the man you've become. I wish that we had time to
reconnect and I had the opportunity to apologize to you in
person. That won't happen, though, because I am nearing the
end of my life. Don't feel guilty for me going. Don't mourn me. I

am not worth that from you, and I accept my part in the way we are now. Feel free to throw me away, dump me in a landfill, or leave me on the side of the road. It is what I deserve. Just know that I do love you.
Mom

"Fuck," I muttered.

She was always selfish, but this... This was something else entirely. This was on a level of horrible that I hadn't seen before. Maybe it was because I was so young when I gave up on caring about her. Probably, though, it was because I could now look at her through the eyes of an adult, someone who took responsibility for his own actions. Okay, maybe not all of them, but at least I figured that out and was trying to do better. It just screamed of her wanting to make me feel bad, even though everything that happened to her was her own fault.

Quentin was right in that I probably needed some sort of therapy. Choosing to do the adult thing, I hopped onto my team email and sent a request for some recommendations. It wouldn't happen overnight, and I probably wouldn't get a response until Monday, but since the team was back in town, I figured I'd head into the ballpark on Saturday morning and have a chat with the manager. Until then, though, I turned the television on and decided to watch the game, something I hadn't done in quite a while.

They were ahead by two at the end of the eighth and brought Strawberry in to close it out. It was good to see Bridge filling in for me at short. He was a good guy, and had actually been decent to me this season, even when I was a crap person to be around. Strawberry was epic, and it only took him five pitches to get the Shamrocks out, even though it was the heart of their lineup. I turned the television off and headed to bed, hoping that I might get a chance to talk to my little Miss Ophelia tomorrow. Thinking better of it, I decided that I would wait to talk to her until I had something lined up for myself. First order of business tomorrow, though, would be a conversation with my manager, which would include a big apology for the way I'd been acting lately.

～

PULLING UP TO THE STADIUM, I HEADED DOWN THE LONG PATHWAY that led to the underground parking garage reserved for team staff and players. I parked my car and pulled the bag from the trunk, making my way into the clubhouse. A handful of players were there, but they mostly ignored me. I didn't blame them; I'd been unruly and deserved to be ignored. Knocking on the frame for the door to the manager's office, I waited for him to look up.

"Hennings," he said.

"Hey," I said. "Got a minute?"

He looked at the bag on my shoulder, then nodded, indicating I should sit in one of the chairs across from his desk.

"Coach," I began, then pulled the box out of my bag and dropped it on his desk. "I'd like for you to meet my mom."

He blinked, then looked at me.

"It's a long story," I said. "She died, apparently recently, and had her remains shipped to me. I haven't talked to her in at least six years, and this is the second contact she's made with me since the start of the year. You remember the letter that came then?"

He nodded, looking a bit stunned.

"Yeah," I said. "That letter said she had cancer. It was bad, and she wasn't expected to make it. I didn't really read much of it other than to realize she was gonna die. This came while we were in Indigo City, and I picked it up on Monday. Pretty shitty homecoming gift if you ask me."

"Should I say I'm sorry?" he asked.

"Nah," I replied. "She was a shrew, a hag, and those are polite terms."

"But she was your mom," he said.

"Biologically," I replied. "She kept me fed and a roof over my head, but everything else was too much work. I bounced when I was sixteen and never looked back. Feel pretty proud of the man I raised all on my own, too."

Coach nodded, taking in what I was telling him.

"I sent an email to medical asking for a referral to a counselor," I added. "I should hear back from them Monday but wanted to make this my first stop. I was a shitty person, and I took it out on you and the team, which was unfair. My life has kind of been turned upside down the last few weeks, and I didn't know how bad I'd been until the night I walked off the field. It got worse, but I did have someone who helped me out."

"I'm glad you have someone," he said.

"Not sure she'll stick around," I countered. "I'm working on that, though."

"You're officially on the IL," he said. "That means you can't come back to the team officially until late next week."

"I know," I said. "I wanted to make sure you knew I was gonna be good to go when the time came. If you'll have me."

"Let me check with medical," he said. "If they determine that you've set up an appointment and are working on getting your shit together, then I'm good with it."

"Thanks," I said.

"Sure thing," he replied. "Might want to touch base with some of the guys. They've been worried about you, even though they'd never outright say anything."

"I've been worried about myself, to be honest," I said. "I'll talk to Bridge. He's the cool headed one of the team, and if I can convince him I'm good to go, it'll help smooth things over."

"Wise choice," he said.

I got up, nodding at him, and walked back into the clubhouse, seeking the man who had been assigned as a mentor to me last season. It was no surprise that he was already there, even though it was relatively early in the day.

"Hey, J," I said.

"Yeah?" he asked.

"Can we talk?"

He looked at me, questioningly, but nodded. I turned and headed over to a less crowded area of the locker room and waited for him.

"What's up?" he asked when he got to me.

"First, I want to apologize," I said. "I've been a shitty teammate, more than just the recent stuff, too."

"Can't argue with you there," he said.

"Not gonna give excuses, but there are reasons my temper has been up," I explained. "Don't know if you want to hear them, or if you even care, but I'll share if you want."

"No need to air your dirty laundry to me," he said. "You doing something to fix it?"

"I am," I said. "I am waiting for a referral from the team for some counseling. Not exactly manly, but it's needed."

"It's actually really manly," he said. "Nothing says you're a man more than owning up to your shit and doing something to correct it."

I took what he said and pondered it, then nodded. "Guess you're right," I said. "Thanks for that."

"So, what's next?" he asked.

"I'm officially out until Thursday," I said. "But I'll be doing 'rehab' with the team starting Tuesday. Coach wants to make sure I have an appointment for counseling, as well as actually making it."

"Sounds good," he said.

"You mind helping me smooth things over with the rest of the guys?" I asked. "I know you're not my biggest fan, but it would really mean a lot if you wouldn't mind."

"Tell you what," he said. "You talk to someone on Monday, then tell me how it went, and we'll see what I can do. Sound fair?"

"I can live with that," I said.

"Good," he said. "And Beckett..."

"Yeah?"

"I'm proud of you," he said. "It takes a lot to look at yourself and realize that you have work to do. Being willing to do it, that's definitely a sign of maturity. Something you were lacking last season, and into the beginning of this year."

"Yeah," I agreed. "I was kind of a dick back then."

"Kind of?" he asked, but he was smiling, so I didn't take it bad.

"Talk to you Monday," I said.

"Sure thing," he replied, then turned to walk back to his locker.

The fact that he didn't blow me off or anything really helped me feel like I made the right decision in going to him first. I appreciated what he said to me, and that he was willing to listen in the first place. Guess he was the unofficial dad of the team. Not that anyone would tell him that.

I headed back to my car, trying to decide how to broach the subject with Ophelia. A text would be the coward's way out, but I wasn't sure I would be able to articulate everything I wanted to say to her. I guess I would just have to fumble through, but not until I got home. I wanted to be able to give her my undivided attention. The question was, would she take my call?

CHAPTER THIRTY-NINE

*F*i...
       I took the back way home, doing my best to avoid the traffic at the dome on the freeway that always seemed to be backed up no matter what time of day it was. The fact that they'd been doing construction on that freeway since before I was born should have given them a clue that it wasn't gonna work. By the time I was home, I was starving, but I also wanted to call McKenzie. I grabbed a couple of string cheese sticks from the fridge, then sat on the couch and made my call.

"Hey," she said when she answered.

"So, what's up?" I asked.

"When was the last time you talked to Beckett?" she asked, and my spidey senses were on high alert.

"Tuesday, why?"

"Did he tell you he was away from the team for a while?"

"How do you know?"

"Did you know?"

"I did," I said. "But how did you know?"

"He flew to Houston," she said.

"He what?"

"Got in touch with the Dragons," she continued. "They set up a meeting for him and Quentin. I was there, and it actually went really well."

"Hold up. He set up a meeting?" I asked.

"I figured you knew," she said. "We met, and he told Quentin he was sorry about what happened when the team was here. Said he really liked you and wanted to know how to fix his fuckup. Hasn't he called you yet?"

"I haven't heard from him," I said. "When was this meeting?"

"Yesterday," she said. "Maybe he's not back yet. I don't know when he was leaving, so maybe that's why he hasn't called you."

"I'm just so confused right now," I said. "He texted me after he blew me off on Tuesday night, but I haven't heard from him at all since then. No texts or calls or anything."

"Give him a little grace when he does call you," she said. "He's had a rough life, and even though he didn't share a ton, I think he could use a shoulder."

"I gave him that," I said. "I told him I'd listen and hear what he had to say, but he just said it wasn't anything to concern me about or something like that. Like, dude, I'm asking because I wanna know."

"He probably wasn't in a place to hear it," she said. "You know how guys are. They have to be the tough ones, the ones who have it all figured out and not show any emotions."

"Which is total bullshit," I said.

"Oh, I know," she said. "But I think he's always had to support himself, never had anyone to do that for him. Maybe he doesn't know how, or maybe he's too ashamed to need help after being so self-sufficient for so long. Either way, it'll be tough for him."

"The question is, do I really want a project boyfriend?"

"Is it the project part or the boyfriend part you're worried about?"

"Both, actually," I said with a laugh.

"Well," she said. "All I can say is that baseball players are a peculiar breed. They need some things given to them with explicit instructions because their brain thinks between the chalk lines. Everything else is a mystery to them."

"You would know," I said. "But I get it. I mean, when I was playing, the most important thing for me was the game. Most everything else fell by the wayside, so it makes sense."

I heard a knock at my door.

"Hey," I said. "Someone's here. Hold on for a minute."

"I'll let you go," she said. "Maybe it's him."

She disconnected the call before I could answer her, because how would he know where I lived? I opened the door and saw a big bouquet of daffodils and I wondered how in the world they were even available right now, since it was the end of July. Then he peeked his head around the blooms.

"Got a minute?" he asked. He looked so genuinely unsure of himself I just kind of stepped back and let him in. Once he was inside, he just stood there.

"Oh, jeez," I said. "Let me take those."

He handed the flowers to me and I stepped to the table and placed them in the center. I turned to see him looking around my apartment.

"Nice place," he said.

"Thanks," I said.

We stood there in awkward silence, just looking at each other—him in his button-down shirt and slacks and me in my leggings and oversized shirt. We were about as opposite as they came.

"Why don't you sit," I said, indicating the couch.

"Thanks," he replied, then went and took a seat.

"How did you know where I lived?" I asked as I sat at the other end of the couch.

"Your friend told me," he said. "Don't be mad at her, though. She wanted to help."

"That explains why she said it was you just now when I was on the phone with her," I said. "She told me to listen to you and give you a chance to explain yourself, so here I am. Explain away."

He looked down at his hands clasped in his lap and I realized that he was shaking a bit, like this was really a struggle for him. I moved closer, sitting right next to him, and reached out and took hold of his hands. When he looked up at me, there were tears in his eyes. I wasn't sure what they were about, but it broke my heart. All I wanted to do was collect him to me and hug him, tell him everything would be all right. But I couldn't do that because I didn't know what was going on with him. Instead, I let my comfort come through my hand holding his and waited him out.

CHAPTER FORTY

*B*eckett...

When she put her hand on mine, it nearly undid me. No one, especially my mom, ever did something like that for me. I looked at her and she was just there, present, and waiting for what I had to say. I swallowed hard, several times, before I found my voice.

"My mom died," I croaked out. She started to say something, but I cut her off. "She was awful," I said. "Other than ensuring I didn't die, she was never truly a mother. I haven't talked to her in more than six years."

I stopped, trying to gauge her reaction, but she wasn't showing any kind of emotion. What I wanted more than anything was to not have to tell her the shit I had been through, but if I wanted this to work, I knew I needed to be honest with her.

"I was also sexually abused," I said, turning away.

I didn't want to see her pity and disgust, but she reached her hand up and cupped my cheek, turning me to look at her. What I saw there made my heart hurt. She looked... I didn't know how to describe it, but it was more than I expected. She rubbed her thumb across my cheek, a gentle pressure to tell me she was there.

"Do you want to talk about it?" she asked. "Or do you just want me to know?"

"I don't know," I said.

"That's okay," she replied. "I'm here if you want to talk, but I understand it's personal and traumatic, so it's okay if you don't, too."

I swallowed again, trying desperately not to cry. I was a fucking man, and I didn't need to be a blubbering fool. She must have seen something in my eyes because she wrapped her arms around me and pulled me close, nearly climbing in my lap.

"It's okay to cry," she said, as if she were reading my mind. "I won't tell anyone. You're safe with me."

That was it, as if she'd flipped some special sequence of switches, just the right ones in the right order, and I was gone. I let it out, years and years of it all just poured out of me. Never, not once, had anyone given me permission to let go of it, leave it out there. No, everyone wanted me to shove it down, put it behind me, forget and move on. But not her, not my beautiful, wonderful, remarkable Ophelia.

I couldn't tell you how long it took, but it seemed like years. Finally, once I felt like I could contain myself, I took a deep breath and let it out on a sigh. She had actually climbed fully into my lap, straddling my legs. My arms were around her waist as she held me, my head on her shoulder, her shirt absorbing all my tears. I lifted my head and looked at her and she smiled. It was soft and sweet, like she was happy, which made no sense at all.

"You good?" she asked, and I nodded.

She went to get off, but I held her there.

"Please stay," I said, and it was raspy with the tears I'd shed.

"Okay," she replied, settling in.

"You keep that up and this is going to turn very different very fast," I said, and she laughed and shifted again. "I mean it," I added.

I wasn't hard, probably couldn't even get there for a while, but if anyone could make me forget my past, it was her. She pulled her arms from around my neck and placed a palm on either side of my face, holding me there, just looking in my eyes. The mess she was looking at was probably horrible, but she didn't seem fazed at all. Instead, she looked enraptured, like I was the only thing she wanted to see.

Slowly, ever so slowly, she lowered her head to mine, pressing her forehead to my own, and closed her eyes, sighing deeply. I took a deep breath and let it out slowly, closing my own eyes. We sat there for a while, at least until my legs started to feel it. She wasn't heavy, I just wasn't used to having someone on my lap for this long. I shifted, and she pulled back and looked at me again.

"Legs are starting to cramp," I said, and she shifted off me, settling beside me on the couch.

"You hungry?" she asked. "I can make up something for dinner."

"If you're hungry," I said. "I'm happy to help or order out."

"I'm not even sure what I have," she said. "Tomorrow was going to be a grocery run."

"Let me order something," I said. "My treat. For putting up with my shit."

"You don't have to," she said.

"I want to," I replied. "What's close?"

I had never been to the little town she lived in and had no idea what the food situation was down here. She grabbed her phone and pulled up a delivery app, giving me free rein on what to order for myself, telling me she'd figure out what she wanted once I picked a place. There was this little mom-and-pop type place called Trotter's that had potential, so I asked her about it.

"They're really good," she said. "Back in the day, they had this giant sundae thing that, if you could eat it all by yourself, it was free. Thing was, it had like thirty something scoops of ice cream in it."

"Yeah, no," I said, laughing. "Not gonna even try that."

We looked at the selections, figured out what we wanted, then I put my card information into the app to pay for dinner, then put her phone back on the coffee table.

"So," she said, just leaving that one word hanging there.

"What should we do while we wait?" I asked.

"I'm sure we could think of something," she said, a blush creeping up her neck as she looked at her phone on the table.

"Are you implying something naughty?" I asked.

She looked at me then and smiled, wiggling her eyebrows.

"You little minx," I said, and she laughed, saying, "Minx?"

I reached my hand over and cupped her cheek, then pushed my hand further around and behind her neck, pulling her toward me. I gave her plenty of time to stop, but she moved faster than I'd planned, capturing my mouth with hers in a fierce kiss, shifting to once again straddle my lap. My hands found her ass and I squeezed the globes, pressing her down on me. While I wasn't fully hard, it was getting there rather quickly. She groaned into my mouth, opening her lips to allow my tongue entrance.

We spent quite a bit of time just kissing, but what a fucking kiss it was. By the time we came up for air, we were both out of breath, gasping to relearn that ever important skill. Her phone buzzed, and she turned to look at it, grabbing it and checking whatever the notification was.

"Food's on the way," she said.

"That's fast," I replied.

"Yeah," she said. "They're really quick, which is great when you're starving."

"How long 'til they get here?"

"Not long enough," she said with a smile.

"Damn," I said, laughing.

"What are your plans for the rest of the weekend?" she asked.

"I have a meeting on Monday, but nothing until then," I said.

"Wanna stay?"

I think she surprised herself with the look she had on her face, but I took the invitation and ran with it.

"I'll stay as long as you'll have me," I said.

There was a knock at the door and she jumped, then laughed and got up and headed to the door.

"Hey, Fi," the kid who was at the door said when she opened it.

Dude looked like he was still in high school at best. He was definitely really young. He glanced over and saw me sitting on the couch. I didn't get up, didn't try to do that whole territorial thing, just sat there waiting for my woman to come back with the food.

"Hey, yourself," she said.

"Your usual, plus one?"

"Yeah," she replied. "I've got a friend over."

"Oh," the guy said and he sounded disappointed.

He probably had a crush on her, which... same, dude. He handed her the bag, and she handed him a folded bill, looked like a ten, but who knows.

"Thanks," he said, still sounding like she'd kicked his puppy.

"See you next time," she said, then shut the door and brought the food over.

"You know he's got the hots for you, right?" I asked.

She looked at me and blinked, completely baffled by what I'd said. Then it all dawned on her and she started to blush.

"Can't blame him," I added.

"He's always the one who brings my food," she said. "I think he's the owner's son or something."

"Well, he likes you," I said. "Like he *really* likes you."

"What are you, twelve?"

She laughed when she asked it, but it did sound like something I would have said so many years ago. That just brought it all back about my life, and my mom, and everything else from then. I think she noticed the change, and she sat next to me, taking my hand in hers.

"I'm sorry," she said. "Probably brought up something bad, right?"

"Yeah," I said. "Something like that."

Watching me, she waited, as if I was gonna say something profound or important, but there really wasn't anything to say. I squeezed her hand a couple of times and smiled, doing my best to hide everything back in the closet, but I could tell she wasn't buying it. Instead of pushing, though, she smiled.

"Hungry?" she asked.

"Starved," I said.

"Let me get some real utensils," she said. "I can't stand the plastic ones."

She got up and walked to the kitchen and I watched her go, admiring the view, but also thankful that she hadn't pushed. Whatever was going on in her head, she didn't push it out, didn't dump her shit on me, and didn't demand I talk to her about my own shit, which was actually really cool. Maybe the two of us could work after all. Only time would tell.

CHAPTER FORTY-ONE

*F*i...

The fact that he'd opened up to me at all was a miracle in and of itself, and I didn't want to push it too hard, so when he got that look, I showed him I was there, but then gave him space. It was hard to not demand he tell me everything, but I certainly wasn't a trained professional and had no tools to give him. Instead, I comforted him and gave him a safe space just to exist.

If I had to guess, his mom had let his father, or some other guy in her life, do whatever they wanted, and accused him of being the one to initiate it. That was the way these things usually played out when they showed up in the crime dramas I watched or were talked about in the podcasts I listened to. I'd never understood how a mother could allow her child to be hurt, and then blame them for what had been done to them. Never known anyone who had actually been through it, though, so I had no actual firsthand knowledge of what exactly happened. All I knew was that the child was never at fault, and Beckett had likely been at the mercy of whoever it was that did this to him, without a parent to stand behind him, help him, or get him counseling.

Grabbing a couple of forks, I headed back to the living room where I saw him watching me. Sure, he had that look of wanting sex, but there was something else there. Appreciation, maybe, or something else entirely. Either way, it was a good look.

"Here we go," I said, handing him one of the forks.

He'd opened the bag and pulled out the two takeout boxes, flipping them both open on the coffee table.

"We can eat at the actual table if you want," I said.

"Nah," he replied. "I can't sit right next to you then."

I smiled and sat as close to him as I could without actually sitting on his lap. He picked up a fork full of his food and stuck it in his mouth, then groaned.

"This is really good," he said.

"Yeah," I replied. "I really like their food."

We ate, mostly in silence with the occasional muffled noises of appreciation for the food. Once we were both done, him long before me, I picked up the boxes and took them into the kitchen, dropping the forks into the sink to take care of later. When I went back to the living room, he had unbuttoned his shirt some, leaving it more open than it had been before.

"Somebody's ready to get the party started," I said.

"I'm always ready for you," he replied, a slight smile crossing his lips. He reached his hand out, motioning for me to come closer, and said, "I want you. I need a distraction from my shitstorm of a life. Can you give me that?"

I took his hand, but pulled, urging him to stand. He did, and I led him down the small hall to my bedroom. It was just a few steps from where we were but felt much more private than the couch. More intimate, which I really wanted. He wrapped an arm around my middle, pulling me back against him, his other hand pulling my hair around and away from my neck, where he proceeded to plant a kiss. I tipped my head, giving him room to explore, and he did so with fervor.

"You smell so good," he said. "Taste even better," he continued, nibbling on my earlobe. "I want to taste all of you. Devour you and make you see the stars for hours."

"Mmm," I hummed, my eyes closing to enjoy his touch and words.

He walked me toward the bed, then spun me around to let me sit.

He kneeled in front of me, pulling my shoes and socks off. He kissed the top of each foot before setting it on the floor. When he looked up at me, kneeling in front of me like that, it was just so much. I didn't know what to do with the emotions that were rolling around.

"You're my queen," he said, and there was a truth to his words that was tangible.

Standing, he reached down and pulled me back up, his hands taking the hem of my shirt and pulling it up over my head, dropping the garment to the floor. He did the same with my tank top, then undid my bra and let it fall as well. The way he looked at me, it was so beautiful I wanted to cry. Like he hadn't seen a million naked women before, but for some reason I was special.

Placing his hands on my waist, he began to shove my leggings down, along with my panties. It was a slow and almost torturous movement, but as he pushed them down, he laid kisses all along my body, starting with my lips, then my chin, neck, collarbone, down to my breasts, kissing each nipple, but not taking them into his mouth, just a chaste kiss at the top. Then my stomach and lower still. He kissed me just above the hair at my pubic region, then moved to one side to kiss my thigh and further down until I had to place a hand on his shoulder to step out of my pants.

When he stood back up, the look in his eyes was one of pure devotion, or something like that. It was the way my dad would look at my mom when she was just doing ordinary things in the kitchen or something. The way he stared at her, loving her without her even knowing he was looking. That was the look Beckett gave me in that moment, and it made my stomach flutter with anticipation and delight.

"I want to worship you," he said, low and deep. "Show you just how magnificent you are. How much I treasure you. Will you let me do that?"

I couldn't speak, just nodded, trying desperately not to let loose the tears that were threatening. He reached around me and pulled the blankets on my bed back, then urged me to sit, then lie down. Without taking his clothes off, he climbed up onto the bed. He'd kicked his shoes off at some point, though I don't know when, and it didn't really matter. His knees were between my own, but he hovered above me, holding himself on his strong arms over my body. Slowly, he lowered himself, kissing me slow and sensuously, lavishing my lips and mouth with his love.

Opening for him, his tongue plunged into my mouth, teasing me with it sliding in and out, a rhythm I was hoping he would continue further down my body. He kept his weight on his own arms, not putting any pressure on me, and he continued to kiss me until I wasn't sure we were ever going to stop. I didn't want him to, either. Finally, he pulled back, both of us breathing heavy. The smile on his face was radiant, as if there was nothing in the world that could break him.

"I could do this all day," he said, then pressed his lips next to mine.

Moving along my jawline, he continued to kiss me, pressing gentle lips to my skin all along the way, moving ever slowly down my body. He paused at my breasts, taking one of my nipples into his mouth. I sucked in a breath, arching my back up to meet him, and he hummed in pleasure, which just added to the sensation. He didn't stay long on the one breast, but moved to the other, lavishing it with the same attention, causing the exact same reaction.

He dipped lower, kissing just below my breasts, then further down to my naval, following the path he'd started, all the way down to my pelvic bone where he pressed his lips against my stomach, just above the hairline there. My eyes were closed, so when he pulled away, I didn't feel him any longer. I opened my eyes, staring down along my body to see him settling between my thighs. He caught me looking and gave me a devilish smile full of promise for things to come.

His arm went over my stomach, across my hip bones to hold me in place, then he dipped his head and licked me from opening to clit, stopping to pull that sensitive nub into his mouth, sucking it and bringing me higher and higher. My eyes fluttered closed and I felt him shift, then he pressed a finger inside me and the sensation was wonderful. He worked me with his mouth and finger, sucking and nibbling on my little nub while his finger plunged in and out of my pussy.

My breathing faltered a bit, stumbling over the sensations happening to me, and I just barely was able to remember the process, each intake coming faster and shorter as he worked me higher and higher. He'd added a second finger, pumping into me, and I could feel that tightening inside as the orgasm built. He bit down and the instant pain pushed me over the edge until I tumbled without form through the cosmos, ebbing and flowing on the waves of pleasure until I finally came back to myself.

As the pleasure subsided, I could feel him moving out of me, away from me, and I felt abandoned until he was back on top of me, his skin pressing against mine. I could feel that he was now naked, but how that happened, I didn't know, or even care. All that mattered was the here and now, and it was perfect. He kissed me deeply, and I could taste myself on his tongue.

"You are so fucking gorgeous," he mumbled against my lips. "I could watch you come over and over again and never tire of the look on your face when that moment hits."

He'd been moving against me, sliding his cock up and down against my pussy lips, and I needed him inside me. I pressed my hips against him, urging him to do what I needed, but he just kept the slow movement going.

"I need you," I begged, finally finding my voice.

"Not yet," he replied, and I moaned my displeasure, but he just kept up with what he was doing.

I could feel myself getting more and more frustrated, which was causing my happy to run away, until he reached his hand down and pulled my leg up on his hip, opening me more than I had already been. He'd pushed himself up a bit on the other arm, and his hand that pulled my leg up was now between us, stroking me and getting my juices flowing even more than they were before. Then, his fingers dipped lower, caressing my asshole. I sucked in a breath and he stopped.

"You good?" he asked.

I thought about it, him still moving his length up and down, but the finger at my back opening was still. Deciding it was fine, I nodded.

"Gonna need you to say it," he said.

"Yes," I said, and he chuckled, but started moving his fingers again.

He was slow, gentle, and very careful to watch my face for any sort of discomfort. The way he was working me, his finger slowly entering my asshole, pressing just the tip, then a little further each time, was ramping me up again for another fall over that wonderful cliff to tumble down into bliss.

"That's it, baby," he said as he kept the rhythm steady. "Come on, you can do this. Let it all go and just feel."

Doing as he suggested, I let go of all my inhibitions and just felt— his cock sliding against me, his fingers pressing into my ass. All of it was so much, and I just let everything else go. Once I did that, the world faded away, and just the two of us were left, connected in a way that was neither physical nor corporeal, just our essences.

Bliss took me, spreading me to the four winds, throwing me into a cacophony of pleasure I had never felt before. He faltered a bit, but then I felt the increased pressure against my asshole and sucked in a breath.

"Relax," he said. "Let me in."

I let go, let him guide me, and finally felt him fully inside me, moving slowly, so slowly, but it kept me on that high and I enjoyed the ride. And what a ride it was.

CHAPTER FORTY-TWO

*B*eckett...

She was high, in that state where we all go when we lose ourselves to the feelings, and I pushed her to let me in. We hadn't talked about this, but she'd let me use my finger before, so figured she'd allow me to dive into her tight asshole this time. I hadn't asked her for a condom, didn't even know whether she had any before we started, so I grabbed the one that was in my wallet. I knew it wasn't the best choice, but it was all I had with me.

I built her up, getting her to that point of pure feelings and pressed into her, and what a glorious sensation when I was finally in. It took time, but I had all the time in the world, so I was slow and steady, but determined to leave my mark.

I pumped in and out slowly at first, allowing her to adjust to me being back there. The angle was just right, and I was able to go all the way, balls deep, which was no small task. Once I started the motion, once that path had begun, I was on my way to spilling into her dark center. Slowly, ever so slowly, I built up speed, gritting my teeth to keep myself in control until I wasn't sure I could hold off any longer. When I heard her keening voice, the one that let me know she was tumbling again, I let go of myself, following her into the stratosphere where we only existed in ethereal forms.

My arms were straining with my weight, and I nearly collapsed on top of her. When I shifted to pull out, her legs wrapped around my waist, holding me in place, not allowing me to leave her. My cock twitched inside her, letting the last of my seed out and into the condom inside her, and she held me firm. Tapping on her thigh, she finally relented, allowing me to pull out and fall to the bed beside her.

"That was…" she breathed, not finishing the statement. "Wow," she finally said after some time.

I just stayed there, catching my breath. Once we were at a point where our breathing had slowed, I pulled the condom off and held it before giving her a nudge.

"Let's go get cleaned up," I said, rolling off the bed and holding my empty hand out.

She blinked a couple of times, but then took my hand and allowed me to help her up. I walked her toward the bathroom that I'd spied when she'd brought me to her room. Flicking the light on, I dropped the used condom in the trash, then started the water in the tub.

"Go pee," I said, pointing at the toilet.

"Umm," she said, hesitating.

"No need to be shy around me now," I said, turning my back on her.

I heard her raise the lid and the seat shift as she settled onto it. I stepped into the tub, pulling the little tab to get it coming out of the showerhead, and grabbed the bottle of bath wash that was sitting on the little shelf thing she had in there. I washed my hands to ensure that I didn't contaminate anything with our foreplay.

She flushed the toilet, then stepped into the shower behind me, my body blocking the water as it rained down. With her head tipped down, her hair was falling in front of her face, so I pulled her to me, using one hand to sweep the hair back and out of my way. Looking up, she had questions in her eyes, but didn't seem to want to give them voice. Instead of asking her what she was thinking, trying to convince her to talk to me, I just shifted us so that she was under the water, then tipped her head back to allow the water to completely drench it.

Picking up the shampoo, I poured plenty into my palm, then began to lather her hair, washing it gently and carefully, allowing the water to rinse the suds from her scalp. Once that was done, I added some of the bodywash to my palm and worked it onto her shoulders, down her front, then reached around and worked it down her back, all the way to her ass. Once I was there, I pulled one of her feet up, so her leg was hitched on my hip. She placed her hands on either shoulder, and I watched to make sure she was okay with what I was doing. She just had this serene look on her face, one that said she was in a good place.

Lathering the soap, I rubbed it between her thighs, carefully ensuring that I went front to back, all the soap heading away from her pussy and toward her ass. I wanted to make sure she was clean, and cleaned up from our play, but I didn't want her to get any kind of infection from it, so was careful with my actions. When I was sure she was clean, I let her leg down gently, then pressed myself against her, kissing her soundly under the spray of water.

"Your turn," she said when we pulled apart, and before I had a chance to argue, she had the bottle of soap in her hand and was pouring a generous amount into her palm.

She rubbed her hands together, then lowered them to my cock, rubbing the soap up and down my length, causing it to come back to attention from her ministrations. I pressed a hand against the shower wall to keep from falling over as she ran her soap-filled hands up and down my length.

"You keep that up, we'll be here all night," I said, my voice tight with restraint.

"Let me take care of you," she said, and the words were like lightning to my heart.

No one had ever offered to take care of me. That was something my mother hadn't even done. But here I was, in this woman's home, and after all the shit I'd put her through, she was offering to take care of me. I'm sure she meant sexually, but there was something else in the words, like she wanted to do more than just satisfy my physical needs.

I wasn't sure what to do with that, but it wasn't something I wanted to ponder at that moment.

Thing was, I didn't want her to just "take care of me" in that sense. I wanted to do that for her. Oh, sure, what we'd just done was absolutely fucking amazing, and I'd do it again any time she wanted. But I didn't want to have that be the only thing we had. That wasn't what I wanted my future to look like. My mom had had a revolving door for the men in her life, and I had found myself well on that same path with women. Something about Ophelia, though, made me want to be different.

For now, though, I would let her take care of this need. Maybe tomorrow we'd be able to talk about the rest of it.

CHAPTER FORTY-THREE

*F*i...

After the second round in the shower, we were both spent, and once we were dried off, we collapsed in my bed and crashed hard. I woke up long before him, and I felt like he probably hadn't slept well in a while with how out of it he was. It was the wee hours of the morning, just after midnight, and I couldn't sleep anymore. I was hungry again, which was ridiculous. Pulling on my leggings and a shirt, I headed to the kitchen to make some toast. It was something quick and easy but would sustain me for at least a little while.

My phone was on the coffee table, but it was almost dead, so I plugged it in into the charger in the kitchen and started to scroll through social media to see what was going on in the world. I hated watching the news, and usually got most of my information through things I saw throughout the day on my socials. If it was something I wanted more info about, I'd do a search and see what articles I could find.

My toast popped and I pulled it out, spreading butter across it before taking a bite. It was crazy how hungry I was, but I ate the piece pretty quick, then ate the second one nearly as fast. Knowing I needed some protein, I opened the fridge and pulled out some string cheese. It was one of those things I had because I loved it, and it was a comfort thing from childhood. When I shut the door, he was standing there. I jumped and nearly screamed but shoved my hand over my mouth before the sound escaped.

"What are you doing up?" he asked.

"I was hungry," I replied, holding out the string cheese for him to see.

"Come back to bed," he said. "I miss you."

As adorable as that sounded, it was kind of nuts. I was only gone for a few minutes, so it's not like he could have missed me that much. Instead of arguing with him, though, I reached out and took his hand, following him back to the room. Once we were there, he held the blankets up for me to climb in, which I did. He climbed in behind me, then pulled me up against him, hugging me to him. It was weird that he was so clingy, but I brushed it off as likely just a one-off thing.

He held me, my back to his front, from the slow, deep breaths he was taking, he was quickly back asleep. I opened my cheese and ate it, tossing the wrapper over onto the floor on the other side of the bed. I could pick it up in the morning. With food in my stomach, and his warm body against my back, I quickly drifted off to sleep once again.

His hand on my breast, kneading it methodically woke me, and I could feel the press of his dick against my ass. While he wasn't actually grinding it against me, he was definitely pressing it, ensuring I knew exactly what he had in mind.

"You smell so good," he whispered in my ear, kissing my neck right beneath the lobe.

I wiggled my hips, pressing my ass against him, and he groaned, pulling me closer than I thought possible.

"I want to fuck you so bad," he said. "Tell me you want that."

Not bothering to say anything, I reached between us and gripped his cock, squeezing and stroking it. The angle was awkward, and I knew I couldn't do this for long, but I wanted to be the one in control this time. He backed off a bit, allowing me to turn onto my back. When he started to move on top of me, I stopped him. Pressing him to the mattress, I climbed up on top of him. I still had the leggings and shirt on from my midnight snack, so he was the only naked person. This gave me the upper hand in that I could stroke and play with him and his access to me was limited.

Stroking him from hilt to tip, I kept up a steady rhythm, enough to make him feel good, but not enough to get him off. I wanted to build it up, and I knew I would need a little work to get myself to a point that I could take him in, too.

"Just like that, baby," he said, his eyes closed, enjoying it all.

I smiled, knowing he was enjoying what I was doing. He ran his hands up and over my thighs, sliding them up and down the material covering them. I could tell he was getting frustrated with the material being there, so I stopped what I was doing and pulled my shirt up over my head, dropping it to the floor. Raising up on my knees, I shimmied my leggings down, leaning back some to pull them all the way off. It was weird, and I kind of fell over on to the other side of the bed, but once they were off, he was right there, stroking me, his hand running back and forth across the junction of my legs.

"Now I'm in control," he growled, latching onto one of my breasts and sucking hard.

"Ooh," I moaned, arching my back against his mouth.

I could feel his grin against my breast, his finger finding my entrance and eliciting another moan from me. He played me like a damn fiddle, working me up to that peak I desired, pressing me further and further with each stroke of his finger, each suck of his lips, his thumb pressing at my clit, rubbing it around and around in circles. I'd started out in control, but he flipped it just that quickly and took over, and I wasn't at all upset about it.

Letting everything else fall away, I just enjoyed his work on me, and fell hard once he'd pushed me over the ledge. I felt him shift on top of me, though I wasn't completely aware. When he slid inside, I opened my eyes and looked at him.

"Condom?" I asked, almost a bark.

"Don't have any," he replied.

I shoved on him, pushing him off me and out of me.

"What the hell were you thinking?" I asked, my anger rising.

"I was in the moment, babe," he said.

"Don't you 'babe' me," I said. "We are not at a point where I am comfortable going without protection. We haven't had any of those conversations, and for you to assume that I'd be down for that just shows that you have some work to do."

I let my anger boil over, and I could see he was flinching from each word I'd said, but we were not at that point. Not even close.

"I should go," he said, moving to stand.

"We should have this conversation," I replied.

He looked at me, maybe trying to decide if what I said was real, or if he should just cut his losses. Neither of which would surprise me at this point. I waited him out, letting him figure his own shit out.

Finally, he asked, "You wanna talk it out?"

"Wouldn't have suggested it if I didn't," I replied.

He took a deep breath, then let it out slowly.

"I don't know how to do a relationship," he said. "If that's what we're doing here," he added, waffling his hand between us. "I'm down for it, but you're gonna have to walk me through it, cause I've never done it before."

I just stared at him, blinking. It was not the confession I was expecting. Didn't surprise me, but it was still unexpected.

"You want there to be an us?" I asked. I mean, I wanted it, I just didn't know if he did.

"I think so," he replied. "I like you. You're fun and crazy, but in all the best ways."

"Okay, calling someone crazy is not the best first step," I said, but was laughing to hopefully take some of the sting out of my words.

"Duly noted," he replied. "What else have I done wrong?"

"What?"

"Obviously I don't know what I'm doing," he said. "I need you to tell me what I've done wrong so I don't do it again."

"That's not how this works," I said. "Sometimes you'll screw up, but so will I. We just have to take each moment as it comes and discuss it."

"Okay," he said, clearly taking my words to heart.

"Let's start with sex," I said.

"I'm down for that," he replied, shifting as if to reengage in our previous activity.

"Slow down there, bucko," I said.

"Bucko?"

"Sorry," I replied. "Dad was raised on a pig farm. I kind of have stupid terms that come out."

"Ah, gotcha," he replied.

"We need to establish ground rules for what we are and are not comfortable with," I explained. "Like, I'm not down for sex without protection yet. I don't know you that well."

"Seems fair," he replied. "What else?"

Oh boy, this was gonna take a while.

CHAPTER FORTY-FOUR

*B*eckett...

"We need to establish ground rules for what we are and are not comfortable with," she said. "Like, I'm not yet down for sex without protection. I don't know you that well."

"Seems fair," I replied. "What else?"

She took a deep breath, then let it out slowly.

"Am I doing this wrong?" I asked. "Because I've never done this before, so have no idea what the fuck I'm doing."

"I get that," she said, and I felt like she actually did understand what I was saying. "Let's start with what we think we want out of this relationship."

"You mean besides hot monkey sex?"

"Hot monkey sex?"

"Come on," I said. "We are fucking amazing together. You know that."

"But monkey..." she said, trailing off.

"Okay," I conceded. "Besides sex, what do we want from this... that's the question, right?"

"Right," she replied.

"Well, I like that I can call you," I said. "The other night, when I first got my mom's ashes, and you came to the bar and brought me home and took care of me, I have never had anyone do that for me before."

"I'm sorry," she said, and it wasn't anything like pity. "You should have people you can count on."

"Easier said than done," I said, realizing that she was about to get the entirety of my fucked-up existence in this little talk we were having.

"Why do you say that?"

"Hard to rely on someone when you don't have any friends," I said, looking at my hands.

"What do you mean?"

"When everyone else was busy making friends, I was busy fending of a creep," I said. "My main goal was to find a way out of the shithole I lived in, and it was no easy task, believe me. By the time I was four-teen, I knew that nothing in this life was easy, and sometimes you had to make sacrifices to get where you wanted to be. For me, that was baseball, and playing at the highest level possible. I was fortunate to have a natural talent, but it was also what made me end up being abused. Being good helped me get further in this business than any of the other shit, so for that I'm thankful. I also learned that sex was just another commodity to be used," I continued. "Never had an issue with fucking someone and then walking away until I met you."

She was surprised at my admission, I could tell, but I kept on, not wanting to stop once I'd gotten going. I wanted to make sure she heard everything I had to say, everything that was bubbling in my soul.

"Sure, I wanted you," I said. "But it was more than just sex. When we met in that bar with your brother, I knew you were hot and would be amazing in bed, but you also had a fire inside you that just seemed to radiate from you, and it drew me to you. Like a siren to a ship captain, you lured me to your cliffs, and I crashed into them, hard."

I watched her, waiting to see what her reaction to my confession would be.

"You deserve to be loved," she said, and a lump filled my throat.

This was it. She was going to tell me my baggage was too much for her, and that she didn't want to have a damaged, broken, good-for-nothing guy in her life.

"I wish we would have met earlier," she added. "Then I could have loved you for longer. Maybe I could have healed your broken before now, but I'm willing to try to help you heal, if you'll let me."

They weren't the words I expected, so it took me more time than it should have to comprehend what she was saying. When it all fell into place, I nearly sobbed. She must have noticed, because she reached out and pulled me to her, hugging me. For the second time in as many days, I let go and just felt, not worrying about what it looked like. She held me, and I let her, releasing all my anxiety and worry and thoughts that I wasn't good enough. Finally, after I'd gotten ahold of myself, I pushed back, looking in her eyes.

"Why are you crying?" I asked.

"I'm crying for that little boy inside you," she said. I cocked my head, not understanding her meaning, so she added, "He deserved so much more than he was given."

"I don't understand," I said.

"Your life has been one fight after another," she said. "You were never given a chance to just be a little kid. Between your mom's abandoning you and the rest of what happened, when were you supposed to just be joyful? To play and explore and learn about the big world around you?"

"My mom didn't abandon me," I argued, latching on to the one thing I knew.

"Didn't she?" she asked. "She was working all the time, leaving you to fend for yourself, and figure it out on your own. When she was home, she was what, drunk? Screwing some rando? How is that not abandoning you?"

I blinked at her harsh tone, wanting for some reason to defend the woman who had given me life, but she was right. Everything my mom did was just for her own benefit. Even after I left home, she was always after me to keep her in mind, to help her out with whatever it was that had happened that day, or week, or month. My sole purpose, according to her, was to take care of her. She'd told me more than once that when I was old enough, I should be the one to take care of her. After all, she'd done so much for me already, it was my duty as her son to become the caretaker.

"Fuck," I said, and it came out angrier than I meant. "Sorry," I apologized.

"I know it wasn't directed at me," she said. "I think you just had a moment of clarity."

"Ain't that the fucking truth," I replied.

It had to be damn near noon, and all of a sudden, I was starving.

"Let's go do lunch," I suggested.

"Now?"

"Yeah," I said. "We're obviously gonna need some time to get through whatever the fuck I have going on up here." I pointed to my head, then added, "Besides, if we're gonna have hot monkey sex, we need to have some calories to burn. And, we need to get some condoms."

She laughed, full on, head back, cackling out loud, laughed.

"Oh my God," she said once she'd settled. "I don't even know what to do with you right now."

"I have ideas," I said, wiggling my eyebrows.

"You are awful," she replied, waving to smack me, but I snatched her wrist and pulled her close.

"You're wonderful," I whispered close to her lips, then slammed into her, taking her mouth by force.

She replied in kind, her own lips opening to allow me entrance. We tangled our tongues around each other and I could tell I was ready to go, which fucking sucked because we didn't have a way to do it without the condoms. Pulling back, I pressed my forehead against hers, collecting my breath.

Pushing me onto my back, she straddled me, then leaned over and pulled the drawer on her night stand open, revealing a pack of condoms hidden there. Her smile when she sat up holding the foil packet was devilish, and I was more than a little turned on by it.

"Those were there all along?" I asked.

"You never asked," she replied with a smile.

"Let's do this," I said, and she cracked up.

CHAPTER FORTY-FIVE

*F*i...

We spent Sunday afternoon in bed, using up all the condoms I had in my apartment. I couldn't complain, other than the fact that I knew I'd be sore on Monday, and my walk into the office might be hard to do. Still, it was a good day, and I felt like we had actually had a good conversation and were making headway into what we both wanted from this relationship.

"I have to head home," he said after a shower that evening.

"Can't you stay?" I asked and was slightly uncomfortable with how much it sounded like begging.

"Gotta go meet with the someone from the team tomorrow," he said. "Not sure of the time, nor how long it'll take."

"Okay," I replied. "I do have to work tomorrow, so there's that."

"You could come stay with me," he suggested.

"And drive from Seattle to Tacoma in rush-hour traffic?" I asked. "No, thank you."

"So quit," he said.

"I'm not quitting my job," I said. "It's something that's non-negotiable. I will have a job, no matter what happens between us. I need to have a purpose, a drive, something to do."

"It's okay," he said, but he was wounded.

"Hey," I said, turning his face to me. "We are just getting started, you and me. There are going to be some learning curves. Sometimes we'll have to agree to disagree, and that's fine. You're still you and I'm still me. We are just also an 'us' from now on."

"Yeah?" he asked, clearly interested in what I was saying.

"Yeah," I replied. "What that 'us' is will grow and change over time."

"As long as you're not gonna abandon me," he said, clearly realizing that his mother had done just that to him.

"No," I replied. "If there is an issue between us, we'll work it out. If it turns out we can't, I will still care about you and want what is best for you. Nothing is going to change that."

"Just promise me you won't go anywhere," he said.

"For now, we're together," I said. "But you need to do whatever it takes to fix the broken in you. That's not something I can do for you."

"I know," he replied. "That's why I'm going to the team doc tomorrow. I'm hoping they can set me up with someone. I'm still on the IL until Friday's game, so won't be playing, but I think I need to be at the games."

"You probably should," I replied. "You need to show your team that you aren't gonna walk away again."

"Yeah," he agreed. "That was pretty shitty of me."

"It was," I said.

"I've done some apologizing, but it'll take time to get their confidence back," he said.

"It will," I replied.

We stood there, him dressed in his button-down shirt and slacks and me in my leggings and a tee shirt, about as opposite as two people could be. He looked at me as if he were trying to memorize what I looked like, and it was a bit off-putting. While I was uncomfortable, I knew he didn't mean anything by it, so I stepped up to him and wrapped my arms around his neck, pulling him to me for a kiss. His arms wrapped around my waist, and he returned the kiss, deepening it.

It didn't take long before he had his hands under my shirt and was working to push it up and off.

"We gotta stop," I mumbled against his lips. "You'll never get out of here if you don't."

He rested his forehead on mine and sighed, his eyes closed. Taking a couple of deep breaths, he pulled back and kissed me one last time, chaste and quick, before turning to go out the front door. I hoped he'd turn back, but then again, wasn't sure if I wanted him to. Just before he turned to go down the staircase, he looked back and smiled, as if the fact that I was still standing there was everything he had been hoping for.

Shutting the door, I headed into the kitchen to make a sandwich. I hadn't gotten to the grocery store that day, so would have to pick stuff up on the way home. Until then, though, I'd have to make do with what I had, which was just enough, thankfully. Sitting down on the couch, I turned on the television and flipped it over to the local channel that was still playing the end of the game. The Cascades were up by one in the top of the eighth, so I got to see at least a little bit of the game. My phone rang, and I nearly jumped out of my skin.

"Hello?"

"Hey, Fi," McKenzie said in a rushed tone. "Don't watch the news."

"What are you talking about?" I asked.

"Wait until your brother calls you," she said. "Something went down at the stadium and I want you to hear it from him first."

"Tell me what's going on," I said, fearing something tragic had happened.

"He's gonna call you as soon as he's out of the building," she said. "I just want you to hear it from him instead of whatever way the reporters are gonna spin it."

She'd barely finished what she was saying when I heard the announcers say something about the Dragons.

"Hang on," I said, turning the volume up a little bit.

"...*that the entire Dragons team is under suspicion of being complicit in this scandal*," the announcer said.

"What scandal are they talking about?" I asked McKenzie.

"I told you not to listen to them," she admonished. "Wait for your brother to call you. He should be able to do that in a few minutes."

"McKenzie," I barked. "What are they talking about? Was Quentin cheating? Was the whole team doing it?"

"Fi, I don't know what all is going on," she said. "All I know is that he texted me and told me to call you and tell you not to watch the news."

"I'm watching the game," I said. "They're talking about it right now. What's going on?"

"Shit," she said. "He didn't want you to find out this way."

"I don't even know what's going on," I said.

"They're saying that there was some kind of device in the stadium," she said. "It was being used to steal signs from the catcher of opposing teams, then relayed to the dugout before being sent to the coaches on the field to tell the batter what was coming."

"Holy shit," I said. "What the actual fuck?"

"Exactly," she replied. "This is why Quentin didn't want you to find out through the news or something. He wanted to explain what was happening, which isn't what they're saying. There was more to it than what is being reported, but I don't know all the details."

"How long has this been going on?" I asked.

"Quentin can explain everything," she said.

My phone beeped, and I pulled it from my ear to see that he was calling.

"He's calling right now," I said.

"Answer it," she replied, then disconnected the call.

"Quentin," I said when I switched to his call. "What the hell is going on?"

"Shit," he said. "I didn't want you to find out this way. I just got off the phone with Mom and Dad and they're pissed."

"I can understand why," I replied.

"It's not like that," he said.

"Really?" I asked. "Because, from what I'm hearing, you guys

237

were stealing signs and using some sort of something or other to do it. You know that's illegal, right?"

"Fi, listen to me," he said, his tone harsh.

"Go ahead," I said. "See if you can explain away your cheating, cause it's not looking so good for you, Quentin."

"I didn't know," he said, and it was so quiet I almost missed it.

"How could you not?"

"None of the players did," he said. "The coaches were using some camera thing to watch the signs being thrown down by the catcher, then they would relay it to the coach, who would then give us a sign. We just knew that we were playing better, hitting the ball better, knowing what was coming before they threw it."

"And you didn't suspect that something was going on?"

"No," he said, and I sort of believed him.

My brother was nothing if not an honest guy. He'd always been good at picking up things, so the fact that he didn't know this was going on was really baffling to me.

"Look," he continued. "I know it looks bad. Trust me, I do. But we didn't know what was going on. At least I didn't."

"I'm not sure I can believe you," I replied.

"Come on, Fi," he said. "You know me. This isn't something I would do."

"But you did," I replied.

I heard him sigh, and I knew he was resigned to the fact that I knew he'd screwed up and I wasn't gonna let him get away with this bullshit of "he didn't know," because they had to have known. There was no way they couldn't know.

"What happens now?" I asked.

"We get a review," he said. "The MLBPA is looking to see if they can do anything to help us, but it just sucks."

"You did that little fuck around and find out, didn't you?"

"Yeah," he said. "We're all kinds of fucked right now."

"I'm sorry you're hurting," I said. "Really, I am. But I have no sympathy as to what you have to deal with. You all knew what would happen. It's one thing to steal signs when you're on base, but this is not that. This is willfully doing something that is against every rule of the game. How long has this been going on?"

He was quiet, which made me mad more than anything else.

"Quentin," I barked. "How long?"

"Couple years," he said, and I could hear the defeat in his voice.

"A couple of years?" I asked. "So, that means your World Series wins were won by cheating?"

"I swear I didn't know," he said.

"Bullshit," I said. "There's no way you didn't know. How the hell did you think you were able to hit better at home than on the road?"

"Fi, listen," he said.

"No," I replied. "I don't even know what to do with you right now. I'm so mad I could punch you in the face. This is against everything we learned growing up. You work hard, you play your best, and if you're good enough, you get the rewards. Instead, you're out there cheating and stealing championships. I'm ashamed of you."

"Fi, please," he tried again.

"I can't talk to you right now," I said. "I'll call McKenzie when I get a chance, but I'm not talking to you for a while."

I disconnected the call and tossed my phone on the coffee table, flopping down on the couch with a sigh. What was he thinking? He knew this was wrong, knew it would get caught, and it would screw his whole career up. Honestly, they may ban them from baseball like they did the Black Sox back in the day. The thing was, this was even worse. They stole the whole fucking championship.

All my life I'd looked up to my big brother as a shining example of how to play the game the right way and here he was, doing everything wrong. He knew how privileged he was to be able to play this game at a professional level. I'd begged and pleaded to get onto boys' teams throughout my life, and I'd done well until I reached high school. Then, I was relegated to the women's teams. Not that it wasn't a good thing to play on those teams, it's just that guys got to go pro, make big bucks, become stars, while women were left on the sidelines.

Things were beginning to get better, especially since women had fought hard to get to be professionals wherever they could, but it was still a long way from how it should be. Basketball had been pro for a few years now, but the rest of the sports were either relegated to what amounted to fluff play or were simply not allowed to go beyond college. There was the option of the Olympics, but that field was so saturated, especially since it was the only avenue for any type of pay.

The fact that my brother potentially threw away this opportunity was mind blowing. Like, he had the chance to do something I've wanted to do as well, but here he was, throwing it all away. I swear, the next time I saw him, I *was* gonna punch him. I really wanted to talk this out but wasn't sure who to call. Beckett came to mind, but I didn't want to do that right now. We were just starting to get things actually figured out, and I didn't want to derail that with my insanity.

"Fuck," I grumbled, then got up and headed to my bedroom.

I needed a shower and to get ready for the week. Maybe I could wash the thoughts out of my head.

CHAPTER FORTY-SIX

*B*eckett...

"*...hits it to the gap and Bridge comes home for another run,*" the announcer was saying on the radio as I drove back to my place. "*This just in,*" he continued. "*It seems the entire Houston Dragons team is now under suspicion for stealing signs.*"

"*That has been done throughout the ages,*" the other announcer said.

"*It appears they have been using some type of device to zoom in to the signs opposing catchers give, then relaying it to the batter,*" the first man replied.

"*Wait, what?*" the second guy asked. "*As in, they are using technology to gain an advantage?*"

"*Exactly,*" the first guy said.

"I fucking knew it," I shouted to myself.

"*Turns out it's been going on for at least the last two seasons,*" the first guy continued.

Instead of heading home, I detoured to drive to the stadium. I knew that there were going to be things we, as players, were going to want to hash out, and I wanted to be part of that conversation. The game faded into background noise as I thought about being in Houston just a couple weeks earlier and knowing that something was going on. Guess my suspicions had been validated, and I wanted to fucking celebrate the fact that they were going down.

Then I thought about how great it would be to rub it into Quentin's face that he was a fucking cheater. Thinking of him, though, made me think about Ophelia. I wondered whether she knew.

"Hey, Siri," I said to my phone. "Dial Miss Belinsky."

"*Dialing Miss Belinsky*," my phone replied, then I heard it ringing.

"*Hey, you've reached Fi*," her voice said, coming from my phone. "*Leave me a message, or better yet, send me a text.*"

I punched the disconnect before the tone could sound. This was not something that I wanted to leave a message about. She'd see I called and would hopefully call me back. By the time I got close to the stadium, they'd already cordoned off all the entrances and made it all one way out of the ballpark. I found a place to park that wasn't too far from the stadium and hoped I could get there without a million people recognizing me. I'd had enough press coverage, especially with my walking off the field the week before, that I worried someone would, and that it wouldn't be a pleasant experience.

I grabbed my pass to get into the stadium on the down low and headed out, hoping to get there before the game was actually over so I didn't have as many obstacles to contend with. Unfortunately, though, I was late enough that I was going against the flow of people who were leaving the ballpark. At least they seemed to be in a good mood from the team's win.

By the time I reached the stadium, the crowd had thinned, so I was able to get into the back entrance and to the clubhouse without many issues. Once I walked in, though, the place was already in chaos. There were a handful of reporters talking to some of the players, but it was clear that no one was going to be saying anything about the Houston team, or their decision to cheat. It took a while, but finally, all the reporters had been kicked out of the room and it was just the players and coaches.

"We all know what we've heard," Coach Johnson said. "What we don't know are any of the actual facts. Until those come out, our answer to any questions about this situation is no comment or something of the like. We don't talk about it, period."

"What *is* happening with it?" Decker asked.

"That's an unknown," the coach said. "Right now, it's in the hands of the league. The cameras or whatever have been disabled, and the powers that be have said that no electronic devices can be used within the dugout. No cell phones, no iPads, nothing. We're completely without them. We also can't have anything that is a live feed of any kind going on in the clubhouse during the game."

"How can we challenge a call?" I asked.

"Glad you could make it, Beckett," Coach said. "Those things are allowed, but they're only allowed specifically in one designated area, and the only time we can connect with the person in that area are immediately after the play, and for only a short amount of time. They know these are things we still need, but everything else is shut down."

"What do you think the outcome will be?" Bridge asked.

"No clue," Coach said. "Decisions will be made once we have all the information. Right now, they are on watch, and anything they do will be scrutinized heavily."

"How long has this been going on?" Huffman asked. "Like, did they steal the World Series?"

"Not an answer I have," Coach said. "Indications are that it has been going on for a while. Some of the players have been talking, and that's not gonna end well for them. But for now, we're just stuck with waiting. When I have more information, I'll be calling another meeting. I just wished this hadn't broken in the middle of our game. Made it a little hard to ensure that we were all on the same page, but I think you guys did well without having any advanced warning of it."

"I just told it like it was," Decker said. "I don't know anything, so I can't answer your questions about it."

"And that's gonna be the company line going forward," Coach said. "You guys are gonna get peppered with questions about this on the regular. You just need to keep to the fact that it is an ongoing investigation, and we are waiting for all the facts to come out and for the league to make a decision on any disciplinary action that may be taken.

When asked your opinion, you can say you don't like cheating, but do *not* say that you knew they were doing it, that you blame them, or anything like that. A non-answer is the best answer."

"But we knew," I said.

"Yeah," Bridge added, and a couple of the other players did so as well.

"You suspected," Coach said. "But even that is more than we want to be spread out there. In fact, Beckett," he continued. "Your questions about it, and the way you were looking at their stadium helped to break this open, so thank you. For now, though, we don't comment."

We all stood, or sat around, waiting to see if there was anything else that needed to be said. After quite a while, the coach finally dismissed us to head home.

"Hey, Decker," I said, walking up to the man. "Can you give me a lift to my car?"

"Sure," he said. "Why didn't you park here?"

"Didn't get here until after the game," I explained. "Couldn't get to the stadium in my car, so had to do a car lot down the way."

"Makes sense," he said, picking up his bag.

We walked out of the clubhouse and down toward the parking area where players and team staff parked. It was a quiet walk with all of us, no one really knowing what to say, and not wanting to voice anything out loud in case someone was listening. We climbed into Decker's truck and headed out to my car.

"Where have you been?" he asked once we were in the enclosed space.

"Had a few things I had to work out," I replied, trying to be as vague as possible.

"This from what happened last week?"

"Yeah," I replied. "But I'm ready to go once I'm off the IL. I'm flying out with you guys on Wednesday to play in the game on Friday."

"Good to know," he said as he eased us to the curb near the parking garage I'd parked in.

"Thanks for the lift," I said before getting out.

"Anytime," he replied. "See you soon."

"Soon," I said, then shut the door.

My phone was vibrating when I walked into the garage, so I pulled it out of my pocket and answered it.

"Hello," I said.

"Hey, you called," Fi replied.

"I did," I said. "Have you seen the news?"

"About the Dragons?" she asked. "Yeah. I've talked to my brother, too."

"I knew it was coming," I said.

"Why didn't you tell me?"

"No, not that," I explained. "I knew they were cheating. I just didn't know how."

"Still, why didn't you tell me?"

"Because I didn't want to accuse your brother without proof," I said. "I called as soon as I found out because I didn't want you to find out by seeing it on television."

"I did," she said. "McKenzie called to warn me, but I'd already seen it. She said that Quentin was gonna call me and to wait for his call before I made up my mind."

"Now that you've talked to him, what do you think?"

"I don't know," she confessed. "It's so not like him to do this, but if they have proof, which it sounds like they do, then he's guilty."

"Did he tell you how they were doing it?" I asked.

"We didn't get into the specifics," she replied. "I didn't want to know too much. Honestly, all of it is too much, though."

"Yeah," I agreed. "I had respect for your brother up until this point. Now, I'm not so sure what to think."

"I'm the same way," she said. "How did you find out?"

"Heard it on the radio when I was heading home," I said. "I made a detour to the stadium and Coach told us that our official response to any questions about this is no comment, so I guess I don't know much more than you."

"I know my parents are pissed," she said. "He called them before he called me, but we didn't talk about what they said. I just told him how disappointed I was that he would do that. I mean, we've been fans of the game for years and there is no way we would do that without being coerced. At least, I didn't think so. It's like PEDs, we don't do them and don't condone people who do. It's just another form of cheating."

"True," I said, because what else could I say. "You doing okay?"

"Not really," she said. "I just don't even know what to think right now."

"If you need me, let me know," I said. "Not sure what I can do, but I'm here."

"Thanks," she replied. "I appreciate that."

"No problem," I said.

"I gotta get to bed," she said. "Tomorrow is gonna suck, but it is what it is."

"Sleep well," I said.

"Thanks," she replied, then disconnected the call.

Tomorrow was already gonna be a shitshow, with trying to get in to see some head shrinker, but to add this on top of it all was almost too much. Hopefully I'd be able to get a good nights sleep as well, but I highly doubted it.

CHAPTER FORTY-SEVEN

*F*i...

"Sleep well," he said.

"Thanks," I replied, then disconnected the call.

I would try to sleep, but whether it would come was another question. I had already changed into my pajamas and was actually sitting in bed when I had called Beckett, but it felt lonely. I'd been on my own since I left for college. Sure, I went home for summers and breaks and stuff, but for the most part, I was a bonified adult with all the adulting things that went along with it. Now, though, I really missed having someone just down the hall to talk to until all hours of the morning. I knew I couldn't call McKenzie because she was likely consoling Quentin, and it was way later there than it was here, so I just settled down to try to shut my brain off.

At some point I must have slept, because when my alarm went off it woke me up. The thing I didn't do was sleep well. No, on the contrary, I slept in fits and starts, tossing and turning most of the night, and felt like death warmed over when I looked at my phone to see it was actually later than when I normally got up. Thankfully, I'd showered the night before, so all I had to do was throw some clothes on and get out the door.

The traffic was bad, worse than normal, even for a Monday morning, and by the time I landed at my desk, it was a couple of minutes past eight.

"Late this morning, aren't we," Carol said, her voice like nails on a chalkboard.

"Not your concern," Jean said, cutting whatever other cruel thing Carol was likely to say off mid-sentence.

Instead of arguing, the other woman nearly stomped off toward her desk, leaving me alone with Jean and my booting up computer.

"Long weekend?" she asked.

"I had a visitor," I said.

"Do tell," Jean urged.

"He showed up shortly after I got home on Saturday," I said. "He stayed until last night, but then something came up and we talked for a while after, too."

"Please tell me that the majority of your time was not spent talking," she said, laughing.

"No," I replied. "Although we did have a good discussion. I laid down some ground rules, and he admitted to some really shitty things he'd had to deal with. It's just that something broke last night in the sports world and I'm kind of all messed up about it."

"Really?" she asked.

"You didn't hear?" I asked.

"Not really a sports fan," she replied.

"My brother is on the Houston Dragons," I said.

"Oh, yeah," Jean said. "I forgot about that."

"Yeah," I said. "Anyway, his team was caught stealing signs."

"Sorry, I don't know what that means," she said.

"The catcher uses his fingers to tell the pitcher what to throw," I explained. "If you are up to bat, knowing what is coming is often helpful in getting hits. With a runner on second base, though, the catchers usually go through several signs to let the pitcher know what pitch to throw. Well, they had some kind of device or camera or something that was used to figure out what they were throwing, then telling the batter what was coming."

"Seems like that shouldn't be allowed," she said.

"It isn't," I replied. "They were caught, though, and there are all sorts of insanity going on with that. My best friend, who is living with my brother and dating him, called to try to make sure I didn't hear about it from anyone else, but they were too late. They announced it during the Cascades game, so I already knew."

"Are you mad or what?"

"Honestly, I'm disappointed," I said. "He knows that this isn't right, and yet he went along with it. Apparently for a couple of years, too, which is even worse. Like, how do you do that, for one thing, but then to just keep doing it? It doesn't make sense."

"Yeah, that's not cool," she said.

"Excuse me," Carol said, coming back over to where we were talking. "I think you guys should probably be working. It's bad enough that you were late, but now you're keeping everyone from doing their job."

"I'm sorry," Jean said in the most condescending tone I'd ever heard. "I didn't realize that you were promoted to our boss."

The pinched look on Carol's face was like a cat butt and I had to duck my head down to keep from laughing outright. She harrumphed and stomped off.

"Oh my God," I said. "How did you say that with a straight face?"

"I fucking hate her," she said and I was shocked.

Jean wasn't the type of person to swear, at least not that I'd noticed, so her outburst was a bit of a shock.

"What?" she said when she saw me looking at her.

"I didn't know you knew those words," I said, then laughed.

"We should probably get to work, though," she said, sitting down at her own desk behind the cubicle wall between us.

She was right, so I started opening the spreadsheets I'd been working on. The numbers soothed me, watching them do exactly as I expected. They didn't lie, didn't change, and were always constant, which is completely unlike the humans around me. By the time lunch rolled around, I was definitely ready for a break.

"You bring lunch?" Jean asked.

"Didn't have time," I replied. "I'm just gonna run across the street to grab a sandwich."

I was already up with my purse slung across my chest and on my way to the elevator when Carol stepped in front of me, causing me to almost fall.

"Where do you think you're going?"

"Lunch," I said, trying to step around her.

She continued to block my path, sneering at me as if I were something stuck to the bottom of her shoe.

"What do you want?" I asked after the third attempt to get around her.

"You should be working," she said. "You were late, and your work has been suffering lately, so you should just be at your desk getting your job done."

"Considering you're not my boss," I said. "And considering you have no authority over me, I think I'll be on my way. Please move."

I wasn't yelling, but I was firm and loud enough that it got the attention of a couple of the other workers in the office. They were all peering out of their little cubicle spaces at what was going on.

"You're new here, so you likely don't know how things work," she said. "But when I tell you to do something, you need to do it. Now, get back to your desk and do your work."

The finality of her voice, and the way she was almost mothering me into doing what I was told just kind of set me off.

"I may be new here, but I am not your subordinate," I retorted. "I work for Mr. Jackson, not you. I don't even work in the same group as you. If my work has been below standards, I would expect to have a conversation with my boss, not someone who thinks they're better than everyone else. Now, as I said, I am on my way to get some lunch. Please move."

I'd raised my voice even more than it was before, which drew an even bigger crowd of people craning their necks over the cubicle walls to see what was going on. It was like she was just realizing what was happening and looked around, seeing the faces of the others in the office looking at her. She stepped aside and I walked past her. I heard her mumble something under her breath but couldn't be bothered to even care what it was.

My phone buzzed as I stepped into the elevator, but I didn't want to look at it or anything until I was outside the building. Nothing good would come of nosey Carol getting into my business.

She is pissed.

Jean had my number and was one of the few people in the office who did.

Any fallout?

If there was, I'd deal with it when I got back.

She's off to complain to HR about being bullied. I've already sent an email stating what actually happened, so you're good.

God, I didn't even want to think about how getting sent to HR in the first few weeks of work would look on my review when it came up, but I couldn't be bothered right now. I was more than just a little hungry and was pushing into that hangry mode. I needed to get food. The office would work itself out or it wouldn't.

CHAPTER FORTY-EIGHT

*B*eckett...

"You must be Mr. Hennings," the woman said as I stepped into the shrink's office.

I'd gotten an email first thing that morning with a time to meet with a doctor, along with an address, and a phone number. Instead of trying to talk myself out of needing this, I went.

"That's me," I said.

"If you wouldn't mind filling this out, we'll get you in to see Dr. Cross," she said, handing me a clipboard with a couple of sheets of paper on it.

I sat in the waiting area and filled out the form with my name, address, all the usual stuff. The second page had questions about why I was in their office, what I wanted to get from these sessions, and whether I thought I would be needing ongoing treatment or just a onetime deal. I filled it out as best I could but had no idea whether I would need more than just one or two appointments.

"Mr. Hennings?" a man said from a door to the side of the reception desk.

"That's me," I said, standing up.

"I'm Dr. Cross," the doctor said. "Won't you come in?"

He stepped back, holding the door open, and I walked toward him.

"Should I leave this with her?" I asked, indicating the clipboard.

"No, I'll take it," he said, holding a hand out.

I handed the papers to him and walked into an office that had all the typical things I expected to see. A desk that was probably worth more than most people made in a month, a leather office chair behind it, and on the top were a few pictures of a nice family, along with all the other things usually found on desks.

"Have a seat," he said, and I looked at the chairs that were opposite the desk, as well as the couch and chair that seemed to be off to the side.

"Where?" I asked.

"Wherever you feel comfortable," he said. "This is just a space for us to talk, so there are no real rules, other than honesty."

"Okay," I said, sitting in one of the chairs by the desk.

He sat behind the desk, but must have thought better of it because he asked me, "Are you good with me sitting here? Or would you prefer I sit in that chair?"

He indicated the other chair that was next to me.

"There is fine," I said.

"Great," he replied, then looked at the papers I'd filled out. "Looks like you recently lost your mom," he said after a bit.

"Yeah," I said. "No great loss, though."

"Why's that?" he asked.

It wasn't an accusation, more a curiosity, like he was fascinated with the fact that it wasn't a big deal that my mother died.

"We weren't close," was all I said.

It didn't seem to faze him that I'd said that. He read the rest of the forms, then set them aside, folding his hands in front of him on his desk.

"Do you mind telling me why you weren't close to your mother?"

"She was a bitch," I said, then realized what had come out of my mouth. "I mean—" I stumbled, but he cut me off.

"Your feelings about her are valid," he said. "Why did you call her a bitch?"

"I don't know if we have enough time to get into that," I said.

"Whatever we don't deal with today can be discussed in the future," he said. "I can't help you if you don't let me in. What was it about her that made you feel the way you do?"

"She was neglectful," I began, then thought more about it. "She was worse than that, though. When I was little, I was basically raised in daycare. I saw her very infrequently, but she was working so much. I mean, she kind of had to since my sperm donor bounced the first chance he got. She had at least two jobs all the time, and when she wasn't working, she was drinking and screwing anything with a dick."

He listened to me, didn't interrupt me or stop my story or tell me the way I felt wasn't right. I didn't know that I'd ever had anyone just let me dump before. By the time my hour or whatever was up, I was exhausted, and the doc had listened to everything I had to say. Sometimes he'd ask a question to clarify something, but for the most part, he didn't stop my word vomit.

"I think we should plan to meet again," he said after he'd said our time was up.

"Probably should," I agreed.

"I'll have Jenna schedule an appointment that will work with your schedule," he said. "I know your work makes it tough, but we can do video or phone consults if you're not in town. Until then, though, I'd like for you to read this." He handed me a couple of sheets of paper that were printed back-to-back. "Don't think of it as homework, but more like something that might help you look at things with new eyes. You can't change who your parents are, but maybe this will give you a way to look at them in a different way."

"Okay," I said, unsure whether I really wanted to see my mother any other way than the person she was.

"I know the saying is that when people show you who they are, you should believe them," he said. "And while that is true, you still should be able to look at them in a way that makes sense to you. I'm not defending your mom or anything she did. I want to make that very clear. I just want for you to find a way to move forward in a healthy way, a way that will make you a better person than you are now. That's what we should all strive to do. Be better. And when we know better, we do better."

What he was saying made sense, but he didn't know my mom. He'd never met her or had to deal with her. Maybe, after I shared everything with him, he'd see her like I did.

"I'll make an appointment," I said, standing up.

He stood and held his hand out to me. I shook it and he said, "Thank you for trusting me with your issues. I hope we can help you find a peaceful place."

"Thanks," I said, then turned and walked out the door.

I made an appointment with the receptionist, then headed out of the office and to my car. The trip to the stadium was slow, but I made it and was able to park in the player parking area. Walking into the building, I saw a few others were already here.

"Hey, Hennings," Bridge said as I walked into the clubhouse. "How did the appointment go?"

"How'd you know?"

"Coach told me," he said. "You don't mind, right?"

"I mean…" I paused, looking around.

"No one else is around," he said. "Otherwise, I wouldn't have said anything."

"Thanks, man," I said. "Meeting went pretty well. Got another one scheduled, too."

"Good," he said. "Therapy isn't sexy, but it's important. Especially with shit that's this important. You need someone to talk it out with outside of the sessions, hit me up."

"Really?"

"Yeah, man," he said. "I know we haven't exactly been on the best terms, but it seems like you've been going through shit. I know that can mess with your head. Not something you need when you're on the field. Been there, done that, got the damn tee shirt."

"How do you keep it out of your head while you're out there?"

"I have no idea how everyone does it, but I just put it off until later," he explained. "You kind of have to compartmentalize it, shove it into a drawer and let it go until you have time to deal with it. At least, that's what I do."

"You make it sound so easy," I said.

"It isn't," he replied. "But you learn how to do it. Some days are easier than others, but once you get into the practice, you just figure it out. It's like when you have a bad at bat. The next time you're up, you can't think about it because it'll just screw this one up."

"That actually makes a lot of sense," I said.

"It took me a while to figure it out, honestly," he said. "But, once I did, it was like a whole new way of thinking came around. I had always been good at forgetting the last at bat, the last error, the last game. My therapist suggested I look at my grief the same way."

"Honestly, I hadn't even thought of it," I said. "But now that you say it, everything makes sense. I have been doing it all along, except I had never been dealing with it. Now that it's kind of out there in the world, I have to really deal with it and come to terms with my life and what it has consisted of up to this point."

"It's work, don't get me wrong," he said. "But it's work worth doing."

"I'm seeing that to be true," I said.

"Good," he said. "Now, let's get out there and get warmed up."

"I'm still technically on the IL," I said.

"Doesn't mean you can't do the work," he said. "Call it conditioning for your return."

"Good call," I said, grabbing a pair of workout pants and a jersey and changing quickly.

The short conversation, and working out with Bridge, really helped me to clear my mind and focus on what needed to happen right here and now. It was also helpful to know that I could work out the other stuff in a safe space with the therapist. Maybe I wasn't as much of a fuckup as I thought.

CHAPTER FORTY-NINE

F i...

When I got back to the office, there was an email waiting for me from HR. I opened it, hoping for the best but expecting the worst.

> *Ms. Belinsky,*
> *I would appreciate it if you would come to my office upon your return from your scheduled lunch break.*
> *Sincerely,*
> *Lisa Franks*
> *HR Coordinator*

Well, that wasn't horrible, but it still left me uneasy. Nothing said what it was for. Nothing indicated whether I'd be there by myself or what.

"You okay?" Jean asked when she came back to her desk.

"HR wants to see me," I said.

"I'm coming with you," she said, and her tone brooked no argument.

I took a deep breath, then stood up, and we walked across the office space to one of the few actual offices on the floor.

"Ms. Franks?" I asked.

"Ms. Belinsky?" she asked back.

"Yes," I said.

"Please, come in," she said. When Jean followed me, she said, "I'm afraid this is a one-on-one."

"I'm a witness," Jean said. "I sent the email, and I would feel better if I was here to ensure that the truth was exposed."

"Exposed?" the HR woman asked.

"Yes," Jean replied, her confidence boosting my own.

"Fine," she said, and Jean stepped into the office, closing the door behind her.

We sat on the two chairs opposite the desk and waited for the HR woman to begin.

"I assume you know what this is about," she said.

"I assume it's Carol trying to cause trouble," Jean replied. "She's pretty much always doing that."

"Ms. Foss said she has been being bullied by Ms. Belinsky," Lisa said. "Indicated that it has been going on from the moment she started."

I sat and waited for more information. First rule, my daddy always said, was let them hang themselves.

"No response?"

"Her saying she is being bullied isn't anything I can respond to," I said. "Did she give specifics?"

"She said you called her stupid," Lisa said. "That you would regularly mention that she is less intelligent than you. You even questioned her sexuality and gender."

"Wow," Jean said, drawing the word out. "She has gone off the deep end with this one. Is she on a smear campaign or something?"

"These are serious accusations," Lisa said.

"And that's just what they are," Jean retorted. "Accusations. Let me tell you the interactions that I have witnessed firsthand. Today, as Fi was heading to lunch, Carol blocked her path and told her that she was not allowed to leave the building and had to keep working through her lunch. Carol is not our supervisor and has no reason to tell us how we should work, or whether a break is necessary. Secondly, we are ahead of our numbers and Mr. Jackson has said many times in the last couple of weeks that Fi seems to be fitting in nicely and doing her work above his expectations.

"Last Friday, Carol told us we shouldn't make plans for the weekend because we were expected to work," she continued. "I personally spoke with Mr. Jackson, and he said that there was no reason for us to have to work over the weekend and to enjoy it. Earlier, Carol tried to start some rumors about a celebrity, and when Fi questioned her knowledge of the actual case, Carol got upset because we didn't believe everything she said. She is nothing more than a gossip, and she tends to bring the morale of the entire floor down."

I hadn't expected such a well thought out and thorough response, but apparently Jean was at her limit, and was all out of fucks to give. I would have stood up and applauded if the situation had been different.

"Well," Lisa said, obviously having underestimated what was actually going on. "Do you have anything else to add?" she asked me.

"While this is my first office job, I am in no way new to cooperative work," I said. "I played sports all throughout school, and you have to work as a team. We played in the little league World Series, as well as going to the college championships. I know how to work well with others. I have been polite to Carol and have never once threatened or challenged her in any way other than to point out that I did not work for her, which is true. She has challenged me, threatened me, and berated me on multiple occasions, though. The most recent one was earlier today when she attempted to block my access to the elevators to leave and pick my lunch up."

"I see," she said. "You have never said anything to her about her personal life?"

"I know nothing about her personal life," I said. "And it doesn't even matter. We work on the same floor for the same company, but that is where our relationship begins and ends. I do not see her outside of work, do not socialize with her, and have no need to. We are not really at the same stage of life. She has been working here for a while, and I am just starting. Our paths simply cross because of the proximity of our working space, nothing else."

"All right," she said.

"By the way," I added. "Almost all of her interactions with me have been hostile, with her being the aggressor."

"Did you want to make a complaint?"

"I just want to be left alone to do my work," I said. "That's what I'm here for. I get paid to do my job, and if there is an issue with my job, my direct supervisor should schedule a meeting to discuss what I am doing wrong so that I can improve."

"You sound like you have your head screwed on straight," she said.

"I feel like I do," I confirmed. "I just don't understand what her problem is."

"She's been like this as long as I've been here," Jean said, and I had honestly forgotten she was there.

"Really?" Lisa asked.

"Oh yeah," she confirmed. "I think she has that long-timers feeling where she is invincible or something."

"Interesting," Lisa said, and it made me think there was more that she knew than what she was letting on. "Well," she added after a moment. "If there is anything else you can think of, please let me know. Otherwise, I think you can go back to your desks and finish out your day. Thank you for meeting with me."

"Thanks," I said.

"If you need anything from us, let us know as well," Jean said as she stood. "And if you need any additional information about what happened earlier today, please talk with those who have cubicles around the elevator. They were all very aware of what happened and can confirm that Ms. Belinsky was not in any way the aggressor in that altercation."

"Thank you both," Lisa said.

We walked back to our desks, and I had that sinking feeling that I was being watched. You know the one where it's like someone's eyes are boring into the back of your head, and you just feel it. I didn't want to look around, because I was sure there were several people looking at me, what with me coming out of the HR office, but my guess is it was Carol, hoping to see me come out of there crying or something. Well, I straightened my back, held my head up high, and walked straight to my desk and got back to work. She was not going to deter me from doing my best. I needed this job, and I wasn't gonna let some woman who had an ax to grind with everyone to push me out of it.

CHAPTER FIFTY

*B*eckett...
　　The guys gave me space in the dugout during the game, but it didn't take long for them to realize that I was back, and likely better than I had been all year. Coach had said I could ride pine until we headed out on our road trip after Wednesday's game. It was actually really great to sit in the dugout and watch the game from that vantage point. Things felt clearer, like I was seeing the game as something new and not the same old same old that I'd been doing for a few years.

"You coming with us?" Huffman asked when he sat next to me after he'd hit a home run in the bottom of the fifth.

"Yup," I replied. "Itching to get back on the field."

"Good," he said, slapping me on my shoulder. "Bridge is good enough, but we need you in there, controlling the middle of the field."

"Oh yeah?" I asked.

"But don't tell him I told you that," he said. "I'll deny it to my dying day."

He laughed and got up, walking further down the bench to talk to someone else. By the end of the night, I think every teammate had come up to me and said something encouraging, which honestly surprised me. None of them had necessarily been standoffish per se, but the fact that so many came up to me and had a nice thing to say, even if it was just that they were glad to see me, was really a boost to my morale. Whatever it was that caused this change, I liked it, and would do my best to not give them a reason to feel off about me again.

"See you tomorrow?" Bridge asked when I was heading out.

"You can count on it," I said.

"Meet me early and we'll run through some drills," he said.

It wasn't a question, but didn't feel like a demand, either. It was an offer, and one I would take gladly.

"I'll be here," I said.

At the beginning of last season, he'd tried to help me out, but my own mind got in the way of what was best for me. I wouldn't make that same mistake twice. Jonathan Bridge had been with the team for years, and if he was willing to work with me, give me his knowledge and show me how to have that same longevity, I was all for it. The walk to my car was longer than I remembered it being earlier in the year. Maybe it was because I wasn't doing what I had normally done, which was analyze every play in my head, figure out what I did wrong, and see what the other guys did that screwed me up. Seeing the way they came to me and welcomed me back, even after the shit I'd put them through, was really eye-opening, and I didn't want to disappoint any of them.

So, tomorrow I'd be up early, get myself to the field with plenty of time to work out with J, and still stay until the end of the game in order to congratulate my team on what would hopefully be another win. I felt good about what was going on with me, and where I was heading. I sent a text to Fi as soon as I got home, figuring I wouldn't hear back from her until the next morning, which was totally fine. When I got home, I put my shit away and went to bed. I was embarking on a new life, and it felt really good.

"Before we head out to the field, we have a few things we need to talk over," Coach said as we sat around the clubhouse. "First, we do not throw anyone under the bus. No other player, team, coach, anyone. We don't know who started it, who set it up, where the instructions came from. What we know is that Houston is a good team, and that whatever happens is up to the league, the commissioner, and the MLBPA. We're not in charge of the rules. They are not within our prevue of our jobs, and we have no other comment. When a reporter asks your opinion, which they will, the standard answer is that we are waiting for the results of the investigation. Are we clear?"

"Yeah," I said, along with a mumbling of other affirmative responses from the rest of my teammates.

"When will the investigation be over?" Decker asked.

"We don't know," the coach responded. "It's gonna take some time, and there will probably be fines and repercussions coming down from all the higher-ups."

"So, we really don't know anything," I said.

"Unfortunately, everyone involved with this has been tight lipped," Coach said. "No news is coming out from anyone, other than it is under investigation."

"I fucking hate cheaters," Huffman said.

"We all do," Bridge responded. "It's not what we stand for, and the players who were complicit in this need to have a serious 'come to Jesus' moment. From the time I was in little league, I knew the rules and was taught to play by them. If you can't do that, you don't belong in the game."

"Exactly," Decker agreed.

"For now," Coach said, waiting for us all to look his direction. "The status of our answers is that we are waiting for the league to make a decision. I know you all want to blast the cheating, which I get, but we need to let the higher-ups do their duty and figure out where it started and who knew what."

"More like cover their asses," I mumbled, not loud enough for anyone other than the couple of guys sitting right next to me to hear.

Decker looked over at me and nodded, agreeing with my sentiment.

"All right," Coach said, clapping his hands together. "Let's get out there and get ready to take game two."

He walked off, leaving us to deal with our own emotions and what-ever. Honestly, I was glad I wasn't gonna be playing for the next couple of days. It gave me a way to not be in the line of fire when the questions started being thrown around. One by one, the rest of the team started grabbing their gear to head out for batting practice. I picked up my glove and walked in that direction as well. Might as well work out what I could since I wasn't gonna get a chance to do much else for the next couple of days.

The game was tight until the bottom of the eighth when Huffman knocked one out of the park and gave us a two-to-nothing lead. Top of the ninth was handled without incident by Strawberry, and we were done and heading into the clubhouse. I hung around in the dugout, waiting to see what the reporters would ask the stars of the game.

"We have no comment," Huffman said when Jenn, one of the local sports announcers, asked him about the situation. "The league is aware and investigating. I don't wanna say anything that would harm that."

Of all the people to ask, he was so not the person. Ask him about his hits, ask about fielding, hell, ask him about coffee, and you'll get a great interview. But ask him something you know he's not gonna talk about and you get nothing. Just a deadpan answer of "no comment." When I was cleaned up and dressed to leave, he came up to me.

"You still hooking up with their short stop's sister?" he asked.

"Yeah, why?"

"What's he saying about this?"

"I haven't talked to him," I said. "His sister isn't really sure what's going on, either, as far as I can tell."

"Damn," he muttered. "I was hoping you'd know what the hell they were thinking. Like, do they seriously have their heads shoved so far up their asses that they thought this would fly?"

"My guess is it was management," I said. "And I'm not talking Tricky Dick, their coach. No, I think it was someone in the front office that set this all up. The managers and players were just supposed to go along with it. Hell, maybe the players didn't even know."

"You think?"

"I don't know," I said. "If I was on the team, and someone started this shit, I'd call them out on it and refuse to play. I'd also go to the media or someone and make them aware as soon as I knew."

"You'd risk your contract for that?"

"You wouldn't?"

"You know what," he said after a minute. "I think I would. Maybe leak something to the press and let them get on it. Wonder exactly what happened there, though."

"No clue," I said. "I know that it wouldn't surprise me if they were all in on it and just hoped they wouldn't get caught."

"We may never know," he said, then thumped my shoulder and headed to the parking lot.

I followed, but at a slower pace. I really wanted to see Fi before we left, but I didn't want to screw her schedule up. I shot a text and let her know I wanted to see her, asking her to either text or call me when she had a minute. This was gonna be a long road trip, especially since I wasn't gonna get laid the whole time. I didn't want to do that to her, which was a really odd thing to be thinking, but there it was.

CHAPTER FIFTY-ONE

*F*i...

I woke up Wednesday morning to a text from Beckett asking me to call him. Unfortunately, I was late getting up, again, and didn't even have time to shower, let alone make a phone call. I shot a quick text letting him know I could call him on my lunch break. Thankfully, traffic was light, and I made it to the office without incident. I didn't want to deal with Carol and her bullshit reasons to harp on me. What she had against me, though, was anyone's guess.

"Hey," Jean said when I got to my desk. "Check your email. Things are wild."

"What's up?" I asked, but she just pointed to my computer.

Booting the machine up, I tucked my purse into my drawer and logged on once it was alive. I had a handful of emails waiting when I opened the program, but I knew exactly which one she was talking about when I saw it. It was from HR and it looked official. Honestly, though, I wondered why Jean knew what was in my emails.

Staff,

It is with great sadness that we announce the retirement of our wonderful employee, Carol Foss. She has decided to retire

early. We will miss her laughter and kindness but wish her the
best of luck in this next chapter of her life.
Sincerely,
Lisa Franks
HR Coordinator

"You see it?" Jean asked, damn near giddy.

"I did," I said. "I kind of feel bad for her, though."

"Why?"

"She's just so stuck in her own need to be right that she ended up losing," I said.

"You really are a great person," Jean replied. "I don't know anyone else in the office who will actually miss her, but here you are, thinking she's gonna get you into trouble, feeling sorry for her."

"I mean," I said, shrugging. "I guess I just don't want to cause waves."

"Too nice," she said, shaking her head and sitting back down.

I wasn't being too nice, though. I had just told the truth of what happened, and the company decided that she was too big a risk. I'd heard about how HR was all about protecting the company, and it wasn't a help for the regular Joe, but I think this was one of those times where the regular Carol screwed herself. She pushed and pushed at me because I was new, and when I didn't bend to her will, she went straight for the throat, hoping her tenure at the company would save her. She fucked around and found out that she was not so irreplaceable as she thought she was.

While I felt bad that she had to go, I couldn't completely feel guilty about the manner of her leaving. She hadn't been at her desk when I came in, but I never really bothered to look for her. Guess I had just missed the fact that she had been completely gone—no goodbye party, no pleasantries of happy retirement, no gold watch, just a 'there's the door' send off with her box of things from the office.

I'd tried to reach Beckett by phone when I was at lunch, but it went straight to voicemail. Checking the schedule online, they were playing a day game, then heading out to their next stop, which was in Houston.

Maybe my brother would let me crash at his and McKenzie's place if I flew out on Friday night. I shot a text off to her to ask and see if it was possible before heading back into the office.

At around four or so my phone rang, and it was him.

"Hello," I said when I answered.

With Carol gone, I felt a bit more at ease answering at my desk.

"Hey," he said. "I miss you."

"Oh yeah?"

"Definitely," he said. "I'm on the bus heading to the airport right now, so that means it's gonna be more than a week until I'm back."

"I saw that," I said. "You're going to Houston first, though, right?"

"We are," he said. "Gonna be interesting to say the least. Wonder how much insanity the press will bring."

"Hopefully not a lot," I replied. "I gotta go, though. I'm still at work."

"Okay," he said. "If you're cool with it, I'll call you when I land."

"That works," I said. "About what time do you think it'll be?"

"Probably won't get to the hotel until about nine here," he said. "So, not terribly late."

"Yeah," I said. "That's not too late. Although, I am gonna have to make it a short call. It's been a long week and I'm beat."

"Wanna take a rain check?"

"Nah," I said. "But I do have to go."

"Okay," he said. "Talk to you soon."

"Sure thing," I replied, then disconnected the call.

I finished up my work and was heading home when McKenzie called. I answered it with my blue tooth system in the car.

"Hey, girl," I said.

"What's up?" she asked.

"Thinking of a weekend trip," I said. "You up for some girl time?"

"Honestly, it's been a nightmare here," she said. "I could definitely use the distraction, but I'm not sure what Quentin has going."

"I would fly in late on Friday night and have to head home by Sunday," I said. "Check with him and see if it'll work. I can either stay with you or at a hotel, whatever is easier."

"I'll check and let you know tonight," she said. "We can even go to the game on Saturday."

"That's what I was thinking," I said.

"Cool," she said. "Talk to you soon."

"Hopefully see you soon," I replied.

She disconnected the call and the rest of the drive home was filled with the sound of my favorite podcasters talking about the latest case they were covering.

CHAPTER FIFTY-TWO

*B*eckett...
With as much traveling as I'd done in the last couple of years, what with the minor league games as well as the majors, one would think I would be used to it and would handle it better, but I swear the flight to Houston was the longest in the history of long flights. We landed, and it took time to get to where we could disembark. Then the bus wasn't even there to take us to the hotel. Once at the hotel, there was a glitch in the system and they had to split us all up all over the hotel to get us accommodated. Normally, we had a couple of floors to ourselves, but not this time. I think there were like three other guys on my floor, and the rest were scattered around. It wasn't even the same hotel we'd been at the last time we were in town.

I got settled in my room, then went to call Fi, but my phone was dead for some reason. It was like a comedy of errors or something. I plugged the phone in and it wouldn't charge. I grabbed my key card and headed down the hall to ask Decker if he had an extra charger, or if I could at least charge it up a little bit for a call, but even his charger didn't work. Instead of getting mad, I decided to see if there was a cord in the gift shop. Sometimes hotels had them, and I was hopeful this one did.

"Shit," I said as I stepped to the gift shop only to find the gate down and it locked up. I walked up to the check-in desk and asked the guy there about it.

"They close at nine," he said. "They will be open again at nine tomorrow morning."

"Do you know if they have phone chargers?"

"I don't usually work when they're open, so have no idea," he said. "I'm sorry. You want to try my charger?"

"Sure," I said, taking the cord he offered.

I plugged it into the phone, and it didn't respond.

"Looks like your phone is dead," he said.

"It worked fine when I left Seattle," I complained. "Any chance there's a store around that is open that I could get a new one?"

"I'm afraid most of those places close at eight," he said. "Let me do a search and see what I can find for you. Who's your carrier?"

I told him who my phone plan was through and he started hunting. He seemed to be about my age, but he was a whiz with the computer, clicking and typing and shit so fast I couldn't keep up.

"Looks like there's a store just a few blocks away that will open at ten tomorrow morning," he said, looking hopeful.

"How far?" I asked. "I have a game I have to get to, so don't want to be going all over downtown Houston on a hunting trip."

"It's actually not super far, but we do have a shuttle that might be able to drop you there," he said. "Want me to schedule you on the bus for tomorrow morning?"

"Yeah," I said. "Probably should. Can you also set up a wake-up call for me for about nine?"

"Can do," he said. "What room?"

"Damn, I don't know," I said, pulling my keycard out of my pocket.

"Looks like it's room 624," he said after running my card through some machine. "What's your name, so I can make sure it's the right room?"

"Beckett Hennings," I said.

"Matches up," he said. "I've set up the call and have you on the shuttle that will leave at ten to head that direction. Anything else I can do for you?"

"Unless you know a magic way to get someone's phone number out of a dead phone, I can't think of anything else," I said.

"Damn, that sucks," he said.

"Yeah," I agreed. "Someone's expecting my call, and I'm just gonna disappoint her. Kind of what I've done a lot of, unfortunately."

"Hope you get it all figured out in the morning," he said.

"Me, too," I said.

I rode the elevator up to my floor and walked down the hall to my room. Somehow, I'd ended up with the room at the far end of the floor. Normally, I'd just do the stairs at that end of the hall, but I was not gonna do six flights, so a longer walk down the hall was what I had to do. I just hoped I would be able to get a new phone and call her tomorrow morning, or at least send her a text. If not, it'd just be one more thing I fucked up, and this was one that I didn't want to do. No, I wanted to ensure that I was doing the right thing by her, and breaking promises was not the way to go about it. Worst-case scenario, I would beg Belinsky to give me her number so I could call her. Maybe he'd be nice about it. After all, we did just bury the hatchet.

"LOOKS LIKE THERE WAS A SYSTEM FAILURE ON YOUR PHONE," THE GAL at the store said. "That means that all of your data is likely going to be lost unless you had a backup somewhere else."

"I thought everything went to some cloud or something," I said. "Like, I've never had an issue with everything just showing up on my new phone from the old one."

"Usually they do," she said. "Unfortunately, it looks like yours has been on the way out for a while and it just finally bit the dust. Older stuff will still show up, but anything you've added since the system started to fail will probably be lost. I'll see what I can do to recover it, but it might not work."

"Just do what you can," I said. "How long is this gonna take?"

"I should know in just a bit if it'll be recoverable," she said. "I'm gonna try to use the SIM card to get the data. I just want you to be prepared for it to not work."

"Story of my fucking life," I muttered and went to sit on one of the chairs they had scattered around the store.

With no phone to distract me, time slowed to a pace that nearly drove me mad. Finally, after either a few minutes or years, the gal came back with my phones.

"I was able to save some of the data, but not all of it," she said. "It's surprising that it actually saved any of it. Take a look and see if you have everything you need."

I took the phone and pulled up my contacts, but she wasn't there. The only thing I really wanted from the old phone was her number. I checked the text messages that transferred and there wasn't anything from her there, and nothing on the call log, either.

"Not everything," I said. "And not the thing I really wanted."

"I'm sorry," she said, and actually sounded sincere. "Here's a website you can go to that may be able to help you recover other data, but it isn't guaranteed."

"It's fine," I said. "I'll just have to figure it out. Thanks."

"No problem," she said. "Do you need anything else?"

"I think this is it," I said.

"Your receipts should email to you," she said. "If you have any other issues, please give us a call."

I walked out of the store with my old, dead phone in one pocket, and my new, yet not fully restored phone in the other. The guy at the counter the night before was right in that the store was only a couple of blocks from the hotel, so I opted to walk back. It was still early enough that it wasn't too unbearable with the heat, but I knew the game would be rough, and the harder one would be the day game we had scheduled in a couple of days.

When I got to the hotel, Decker was in the lobby, looking at something on his phone.

"Hey, Hennings," he said.

"Yeah?" I asked, walking up to him.

"You did bury the hatchet with Belinsky, right?"

"When I was off, yeah," I said. "Why?"

"Look at his Twitter feed," he said, turning his phone to me.

I scrolled through the posts and saw that he sent a tweet about his sister deserving to be treated better than trash, and that when he saw me, he was gonna let me know exactly how he felt.

"Fuck," I said.

"Yeah," Decker said. "This doesn't sound like him. Normally he's all about the team and his game, and doesn't usually post personal stuff."

"I mean, he's right," I said. "His sister is worth more than that. But my phone was dead, and you can vouch for me. I just got the new one, but her number didn't transfer over. Guess I've just fucked up one more time."

"Nah, man," he said. "It wasn't your fault. I'll be there to back you up."

"Thanks, man," I said. "I gotta go grab my gear. What time is the bus supposed to be here?"

"They're taking us to the stadium in half an hour," he said. "You've got time."

"Be back in a bit," I said, then walked to the elevator and took it up to my floor.

I grabbed my bag, straightened up the rest of my shit, and headed back down to the lobby. I just hoped that Belinsky would be kind and give me Fi's number. I really did owe her an apology, and I wanted to do it sooner rather than later.

CHAPTER FIFTY-THREE

F̧i... McKenzie had sent a text saying Quentin was fine with me crashing at their place over the weekend, and that he would be happy to see me. I was home and getting things set up for the weekend flight, packing a bag so it was all ready to go with me to work on Friday morning.

I was so distracted that I didn't even notice that it was almost eight and I hadn't heard from Beckett. I called his number, figuring he was just distracted, and it went directly to voicemail. Maybe they got in later than he thought, and he had gone straight to bed without calling. I was disappointed, but I could live with it.

When I had everything packed except the things I needed up until I left, I hit the sack, knowing the next couple of days were going to be rough. But having this trip ahead of me made it seem like it would be worth it. There was no text or voicemail when I got up the next morning, but figured he'd been busy, or wasn't up yet, so didn't think anything of it. I got up, showered, dressed, and headed out the door to my office with my packed lunch, figuring I'd hear from him at some point.

"You look chipper," Jean said when I sat down at my desk.

"Planned a trip to see my brother this weekend," I replied.

"Nice," she replied. "I know I should know, but where is he again?"

"Houston," I said. "I'm gonna stay with him and my best friend. They're living together. We'll go to the game on Saturday, too, which means I'll get to see him play."

"Will your boyfriend be there?"

"He's not my boyfriend," I said, then stopped and remembered. "Okay, maybe he is, but, yeah, he'll be there. The Cascades are playing the Dragons starting tonight."

"Then you better have a good time," she said, laughing. "And when you get back, you can give me all the details. You know I'm living vicariously through you, right?"

"You're ridiculous," I said. "My life isn't one that should be lived vicariously through. It's boring and ordinary."

"Except for the hot baseball players in your life who make it so much more than just ordinary," she said.

"Okay, fine," I said. "But I still think it's pretty boring."

"We'll have to agree to disagree," she said, then sat down at her desk and disappeared from my view.

I booted up my computer and got things going while I made my way to the break room to drop my lunch in the fridge and get some coffee. By the time I got back to my desk, my computer was all ready for me to log in. Before I began, I made another call to Beckett, hoping to catch him to let him know I was going to be heading down, and to find out where he was staying, but it went to his voicemail again. I sent a text to my brother asking him to ask Beckett to call me. My phone rang almost immediately.

"Hello?"

"Hey, sis," Quentin said. "What's up with the douche canoe?"

"What?" I asked. "I don't know what you're talking about."

"You asked me to have him call you," he said. "Can't you call him?"

"I tried," I explained. "The call just goes straight to voicemail, though. I figured you'd see him and be able to have him call me."

"First, I'm not his secretary," he said.

"I didn't mean—"

"Nah," he said, cutting me off. "I don't do errands for him. I don't take messages for him. If he can't man up and contact you on his own, he isn't worth your time. You need someone who will put you first, not someone who ignores you."

"I don't think—"

Again, he cut me off, saying, "He's a dick. You never should have hooked up with him because he isn't worth it. You deserve better."

"Quentin," I said. "You aren't even listening to me. He flew in late last night, so it was probably too late for him to get back in touch with me. Not a big deal. It's early morning now, so he probably isn't even up, which is also just fine. You need to calm down before you give yourself a heart attack. If you don't want to talk to him, that's fine. But don't be shitting on him when you don't know what you're talking about. I'm sorry I bothered you."

I hung up before he had a chance to respond.

"What was that all about?" Jean asked, popping her head over the wall between our cubicles.

"My brother being an asshole," I said. "He thinks he knows what's best for me but has never bothered to ask what I want."

"Sounds like my brother," she said. "Sticking his nose in where it doesn't belong."

"Exactly," I said. "I just asked that he have Beckett call me when he saw him at the stadium today. Instead of doing this favor for me, he tries to bash the guy without even knowing anything. Like, maybe his phone died. Maybe he's not up yet. There are a number of things that may cause him to not be able to call or text me. My brother just wants to see the bad in everyone."

"I'm sorry he's an asshole," she said.

"Yeah, me, too," I replied.

I spent the day doing my duties, entering payments into my spreadsheets, and logging all the invoices to be paid. I wasn't sure who printed the checks, or mailed them out, or any of that stuff. I just crunched the numbers and did my journal entries so that whoever was in charge of that piece could get it done timely.

The day drug on, and I was in my numbers so much that I simply took a quick break to go grab my lunch to eat at my desk. I ate in silence, perusing social media to see what was going on in the world. I'd forgotten all about my brother and his asshole ways and was almost ready to dive into my numbers again when I caught his rant on Twitter. He was going on and on about how people need to man up and take responsibility. I really wanted to call him out on it but decided to let it go and deal with it when I got down there.

CHAPTER FIFTY-FOUR

*B*eckett...

"What the fuck is wrong with you?" I asked when I saw Belinsky on the field.

"You," he replied, stepping up as if he was trying to scare me.

Sure, he was a good half a foot taller than me, and probably had about thirty pounds on me, but that hadn't stopped me from taking him down the last time I was here. Instead of cracking to his intimidation tactics, I pushed forward.

"You don't need to go airing out all my dirty laundry on Twitter," I said. "For your information, my phone became a brick on the flight down here. And because this town is such a shithole, I couldn't get a new one until this morning. When I did, not everything transferred over, including your sister's number. I was gonna ask you for it, but obviously you don't want her to be happy, so I'll just let you soak in your own shit and figure out another way to get her number. I have resources, too."

I turned around and walked away from him, ignoring everything he tried to hurl at me, which included some pretty shitty words. While I wouldn't get to play today, I intended to make up for it the next day. If things went the way I wanted, I'd be hitting a line drive off of Quentin

Belinsky's head. Probably wouldn't be that lucky, but it was fun to pretend.

Dropping down into the dugout, I headed back to the locker room. Maybe she'd called me and left me a message, or a text. One could only hope. Unfortunately, my phone was without any contact from her, so I still didn't have her number. I changed into my uniform pants and a shirt for watching the game from the dugout and headed back out. While I couldn't do anything on the field to help my team, I could support them from the bench, and I would do that.

We played well, paid attention to what they were doing both on the field and in their own dugout, watching for any additional cheating on their side, but it was quiet, and we ended up edging out a victory by one run. The guardian was on fire, throwing a perfect nine-pitch ninth inning to strike out the side and give us the victory. I was happy with how horribly Belinsky played, too. He'd gotten the golden sombrero, four strikeouts on twelve pitches, including the final out of the game. I couldn't ask for a better game for him.

I pulled my phone out of my bag in the clubhouse and saw that there were still no calls or texts from Fi, and I began to wonder if she was waiting for me. If she was, I was in trouble, because I couldn't call her. Hopefully, she'd figure it out and at least send me a text so I could let her know what happened with my phone. We climbed onto the bus and took the short ride back to the hotel. As I was walking in the door, my phone rang.

"Hello?"

"Beckett?" she asked.

"Oh, thank fuck," I said. "My phone actually died, and I didn't have your number anywhere but in my phone, so I couldn't call or text. I'm so sorry."

"I figured something like that happened," she said. "I asked my brother to have you call me, but I'm guessing he didn't give you the message."

"You would be correct," I said. "Hey, I'm just heading up to my room. If I lose you, it's because I'm in an elevator."

"No problem," she said as I stepped into the small box. "He wasn't really sounding like he was gonna tell you, so it doesn't surprise me. Oh, I saw you guys won tonight."

"We did," I said. "And your brother failed, which, not gonna lie, kind of made me happy."

"He deserves to have a crap game every once in a while," she said. "Especially when he's an asshole."

"Isn't he always?"

She laughed, but then the phone cut out.

"Shit," I muttered as I waited for the old box to get me to my floor.

When it finally rumbled to a stop, I stepped out and my phone was ringing again.

"Hey," I said when I answered it.

"Stay away from my sister," Quentin shouted into my ear.

"She's an adult and can choose her own friends," I said. "Besides, you're not her daddy. And if you were wanting to play that role, I just don't know what to tell you other than you're a sick son of a bitch who deserves the worst thing imaginable."

He sputtered and stuttered, but I just disconnected the call. I went to my call log and found the number she'd called me from. Before returning her call, I added it to my contacts and emailed it to myself so I'd have it in at least one other place if my phone decided to take another shit on me.

"Must have had the call drop," she said when she answered my call.

"Yeah," I said. "Also got a call from your brother. He told me to stay away from you."

"I'll call you back," she said. "I'm gonna give him a piece of my mind."

She disconnected the call before I could argue, so I continued the long walk down the hall to my room, using the key card to get me inside. I plugged my phone in, then dropped my bag and kicked off my shoes. If I was lucky, she'd let me do a video call and maybe we could have a little fun. I had my jacket and shirt off and was working on my pants when my phone lit up with a call.

"That was fast," I said.

"It didn't take long to talk some sense into him," she said. "What hotel are you staying in?"

"Why?" I asked.

"I'm coming down tomorrow night," she said. "I was supposed to stay with Quentin and McKenzie, but he's being a dick and I don't want to anymore."

"I wish you could just stay in my room," I said.

"That would be great," she said. "I know the rules, though, so won't ask."

I gave her the name of the hotel, then added, "You should pack some condoms."

"You don't have any?"

"No need," I said. "You weren't gonna be with me, so why would I need them?"

She didn't respond. Honestly, I couldn't even hear her breathing. I thought the call must have dropped, but then she spoke.

"You really didn't plan to hook up on this trip?"

"Thought about doing phone or video sex with you," I said. "Not sure if you're into that, but I'd be down."

Another stretch of silence, where I guess she was thinking about what I'd said. I waited, not wanting to push her, but desperately wondering what was going on in her pretty little head.

"I don't know what to say," she said, and I wasn't quite sure how to answer her.

"Just tell me if you're down," I replied, hoping it was the right thing.

"No," she said. "I mean, the fact that you hadn't planned ahead to hook up. That's really, well, not like you."

"Trust me, I know," I replied. "But there's this beautiful woman I met who has me doing all kinds of crazy things, making me change my ways and want to become a better person."

"Really?"

She sounded so surprised that all I could do was laugh.

"You've messed with my head," I said after a while. "Made me think about a future, about settling down, about making a permanent thing out of you and me."

"What are you asking?"

"Not really asking much," I said, but the truth was, I wasn't even sure what I was asking. I'd never done anything like this before. I was a fuck-and-run kind of dude, but that wasn't what I wanted with her. "Maybe we can talk more when I get back to town?"

"Or tomorrow after the game?" she asked.

"Oh, yeah," I said. "You're coming down. I forgot you were coming so early."

"Yeah," she said. "So, I'll see you tomorrow?"

"When do you get in?"

"Hang on," she said, and I could hear her messing with her phone, I assume finding her flight information. "Ugh," she said after coming back on the phone. "I forgot I booked a red-eye flight, so I don't actually land until Saturday morning around five."

"That's ugly," I said.

"Tell me about it," she replied. "At least I'll get about four hours of sleep on the flight. That's one good thing about being able to sleep on the plane. I know some people can't do it, but I have no problem. I guess that means I'll see you for breakfast instead of a late dinner."

"I can do that," I said.

I wanted to tell her I missed her, that I really wanted her with me all the time, and that I'd do anything she asked if she could guarantee she'd stay with me. I didn't want to scare her off, though, so didn't voice those desires out loud.

"So," I said after a bit. "You down for phone sex?"

"Umm," she hummed.

"No pressure," I said, although I really wanted to.

"I think I'd rather wait until I see you in person," she said, and I could almost hear the blush running up her cheeks.

"I can do that," I said. "See you soon."

"See you Saturday morning," she said.

She disconnected the call, and I set my phone down and groaned. I was definitely gonna have to take care of myself if I ever wanted to sleep.

CHAPTER FIFTY-FIVE

F i...

I disconnected the call and let out a breath, thinking back over the last few minutes. Beckett hadn't packed condoms and said he hadn't planned on hooking up while he was on the road trip. From what Quentin had told me, that was not like him. Quentin, of course, had ulterior motives. He hated him, so now I had to look at everything he'd told me through that lens. It could be a lie, just blowing smoke up my ass, but he sounded sincere, like he really hadn't planned on doing anything.

Phone sex was never something I'd wanted to do, and wasn't sure I ever would, but who knows, Beckett was pretty persuasive and he might just talk me into it. I was actually looking forward to the trip more now than I had been before talking to him. I thought about the call I'd had with Quentin after Beckett told me what he'd said.

"I told you he was bad news," he'd said. *"You need to break it off with him. He's not worthy of you."*

If anything, Beckett had shown just how worthy he was. He apologized about not calling me and explained the reason, and I believed him, too. He was kind, generous, especially in bed, and actually pretty funny. Oh, sure, some of the things he'd said were crass, but every guy has that side to them. Besides, that was when he first met me. After we'd gotten to know each other, he'd been nothing but kind with no bullshit, which was really refreshing. Sure, he wanted to get into my pants as often as possible, but I was down for it.

Luckily, it was only one more day of waiting until I climbed onto a plane and headed down to see him. This whole day job thing was cramping my style in wanting to travel all the time, but it was allowing me to afford it, which I couldn't complain about. I'd been fortunate to find a job right out of school, which also let me have a little time between graduation and starting to play. The full ride scholarship meant no school loans, and I was able to find the tiny apartment close to my parents for a super cheap rate. All that meant that I had more disposable income than most people my age, and I planned to spend it wisely, on traveling when I could.

My phone rang, and I saw it was McKenzie, so I answered it.

"Hey, girl," I said.

"Your brother is pissed," she replied. "Like, I've never seen him this mad before."

"He's just mad I'm not letting him run my life," I said. "I understand he wants to protect me, but I'm doing just fine on my own. He would die if he heard about my college days, because those were way wilder than what's going on with me and Beckett."

"I don't understand what his beef with this dude is," she said. "Were they rivals in little league or something?"

"Nah," I said. "I don't think Beckett's from here. Not really sure where he grew up, but I would put money on it not being in our neck of the woods."

"It's like there's something there that's making this a big deal," she said. "I've asked him what the issue is, but he just says that the guy is a dick, a player, and is just out to hurt you. Honestly, it's making me wonder what he knows that you don't."

"I probably know more about Beckett than he does," I said, sitting down on my bed. "They play against each other, and they're sort of rivals in that respect, but seriously, I have no idea why he's so dead set against him."

"I'll see if I can find anything out for you," she said. "You know I got you."

"I know," I said. "I appreciate it. Oh, I'm gonna stay in a hotel so I don't have to deal with him. We still good to do something Saturday morning?"

"For sure," she said. "I definitely want to have me some girl time. I miss you."

"I miss you, too," I said. "Maybe you could come up here some time and see me. We could hang out and I can show you my apartment."

"Work is insane, though," she said. "I mean, I have weekends off, but seriously, if I could work on the weekends, I just might catch up."

"Ugh," I groaned. "I feel fortunate to be doing what I do. No extra hours, no rush to get things done. As long as I stay focused and do my job every day, I am all good."

"Which is why you are in finance and I am not," she said, laughing. "I couldn't do numbers to save my life."

"Well, I can't draw to save mine," I replied. "So, I guess that makes us even. You do you and I'll do me and we'll each be happy."

"For sure," she said. "I gotta get, though. It's kind of late here."

"Yeah," I agreed. "It's not that late here, but I have a busy day tomorrow. Don't want to miss my flight and get my nap in."

"That's right," she said. "You're flying overnight. I can't do that, like, at all. Don't know how you manage to sleep in those uncomfortable spaces."

"I can sleep standing up in a corner," I said.

"Lucky," she replied. "Well, I'll see you on Saturday."

"See you then," I said. "I'll text you when I get to the hotel and we can plan the day."

"Works for me," she said. "Love you."

"Love you, too," I replied, then disconnected the call, flopping back on my bed.

Quentin and I were gonna have to have it out at some point, and I figured the sooner the better. I didn't want to screw up his game, but he was messing with things that were none of his business. No, while I was in Houston, we were gonna hash things out one way or another. If he couldn't figure out how to be happy for me, then he was gonna find himself with a sister who wasn't so sure she wanted to be around him. Harsh? Sure. But I was tired of living my life the way he wanted me to.

CHAPTER FIFTY-SIX

*B*eckett...

"You good to go?" Decker asked as we walked down the hall toward the elevator.

"You know it," I replied. "I've been itching to get back out there. This delay's been a struggle."

"Coach never did say what your injury was," he said as we stepped into the box to take us to the lobby.

"Not sure how to articulate it," I said, trying to keep it as vague as possible.

"Well," he said as the doors closed. "Good to have you back. J is good and all, but I know you're better out there up the middle."

"He's been playing really well," I said as we stopped at another floor and a couple of other players got on. "Just really miss being part of the action."

"Glad you're back," Huffman said.

"Thanks, man," I replied.

The dude was a giant, both tall and wide. How the hell he ran so damn fast in the outfield was a mystery that I didn't think could be solved. The amount of space he took up in the elevator meant we weren't able to add anyone else at the other floor we stopped on. By the time we got to the lobby, I was ready to run to the bus. I kept it cool, but just barely.

"Welcome back, Hennings," Coach said as I stepped up onto the bus.

"Thanks," I replied.

The rest of the team filed in quickly and we were on our way to the stadium for batting practice, as well as fielding for those of us that needed it, which I definitely did. I'd decided that I was just going to ignore Belinsky for the day, let him figure his own shit out, and stay away from him. Obviously, if either of us got on base, we'd likely have to be near each other, but if I could help it, I would do whatever it took to not let that happen.

Fielding was a struggle, especially since it'd been more than a week since I'd done anything athletic that didn't involve sex with a certain lady, but I was holding my own with Coach Rodriguez. He was beyond amazing when it came to teaching us all the techniques that had earned him a spot in Cooperstown. After infield practice, he sent me up to the batting cage to get my timing down in order to be the "fully rounded player" he knew I could be. Those types of compliments were always hard for me to hear, particularly with my history, but this guy had always been aboveboard and beyond reproach in every interaction we'd had. We headed back into the clubhouse to get ready for the game, and Bridge came up to me.

"You good?" he asked.

"I am," I replied. "Better every day. Thanks for recommending therapy."

"No problem," he said.

We'd built a pretty good relationship after I'd fucked everything up, but he seemed to realize that I had issues I needed to work out and didn't hold that against me any longer. I'd apologized, sincerely, to him about everything when I first got to the team. Told him I'd appreciated everything he tried to do for me, and that without his help, I probably wouldn't be here right now. While he'd agreed with me, it wasn't in an "I told you so" kind of way. It was more the way an older brother or father would be with a kid that had figured it out on their own. I guess there was a reason he was called the father of the clubhouse.

Hitting sixth in the lineup wasn't my normal spot, but having missed the last ten days, it made sense that I'd be starting lower down. At least I would be out on the field, which is something I sorely missed during my hiatus. Again, we watched their team, both on the field and in the dugout, looking to see if they were still trying to get away with shit that was both illegal and immoral. Fortunately, they seemed to have stopped everything. I guess getting caught really made them change.

They seemed to be on edge when the game started. It was like they were just waiting for something. They'd changed their pitcher to start with an opener, likely just for the first inning, but something felt off. After a hit by Matsui, Huffman stepped up to the plate with two outs. Their pitcher kept shaking off the signs from the catcher, obviously not wanting to do whatever it was that was being called. Watching their manager, I could tell he was getting pissed that his calls weren't being heeded. Honestly, I wasn't sure exactly what he was calling, but it didn't sit right with me.

I was standing on the top step in the dugout, waiting my turn to head to the on-deck circle when their pitcher finally nodded, then threw at Huffman. No, he didn't throw at him, he threw behind him, like by a long way. Their catcher missed it and Matsui trotted over to second, but still, it wasn't right. After time was called, the home ump gave everyone warnings.

"What the fuck are you warning us about?" Coach shouted. "We haven't done a damn thing. Why the fuck are they throwing at us, and why don't you throw him out right now?"

The whole team was up on the rail, shouting their agreement with our coach and asking for more to be done, but the ump said that he couldn't do anything until the warning was handed out.

"That's bullshit," Coach said in response, and he was told to watch his mouth.

They ended up walking Huffman and Cameron struck out, leaving me in the on-deck circle, coming up first in the top of the second inning. We all trotted out to the field, ready for action. Kors was killing it on the mound, throwing nasty pitch after nasty pitch, and I was here for it. He ended up getting their leadoff hitter to ground out, then struck out the next two, including Belinsky to end the inning.

I was up first, and their opener was still in. The hairs on the back of my neck were standing up, and I knew something was gonna happen. I wasn't sure what, but I knew it was gonna be bad when it did. A chorus of "boos" echoed around the stadium as I stepped up to the plate, grinding my back foot into the box, getting set to take the first pitch.

Just like last time, everything slowed to a snail's pace, the ball coming out of the pitcher's hand and tailing into me. I kept expecting it to drop or break or anything, but it just kept coming. I turned my head just as it hit me in the back of the helmet. The crack echoed inside my head, the helmet flying off and away from me, and I dropped to my knees.

The trainer was just there, inside my field of vision, as if appearing out of thin air. He was talking to me, but I couldn't really hear him or make out what he was saying. My ears were ringing, and I put my hand to the side of my head and it came back bloody. I blinked a couple of times, trying to figure out exactly what the fuck was happening, but I couldn't make sense of it.

Finally, after forever and a day, I could hear both the trainer and the coach asking me questions. I looked at both of them, then turned my attention out to the field. I was in shock. The entire team was out there, actually both teams, and they were going at it pretty hard. I could see fists flying, people tugging on jerseys, everything was just mayhem.

"What the fuck was that?" I finally asked, looking at the coach.

"Not really sure," Coach said. "We need to get you looked at."

"I'm fine," I lied, feeling a pounding in my head I'd never experienced before. "I need to make sure they know I'm behind them. I want to make sure they know I support them."

"Son, there's nothing you can do," Coach said. "Come on."

He and the trainer helped me to my feet, and I wobbled more than I would have liked, but steadied pretty quick. It was eerily quiet in the stadium, though, like I couldn't really hear anything—no shouting, no yelling, no cheering, nothing. I started to shake my head, but the trainer grabbed it.

"No, no," he said. "We're not gonna do any of that until we know what's up."

His voice was warbly, though, like he was talking through water or something.

"Yeah," he said when I looked at him. "I think you've got a concussion, maybe something more. Let's get you to the clubhouse and check you out."

I followed him obediently but didn't like leaving my team out there, fighting my battle for me. That wasn't what this team was about. I'd let them down enough, and now I was doing it again. The walk to the clubhouse and back to the training offices was the longest walk I'd done in quite some time.

CHAPTER FIFTY-SEVEN

*F*i...

Climbing into my car and heading to the airport, I turned on the radio instead of listening to my usual podcast, hoping to hear the game. They were just finishing the pregame show and giving the lineups for the game. I knew I wouldn't be able to hear the whole thing and would likely miss some of it while I was getting through security at the airport, but I would listen to what I could and maybe watch what I could on my phone, or if I was lucky enough, they'd have it on one of the televisions throughout the airport.

"*I think this should be a good game tonight,*" one of the announcers said.

"*These two teams have been fighting hard the last couple of meetings,*" the other guy commented. "*It's been a struggle for both teams to find footing in this west division.*"

"*And with it being one of the harder divisions to get a wild card contender out, each game matters,*" the first guy said.

I wound around the back streets and got onto the freeway, heading toward Seattle and the airport. Traffic was going to be a nightmare, but at least I would be leaving it all behind and getting time with my bestie and watching the boys play.

"*The Dragons are taking the field to get ready to start,*" the announcer said. "*We'll take a quick break and be back for the first pitch.*"

A commercial came on for one of the local car dealerships, then one for an eye surgeon who was doing those laser surgeries with one of the former players who sometimes does the pregame show, saying how amazing their surgery went. After that it was for the morning show on the sports station that the games were on.

"*It's interesting that they slotted an opener in for today's game,*" one of the announcers said as they came back on the air.

"*Usually, that's saved for when the starter doesn't do well more than a couple of times through the lineup,*" the other guy said. "*But Brooks has been doing really well in the last couple of starts.*"

"*And the opener they chose,*" the other guy added. "*Velasquez has been a fill-in guy with not a lot of experience at this level. It's as if they're just trying him out to see what he can do.*"

"*Well, we're gonna see what he can do right now,*" the first guy said.

I kind of hoped that the game would be boring and nothing would happen.

"*We've got Adams up first,*" the guy said. "*He's been doing well since they put him up at the top of the lineup.*"

"*I agree,*" the other guy replied. "*It's like he was waiting to show his full potential until he was in the spotlight at the top.*"

They droned on and on while I made my way, slowly creeping along in traffic. The first guy grounded out to first. The next guy up hit a pop fly to the outfield, so we had two outs at that point and I figured it would be a quick inning.

"*The first pitch to Matsui comes in, right in the middle of the plate,*" the announcer said. "*And Matsui swings and sends it out into the outfield for a base hit.*"

"*Not a bad way to get things going here in the first,*" the other guy said, and I agreed.

"*Matsui turns, and the ball is thrown back in to Belinsky, their*" *short stop, who's at second. He was just itching to tag Matsui off if he tried to stretch that single,"* the first guy said.

"John Huffman has been on a tear in the last week or so," the other guy said. *"He's been really hitting the ball well with an eight-game hitting streak. He steps into the box and waits for the pitch."*

"Velasquez lets go and look out, the ball goes behind Huffman," one of them said.

"I'm not sure whether that was intentional or not," the other one said. *"But, from what I'm seeing on the face of Huffman, it appears that it was absolutely intentional."*

"Brian Finn, the home plate umpire, is now giving each bench a warning," the first guy said. *"Do you remember anything happening last night that would make this happen?"*

"Nothing that I can remember," he replied. *"I don't remember us even brushing one of their players back, so this is out of nowhere."*

"Huffman is barking at Velasquez," the first guy said. *"Saying that he needs to watch what's going on."*

"Which is what everyone is going to do now," the other replied.

"Stupid boys," I said, merging onto the freeway to head north.

The traffic around the dome in Tacoma, where freeway repairs and upgrades had been going on for as long as I could remember, was always bad, which made the drive take that much longer in that stretch. The rest of the inning was pretty uneventful, and Beckett was left on deck and would be up the next inning.

More commercials came on as the teams switched spots, with the Cascades taking the field and the Dragons coming up to bat.

"We're back with you," one announcer said. *"And we've got Nelson coming up first."*

"Another player who has been hitting well as of late," the other guy said. *"He also has a hitting streak going, but his is only four games. Let's see what Kors can do."*

"Kors has been really pitching well in the last few starts," the guy said. At this point, I didn't know who was who, and honestly didn't care.

"*He has been,*" one guy said. "*He's going to rely heavily on his breaking ball, that slurve that he's got has been his go-to pitch to get out of things.*"

"*That's a pitch he developed in the off season,*" the other guy said. "*And the work he's been putting in has really showed promise.*"

I'd finally reached Fife where the freeway opened up a bit, and I was cruising at faster-than-a-snail's pace. I listened to the guys talk about the pitches that this guy was throwing, how he was so much improved over the previous year, and when the Dragons' first guy came up, the pitcher got him to ground out on the first pitch. After that, the next two players, including my brother, were struck out, retiring the side quickly.

"*Definitely a relief to get on and off the field so quickly,*" one of the announcers said after they came back from the commercial break.

"*And Velasquez is back out there to start the second inning,*" the other one said.

"*Hennings, just back from his ten-day stint on the IL, is looking to come back hard,*" the first guy said.

"*There was no cause given for his break,*" the other one said. "*Inside sources indicate that it was a family emergency of some sort, but they're all being tight lipped about it.*"

"*He was hit pretty hard by Belinsky when he slid into him in Seattle the last time the Dragons were there,*" the first guy said.

"*That's true,*" the other one replied. "*Let's just hope his timing is up to it and that he picks back up where he left off.*"

"*Which is what we're all hoping for,*" he said. "*He's coming into the box, grinding that back foot in right at the line at the back of the box, and giving his practice swings before stepping in.*"

"*Velasquez is on the mound and set,*" the other one said. "*He shakes off the first pitch, then another and another, and now he's stepping off.*"

"*Scouting reports are pretty established by this point in the season,*" the first one said.

"*Whatever Douglas is throwing down, Velasquez isn't wanting to throw,*" the other one replied.

"*I never understood this at the top of the inning,*" the first one said. "*You come out of the dugout and should know what you're gonna throw. It's a strategy you come up with while you're on the bench. So why is he shaking him off?*"

"*Normally this isn't an issue,*" the other one said, and I seemed to remember he played for the team at some point in time. "*When we'd come off the bench, we all knew what the first couple of pitches were going to be.*"

"*Do you think Velasquez is second-guessing the coach?*"

"*At this point, I don't know,*" the guy replied.

"*Well,*" the first guy said. "*Looks like they're on the same page now. Velasquez is toeing the rubber and coming set. The wind up and here comes the pitch.*"

"*Whoa,*" the other guy said. "*That hit him and he's down.*"

"*And here come the players, all coming out onto the field,*" the first guy said.

"*I don't know what just happened,*" the other one said.

I couldn't pay too much attention to what they were saying because the traffic took that moment to bog down through Federal Way. I wanted to be watching the game but was stuck listening to these two guys tell me what was going on. Problem was, all they were saying was that Beckett was hit and everyone was on the field fighting.

"*Oh no, here we go again,*" one of them said.

"*Whatever happened, it's blown up into mayhem on the field,*" the other replied.

They were talking about the guys on the field fighting, but weren't saying anything about Beckett, and that's all I really cared about. I drove through the slog and the freeway opened up again, but slowed down almost right away when I got closer to the exit I wanted to take for the airport.

Most people took the one that led them down and around through the drive at the parking garage at the actual airport. I too the earlier exit at 188th and followed it down to International Boulevard to get me to the parking places where you could leave your car for far less than parking in the long-term parking at the airport itself. By the time I got closer, it seemed like the fighting on the field had died down.

"*We're not sure why,*" one of the announcers said. "*First was the pitch behind Huffman. Then they threw right at Hennings.*"

"*Throwing at a player is part of the game,*" the other guy said. "*But you never, ever, throw at their head.*"

"*You also throw a breaking ball of some sort, not a fastball,*" the first guy replied.

"*Exactly,*" the second one agreed.

"*This was completely uncalled for,*" the first guy said. "*There is no reason for them to be throwing at our players, especially in the first and second innings.*"

"*That's what I don't understand,*" the other guy said. "*If there had been something that had happened, if this was halfway through the game, then maybe you throw inside to brush guys back. Throwing at someone just because makes no sense.*"

"*It looks like things are finally cooling down,*" the announcer said. "*Let's hope better heads prevail in this volatile situation.*"

"*We know that at least their pitcher will be ejected, as well as the manager,*" the other announcer replied. "*What we don't know is who, or how many. We'll also get an update on the Cascades' shortstop, Beckett Hennings when we hear something. Our announcer, Jenn, is on the field, so let's go to her to see if she knows anything.*"

"*Thanks, Brad,*" she said. "*From my vantage point, all I saw was the hit to Hennings and him dropping. I heard Huffman shout something from the dugout and that's when everyone piled out. I can't repeat what he said, though, because we can't have that on the air. But let's just say that he was unbelievably upset that they hit his teammate, suggesting it was over something that may not even have happened this game, or in the last few games.*"

"*What do you mean?*" the announcer, who I assume was Brad, asked.

"*Some of the rumblings from the dugout have indicated that this has more to do with the scandal that's surrounding the Dragons,*" she answered. "*It wasn't said clearly, so it may be all in my head, but I did hear Rob, the manager, say that Houston was blaming the Cascades for the incident.*"

My phone rang, and I picked up right away, using the Bluetooth system in my car.

"Beckett?" I asked.

"Hey, no," McKenzie said. "I wanted to make sure you knew what happened."

"I just heard it on the radio," I said. "They're saying something about this being related to the cheating thing. Is that true?"

"Oh, God," she said, sighing. "Quentin said something about Beckett being the one who found something and snitched on them, but I didn't believe they'd do anything about it."

"He knew?" I asked, shouting. "He knew that Beckett was going to be hit, and he didn't bother to tell me?"

"I don't think he knew this was going to happen," McKenzie explained.

"He knew they were gunning for the team," I said. "I swear to all that is holy, if he knew they were gonna throw at Beckett, and he's hurt more than just a bump, I am coming after him."

"Fi, I don't think he knew," she said, but I couldn't be sure.

"Tell him when you see him that he is on my shit list," I said.

My phone buzzed, and I looked and saw that it was Beckett calling.

"I gotta go," I said, then switched to the call from Beckett. "Hey, you okay?"

"Fi?" a man asked.

"Yeah, that's me," I replied. "Who's this?"

"My name is Jonathan Bridge," he said. "I filled in for Beckett when he was on the IL. I wanted to let you know that they've sent him to the hospital and wouldn't let him take his phone. I have it with me and will be going to the hospital as soon as the game is over to give it to him. I didn't want you to not know what was going on, though."

"Thanks," I said, sighing in a little bit of relief. "Do they know how long he'll be there? I am flying down tonight. I'm actually on the way to the airport right now."

"The hit was pretty hard, and I think he'll probably be in there a day at least," he said. "I have to go now, but I wanted you to know what was up."

"Thanks," I said again, and the line cut out.

The radio came back on and they were still talking about what happened, and it appeared that the game hadn't restarted yet. Ugh, this was gonna be nuts.

CHAPTER FIFTY-EIGHT

*B*eckett...

"This is ridiculous," I shouted.

"Sir," the attendant at the hospital replied. "You have a head injury. Those are taken very seriously."

"I'm fine," I barked, anger filling me. "I just need you to get these stupid tests done so I can go back to the game and help my team."

It was one thing to have to leave my team on the field to fight my battles, but it was another to not let me have any of my personal items, especially my phone, so that I could tell Fi what was going on.

"We'll be able to determine whether you're fine or not once we can take these scans," the attendant reiterated. "If you would let us do them, we'd be done faster."

"I'm not a fucking toddler," I shouted.

"But you're acting worse than the two-year-old we had in here last week who fell off a bed," the attendant replied in a cold voice. "If a toddler acted better than you, an adult, that should tell you something about your behavior."

"Fuck," I muttered.

I'd already done x-rays and a CT scan, but now we were doing the big MRI. Neither of the other tests had come back with any conclusive injuries, so they wanted to do this next one to rule out soft tissue damage, as well as a possible brain bleed. The number of questions they had to ask before they even put me in the room was ridiculous, but I guess it was needed to ensure that they didn't suck some random piece of metal out of my body with the big magnet.

After they ran me through the machine with its whirs and beeps and shit, they wheeled me out into the hall where they again transferred me to the gurney I was on initially. Once that was done, I was sent back to the emergency department where I lay in a room for an eternity before anyone bothered to come in and check on me.

"Mr. Hennings?" a young guy asked, stepping into the space.

"That's me," I replied.

"I'm Dr. Miles," he said, stepping closer to the head of the bed I was in so I could see him easier. "I'm the orthopedist on duty tonight. I understand you were struck with a baseball on your helmet and possibly your head?"

The way he said it made it clear it was a question, so I answered with a simple, "Yeah."

"I see," he said, looking at the papers he had in his hand when he walked in. "I've looked over your scans and it appears that nothing was broken, which is good. My only concern is that there is some soft tissue damage at the base of your skull, just on the right side of your spine. Under normal circumstances, this wouldn't be much of an issue. The fact that it was caused, potentially, by being struck, has me a little concerned about additional damage coming later on."

"What do you mean?" I asked, realizing that this was more than what I initially thought.

"I mean," he said, looking at me pointedly. "We are going to keep you here at least until tomorrow when we can do another scan to rule out any increase in damage. At that point, we'll be able to determine whether this is something that will heal on its own, or if it will require additional action to help it."

"You mean surgery," I said, and I'm sure the blood ran out of my face.

"Possibly," he said. "We won't really be sure for a while. If things stay the same, though, I'll just recommend that you take a break for a week or so and follow up with an orthopedist closer to your home for more testing and determinations."

"So, I'm benched," I said, and couldn't keep the disappointment out of my voice.

"For now, yes," he said. "But it looks like you should make a full recovery, as long as nothing changes in the next few hours."

"Damn," I mumbled.

"I'm gonna get them to get you up to your own room and out of the ER," he said. "Do you have family you can call?"

"My team is here," I said. "But I can't call anyone because I don't have my phone."

"If they're your team, they probably know where you are," he said. "I'll make sure the nurses know you're expecting them late."

"Thanks, doc," I said, and he walked out the door. "Fuck," I muttered after he'd gone.

CHAPTER FIFTY-NINE

*F*i...

By the time I actually got to the car park, the game had restarted, but they hadn't given an update on Beckett. I was honestly getting worried about him, wondering what I would find when I got to the hospital. I left my keys with the guy and took the shuttle over to the airport, heading straight for security. Thankfully, I only had my carryon with me, so didn't have to deal with the nonsense of checking a bag.

While the line was long, it was pretty quick, which was unusual for this airport. The number of airports I'd been to weren't big, but Seattle's seemed to have the longest lines and the worst service. When I got to the front of the line, the agent waved me over.

"Ticket and ID," he said.

I pulled up the boarding pass on my phone and showed it to him. He scanned it on his device, then looked at the picture on my ID and back at me a couple of times, before handing it back to me, and waving me through to the machines. I dropped my suitcase onto the belt, picked up a bin, and dropped my phone and shoes, along with my purse, into it, shoving them through the x-ray machine behind the people in front of me.

Slowly, we moved forward, each stepping into the big box with their hands up over their heads while the thing whirled and took what-ever image it did before they stepped out. When it was my turn, I stepped in, turned to the side, put my feet onto the spots on the floor and raised my arms over my head. It spun the little image thing around, then the agent told me to step out. I did so, waiting in the smaller section while whoever was in charge of looking at things made sure I didn't have whatever it was they didn't want me to have on me.

"Okay," she said, then motioned for me to go ahead and grab my bag and shoes.

I snagged my phone and shoved it into my purse, pulling it over my head to lay against my body, then picked up my shoes and suitcase and walked toward the seats. Setting my bag down, I dropped my shoes and slid into them, then turned to make the walk down the concourse.

By the time I made it to my gate, I was wound up tighter than a drum. There were no televisions around for me to see if I could see the game, so I pulled out my phone and pulled up the app for the league and found the game. When I pulled up the view to see it, I could see that they were already in the fifth inning and we were ahead. I looked through the box to see who had been thrown out and it appeared that Beckett was out, and they'd tossed the giant, Huffman. I assumed the coach had been tossed, as well as their pitcher and coach. I flipped teams and looked at the Dragons' players and was not at all surprised to see that my brother had also been tossed, along with another player that wasn't the pitcher.

Instead of waiting around to see what happened, I pulled my phone app and called my brother.

"Hey, sis," he said, sounding almost happy.

"What the hell were you guys doing?" I asked.

"What are you talking about?"

"You hit Beckett," I barked. "You knew something was gonna happen, and you didn't bother to tell me. I had to hear about it on the radio on my way to the airport."

"It's just part of the game," he said.

"No," I retorted. "You hit him in the head. With a fastball. Are you fu-freaking kidding me?"

I stumbled over the word because I didn't want to swear while shouting into the phone at the airport.

"Come on, Fi," he said, but I shut him down.

"Don't you do that to me," I said. "You knew this was gonna happen. Hell, you probably were the one to tell them to hit him in the first place, just because you don't like him. Are you jealous or something?"

"Are you kidding me right now?" he asked.

"I know you don't like him," I said. "But come on, you're the one who introduced us. It's your own damn fault that we're together."

"No way," he said. "This is not what I wanted."

"Really?" I asked. "Because I remember pretty clearly that you wanted me to hook up with him to get some super secrets out of him. To me, that sounds like you're jealous or don't think you're as good as him."

"Come on," he whined.

"Look," I said. "I get that you're rivals in some way. You play the same position, and you're from here, so you're probably a little upset that your hometown team didn't draft you. But seriously, you need to let it go. You're better than this, Quentin. Don't let your cheating team pull you down to their level. Man up and take control."

"Wow," he said on a rush of air. "You really think that little of me?"

"Prove me wrong," I replied. "Show me that you're not the same as the rest of your cheating teammates. Prove that you're above all of that and are solely in the mindset of 'may the better man win.'"

"You think I want to be known as a cheater?"

"You don't seem to be denying it," I replied.

"Fuck," he said and I could hear the disappointment in his voice.

"I always looked up to you," I said, quieter now. "You were someone I wanted to be like. But this new you, the one who would willingly cheat at a game to get ahead. Nah, that's not someone I want to be associated with at all."

"I..." he began but paused. I waited him out until he finally said, "I guess you're right. I have failed at being the better man."

"Acknowledging it is the first step," I said.

"Yeah," he said, but didn't say more.

"I'm getting on a plane to head down there," I said. "I'm going straight to the hospital when I land to see Beckett. I'll see you tomorrow, but be prepared to show me how you're gonna change, okay?"

He sighed, but then said, "I will."

"I love you, big brother," I said.

"I love you, little sister," he replied.

I disconnected the call and sat there, staring at my phone, and realizing that my big brother, the one I felt could do no wrong, had stumbled into the wrong crowd and hadn't realized how far down the wrong track he'd gotten. I pulled up the baseball app again and kept an eye on the newsfeed to see if any news would come in on Beckett. I had a couple of hours to kill before I had to board the plane, so I fished out my charger and plugged it into the outlet next to my seat. The long wait had just begun.

CHAPTER SIXTY

*B*eckett...

I'd finally been moved to a private room where I turned on the television to see if I could watch the rest of the game. After several searches, it didn't look like it was available here, so I buzzed the nurse.

"Hey," she said when she came in. "What's up?"

"Do you know if I can watch the baseball game on this thing?" I asked.

"Oh, sure," she said, taking the buzzer contraption and fiddling with it until the game came on. "There you go."

"Thanks," I said.

"No problem," she replied. "You all good now?"

"Any chance I can get some water?" I asked. "And maybe a snack?"

"Water shouldn't be a problem," she said. "Just have to check the chart to make sure they aren't thinking surgery might happen. That will also tell me if you can eat anything. Be right back."

"Thanks," I said as she walked out the door.

I turned up the volume on the television and saw that we were ahead. It was the top of the eighth and J was up, which meant that he must have come in for me once everything settled down. Hopefully he was able to get into my phone and call Fi. I didn't know what she had seen or heard, and I wanted to make sure she wasn't worried about me. No one needed to worry about me. I was fine.

The door opened, and another woman came in with a tray full of stuff.

"I've got your water," she said, setting the tray onto the edge of the table, then pulling the plastic pitcher thing off with a cup and straw. "We weren't sure what you liked," she continued. "I've got some crackers, some fruit, a sandwich, granola bars..."

She listed things off the tray that were there, and I was honestly surprised at how much variety they had available in the middle of the night like this. I told her what I'd like, and she pulled those off the tray, then headed back out the door. I snacked on some fruit and ate the sandwich while I watched the team take their anger out on the field.

Coach had been tossed, but that didn't surprise me. They always tossed the manager when a fight broke out—something about not being able to control their team. It was bullshit and they knew it, but it was one of those unwritten rules, you know, like not throwing at someone's head. I guess the Dragons hadn't read that rulebook.

The phone next to the bed rang, and I stared at it for a minute, unsure who would know where I was, or even how to find me. They'd checked me in as private to keep the anonymity for me, what with the way the press tended to hound anyone to get a good story. I'd given them a list of people who I was fine knowing I was there, so this must have been someone on the list. Finally, I answered it.

"Hello?" I asked, unsure who it might be.

"Beckett?" Fi asked, and I sighed in relief.

"Hey, baby," I said with a smile. "I thought you were flying in."

"I'm waiting to get on the plane," she replied. "There was some sort of mechanical issue, so they needed to fix it before we could get on."

"You sure it's gonna be safe?" I asked, concern for her seeping into my voice.

"Oh yeah," she replied with a laugh. "Apparently, someone was not so careful when they used the bathroom on the flight in. They're supposed to be able to fix it, but even if they can't, it won't stop the plane from being fine to fly."

"Glad I wasn't on that flight," I said. "I hate the bathrooms on planes. I mean, the stench that comes out of them sometimes is awful."

"For sure," she said, and she sounded like her mood was better. "So, how are you?"

"I'm fine," I said. "Got me a snack, some water, and am watching the game. Got the whole room to myself, which would be great, except I'd like it better if you were here."

"I'm planning on coming straight from the airport," she said. "They say that we should be able to leave soon, so that would make it just after six when we land."

"You're not gonna drive tired like that are you?"

"Oh, no," she said. "I'm taking an Uber. Besides, I plan on sleeping on the plane, so it'll all be good."

"As long as you're safe," I said.

"I will be," she replied. "So, seriously, how are you?"

"Nothing's broken, just a bump on the head," I said, downplaying the concern the doctor had given me before he left. "I'll be fine in no time."

"Don't they have to watch you for a while?" she asked. "I mean, after a head injury, don't they worry about concussion symptoms?"

"Doc said he'll do another test in the morning," I said. "It will show that I'm just fine and I'll be released. May be able to go as soon as you get here."

I didn't want her to worry, not about me. I'd be fine. I always was. There was no need for her to have to suffer over me.

"I hope so," she said. "But if not, I'll stay with you all day tomorrow. You'll probably be sick of me and tell me to leave by noon."

"I could spend all day, every day with you, and never get sick of you," I replied, and it was the truth.

"Crap," she said. "I gotta go. They're boarding."

"See you in the morning," I said.

"See you then," she replied. "Love you."

She disconnected the call before I even had a chance to respond. I was sure it was an automatic response, that she didn't mean it, but for the moment, I would hold those two words close to my heart in hopes that someday I would live up to her love.

CHAPTER SIXTY-ONE

$\mathcal{F}$i...

"Crap," I said. "I gotta go. They're boarding."

"See you in the morning," he said.

"See you then," I replied. "Love you."

I stuffed the phone into my pocket as I scrambled up to the gate with my bag. They'd said they wanted to load as quickly as possible to try to save some time and get us to Houston as close to the scheduled arrival time as possible.

The guy at the gate scanned my boarding pass from my phone that I'd pulled back out and sent me on down the jetway to the plane. I had become a master of getting onto the plane, stowing my suitcase above the seats, and getting into my seat as quickly as possible, so this was easy to accomplish, even with everyone around me doing the same.

Sure enough, we were loaded, seated, and being pushed back from the gate in record time. I guess everyone was ready to be on the way. The flight attendants gave us the safety instructions, then we were off. I swear it was no less than ten minutes from the time we pushed back until we were in the air, and I was in absolute shock at the speed we'd done it.

Once the plane leveled off a bit, I leaned up against the window and closed my eyes, hoping to crash as quickly as possible to get as much sleep as I could before we touched down. Somehow, I must have crashed quickly because I had no more than closed my eyes than the sun was coming in from the small portal in front of me, waking me with the early morning light of sunrise. It took a minute to orient myself, but when I looked out the window after pushing my shade up, I saw the unmistakable skyline of Houston as we began to descend into the city.

Pulling my phone out, I realized that I would probably need to charge it for a couple of minutes at the airport before getting a car to take me to the hospital to see Beckett. I pulled the cord from my purse and plugged it into the seat to get a little bit of juice before we landed, unplugging it as soon as they announced it on the speakers. Once we touched down, I plugged it back in, knowing it would be at least a few minutes before we made it to the gate.

"I want to thank you all for your assistance in Seattle," the pilot said. "With your speedy loading, we were able to make up nearly all of the time we were delayed and are arriving in Houston just fifteen minutes late. Now, as you may know, some of the passengers have connecting flights, so if you don't have one, we'd appreciate it if you would remain seated until all those who have to make that mad dash are able to get off the plane first. Again, thank you for flying with us, and enjoy your stay in Houston."

We taxied to the gate pretty quickly, and since I wasn't going anywhere else, I just stayed in my seat and waited for the rest of the folks to get up and grab their stuff before I finally unplugged my phone, stood up, and pulled my suitcase from the overhead compartment. While I wasn't the last one off the plane, I was definitely near the end of them. My phone was actually fairly well charged by the time I made it to the terminal, so I pulled up the app for the car service and checked to see if I could get one. Realizing I would have to have the address where I was going, I decided to wait until I got closer to baggage claim to order the car.

I looked up the hospital where Beckett was and then plugged it into the ride share app and ordered a car. I was surprised that there was someone already there, so I stepped out to the pickup location and greeted the driver.

"Hey," I said when the driver stepped out.

"Are you Ophelia?" he asked.

"I am," I said, stepping toward the car.

"Just the one bag?"

"Just this one," I confirmed.

He picked up the bag and set it into the trunk of the Prius he drove as I climbed into the back seat. Before shutting the door, I made sure there was a handle on the inside and that the window would roll down. Call me paranoid, but I listened to too many crime podcasts to not think of these things. Satisfied that I wasn't going to be kidnapped, I closed the door, and the driver got into his seat.

"Would you like music?" he asked, turning in his seat to look at me.

"Doesn't matter," I said. "I'm off to see a family member in the hospital, so just want to get there as quickly as possible."

"No problem," he said and turned around, putting the car into gear, and pulling out into traffic.

I was thankful that he just put on some classical music at a low level and didn't bother to talk to me again until we were getting close to the hospital.

"Should I drop you at the ER?" he asked.

"Just the front entrance," I replied. "They've already been admitted."

"Okay," he said, pulling his car around the building to what I assumed was the main entrance.

He parked and opened his door, popping the trunk. By the time I got out of the back seat, he already had my suitcase out and sitting on the curb.

"Hope your family feels better," he said.

"Thanks," I replied, grabbing my suitcase and heading to the door.

It swooshed open, and I stepped inside, shoving the sunglasses I had on up on top of my head. I went to the desk and waited for the guy sitting there to look up.

"Can I help you?" he asked.

"I'm here to see Beckett Hennings," I replied. "He's my fiancé."

I added the last bit just to ensure that the "family" rule that some hospitals had wouldn't be an issue. He clicked on his keyboard then looked up at me.

"Can I see some ID?" he asked.

I pulled out my driver's license and handed it over. Hopefully, Beckett had made mention of me coming to see him and they'd let me in. I mean, I was able to get to him by phone before I got onto the plane, so I assumed he had.

"He's in room 1128," he said, handing my ID back. "If you follow those lines, there is an elevator just down the hall. Take that to floor eleven and you can check in at the nurses' station for additional directions."

"Thank you," I replied and turned to follow his instructions.

I found the elevators, pressed the button to call it, and waited. Once it arrived, I let the couple of people in it get out before stepping in and pressing the button for the right floor. When it stopped, I walked out and saw the nurses' station, but there was no one there. I looked around to see if someone was close by, but it was like the place was deserted. Scanning the numbers on the doors around, I figured out pretty quickly where Beckett's room was and headed that way, stepping into the dim space.

There was a curtain just inside, the kind that is on a track with the chains holding it in place. I stepped to the end of it and pushed it to the side just a little bit to step behind it, and there he was. He was facing the door and was sound asleep, his face slack and soft. I just wanted to stare at him for a moment, gather this vision into me and save it for later.

The door opened behind me and the curtain whooshed to the side, pouring light from the hallway onto his face. He squinted and shaded his eyes with his hand.

"Oh," a young woman said. "I didn't realize he had company."

Before I had a chance to say anything, Beckett spoke up.

"You made it," he said, reaching a hand out to me.

I drug my suitcase over to the wall, then went to him, taking his hand in mine. He pulled me down and kissed me long and slow. I'm not sure what the nurse or whoever she was thought, but it didn't really matter. No, what mattered was I was here, and he was okay.

"Let's not raise his blood pressure too high," the woman said behind me and we broke apart.

"Sorry," I said, but Beckett pulled me to him, urging me to sit on the edge of the bed.

"Need to get his vitals," she said, pulling the little cart with the blood pressure cuffs and such on it over to the bed.

"I'll move," I said, but Beckett held me firm. "Beckett," I admonished and he finally let me go.

I stood and walked to the other side of the bed where there was a chair I could sit on and wait until the nurse was finished. Beckett didn't take his eyes off me the whole way and didn't even acknowledge the nurse as she pulled his arm up and plugged the cuff that was there into the machine. She took his other hand and put the little oxygen meter onto one of his fingers, then swiped the thermometer around his forehead and behind his ear. The machine beeped a constant rhythm until it gave a final one to indicate it was done measuring things.

"Not too bad," the nurse said, pulling the plugs from the cuff and removing the reader from his finger. "Remember, you had a head injury. Don't be getting out of bed on your own."

"Don't plan on it," he said, but never wavered in his staring at me.

"Thank you," I said as the nurse walked back to the door, pulling the curtain back into place and closing the door behind her.

We were dropped into a quiet stillness, him lying there, staring at me.

"Come here," he said, reaching his hand out to me.

I scooted the chair closer, thinking that was what he wanted, but he grabbed me around the middle and pulled me nearly on top of him. I squeaked but ended up landing next to him on the small bed.

"I missed you," he said, pushing my hair out of my face where it had flopped.

He pulled my head toward him and kissed me soundly, my arm

going over his body without my even thinking about it. The kiss was long and slow and so damn enthusiastic that I wished we were in a hotel or somewhere, anywhere but in a hospital right at that moment.

"I want you," he said, his hand smoothing my hair back more, the other one roaming slowly down my side.

"You're in the hospital," I replied.

"So what," he said. "I'm not dead, yet."

"You're awful," I said, laughing.

"Grab a condom," he said, and I looked at him, confused. "Unless you want to go without."

Instead of arguing with me, he pulled me back down and kissed all sense out of my head while his hands roamed down and pushed the blanket down from between us, then pulled the gown he was wearing up. I was keening into his mouth, feeling him already hard and ready for me. Instead of resisting, though, I went with it. I mean, who would know?

Shoving my purse around so it was sitting behind me, I inched myself up, pulling my skirt higher as he continued to shove the blankets down. It was awkward to say the least, but somehow, right in the middle of that hospital room, he pushed my panties to the side and slid inside me, and oh, God, was it wonderful.

We moved slowly at first, but it didn't take long for me to feel that building pressure. He'd slid his hand between us and used his thumb on my clit, rubbing it in small, quick circles as he wound me up higher and higher. Then, all of a sudden, as if out of nowhere, I crashed, crying out in pleasure as his mouth captured the sound. I felt him shudder beneath me and could tell he had come right after me.

When I pulled away from his mouth, he looked upset.

"What's the matter?" I asked.

"No condom," he replied.

"IUD," I said, then added, "But I appreciate your concern."

"I don't think I want to have kids," he said, and the confession was almost out of nowhere.

"There's plenty of time to discuss those things," I said, not wanting to ruin the moment we had just experienced.

He heard it before I did and snatched the blankets, pulling them over the both of us. The curtain whooshed over and I closed my eyes, not wanting to see whoever it was that came into the room. I did not need that embarrassment.

"Mr. Hennings," a man said, then added, "Sorry. I'll be back in a minute."

I heard the door close and Beckett was just laughing.

"You asshole," I said, slapping his chest as I righted myself and got off the bed. "Oh my God. Why didn't you warn me?"

He just laughed as I climbed down and shoved my skirt down over my now very wet and filling panties.

"I'm going into the bathroom," I said, walking over to the small space in the corner of the room.

I shut the door and sat on the toilet, burying my face in my hands. I was never gonna be able to live this down, and I was sure that Beckett would bring it up any chance he got. Fuck my life.

CHAPTER SIXTY-TWO

*B*eckett...
   I couldn't help but laugh. She was so embarrassed, but it was absolutely adorable on her. I mean, yeah, the sex was good, but it paled in comparison to past experiences. Hopefully I'd be out of here today and could show her exactly what she meant to me. I had to admit, though, that going without a condom was very nice.

"Knock, knock," the doctor said by way of warning.

"Come on in," I replied, not able to keep the chuckle out of my voice.

"She gone?" he asked after looking around the room.

"In the bathroom," I supplied. "She's embarrassed."

"No need for that," he said. "I'm glad you feel up to... 'company.'"

The way he said the word made it almost sound dirty, so I had to correct him.

"She's my girlfriend," I said, and even though the word was foreign to my lips, it sounded right to my ears.

"Just be careful," the doctor said.

"Always," I replied. "So, tell me the good news."

"First, we need to have another look inside that head of yours," he said. "I've ordered another MRI and when we have the results of that, we'll be better able to tell you what is going on."

"She can stay here while I'm gone, right?"

"Sure," the doctor said.

The bathroom door opened, and she stepped out, still blushing, but obviously feeling brave.

"Hey," she said, walking over to the chair by the bed.

"Good morning," the doctor said, not at all mentioning what he'd walked in on earlier. "As I was telling Mr. Hennings, we need to do another scan, and once we have the results, we'll be better able to determine where we go from here."

"Is he in any danger?" she asked, and my heart melted just that much more.

"With brain injuries, there is always a danger," the doctor explained. "But it looks like the helmet did its job and protected his brain, which is what we always want to see. I'm just being extra cautious to ensure that there aren't any underlying issues that may blossom in the future."

"Oh, okay," she said.

She'd grabbed my hand when she sat down and had been slowly squeezing it tighter and tighter with every word the doctor said. She finally loosened it up when he said things looked good.

"How soon until they come to get me?" I asked.

"Pretty soon," the doctor said. "Mornings are usually pretty open, so shouldn't be too long. Once you're done, I should have the results pretty quickly, too. Might even get you out of here before lunch."

"I'd like that," I said.

"Me, too," she agreed.

"I'll see what I can do," he said, then left.

I gave her hand a little squeeze and said, "I'll probably have to go home when I get out."

"I fly out tomorrow," she said.

"Maybe we can go together," I said.

She smiled and pulled my hand to her lips, kissing my knuckles.

CHAPTER SIXTY-THREE

*F*i...

They'd come to take him to get the test done shortly after the doctor left, so I was stuck in the room just waiting for him to come back. I had pulled my charger out and plugged the phone into the wall so it would be fully charged for the day.

"Oh, hey," a man said as he entered the room.

"Can I help you?" I asked.

The guy didn't look like he worked here, what with wearing dress slacks and a button-down shirt.

"I was looking for Hennings," he said.

"He's getting a test done," I replied. "I'm Fi."

"Good to meet you," he said, walking closer. "I'm Jonathan. I called you last night."

"Oh, yeah," I said, placing the face with the voice. "Thanks so much for letting me know what was up. I really appreciate it."

"No problem," he said. "I wanted to make sure he had his phone when it was time for him to leave."

He pulled a phone out of his pocket and held it out to me.

"Thanks," I said, and realized that it was nearly dead. "I'm just gonna plug it in so he has a charge in case he needs it."

"I didn't even think about that," he admitted. "How's he doing?" he asked after I'd plugged Beckett's phone in.

"I think he's doing good," I said. "The doctor said that if the test comes back good, he might be able to leave today."

"That's great," Jonathan said.

"Hey," Beckett said as they wheeled him back into the room.

"How's it going?"

"Let me tell you," Beckett began, but then stopped.

I wasn't sure what he was gonna say, but whatever it was died on his lips. The nurse wheeled his chair over to the bed, then helped him to make the move. Once he was settled, she left. He cleared his throat and began again.

"I see you met my girl," he said, indicating me.

"Talked to her last night," Jonathan replied.

"You did?"

"You told me your password for your phone and told me to call her," Jonathan said. "Do you not remember?"

That made me worry.

"Just forgot," Beckett said, but it was clear he was thinking something else.

"Doesn't surprise me," Jonathan said. "You were pretty out of it when they wheeled you away. I brought the phone back and Fi plugged it in, so you should be good to go in a bit."

"Thanks, man," Beckett said.

I watched the interaction between these two and realized that there was some sort of mentorship going on. Jonathan was obviously older than Beckett, but I didn't think he was a coach, so wasn't sure what the deal was with them. I didn't want to ask, either, because if they wanted me to know, they would tell me.

"I gotta get," Jonathan said. "Let me know what happens and I'll make sure Coach knows and can let the rest of the team know."

"Will do," Beckett said.

"Nice to meet you, Fi," he said, reaching a hand out for me to shake.

"It was good to meet you, too," I replied, shaking his hand.

"Thanks for calling me last night. I'm glad I had more insider information."

"Keep him safe," he said before turning and walking out the door.

I waited for Beckett to say something, anything, but he just stared out the door after his teammate.

"You okay?" I asked after a bit.

"Fine," he said, finally turning his face to me.

"Hey," I said, realizing that there were tears in his eyes. "It's okay. I'm here."

He swallowed hard and I went to him, lying down next to him on the small bed, pulling him to me. It took a minute or two, but he finally let go and I could feel the sobs coming out of him, felt the wetness of his tears on my bare shoulder, and I just held him and let him let go.

We stayed that way until I heard the doctor knock on the door. Beckett pulled back and used the sleeve of his hospital gown to wipe his face clean.

"We all good?" the doctor asked as he came in.

"Just holding my girl," Beckett said, trying to sound like he wasn't just bawling.

"Good, good," the doctor said, not mentioning the scratch in Beckett's voice or the redness of his face. "I got the results and everything looks fine. I want you to go see your regular doctor once you get home and would prefer it if you would call and make an appointment before you leave so I can get them the results of the testing and such."

"Not really sure where to go," Beckett said. "The team always arranges things like this."

"I'll reach out to the trainer at the stadium and see what he wants you to do," the doctor said. "When I have an answer, I'll let you know."

"Thanks," Beckett said, and the doctor walked out. "I'm sorry," he said to me, and I looked over at him.

"What for?" I asked.

"Being a baby," he said.

"You literally got hit in the head," I said. "It could have killed you. You have the right to be a little upset about it all."

"I shouldn't be such a crybaby, though," he argued.

"Bullshit," I said. "I would feel like I wanted to cry, too. I mean, this could have changed everything for you, so having an emotional reaction is not at all out of line."

He closed his eyes and sighed. I assumed he was trying to get himself back into the unemotional person he usually was.

"Don't," I said.

"Don't what?" he asked.

"Beat yourself up," I said. "There is nothing wrong with crying, and there is nothing wrong with being emotional."

"I just saw everything slipping away from me," he admitted.

"Like your career?" I asked.

"That, and you," he said. "I couldn't imagine my life without you."

"Where am I going?" I asked.

"Why would you want to be with me if I was such a failure?"

"Okay, first of all, you're not a failure," I replied. "You were injured. It wasn't your fault. If you were hurt so bad you couldn't play, we'd figure it out."

"Really?" he asked, his eyes wide.

"Sure," I said. "I mean, we could always crash at Quentin's place. Especially since it's probably all his fault."

"What's my fault?" my brother asked as he came into the room, McKenzie right behind him.

I blinked and looked at him, trying to figure out how to blame him for what happened.

"You didn't warn me," I finally said. "If you had, I could have warned Beckett to watch for it. Maybe then he wouldn't be lying in a hospital."

I had tried to get up, but Beckett held me down. I was surprised at how strong he was, but realized that just because his head was injured, it didn't have anything to do with the rest of his body.

"I didn't know," Quentin said.

"Bullshit," Beckett replied.

"They said they wanted to punish you guys," my brother continued.

"Said they wanted to show you what cheating was actually like. I told them to let it go and move on, but some of the guys are really pissed."

"But why Beckett?" I asked.

"Because I blew the whistle," he said, and I looked at him. "I figured out they were stealing signs. I didn't know exactly how but had my suspicions. When we found something that looked like a camera in the batter's eye, I told my coach. He told me to let it go and that he would take care of it."

"He certainly took care of it, all right," Quentin said.

They'd come further into the room but were still standing a bit away from us.

"You shouldn't have been cheating in the first place," I said. "If you hadn't, none of this would have happened."

"Fi, you don't understand," he said.

"What don't I understand?" I asked. "That you were cheating and everyone should just let you keep at it? That you winning those World Series games was probably because of that cheating and you really aren't as good as you think?"

"Fi, come on," he argued.

"No, you come on," I said, getting angrier with each word. "You nearly killed him. He could have died. Did that even cross your mind? How about the pitcher? Did he think that a fastball to the head would just be able to be walked off? Because that's not how we were raised."

"I know," he said, and sounded dejected.

"So," I began. "What are you going to do about it now?"

"Ask for a trade," he said, and I stopped short.

"A trade?" I asked and could feel Beckett gripping my arm where it rested on his chest.

"Yeah," he said. "I can't condone what they did. Should have said something a long time ago, but I wasn't sure how to go about doing it. We were winning, and I was just kind of caught up in the mentality of the team. Now, though, they've pushed it too far."

"Ya think?" Beckett asked.

"I know we don't get along," Quentin said. "We're just kind of that way, but I never in my life thought they would do something like this. I would never want to see anyone get hurt like that. Not even you."

"Could have fooled me," Beckett retorted.

"I'm sorry," Quentin said and my mouth dropped open. "I should have stopped it a long time ago, so for that I'm sorry. I'm also sorry that they targeted you. You were looking out for your team, which is what we're all supposed to do."

"And you were just covering your ass," Beckett said, but there wasn't the harshness he'd had before.

"I was," my brother said. "You're a damn good short stop and a damn good guy, from what Fi tells me. So, I'm sorry I tried to ruin what you two have, too."

"You saying you approve?" Beckett asked.

"No," my brother said, then laughed. "I don't think I would be happy with anyone dating my baby sister."

"Not a baby," McKenzie, who had been quiet for this entire exchange, said.

"Definitely not a baby," Beckett agreed, and I laughed at the look on my brother's face.

"Am I interrupting?" the doctor asked as he stepped into the room.

"Not at all," Beckett replied. "Good news?"

"Talked to the trainer and found someone for you to see when you get back," he said. "I've scheduled an appointment and will give you all the information when you're discharged. But for now, you're good to go. I don't want you driving or drinking until after you have a chance to discuss this with Dr. Thomas. Do you have a way to get around when you get home?"

"I can drive him," I said.

"Good," the doctor replied. "Now, let me see if we can get you out of here."

"Thanks, doc," Beckett said, and the doctor walked out of the room.

"I gotta go, too," Quentin said. "Need to head to the stadium and see what my suspension looks like."

"Where are you wanting to get traded to?" I asked.

"I would love to come home," he said. "But, with this guy, it's not likely to happen."

"Sorry, dude," Beckett said. "Not giving my spot up for anyone if I can help it."

"I know," he said. "Well, I gotta get."

"Bye," I said, getting up off the bed and walking over to give him a hug.

"Next time you come down, we can do a girls day," McKenzie said after hugging me.

"Unless you've moved," I replied.

"Yeah," she said. "But that would just mean a whole new city to explore."

"True," I said, and watched them walk out.

"Come here," Beckett said, and I turned around to see him sitting up more in the bed.

I walked over to him and sat on the edge of the bed.

"I know we haven't talked about any of this, but I have a question," he said.

My stomach did a little flip and my heart started to race.

"What is it?" I asked.

"It looks like I'm gonna be laid up for a couple of days at least," he said. "I was wondering whether you wanted to stay at my place. If you don't, that's fine, but I wanted to ask."

"That wouldn't be a good commute for me," I said. "But you could stay at my place instead. I could take care of you and even get a day off to take you to your doctor appointment and stuff."

"You'd be willing to do that?"

"Of course I would," I said. "Why wouldn't I?"

"I've just never had anyone really care," he said.

I blinked, unsure what to say. I did the only thing I could think to do, which was to pull him into my arms and hug him.

CHAPTER SIXTY-FOUR

*B*eckett...

"You're good to go," the doctor said about an hour after he'd been in before. "I do have a list of things I don't want you to do, but you should be good to go home."

"So, I can fly?" I asked.

"Sure," the doctor said. "Once I get the final discharge paperwork for you, we'll let you out."

"Should I order an Uber?" Fi asked.

"Unless you have a car, I would suggest either that or a taxi," the doctor said. "I don't want him doing too much activity for at least a couple of days, but he should be good to go come the time his doctor appointment is. No driving until then, either. I don't want something to come up and cause an accident."

"I don't either," I said.

"Go ahead and get dressed and I'll have the discharge nurse come in to get you on your way," the doctor said.

"They cut my clothes off in the ER," I said.

"I'll find you some scrubs," the doctor said and headed out the door.

"They cut your clothes off?" Fi asked, her eyes wide.

"Yeah," I said. "Couldn't exactly undress myself at that point."

"But still, they cut them off?"

Her pitch went higher and her eyes opened further. It was comical to look at so I laughed.

"Why would they cut them off?" she asked, clearly confused and concerned.

"Baby," I said, taking her hand in mine. "It isn't surprising. I've seen them cut clothes off players on the field. They have to do what they have to do, and if you can't help them, then they just have to make decisions. They were worried about my balance, my ability to stand, and my ability to roll over even, so they just had to make do with what they could. Cutting my clothes off was the least of their worries."

"But what it if was a special shirt or something?" she asked. "What if it was something important and they just cut it off?"

"I'd rather they cut my clothes off than shift me and make me para-lyzed or something," I said. "Besides, it's just my uniform."

"What about your shoes?"

"They're in the closet," I said. "They didn't have to cut those off, just untied them and slipped them off into a bag of what they could salvage."

"Oh, okay," she said, and I could see that her sense was coming back to her.

Just then, one of the nurses stepped in and said, "I've got your discharge paperwork. You ready to go?"

"He doesn't have anything to wear," Fi said.

"No worries," the nurse said. "Let's go over your instructions and upcoming appointments. By the time we're done, someone should be here with something for you to wear."

The nurse then went about giving me instructions on how to handle the small cut that was at the base of my skull, what foods I should avoid, a prescription for pain medication, but suggested that I not take it if I didn't need it as it was addictive. There was the information about my appointment with the doctor in Seattle that they had sched-uled for me with an address and a phone number.

"If you have any issues, or have any difficulties, call this doctor, or dial 9-1-1," he said. "But you should be good as gold in no time. You're fortunate that you were wearing a helmet. That could have been much worse."

"Tell me about it," I said. "Not the way I wanted to spend my first day back in the lineup, but hey, I'll live."

"That's the spirit," he said as another nurse walked in, carrying a set of clothes the nurses wore.

"These should work to get you back to where you have your own clothes," she said.

"Do you need help getting dressed?" the nurse asked.

"I think I'm good," I said. "Besides, she can help if I need it."

"Oh, yeah," Fi said. "I can totally help him."

"Then I'll leave you to it," the nurse said. "Just buzz when you're dressed and we can get you wheeled to the entrance."

"Where should I have the Uber come?" Fi asked, phone in hand.

"The main entrance is the best place," he said. "Let them know when they wheel you out that you're waiting for a car."

"Thanks," I said, and they both walked out the door.

"Ordered," Fi said, then looked at me.

"You want to undress me?" I asked.

"Beckett, that's awful," she said.

"So, you don't want to undress me?"

"Seriously," she said, rolling her eyes. "Are you twelve?"

"Come on," I said. "Let me at least have a little fun. I'm injured and need help."

I tried to give her some sort of look to say that I was pathetic, but it apparently turned into something so funny that it took her a good five minutes to stop laughing. We did finally get me dressed into the scrubs and in my cleats. By the time they got back with the wheelchair to take us to the lobby, we had contained our humor and were back to acting like the adults we were supposed to be.

CHAPTER SIXTY-FIVE

F i...

I was able to change my flight pretty easily, and the team booked Beckett on the same one so he would have someone to help him with his luggage and such. They really didn't seem to want to have him hurt further, which was a really nice thing. He'd been able to change into real clothes at the hotel before we checked out. By the time we got on the plane, I was beat and ended up falling asleep on his shoulder.

The drive to my place was uneventful as well, and he seemed to be doing fine, but had a pinched look on his face every time he moved his head. When I'd asked him about it, he'd said it was just stiff. While I was concerned, there really wasn't anything I could do about it.

I'd called my boss and told him that I had a family member that had been injured and asked if there was a way for me to either not work, or work from home. Since I hadn't brought my laptop home with me, he said that I could skip Monday and if things looked like I would be out for a while, that I could get my laptop and we would work out the work-from-home option until my family was better.

"You know I can handle a day on my own," Beckett said. "I'm not a complete invalid."

"It's fine," I replied.

"You could just quit," he suggested.

"I worked too hard to get where I am," I said. "I know it's my first job with my degree, but it is important to me. Besides, I don't want to be a kept woman."

"I plan on keeping you, so there's not much you can do about it," he said, laughing.

"You know what I mean," I replied, playfully slapping his shoulder.

"Ow," he said, and I looked at him, but he was smiling in that way that said he got me.

"Just for that, I should hit you harder," I said, laughing myself.

"There are some things I'd like to do to you that are hard," he said and there was heat in his eyes.

"You up for it?" I asked seriously.

"Always," he said. "I could never not be ready for you."

Again, his eyes held a heat, but this was more than just the need to fuck me. No, this held a promise of something much bigger, and I was here for it.

"Don't promise something you aren't prepared to back up," I said.

"Wouldn't dream of it," he said. "Now, take me to bed. We've got some things to do."

"Things?"

"Yeah," he said. "Several things, in all sorts of ways. I anticipate it will take most of the rest of today, and well into tomorrow to get them all done."

"Let's start slow," I said. "We don't want to wear you out. I want you to last for a long, long time."

"I'm ready for that," he said. "I'm ready for forever if it includes you."

I stared, unsure how to respond, but then saw him smile and realize what he'd just said.

"Not marriage," he said. "Not yet. I've still got demons to slay. Will you help me slay them?"

The serious turn his words took were drastic, but I knew what he was talking about.

"I'll be your shield maiden," I said. "Where you go, I'll be right by your side."

"I knew I could count on you," he said. "Now, let's get in there and make a mess of your bed. I want to get you all kinds of dirty."

He didn't have to say anything else. I took his hand and led him to my bedroom where we could spend however long we needed indulging our pleasures.

EPILOGUE

*B*eckett...
She was warm next to me and I loved it more and more every day. I'd moved in with her full time after about a week of us coming home from Houston, and it was clear that we were meant to be together. She'd suggested that I keep the apartment and sublet it until we were sure, but I already was. Nothing would pull me away from this beautiful woman who was breathing deeply in her sleep next to me.

My doctor had declared that I could go back to the team as soon as my ten-day stint on the injured list was over, as long as I wore a helmet while up to bat as well as while I was in the field. I didn't like it, but there had been a few other players who had done this before, and they'd even instituted the rule for the base coaches to wear them during games, so I guess I could deal with it for a while.

The team had played well, but we just couldn't get over that hurdle to get us into the post season, although we came close this year. Maybe next year we'd make it.

Now that it was the off season, I was going to take full advantage of not having anything I needed to do for at least a month other than going to the gym and keeping myself in shape. No, I planned to spend as much time as I could with Fi, getting to know her better and learning everything there was to this beautiful woman.

"Hey," she murmured as she shifted and looked up at me.

"Hey, yourself," I replied.

"Been up long?"

"Just a little while," I replied. "Why?"

"Trying to figure out why you're staring at me while I'm sleeping," she said, then yawned wide.

"I'm just memorizing your everything," I said. "I don't ever want to be away from you, and when I have to be, I want to be sure that I know what I'm missing."

"Not planning on going anywhere," she said, stretching like a cat, long and languid.

"Coffee?" I asked.

"Please," she replied and the way she said it sounded like it was the only thing she needed to keep her going.

"Be right back," I said and got out of bed.

I padded to the kitchen, pulled down two mugs from the cupboard, and started the coffee. I doctored hers up like she liked and added a little sugar and milk to mine as well, then took both back to the bedroom. When I stepped in, the bed was empty, but then I heard the toilet flush. I set her mug down on her side of the bed and climbed back in with my own mug.

When she stepped from the bathroom, my jaw dropped. She was completely naked and her hips swayed as she walked toward me. Don't get me wrong, I'd seen her naked plenty of times in the last several months, but there was something about this time that really just knocked me over.

"What?" she asked, stopping dead in her tracks.

"You are the most beautiful thing I've ever seen," I said. "Absolutely nothing in the world compares to your beauty, and I'm damn lucky to get to spend time with you."

She blushed all the way up to her roots, but then continued walking to the bed. I set my mug on the end table next to me and opened my arms to allow her in. She climbed on top of me, straddling my legs, and

I could feel her warm, wet heat against my already hard cock. Sliding up and down my length, she stared into my eyes as if trying to gauge something I didn't know.

Pressing her lips to mine, she kissed me deeply and my arms went around her, pulling her closer to me. With one hand on my cheek, the other dipped between us and she gripped me in her hand, working my length over and over from tip to base, then she shifted and started to slide me into her.

"No condom," I mumbled against her lips. We'd been using them, aside from the one time at the hospital, since we'd come home, so this was something I knew was her line to not cross.

"No need," she replied, continuing to press me so that I entered her, and my God, it was better than I ever could have imagined.

"Oh, yeah," she sighed once I was fully seated inside her.

She began to move, her eyes closed, her hands on my shoulders. My own hands were at her hips, keeping her steady as she rode me. While I wouldn't likely get off this way, I didn't even care. I wanted to watch her ride me, be the angel I knew she was, and see her get those wings she got when she floated away on her ecstasy. She'd rescued me from a hole I didn't know I was drowning in, and I would never let her go if she would allow it.

For now, I would just let her find her pleasure, her release, and watch her explode into a million tiny stars scattered across the universe before gathering back together in my arms. I'd finally found my home, a place where I was wanted, and I didn't want to ever leave it.

NOTE FROM AUTHOR

Images and Blurbs available upon request.
I would ask that you obtain high quality headshots and cover art images directly through me, rather than taking them from either my website or Amazon, however, blurbs are readily available through both places.

ABOUT THE AUTHOR

Born and raised in the Pacific Northwest, CM Kane was fed a steady diet of sports, particularly baseball. Having this love of the game instilled in her at an early age, she found that nothing was better than getting lost in the game. Storytelling was another gift that was encouraged in her youth, and she's taking to the written word to explore a new aspect to the game she loves.

Social Media and Website Links:

Website:
https://www.authorcmkane.com

Facebook:
https://www.facebook.com/AuthorCMKane

Instagram:
https://www.instagram.com/authorcmkane/

Amazon:
https://www.amazon.com/author/cmkane

BlueSky:
https://bsky.app/profile/authorcmkane.bsky.social

ALSO BY C.M. KANE

Seattle Cascades

1. Extra Innings

2. Caught Stealing

3. Backstop

4. Power Hitter

5. Double Play

6. Find a Gap

7. Sweet Spot (Coming Soon)

8. 7th Inning Stretch (Coming Soon)

New Orleans Magicians

1. Choke Up

2. Caught in a Pickle

3. Brand New Ballgame (Coming Soon)

4. Fan Interference (Coming Soon)

5. Flashing the Leather (Coming Soon)

Austin Aces Hockey Club (Shared World)

Power Play

Anthologies

Unnerving: Eclipse

Street Justice (Limited Time)

Fooling Around (Coming April 1, 2025)

Neon Lights & Country Nights (Coming June 1, 2025)

Stand Alone Titles

A Switch in Time

www.ingramcontent.com/pod-product-compliance
Lightning Source LLC
Chambersburg PA
CBHW071518260626
47170CB00002B/416